OCTOBER HOUSE BOOKS

Copyright © Jo Wesley 2019

Jo Wesley asserts her right under the Copyright, Designs and
Patents Act 1988 to be identified as the author of this work. This
novel is a work of fiction. The characters portrayed within it are
the work of the author's imagination. Any resemblance to actual
persons, living or dead, is entirely coincidental.

All rights reserved. No part of this publication may be reproduced,
stored in a retrieval system or transmitted in any form or by any
means, mechanical, electronic, photocopying, recording or
otherwise, without the prior written
permission of the author.

ISBN: 9781078294195

60000 0001 59075

Chapter 1
- late November -

HIGH-PITCHED BEEPS POUNDED MY EARS. And the smell? That wasn't right. Like petrol on a barbeque. Something felt wrong... horribly, out-of-place wrong. Shit. Not a dream. I threw the duvet to one side and leapt from the bed. Through the crack in the curtains, moonlight tinged the room grey, but the flicker of orange from the open bedroom door lit the hump in the bed.

"Jez, wake up!" I shook him. "Jez. Don't play silly buggers."

The children! He'd have to wait. I pulled my t-shirt over my nose and rushed from the room. My skin prickled with the heat and smoke swirled around the landing, searing my eyes, while below the hallway glowed.

Fire! Please God. This couldn't be happening. My children, I had to save my children.

"Lily, Char..." Coughing, I dropped to my knees on the bare floorboards. Keep low, that's what they said on the TV. Stinging tears streamed down my face and a muzziness numbed me.

"Mummy." Two terrified voices merged into one.

They were alive! The floor shuddered as they rushed over. Lily's fist curled into her mouth and she coughed. Holding their trembling bodies tight, I turned from the heat and fled back to my bedroom. Their hearts thudded and they trembled as if chattering with cold.

As flames licked the stairwell, I kicked the bedroom door shut, muffling the crackling and dulling the beeps, but smoke rolled through the gap at the bottom. Frantically, I stuffed Jez's dressing gown into the space and jumped to my feet to find the twins gazing at him. Why wouldn't he wake? I wrenched the window open and gasped thick lugs of frosty air, before heaving each of them onto the windowsill. Charlie whimpered as I lowered him onto the flat roof of the old toilet while the breeze cut through the nylon of Lily's princess nightie, making her shiver. They'd freeze out there.

I grabbed the pile of clothes from the chair and threw them outside to litter the roof where the children cowered.

Get out, just get out, my mind screamed. But I couldn't. Not yet.

"Stay there. I won't be a minute."

"Mummy?" Lily's cry ripped through me.

I wavered, drawn between the desperate urge to flee and save my children or to risk precious minutes more to save Jez. But I had no choice. I couldn't leave him.

He lay still, his mouth open. I shook his shoulders. Wake up! I thumped his chest and yanked his arms. Cool, heavy, like the stress ball he squeezed. Beneath the smell of burning I caught the tang of whiskey on his lips. *Not again. You bastard, Jez.* You promised.

But then my heart stopped as I caught the glint of moonlight on the tin of baccy on the bedside table and the prescription bottle which lay open on its side. I snatched it up, slammed it to the floor. Empty. Was he… was he?

"Shit, Jez. What've you done?"

I slapped his face. *Please, please wake up!* His eyelids didn't flicker. Bloody hell, he'd finally gone and done it… I dabbed my t-shirt to my leaking eyes and sniffed back the threatening spill. What should I do?

"Mummy?" Lily and Charlie!

"I have to go. Please forgive me." My throat tightened from fear and pain, stopping me from saying more. Instead I

4

bent down to kiss him and, brushing away the tear that splashed his cheek, I forced myself to my feet.

My jeans lay on the floor. As I pulled them on, I spotted Jez's mobile and car keys on the side and snatched them up, but on reaching the window I hesitated. His tin! It had to be where he stashed his money. But what if Jez wasn't... what if he woke up? Well, I'd give it back. Crouching down, I jammed a key into the corner join of the wardrobe skirting. The plank clattered to the floor and I bent low to reach into the space, drawing out the metal box.

Somewhere glass shattered and I leapt up clutching the tin. If I was doing this, I had to go. Now.

I clambered onto the windowsill and took one last look. He'd become a black shape in the grey. The bump on his nose, the flag of St George tattooed on his arm, the thick scar on his forearm from an old bike accident. I didn't need to see them to know they were there. I swallowed.

"Goodbye, Jez," I whispered. "I'm so sorry."

The children's arms wrapped round my legs, pulling me onto the safety of the flat roof. Except we weren't safe. Even though frost bit my toes and no light flickered through the kitchen window, the crackle of splintering wood warned that the fire could soon be raging beneath our feet. Worse, what if the roof collapsed under us? As I knelt, grit dug into the knees of my jeans making me wince, but I took Charlie's hands and gave them a squeeze. His trusting blue eyes held mine and I smiled to show him he didn't need to be afraid, but I felt sure he'd see my shaking hands, see the terror inside me. We had to get out. My children didn't deserve this. No matter what choices I'd made, they were innocent. Please let them make it, I prayed. *Please.*

I clung tight to Charlie, lowering him to where I could make out the shape of the wheelie bin. His eyes widened

5

with fear.

"I'm not going to drop you." My voice quivered. "Kneel on the lid and then slide down."

I inched forward into the darkness, the gravel tearing at my bare stomach, while my underarms stung as they scraped the heavy felt of the flat roof. It couldn't be much further. Charlie's arms bowed and he let go of my fingers. The bin clunked, then a thump as he dropped to the ground.

One down, one to go. I swung round to Lily.

"Ready?"

She shook her head. I hugged her trembling body and kissed her cheek. "You can do this. Hold on tight."

A huge crashing sound came through the open window above, making us both jump. We had to hurry. Heart pounding, I lowered her down. When Charlie called to say he had her, I snatched the clothes and dropped to the ground. Pain wrenched my ankles, jarred my knees. Grimacing, I grabbed the twins and hobbled past the garage to the car parked beside the back gate.

The children clambered onto the rear seat. Once clipped into their seatbelts, I bundled the clothes around them and dragged Jez's hoodie over my head, welcoming the smell of fabric conditioner and the hint of his aftershave. Out in the open I kept his hood up, telling myself I felt closer to him that way, but I lied. The cold metal box hugged to my chest was proof of my guilt. With a shaking hand, I tapped out the numbers on Jez's phone and jumped into the driver's side, throwing the tin onto the passenger seat.

"Fire," I said, when the woman answered. It felt like a cheese grater had shredded my throat.

My eyes watered, my teeth chattered. I turned the ignition key and twisted the temperature dial round to the hottest setting. Cold air blasted out.

"Hurry!" The gravelly voice didn't sound like mine. Probably a good thing. "There's a man stuck in the house. In the back bedroom. Just him, no one else." I ploughed on, ignoring her questions. "Listen. It's 23 Stephen Langfield Way, Beeches Estate. Got that? Yes, 23. A man trapped inside. Upstairs, back bedroom."

Then I cut her off.

"He'll be…" My words of comfort to Charlie and Lily died on my lips. They sat wide-eyed; their little strained faces turned towards the house. At hell. I could just make out the two upper windows. Still dark, thank goodness, which meant the fire hadn't reached the back. Maybe there would be hope for Jez. Unlikely though. The memory of the empty prescription bottle told me as much. Blue streaked the sky behind the darkened roofline. Someone else must have called before I did. I glanced at the tin and at the road ahead, where the fire engine would soon come. I had to get away.

"Take your time," Jez had said when he'd been teaching me to drive. Could I do this alone after just five lessons? Biting my bottom lip, I pressed the clutch pedal and pushed the stick into gear. The car juddered, but I breathed easier as it picked up speed.

At the end of the street two men sprinted through the light of a streetlamp, arms pumping. One swerved from the path, leaping from between two parked cars into the road.

"Oi!" I heard him shout over the noise of the engine.

He sounded like one of the yobs outside the Duke of York at kicking out time, fuelled and ready to fight. I hit the accelerator, then the clutch, thrusting the gear into second. I waved my arm – move aside – but still he ran. Now the other one followed. Why were they running towards me? Surely, they'd want to save Jez? Their mouths were ferocious squares, their fists clenched. If I stopped, they'd frighten the children. Or worse.

I jammed my foot on the accelerator. The engine screamed as we headed straight at them. Move, move. Their snarls turned to shock and they jumped aside, too late as a fist or a foot smacked the side of the car, while from the back seat came a child's shriek.

"… bloody money … you bastard…"

In the rear-view mirror I watched them standing in the road, arms raised, until a siren belted out and they sprinted away from us and away from the house and Jez.

"It's okay," I told the children. "We're safe now."

But from what? As I slowed for the junction, jerking sobs reached me from the back seat, masked by the blast of the siren. To my right, houses flashed blue as the fire engine came closer.

Clutch, accelerate, take your time. Where should I go? I turned the car in the other direction, towards home. Something I hadn't called my old flat for weeks now. But what if those men knew it was me driving and hunted us down? Were they the ones Jez had been worried about? The reason he… A tear rolled down my cheek and I brushed it away. Don't blubber now.

We needed to go somewhere safe after I'd collected our old belongings. Somewhere we wouldn't be found, while I tried to work out what was going on. My mum's? I shook my head, unable to believe I'd connected her with the word 'safe'. But she was my only hope. No one here knew the old me. I was Karis now.

I looked in the mirror at the children, forced lightness into my voice. "Fancy a trip to your nan's?"

They looked as blank as I felt. They didn't know what a nan was, poor sods. I grimaced. Knowing my mum, they were better off that way.

Chapter 2
- starting Year 6 -

I OPENED THE FRONT DOOR to the haze of fag smoke and a disgusting smell. With my arm over my nose, I went through to the kitchen where newspapers littered the floor beside the back door. Upside down on the soggy paper sat Bill's manky trainers. I smirked, then felt bad. Poor Tibbles would be in for it. I swung my school bag over my head, chucked it to the floor of the larder, and got out of there.

Mum sat on the settee, thumbing through the TV Times, her feet tucked under her legs. She'd put on a bit of red lippy, the same colour as her long nails. They shone as she picked her cigarette from the ashtray and flicked it to leave a fag-shaped line of ash.

"Nothing on," she said. "Bill's stopping out with his workmates now, but I can't be arsed to go down the club with Julie."

"Tibbles been at it again?"

She took the stub from her mouth and exhaled a long puff of smoke, which drifted upwards, clouding her black fringe.

"If that cat shits in his shoes one more time, it's dead." She pointed her fag at me. "You wanted it, you sort it."

I threw myself down on the other side of the settee, my elbow banging against the wood beneath the thin foam of the arm rest. I knew it was foam, because I'd caught myself picking at it through the hole in the fabric the other day. The hole was down to me too, after I'd pulled at the brown threads that hung loose. Guiltily, I checked the gap to make sure the jagged bits of yellow were tucked away. No point annoying Mum more.

"I'm going round Nina's later. Her mum says I can stop over. We might go down town tomorrow."

Mum shrugged and twisted the butt in the ashtray. "You better hope that cat behaves while you're gone."

♦

I was sitting on the old lawnmower when I noticed the new boy next door leaning on a concrete post, watching me from the other side of the fence. How long he'd been there, I didn't know, as I'd got to an exciting but scary part in my book. If I hadn't looked up to check real fog wasn't creeping in, he could have been and gone without me ever knowing. To think only a year ago I dreamt about joining the police when I grew up – a secret I'd kept to myself as it wouldn't make me popular – but I'd be useless. The police had to notice things, like the grass stains on the knees of his white trousers and the fact that his white top wasn't too clean either. If his mum was anything like mine, she'd moan her head off.

"James Herbert," he said. "Mum won't let me read stuff like that."

He talked different to most people round here. All his words ending with a 't' sounded like they had one.

"Why?" I checked the page number before letting the book drop into the grass beside my cassette player. Unnoticed, the tape had reached the end.

He blushed, then shrugged. "You know."

My neck ached from staring up at him, so I stood up. "She doesn't like books?" That made sense. No one else read them round here.

"Different sorts of books. She says reading James Herbert won't help me pass the eleven plus."

Eleven plus? The teachers all went on about that. It's not about winners or losers, pass or fail, but everyone knew it was just talk. Us failures would be going to Sir Roland Boyce Seccy School. Mr Hall, my teacher, said I'd do really well, but he was just being nice. At any rate, I wanted to go to school with my friends.

"You're going to Grammar?" I whistled. Then I nodded towards his house. "You like it here?"

Again, he shrugged. "Dad lost his business. Then he and Mum split up. So we had to move."

"But you've bought it. That's something."

He shrugged. "My name's Troy, by the way," he said, with that fancy voice of his. "What's yours?"

"Troy?" I choked back a giggle. We'd learnt about the Trojan Horse in Year Four. His mum must have called him Troy because she hoped he'd grow up to look Greek or something. Well, she'd got that wrong. I looked more Greek than him. He was fair, with freckles. Loads of them.

"And you?" he repeated.

I hated this part. Lowering my voice, I confessed, "Cindy."

Now he smiled. "Like the doll?"

I did the eye-rolling thing. Everyone said that – even though my name was spelt with a 'C' – or they asked if it was short for Cinderella. Luckily most of them didn't ask what it was short for.

"Why are you sitting out here anyway?" He looked around at the murkiness. "It's nearly dark."

"You know." I waved my hand around, like that explained it. He didn't say anything though, so I had to go on. "I'm waiting for my cat. I was going round to a mate's, but Tibbles pooed in my mum's boyfriend's trainers again. I think he's scared to come back."

11

I'd said it without thinking, but fear must be the reason. Tibbles usually appeared soon after I got back from school. His favourite trick was tripping me up when he padded around my legs, wrapping them in his tail and purring until I fed him. Even though I'd been so stuck in the book I hadn't seen Troy, Tibbles wouldn't have gone past without saying hello, especially as he'd be hungry and needing his dinner. That was my job even though he was my big sister's cat, but she'd left him behind when she moved in with her boyfriend, Simon. Mum called him Slimeball Sime behind Mandy's back but I liked him, especially when he gave me money for sweets and stuff. My mouth watered. How long was it since I'd had something to drink?

The pink sky had faded to grey turning the tall hedge at the back of the garden – the one Tibbles usually came through – into a silhouette of peaks, while Troy's white clothes now glowed in the dark.

"If you see Tibbles, let me know. He's an old Tabby. He's got a chunk missing from his ear." I pulled at the top of my right ear to show him what I meant. "You going to Redhill Primary?"

He nodded.

"Great. Walk with me."

I'll look after you, I wanted to add. With a name and voice like that, he'd need it.

♦

As I opened the back door, the smell hit me. Different to earlier, the kitchen now stank more like sweat and damp. I pulled a yuk face and tugged my top over my nose while I grabbed a can of Coke and a bag of crisps.

"Mum." I wandered into the lounge. "You seen Tibbles

yet?"

"Nah." She didn't move her gaze from the TV.

"Troy next door reckons he's going to Grammar School. If I pass, can I go?"

"Troy? What sort of name is that?" She sniggered and popped a fag in her mouth. Her cheeks hollowed inwards as she flicked her lighter twice and dragged hard on her fag so its tip smouldered. Nina and I used to practise that with our pencils, so we'd get it right and not cough like Mandy did when she had her first go.

"Teacher says I'm good enough."

She put the fag packet back on the coffee table and rearranged the ash tray, so it lay flat on the settee arm. "Why on earth would you want that? You'd lose all your friends. Nina and that lot won't be there – and don't think I can pay for a posh uniform for you either. I can't afford living as it is."

She settled back into the settee, her eyes glazing over, while I sipped at my can, enjoying the fizz of bubbles on my tongue.

"Seriously, Cindy. I can't afford for you to be thinking that sort of shite. People like us don't go there. For a reason."

She rubbed her fingers together. Money. No one round here had any of that. Troy's mum neither by the sound of it, so how come he could manage to go? But then they'd bought their house. Mum's mouth opened like she was about to say something else, when the doorbell rang.

"Who the hell is knocking this time of night?" She unfolded her legs to stagger from the settee.

I followed her out. Maybe we'd locked the door and Bill had forgotten his key? But he never came home so early on a Friday night.

"Is Cindy there?" Troy said. He stood at the door

13

holding what looked like a baby wrapped in a pink fleece. "I'm sorry. I found him under the bush in my garden. I thought he was asleep, but…"

Please, not Tibbles. My face crumpled, even though I didn't want it to, and Troy's face became a blur. I couldn't cry, not in front of him. I swiped my arm across my eyes and forced a smile.

"Thank you." I sniffed and held out my arms, so he could place the bundle into them carefully as you'd do with a baby.

He smiled at me. Sad, like he knew how I felt and turned away.

"Thank the Lord for that. No more crap in the house." Mum closed the door. She looked from my face to poor Tibbles, cold in my arms, and patted my shoulder. "You have to look on the bright side, love. He *was* old."

Chapter 3
- late November -

As I went to close the front door to my old flat, I remembered the folders I'd left tucked at the bottom of the electricity meter cupboard. How could I have been so stupid? My hiding place would be the first place people would go if they noticed the flat was empty. Thank goodness they hadn't already. I jammed the precious folders into one of the carrier bags heaped on the walkway floor and locked the door for the final time.

My neighbour's kitchen light was on and a shadow moved behind the net curtains. She must have had the baby, I guessed. The last time I'd seen her she'd been waddling, breathless along the walkway. With a smile, she'd rubbed her belly and told me not long now. That was – what? – nine weeks ago? All the time I'd been given with Jez.

Don't think of him. Just about Lily and Charlie and what had to be done.

I slotted my hands through the carrier bag handles and hoisted them up. My legs quivered like a weightlifter and the thin plastic cut into my fingers. Thank goodness it was the final run – not that there was much to take as most of our things had been at Jez's. Glancing over the brick wall of the walkway I checked for signs of movement. Lamp light reflected on the roofs of cars below, while the block opposite stood silent and grey but for the blue shimmer of a TV in one flat and the imprint of a naked bulb that blazed a crimson circle through the curtains of another. Apart from the occasional hum of a passing vehicle on the main road outside, it felt as though a hush had fallen over the area. As if something lurked, breath held, waiting.

Fighting back my nerves, I rounded the corner to the stairwell where a yellow flickering light cut through the gloom. No one there. But would they hide here surrounded by flats or would they be staked out where I'd tucked Jez's car in the area for the next block? Where Lily and Charlie slept. Why on earth had I thought it better to leave the children than to wake them?

I clattered down the concrete steps, down one flight, then another. At the bottom, I held my breath while I rushed past the bin room – the stink always reminded me of Mum's house – while praying someone wouldn't leap from the darkness. My bags bashed the sides of the corridor while the corner of something sharp – the photo album – smashed my shin. Sh… I gritted my teeth and twisted my hand round, so the softer clothes knocked against me.

Out in the open, the chilled air nipped my face and the sharp echoes of footsteps on concrete were stifled as I crossed the grassed area to reach Jez's car. In the distance someone called out, while in the road a car rattled past ready for the knacker's yard. That's what my breath sounded like too. I should have brought water with me, something to ease my throat. When I'd crammed the bags into the boot, burying the stuff I'd fetched on my earlier trip, and stashed the carrier bag containing the photo album and my folders beside the tin in the well of the front passenger seat, I pressed the lock on the driver's door.

Behind me the children slept. I muttered a silent prayer of thanks. Thanks to me they could have died tonight. If only I hadn't fallen for Jez's promises and we'd stayed here in our flat. But tonight the 'if onlys' would have to wait. I had a job to do.

Fingers trembling, I turned the key in the ignition, my heart jolting with fear as the engine screech ripped the silence. I checked the door locks were down and nothing moved in the nearby shadows. Now all I had to do was get the children to mum's in one piece. Bloody hell. Over fifty sodding miles.

Breathing deeply, I clamped my hands around the steering wheel. Don't go too fast or too slow, push the clutch down and shove the gear into reverse, careful on the accelerator, now brake and do it again, but this time with the gearstick in first. I got all the way to the Three Horseshoes junction before stalling. Frantically I fired the engine. The police could be out there somewhere. Or those men. This time I jabbed the pedal, keeping the engine revs high, so the second the lights turned green we jerked away.

Once out into the open roads I relaxed, slowing for winding lanes and hushed villages, until it struck me: I had to go via the M25. How else would I do it? I hadn't a clue about how to get to Mum's along the side roads and I could hardly stop and ask. As I followed the blue signs and turned the car onto the slip road, fear sapped the strength from my arms and legs.

"Don't be silly. You can do this," I muttered over and over.

Tears swam in my eyes. Shit, I couldn't cry. Not now. I had to see.

The revs crept up towards the red line but I continued to press down on the accelerator. A smell of engine fumes filtered into the car. Petrol? I shoved the gear stick into fourth and made it onto the carriageway, just behind a white-sided HGV with a yellow sticker on the back asking if I thought he drove well. If he did, I was sticking behind him.

Was that the smell in the fire? The red lights of the truck in front blurred into a burning glow and the tang of petrol seared my nose, burning my throat, while questions blazed

17

round and round. Someone had tried to kill us. All of us or just Jez? Did they know I was in the house? That little Charlie and Lily slept in his mum's old room? Did they care?

Those men – the ones who'd chased after us – they wanted money. That's what they'd shouted. Jez had been scared these past few weeks, checking the doors, peeking through the curtains at the slightest noise, monitoring his mobile. Three times in the past week I'd woken to find an empty bed at two in the morning and him downstairs sitting at the kitchen table, staring at the wall.

"What's the matter, Jez?" I'd brushed my hands through his bed hair.

"Nothing," he'd said. "Don't worry."

But how could I not when the shadows cut deep beneath his eyes and his fingers entwined on the beige Formica top? He was praying because he knew, *he knew* he had reason to be fearful. I clenched the wheel, like I was gripping his shoulders, shaking him.

So, what the fuck did you mean by 'Nothing'?

♦

Kingsley Road. For the first time in my life I was pleased to see that sign, unable to believe I'd made it in one piece after just five driving lessons with Jez. I yawned wide, my skin so taut it felt it could split like an old elastic band. Bed would be good. That's if there was one. Knowing Mum, she would have installed a new boyfriend with a fetish for train sets or something. And what about Ella? How could I have forgotten her?

My teeth scored my lip as I turned the steering wheel this way, then that, inching the car between the vehicles parked on both sides. Apart from all the cars, the street still

18

looked the same as it did over a decade ago; a mix of 1950s semis and terraces, with brown bricks and moss-covered tiled roofs. The council had changed all the windows and doors to uPVC before I left, except for the ones that were bought. Like Troy's. Even in the murky morning light, I could see his old house had the same door from years ago, still painted sky blue with nets behind the glass in the top half of the door. Did he and his mum still live there or had they fulfilled their dream and got away? I hoped so. They deserved happiness.

It wasn't until I'd reached the turning circle at the end of the road that I found a space I could fit into without having to worry about parallel parking. Once out of the car, the chill cooled my flushed cheeks and I breathed deeply, welcoming the freshness after the claustrophobic feel of the car.

I bent to wake the children. Startled, they gazed around, taking in the unfamiliar scenery.

"Where are we?" Charlie murmured as I lifted him from the car.

"Your nan's."

Lily bum-shuffled across the seat, knocking Jez's jumpers onto the floor. *Jez.* Did they manage to reach him in time? I shook the thoughts away. They'd have been too late. He'd gone hours before. Fingers of icy air brushed my skin and I shivered. With the children half-running beside me, I strode across the frosted grass verge which crunched beneath my feet and along the path, past Mrs Dibb's, past Frank's, past the house with the man who'd scared me as a child with his banging on the window and yelling at us to 'Clear off!' if we so much as touched his fence. I reached Troy's, then Mum's.

Her gate scuffed the concrete path as I pushed it open.

In the middle of the front garden I could make out the tip of a chipped red hat, the rest of the gnome hidden in the tangle of grass and blackened nettles. I pressed the doorbell, but it didn't ring, so I tried the tarnished knocker which managed a half-hearted clang. Didn't anyone visit Mum anymore? Standing back to check her bedroom window, I half-expected her to pull back the curtain and grumble, "Who's bloody calling at this time in the morning?".

But what about Ella? I banged the knocker again. How old must she be now – thirteen? Not old enough for the stage where nothing could rouse her before midday. So, why didn't she get the door?

"I'm cold," Lily whined. Her teeth clattered together, fuelled by the brrr noise she'd been making since we'd stepped from the car.

I hugged them both tight. We'd have to go back to the car and wait until Mum woke up. Then, I remembered.

"Stay there!" Their alarmed expressions told me they would rather follow, but they did as I'd asked.

A lawn mower protruded from the wilderness that Mum's back garden had become, overshadowed by the hulking Leylandii which bordered the rear. Near a mildewed statue embedded face down in the dirt, I bent to tug free a small slab of crazy paving. Beneath it, on pieces of broken concrete littered with fleeing woodlice, sat a rusting key.

The children smiled with relief when I returned. I wiggled the key in the lock, muttering, "Please, please work."

It turned and the door scraped open. And that smell, the stink of home, hit me again.

Chapter 4
- Summer term. Year 9 -

TROY'S HOUSE SMELT OF BAKED CAKES. His mum said cooking was one of the few joys she had left. That and her books. It seemed every time I walked into her kitchen she'd be standing by the oven, where she'd wipe her floury hands down the front of her apron and point to a fresh batch cooling on the side. This morning was no different, even though it was just ten o'clock.

"Take them while they're still here." She nodded towards a tray of butterfly cakes that sat on the grey worktop in front of a row of cookery books. "I'm on coffee duty at church today, so they'll be going with me."

I took one and smiled at her, as if I knew what she was going on about. Church. Another thing no one else in our road did – not even my nan when she'd been alive – except for Mrs Davies, three doors down, who got picked up every Sunday morning to go to the big church in the centre of town. I went there once for a christening. It smelt musty. The vicar droned on and we sang boring songs, like the ones I'd sung at primary school where the music teacher's head would bounce up and down as she banged away on the piano. Maybe that was it. You had to be old to enjoy stuff like that. After all, the woman giving Mrs Davies a lift looked about one hundred and her ancient banger wasn't far off too as its engine sounded like a clapped-out ice cream van with all the jangling.

Troy's mum looked old. Different to when she first came here, when she waltzed about with her matching outfits and shiny stilettos. Back then she'd clipped along the road looking up as she walked, when everyone knew you kept your head down to check for dog mess. Now grey streaked her hair and she tied it back – not tight like mum where it lifted her eyebrows – but looser so wispy bits littered her forehead. She didn't wear make-up anymore, which was good what with all that arm sweeping she did to keep the flour from her face, and her stilettos had been replaced by brown granny shoes the same colour as her tired eyes. While she wore the same dresses and trousers as always, the pinks and yellows were faded and the hem of her jackets hung out of shape at the back.

I popped the last of the cake into my mouth, threw the captured crumbs into the sink and sat fidgeting with my handbag.

She gazed at it, as if she knew what I had stashed in there. "That's a pretty bag."

"Yeah, Mandy gave it me."

"Troy says she might be moving back home."

I shrugged. "You never know with my sister. One minute they're on, the next off. She stopped at ours last night, but Simon's just come round to fetch her back."

Mrs Hamilton smiled and turned to her cakes. As the floorboards creaked above, I prayed Troy would hurry up. She probably did the same. She was strange about things like that. She'd make me stand in the kitchen with neither of us knowing what to say, rather than send me upstairs to chat to Troy. Stupid really, as he came straight up to my room round my house even when Mum wasn't home (which was most times).

"Going anywhere nice?" she said as Troy walked in.

"To the park," he said.

His hair stuck up where he'd gelled it and damp stained the collar of his beige t-shirt.

"Don't forget your sunscreen."

Troy grinned so his nose crinkled along the patch he'd sunburnt yesterday. It had turned the same colour as his reddened forearms but shinier. He needed my colouring. I straightened my arms to check my tan was still a nice golden glow. Perfect. By this evening it would be even darker, so I could show off in my new short-sleeved blouse at school tomorrow.

"Ready?" I said, as Troy nicked one of the cakes. "Bye, Mrs Hamilton."

We were nearing Troy's front gate when Simon stomped out of my house. He mouthed something starting with the 'f' word and yanked the door shut so the knocker clanged, but then he saw me and whistled – one of those long low ones the men on the building site near the school did.

"Looking good, Cindy girl." His gaze ran from my sandals to my denim shorts. "Nice tan."

"I said I'd go browner than you. You'll owe me a fiver by the end of today."

Troy stiffened beside me. I ignored him and walked over to the fence where I leant forward so Simon could see the hollow between my boobs. He'd told me in secret that mine were nicer than Mandy's, even though they were tiny compared to hers. Perter, he'd said last week, and he'd run his finger between them so a shiver ran up my back.

"Oi, leave off!" I'd shoved his hand away. "Cheeky."

His dimple had cut into the side of his cheek. "Sorry, I just can't help myself."

When I saw him a few days later, he'd winked and slapped his own hand, like he was telling himself off for being naughty. I liked that. Mandy was so lucky. If I was her, I'd be nicer to him. Now he gave me that same cute grin, the one where one side of his mouth lifted higher than the other and his dimple showed and his grey eyes with flecks of yellow moved from my chest to my face.

"You'll have to come round to mine to collect it. No doubt she'll tell you everything." He held his smile as he jerked his head towards my house, but his face darkened and his knuckles whitened in his clenched fists. Mandy must've really done it this time.

"Come on. We've got to go," Troy said. He stood by his front gate shielding his eyes to look back at me. I checked my watch. We'd promised Nina and the others we'd be there by ten thirty and it was nearly that now.

"See ya later," I said to Simon and headed towards Troy.

We walked in silence to the end of the road. Troy was annoyed, I could tell. Once around the corner, I pulled a ciggie from my bag and sparked up.

"You should take care with him," he said. "First he gets you hooked on them." He pointed at the cigarette, ignoring the perfect circle puffs of smoke I'd mastered in the few weeks since I'd started. "Then he's looking at you, like, like…"

He ripped leaves from a bush and threw them to the ground. "He's your sister's boyfriend. He's twenty-eight."

"Twenty-seven. And he's with my sister, so give me some credit, won't you?"

He wrenched more leaves from a hedge, lobbing them angrily into the air. "You're not exactly making it easy."

I went to argue, then realised he was right. But I quite liked the attention.

I shrugged. "Whatever."

Chapter 5
- late November -

THE BRRR OF LILY'S CHATTERING TEETH hushed as we stole into the house. To our right the stairs rose into the dark landing, while ahead the hallway led through to the kitchen. The silence closed in on us. As I shut the front door, holding it so it didn't bang against the frame, I realised with a start that the temperature hadn't changed from outside. I touched the hallway radiator – ice cold – but Mum loved the heat. Please say she hadn't moved and we'd broken into someone else's house.

The twins clung to me as, heart thudding, I crept into the lounge. In place of the beige velour settee sat a green leather couch crushed between two armchairs. The curtains were different too. Half open at the back of the room, they allowed a glimpse of the garden through the nets, while at the front they were drawn tight. Even in the gloom the stripes clashed with the carpet, all swirls and leaf shapes just like Nan's which had 'hidden the dirt'. Except Mum would be fifty-odd, not ninety.

Then I spotted the picture on the mantelpiece of a young girl in her school uniform. A younger me. But not me. I picked up the grey mount and wiped my arm across the photograph to clear the dust. Her dark hair curled over her shoulders and trailed down her blazer. A strand touched the Elmhurst High School emblem, like a finger pointing: *look at me, look what I've achieved*. I swallowed. Like me, Ella had passed, but she'd gone one better and made it to Elmhurst. That's if this was her. *Who else could it be, stupid?* Her face was heart-shaped, like mine, with a mole on the side of her mouth, but while her eyes were wide, they weren't my deep brown. Again, I swallowed, forcing back the ball of hurt that threatened to choke me. I'd forgotten. How could I have forgotten her beautiful smile, that dimple cutting into her cheek and those gorgeous eyes, grey, flecked with yellow?

I put the photograph down and wiped my dusty fingers on my leg. Before turning back, I checked my face in the mirror above the mantelpiece and forced a smile.

"You stay here, while I go upstairs," I whispered as I lifted the children onto the settee.

"Your eyes are all red," Lily said. Her finger traced the curve of my cheek. "You look sad."

"I'm tired."

She stared at me, the horror of the fire reflected in her eyes, her face tinged grey. What was she thinking? This time yesterday she'd been in her reception class with Charlie, painting splodges that she'd said were our family, but now we were minus the fourth blob. Neither of them had asked the question I dreaded. Why did we leave Jez behind? I knew what I'd tell them. The firemen would have saved him – that's what I told myself – they wouldn't have allowed those flames to reach him, to blacken him.

Charlie gripped the settee arm as if to stop himself from sliding to the floor. I ruffled his hair.

"I won't be a moment. I'll just wake your Nan."

As I started my slow climb my palm grazed the handrail and specks of white fluttered to the worn carpet. The paint on the bannister had chipped away to reveal yellowing layers. No matter where I trod, the stairs creaked. At the point they curved round, I paused at the window to gaze down at Troy's kitchen door which faced Mum's. An image rose: us stepping outside, laughing as his mum told us to take care – like she always did – before she closed the door and cut off the waft of baking. I moved away before the memories rolled on.

All three of the bedroom doors stood open. As I inched towards Mum's room the smell of stale cigarettes grew stronger. Her curtains were closed but light pierced the thin material turning the room a murky grey. Unnerved by the stillness, I tiptoed inside.

"Mum," I whispered, as I lifted a corner of the curtain to let in light. "It's me."

The duvet lay flat until it rose over a mound of pillows, bulkier on the side which bordered the solitary bedside table. Mum's. I could tell by the glass ashtray, empty but for a veneer of ash. I moved onto the next room, where a bare mattress lay on the bed, its centre sagging and worn. The pink walls were littered with blue tack and jags of paper from old posters. One still hung in place above the bed, its corner curled over. Some boy band or other, all jutting jaws, muscular arms and arrogant eyes. The name came to me. Hadn't they split up two or three years before? The wardrobe was empty but for a couple of dresses which hung to one side. I lifted one of them out, trying to picture myself at thirteen. I'd been smaller than average but, even so, no way could I have fitted into this and it was far too girly for a teenager.

With a deepening sense of unease, I moved onto the smallest room. The one that had become mine after Mandy moved back home. Opposite the bed the magnolia paint failed to camouflage a wall pocked with streaks and dips from where I'd lost my temper that awful day. My legs crumpled and I dropped onto my old bed puffing a cloud of dust from the duvet. In the bleak light the particles rushed, giddy with freedom, until falling slowly and fading away. The carpet was different. Gone were the streaks of paint which had matted to the fibres and scratched my feet. It

27

seemed like no time since I'd sat staring at the arcs of purple and red splatting the walls and floor, feeling this same fear and despair. I pressed the heels of my palms to my eyes. *The memories. That poor girl.* I shouldn't have come back. A shaft of pain gripped me like the talons of a hawk and a dark weight settled.

Downstairs the children were asleep, heads at opposite ends of the settee, legs tangled. I wanted to lay down with them and hold them tight while I worked out what to do but instead, afraid to wake them and desperate to ease my burning throat, I went through to the kitchen where I let the tap run while I searched the cupboards for a glass. The water taunted me, splattering the sides of the metal sink before it gushed down the plug hole. Nothing was where it used to be. Finally, I found the glasses tucked behind a stack of plates in what was once the crisp and biscuit cupboard. The chilled water set my teeth on edge but soothed my throat.

I'd forgotten just how odd the downstairs space was. The bathroom, reached by a door in the hallway, ate into the kitchen space, while the larder sat beside the back door making for a narrow exit. Mum had always said she'd get the council to move the bathroom upstairs as soon as she had a spare room but, by the look of my duvet cover and the bare mattress in the second bedroom, she'd had several for years.

The bottom of the toilet bowl was stained brown – I couldn't remember a time it was white – and the cistern clanked when flushed. At the sink, green water marks lined the ceramic behind the taps. I splashed cold water over my face and used the hem of Jez's sweater to pat my dripping chin. Back in the lounge, I slumped into the armchair to think. I'd have to stay, at least until I found out what had happened to Mum and Ella. Where else could I go? Certainly not back home, especially if those men were looking for us.

On the settee, Charlie murmured and twisted round, clutching Jez's jumper. The children's clothes were in the car. Once I'd fetched them, I needed to hide the car somewhere in case we were associated with it, but I couldn't do that until Lily and Charlie were tucked in bed for the night and wouldn't notice me missing. A shiver ran down my spine. Was I really thinking of leaving them alone, even for a few hours?

"Think!" I hissed to myself. There must be another way.

For now, I'd have to grab our stuff and risk the car being spotted. Knowing my luck, some of the old neighbours would still be living here, the ones who got up at the crack of dawn to spend the day nosing through their nets. Would they recognise me? I brushed my hands through my hair. The bristly feel from years of peroxide gave me hope.

I crept out, twisting the key so the front door didn't bang and wake the children. My footsteps pattered along the garden path. In the distance, a car droned. A breeze had picked up making me shiver as it cut through Jez's sweater but the goosebumps prickling my neck weren't just from the cold. While the blank windows of the houses with their curtains drawn should have reassured me, I could feel watching eyes. I leaned over the gate to check up and down the road. Nothing. This time I lifted the gate so it didn't scrape on the concrete.

A flash of blue caught my eye. From behind a privet hedge a man in jeans appeared, hands tucked into the pockets of his jacket as he strode along the footpath. My heart thumped. I knew that walk! How could I forget it? Our eyes met – I couldn't tear myself from his gaze – but he leapt back as if I'd slapped him.

"Cindy? Is it really you?"

Chapter 6
– Summer term. Year 9 –

THE TWO OF THEM SAT ON THE SETTEE, feet tucked under their thighs, gazes planted on the telly, puffing out plumes of smoke like steam engines. In her free hand Mum gripped two lottery tickets, while Mandy's ticket lay beside her on the settee arm. I watched, fascinated by their perfect coordination as they took another drag. I so wanted to join them and show off my latest smoke trick where it would puff from my nose. Troy said it was disgusting, but Nina loved it. As Mandy caught me staring, I shot round pretending to watch the TV. How could they get excited about a load of balls bouncing around? In Maths the other day Mr Smith told us we had more chance of being murdered or struck by lightning than of winning the lottery. The way I looked at it, if I did win I had a high chance of the rest happening, so best not chance it.

Mum screwed up her tickets and dropped them onto the coffee table. "Load of shite. Why I bother, I don't know. You got any numbers, Mand?"

"Nah," Mandy said. She stretched, arching her back so her boobs stuck out, and picked up her can and shook it. "Get us another drink, Cind. There's two Fosters left at the back of the fridge."

When I came back with the cans Mum had switched the telly over to a film.

I yawned. "I'm going upstairs."

Mum waved but her gaze never left the TV, the flickering images reflected in her eyes. Next to her, Mandy used her teeth to lift the ring pull so she could jam her stubby fingers under. As the lager fizzed, she slurped the top of the can.

"Making the most of your room, are you? Exciting day tomorrow."

For you, I wanted to say but I just shrugged. It was like she was needling me all the time, even though I'd said yes, you can have your room back. Yes, I'll chuck out my stuff because it won't fit in my old room. I stomped upstairs and threw myself onto the bed. She reckoned I didn't need a bedroom just for books, while she needed a bigger room for all her clothes and make up. Selfish cow. No wonder Simon couldn't handle her.

A stack of books sat on my bedside table. My latest hoard from the library. Too depressed to sit up and check them out, I dragged the top one down, taking care not to topple the rest. Nelson Mandela beamed at me. After all he'd gone through I should read it, but I couldn't. Not tonight. Its weight suggested heavy reading and I needed something to take me from this world. I pulled the next one from the pile. Stephen King. More like it.

♦

The second the move was over I headed round to Troy's, first checking through the panes in the back door for signs of his mum. No shadow moved in the kitchen – of course, she'd be at church – so I climbed over the chain link fence between our houses. Mrs Hamilton would kill me if she knew. Only last week she'd moaned about the fence buckling where we leant against it. I rattled the door handle. Locked. Above me, came the splatter of the shower through the open upstairs window and the sound of '*If you want to be my lover*' playing on the radio. I grinned when Troy started singing in a high-pitched voice which, I hoped, was a mickey-take of The

Spice Girls.

My smile faded when I spotted the four bin bags by our front gate. All filled by my helpful sister who'd pointed out I didn't need that, or that, or even that as she squeezed more of my stuff into the bags. The corner of a book strained against the plastic and I resisted the urge to rescue it. Pointless, as I wouldn't have anywhere to put it in my poke-hole of a room.

"Ooo-oooh," Troy squealed. I could imagine the shampoo bottle being used as his mike. Great material for winding him up when he got out of the shower which, knowing him, would be at least an hour.

Tucked in my handbag were the two fags I'd nicked from Mandy's pack. Compensation, I reckoned, for the loss of my room. I went to pull one out and then paused. If Mrs Hamilton caught me, she'd get narky like last time. What was her problem? Just because I smoked, it didn't mean Troy would.

I headed off to the Rec. As I neared the end of the alleyway, fragments of voices echoed. "Here, here. Ref!" I stepped onto the field to applause and the screech of a whistle coming from the black, maroon and white figures that speckled the back pitch.

What a result! The swings were empty, leaving me the whole lower park. I wandered over, side stepping the jagged green pieces of glass around the see-saw, before doing the usual routine of checking the swing seat for gob or chewing gum. With my arms looped around the chains, I pulled a fag from my handbag, straightening the end where it had got crushed and the baccy was coming out. Rocco had been by recently. A sprayed black R tagged a sign saying, 'Under 13s only may use this equipment'. Yeah, right, like little kids were going to come here. I sparked up, took a deep lug and puffed out three perfect smoke doughnuts as Nina called them.

Beyond the trees were rows of rooftops, like steps leading up the hill until they reached Upper Mosston and became tall blocks of concrete. I'd often sat here wondering what it was like to have no garden. We were lucky. I squinted, straining to spot colour dotting the grey where they had to hang their washing over the balcony sides to dry. None today but through the gaps between the buildings I could see a whole two miles to the boundaries of Mosston and freedom.

I took another drag. Troy reckoned he'd get away and go to college before university. When I'd mentioned college, Mum had cackled.

"You live on planet Fantasy," Mandy had said and set Mum off laughing again, as if she'd said something really clever.

Round and round I twisted the swing, so the chain clanked above me and the seat rose forcing me on tiptoes to reach the ground. When I let go, my hair whipped into my face as I twirled, legs outstretched, until the chains snapped open. As the swing jerked back, I found Simon heading over. His jacket dangled over his shoulder, while he'd tucked his other hand in his jeans, so his thumb hung out all casual. As he came closer, I knew he was gazing at my boobs even though I couldn't see his eyes through his Ray-Bans. Well, today he'd be out of luck. I hitched my t-shirt up.

Without asking he sat on the other swing. "You okay, Cindy girl?"

I shrugged.

"Your sister giving you a hard time."

Behind his shades, I could just make out his eyes looking at my face. The corner of his mouth lifted in a sympathetic smile. Of course, he knew what Mandy was like.

33

He understood.

"Lovely tan. You haven't collected that fiver I owe you."

I flicked my cigarette away where it landed beside the see-saw and stretched out both my arms. He did the same. Mine were darker.

"How about double or quits?" he said.

"How?"

"See who can get the swing to go highest. Are you up for it?"

Up for it? I was made for a bet like this.

"Not cash though. Three packs of B&H." No point having money when Sid the newsagent wouldn't serve me.

Simon copied me when I pushed the swing back as far as it would go and leapt on. Leaning back so my hair brushed the tarmac and bending forward so it flipped over my face, I got higher than him. He managed to catch up but his swing did the jerky dropping thing and he bottled it, letting his feet catch the ground to slow down. When I laughed, he poked his tongue out.

"Three packs it is then," he said. "But you'll have to come to mine to collect. I can't be seen giving you them."

He got up and slung his jacket back over his shoulder. "I'll learn not to bet against you again. You're way too good. See you in half an hour."

Three packets. *Three* whole packets! I slid from the swing and headed off in the opposite direction, although I didn't have a clue what I would do for the next half hour. Then I remembered the other cigarette in my handbag and pulled it out. Now I wouldn't have to save it for later. Talk about better than a lottery win. Sixty fags! Nina was going to be soooo jealous.

As I reached the bottom of the alleyway that led into our

road, Troy came out of his front gate. He waved and broke into a jog. His t-shirt matched his trainers, glowing whiter than a toothpaste advert. He slowed as he reached me and his face flushed like he had something exciting to say.

"Great singing," I said. He smelt of aftershave, just like the one Simon wore. Kouros or something.

"Uh?"

"I heard you. In the bathroom. Spice Girls, wasn't it?"

He clapped his hands to his mouth, so I shoved his arm. "I'll keep your secret lover boy. Come on then, who is she?"

He frowned. "She?"

"Yeah, what's with the clothes and aftershave?" I pointed at the navy horse logo on his t-shirt. "Is it real?"

"I saw Dad yesterday," he said. "He's given me money too. Fancy going down town?"

"I can't just yet. I've got to pick up something from Simon."

His smile faded. "Simon?"

"Come with me," I said. "I won't be a minute."

He shook his head. "You go. You know where to find me."

Shoulders slumped, he walked away. He didn't look up as he reached his gate, didn't see me wave to say I wouldn't be long, but I saw him kick the gate open with his new posh trainers and heard it smack against the post.

And I was sure it wasn't my imagination that heard him shout, "Fuck Simon."

Chapter 7
- late November -

HE HURRIED TOWARDS ME, not noticing the shock I knew must be stamped on my face. Cindy. How many years since I'd been called that? The old feeling of nausea rose. No way would I become her again. Troy swept his hand through hair that was still the same sandy colour, flecked with blond. He still had the same green eyes and upturned nose, but the freckles I used to count to annoy him were now camouflaged by a deep tan and, as he smiled, crinkles cut into the corners of his eyes.

"I can't believe it. I thought I'd never see you again."

Arms outstretched, he went to hug me but, nose wrinkling, he drew back.

Instead, he grasped my hand like best friends and not the strangers we were while I fought the urge to snatch my arm away. Not just because I found his friendliness overwhelming, but my skin and clothes reeked of smoke. His voice had an odd twang, still well-spoken but with a hint of something I couldn't define. I'd rubbed some of his poshness off within months of him moving in, proudly teaching him how to talk 'proper' – except back then it was 'proppa' – so he wouldn't get picked on in town. In return, he'd taught me how to speak in front of adults, as he reckoned it was handy to be able to communicate better sometimes. How naïve and stupid I'd been to mock him, especially when speaking so well had come in handy later when I'd needed work with no qualifications, no references, no history.

"You've hardly changed," he said.

I grabbed a handful of hair. "Are you blind?"

My voice sounded different too. Coarser, thanks to the

fire. A picture of Jez lying there flashed to mind, his cold lifeless body at the mercy of those hungry flames. *Please let the firemen have reached him before the fire did.*

He shrugged. "Okay, you've bleached it and it's short now, but there's no mistaking you."

If he recognised me, who else would? I checked the houses around us for signs of nets twitching or shadows lurking behind the windows.

"I've left the children inside," I said. "We've just arrived. I need to get our stuff before they wake."

"I'll help."

There was no point saying no. The Troy of old wouldn't have watched me struggle and I doubted this one would.

He didn't ask why I'd stuffed our clothes in carrier bags or why I insisted on carrying the tin and the heavy bag with the folders and photo albums. He just held out his hands to take the bags and followed me back to the house. As he talked about the weather and how the estate had changed, the bags bashed against his legs and my scraped shins ached in sympathy.

"You still living there?" I jerked my head towards his Mum's house as we passed by.

"Just visiting for a while."

I stopped at the front door. "Thank you. I'll take them."

"It's no bother. I'll bring them in."

"The children are asleep."

He glanced at my outstretched hand. "And your partner?"

"Just the children." His ring finger was bare too.

"Can I come round for a chat after lunch? Or are you going to see your mum?"

"Mum? You know where she is?" I flushed. Talk about dropping myself in it. Before he could query it, I added,

"After lunch would be good."

I dropped the bags in the hallway and closed the door. Through the patterned glass pane, I watched him walk down the path, turn and disappear. My body ached with tiredness and fear. To him and everyone I'd be Cindy girl again. Memories punched me. Again and again. Please God, no, no, no. Take them away.

I slid down the wall and huddled like a child on the floor. A sour taste filled my mouth. Fucking Cindy girl. As hot tears broke free, I buried my face in my hands, and sobbed.

Fuck Cindy girl.

They did just that.

♦

It took a while to work out that the bits of black were pieces of fluff littering a carpet and not my bed. Carpet? Then it hit me. I was at Mum's, asleep on her hallway floor. Clutching the radiator, I eased myself to my feet and brushed myself down. Then the rest came flooding back: Troy, them and poor Jez. Strengthened by sleep, I forced back the memories.

Sunlight broke through the net curtains at the back of the lounge, lighting the area where the children lay asleep on the settee. Their little faces were tinged grey – from tiredness, shock or soot, I couldn't tell.

Upstairs I dumped the bags in the second bedroom, before flicking on the immersion heater and searching for bedding amongst the tangle of sheets and towels on the shelves above the tank. In the end I dragged the whole lot out, upending it on the bare mattress in Ella's old room where I set about separating it into piles. Everything smelt musty – worse, of urine. Better get used to that smell. I shivered as whispers from the past threatened to shout and shadows lurked in the doorways ready to spring to life. I gripped the bed frame and anchored myself to the present.

When Troy arrived an hour later the washing machine drum was banging as it whirled, while the twins splashed in the bath. I heard his tentative knock and shouted for him to come round the back but, as he tapped the door for the second time, I found myself doing something I'd always sworn I'd never to do again and left the children alone in the water – just for a second, I told myself, knowing what had happened when I'd said that before.

"The twins are in the bath." I rushed back to the kitchen, leaving him to make his own way inside.

He came into the kitchen wearing the most ridiculous grin, while all I could offer was a flickered smile.

I had to raise my voice over the din of the spin cycle and the children. "I found some old coffee and tea bags, but no milk."

"I can manage black coffee," he said in his strange twang.

The children sat at either end of the bubble-filled bath, in a haze of steam. Little Munchkin Men with blond twists sticking up from where I'd shampooed and rinsed their hair after raiding Mum's bathroom cabinet.

"Look Mummy," Lily said as she smacked the water. "I'm playing piano."

"Mine is better," Charlie said, thumping his hands so water splatted over the side of the bath.

Troy came over to hover by my shoulder, the warmth of his breath brushing my cheek. I had to clench my fists to fight the urge to push him away. Hopefully, the change of clothes and quick wash had removed most of the stink of smoke.

"Hi guys," he said. "I'm Troy. I used to know your Mummy."

The children stopped pounding as they took in the stranger beside me. Too close. It wasn't just his voice that had changed, his aftershave had too.

"Tell you what." I manoeuvred myself so I could speak to him without having a mouthful of his sweater. "Why don't you make the coffees while I get them out?"

As I held out the least musty bath towel I'd managed to find, Lily folded her arms threatening a sit-in.

"I said ten minutes more and it's been at least twenty."

Once the children were dressed we went through to the lounge, where they sat on the settee, legs stuck out straight so their little feet hung over the edge, watching us. I switched on the TV, grateful to see Mum had Freeview, and pressed the numbers for the twin's favourite channel. Fireman Sam waddled across the screen.

"We had a fire," Charlie said.

"We did, but Lily didn't like the loud bangs of the fireworks, did she?" I kept my voice light, as if Charlie was discussing any old Bonfire Night and walked over to him.

"But…" he started to say.

My knees cracked as I bent down to him. Keeping my back to Troy, I put my finger to my lips. Bewilderment reflected in his eyes.

"Why don't you tell Troy about your school?" I said.

Lily jumped in, eager to speak while I found a different channel – one with an animated film. Poor Charlie still looked confused and kept opening and closing his mouth as if I'd misunderstood him and he needed to explain, so I perched on the edge of the settee, beside the armchair where Troy sat, becoming a buffer between him and the children.

When Lily's voice slowed and she trailed off mid-sentence, her attention absorbed by the film, Troy waited for her to continue with her breathless chatter about school.

"I take it you don't have children," I said.

He shrugged. "Too busy. I'm only back for two months, until the New Year."

"Back?"

"I emigrated about eight years ago. I live in Canada now. Halifax. What about you? Are you visiting your Mum?"

I knew he was desperate to get away from this estate – weren't we both – but Canada? The thought of him living so far away left me feeling out of sorts for some reason. His gaze drew me back. He was waiting for an answer but what would I say? I couldn't keep up an outright lie, not to him.

"She didn't know we were coming. Where is she by the way?"

He hesitated, throwing a glance towards the children, but I signalled for him to go on. They were engrossed in the film.

"I'm sorry, Cindy," he said.

I flinched. I wished he'd stop calling me that. It dragged shocking memories to the surface: ones that left me breathless, me sandwiched between those lecherous faces…. Then it hit me, he'd said 'sorry'. Did that mean she was dead?

"My Mum said she'd had a stroke about two months ago. I think she's in a care home or something."

"So, she's..." If I said any more the tears would spill. From sadness, from relief?

The warmth of Troy's hand seeped through my fleece. I jumped up and walked over to the back window. Close up the nets were yellow and smelt musty and stale – of Mum. Strange how I thought of her and of this place by smell. The only way to keep the dark cloak shrouding the past.

The sun had disappeared behind a cloud and the tips of the Leylandii swayed in the breeze. A fat pigeon sat on the lawnmower arm, its plumage ruffled as it twisted its neck, ever watchful. It flapped off in the direction of Troy's house.

Troy was back, standing behind me, looking out for me. He'd always been good like that – when I'd let him – but we weren't kids anymore. Thank goodness.

I needed to breathe. I swung round, forcing him to step backwards so I caught a glimpse of the school photograph and the smiling girl with the dimple.

"And Ella," I said. "What happened to her?"

He shrugged. "I'll ask Mum. Is there anything else I can find out?"

If I sat him down and asked a million questions, it wouldn't be enough, but now wasn't the time. I had to deal with the future.

"Not so much find out, but there is something else," I said. "Have you got a car?"

Chapter 8
– Summer term. Year 9 –

I CHECKED THE AREA FOR NOSEY PARKERS. The last thing I needed was someone telling Mum I'd been seen going into Simon's place when Mandy didn't live there anymore. She'd want to know why and then she'd nick my fags off me. On the wall opposite, a steaming mug sat beside a pair of dirty gloves and a garden fork. While no shadows lurked behind dark windows, whoever they belonged to had gone inside, probably to take a phone call or something, which meant I had to be quick.

Unlike ours, Simon's gate didn't need to be picked up to open it. I gave it a little shove and it flew open, bashing against a rock on the side of the path before it juddered back. What sort of person put a stupid rock in the path? I flushed, realising it had probably been put there to stop people like me smashing the gate off its hinges.

Mrs Norris peered through the window of her ground floor lounge. I groaned. Mandy said she was a right witch, always going on about her and Simon making a noise. Apparently, she had this broomstick she'd thump on her ceiling until they turned down the TV. She looked the sort, with her downturned mouth and glaring eyes. I hesitated, half-expecting her to shove the window open and yell about the gate, but she shuffled away into the gloom. Her cat was cute though. Mandy moaned he shat on the flower beds, but I liked him. He reminded me of Tibbles, the way he wrapped himself round my legs and purred while I waited for Mandy to answer the door. He'd try to come inside and she would shout 'Ger-out' and go to kick him, forgetting she was meant to be a cat lover what with her owning Tibbles first. When I pointed that out, she'd say it was my fault for encouraging him. By the time I made it into her house, she'd be in a right strop.

Simon's front door was next to Mrs Norris's. Her little porch was covered with little animal ornaments: a stone cat, a grey tortoise and a dog wearing a chain which said 'Welcome' and – my favourite – a man holding a wheelbarrow filled with pansies.

Apart from a bristly mat, Simon's porch was empty. No sign of the cat either. The doorbell buzzed when I pressed it; along with the first tremors of nerves. Mandy would kill me if she knew I was here. She'd say I should be on her side and not having anything to do with a louse like him. The stairs creaked and the door opened and Simon stood there, a lopsided smile spreading across his face.

"You're eager," he said.

He ushered me up the stairs, past the kitchen and into the small lounge. Since Mandy had left he'd changed it around. Now the armchair and two-seater settee sat on this side of the room, while the TV and video were opposite beside the fireplace. I could see why he'd done it. Without the chair in the way there was more walkway space through the alcove which led to the two small bedrooms and bathroom.

He knelt to fold away a copy of The Sun left open at Page 3. As he picked up a mug and a full ashtray, he signalled for me to sit down on the settee.

"I can't stop long. Troy's waiting."

"Is he?" He craned his neck to look through the window.

"We're going down town. Shopping."

"You can stop for a quick drink, surely."

I shook my head.

"Aww, come on Cindy girl. I've been stuck here on my own for days. It'd be good to have a chat. Just the one coffee?"

Five past twelve, the clock on the mantelpiece said. Troy wouldn't be happy, but if we hurried we could make it to town by one. That would give us three hours before the shops shut.

"Tea," I said. "Two sugars. I'll have to be quick though."

He came back in a few minutes later with my tea and put it down on the windowsill next to the settee. Then he shot out, returning with a box of Quality Street, which he opened and put on the carpet by my feet.

"Have as many as you like." He sat down beside me on the settee. "Here, you don't look comfortable."

He tucked his cushion behind my back and, laughing, pinged my bra strap.

"I can't get over how fast you're growing up," he said. "Your sister talks about you like you're a child, but you're definitely not that."

He ran his finger down my arm and I jerked away. "Don't do that."

"Tickle, does it?"

"No." I rubbed my arm to stop the tingling. "I'm not ticklish."

"I don't believe it." He leant over the arm of the settee to pick up a pack of B&H. "Double or quits you are."

"We've already done that and I won. Anyway, I don't need more than three packs."

"What about you keep the three packs and get a fiver for shopping? If I make you laugh or you submit you only lose one pack. Or you could pay a forfeit."

His dimple cut into his face as he smirked. He reckoned

he was onto a winner but I could hold my own. While Troy won all the arm wrestling and word play games – well, he did go to grammar school – I knew more swear words than him, could blow smoke doughnuts and, most important, I was the tickling champ.

He was looking at my boobs again. "No weirdness, right? Just the arms, legs and neck."

"And the stomach, but that's it," he said. "Now lie like this."

He manoeuvred me so my head was on one settee arm and my legs on the other. The fabric felt greasy. I could imagine him and Mandy sitting here eating chips and rubbing slimy fingers along the arms, like I watched her do the other day at ours. I went to sit up, but he gently pushed me back. He ran his hand along each of his forearms, pretending to pull his sleeves up even though he was wearing a t-shirt. When he lifted my top, I snatched it back – no way was he seeing my bra – which made him tut and shake his finger. But he took more care, shifting my top up a few inches. Cool air wafted across my tummy.

Smiling at me, he ran his finger across my stomach. He did it again, circling round my belly button. My skin quivered. Funny sort of tickling, I wanted to say, but if I did he might stop. His tongue poked through his teeth, his eyes flicked from my stomach to my face. As his finger ran along the waistline of my jeans a heat grew between my legs. A tingling – not like before with my arm – but an urge. I needed to be touched down there, to be rubbed or something. Anything to ease this feeling. I flushed, unable to believe I'd just thought that.

I squeezed my legs together. Enough. I couldn't take any more.

"Stop." I pushed his hand away.

He groaned and pressed himself against my thigh. I could feel a hardness. Had I done that?

"No." I sat up. The bits between my legs still hot.

I had to get away, get out of there. But I wanted him to go on, I wanted to find out what it would feel like if he... if he put his hands down there. Was that really what I wanted though? I mean, this was Simon. My sister and him would have... Yuk.

He knelt beside me and put his hands on my knees. "Just two minutes more. Then you'll win."

"I've got to go." I got to my feet.

He shuffled over to the side of the settee and picked up two packets of fags.

"Just remember, the other pack is here if you want to pay a forfeit." He smiled. "It'll be a nice one, don't you worry."

Chapter 9
- late November -

TROY SCRATCHED HIS FOREHEAD. "Promise me we're not doing anything illegal. I mean, this – everything – is very odd."

I shook my head. "You won't be. Anyhow, it's not like I stole the car. Just borrowed it."

"You know I'd do anything to help you but if I get a criminal record, it would make things very difficult."

I wanted to laugh, to tell him not to be so serious. How could following a car be a problem? But I could see his point. Unlike me, he had a future to risk. He thought about things, planned the landing, while I went ahead and jumped. Look where that had got me.

I turned back to the window. I hated telling half the story, but it wasn't like I'd lied. If the police stopped me tonight, I'd be the one in trouble, not him. Anyhow, I had no choice. If it stayed here, the car might as well have a tracking beacon on it to pinpoint our location. Those men probably wouldn't think I'd be so stupid to park it in the same road, but they'd guess we'd be nearby. Not that I wanted to move it.

Once again, I'd have to face navigating Jez's car along the motorway, through towns and villages, gripping the steering wheel while I prayed I wouldn't be pulled over and asked to produce a licence I didn't have. But when I was standing on top of a mountain of poor choices, what were a few more scoops?

"You'll be fine, honest. How about you take the children in your car? That way we don't have to wake them. They'll be asleep in minutes."

He gave me the same look of old. The one he'd given me when he saw me smoking my first cigarette and I'd told him not to stress, I wouldn't get hooked. The one he'd given me when I told him not to be silly, Simon was like a relative to me. I wiped my hand across my eyes to draw the curtain on my thoughts. Why, since coming back here, was that bastard constantly on my mind?

Giving Troy the widest smile I could manage, I kept my voice light. "So, nine o' clock then?"

♦

After Troy left, I went through to the kitchen to search the cupboards for anything other than the three cans of value baked beans I'd found stashed at the back of the larder during my earlier search – now down to one tin after a boring lunch with the twins. There wasn't even a shrivelled potato or rancid carrot anywhere. I shook my head. Fancy thinking I'd find evidence of vegetables. I mean, this *was* Mum's house. But surely there'd be cartons of cereal, biscuits or other cans? Not just beans. Then it struck me. Mandy! About the only thing she was passionate about was her hatred of beans. And if she'd been in here, taking what she could while Mum was stuck in hospital, it would explain the tins left in the larder along with the washing powder.

"Pretty please," she used to say. "Put my stuff on with yours. The colours run for me."

Or she'd come through, sniff her top and hold it out. "Does this smell okay to you? I can't be arsed to wash it. Jessie's coming straight from work. She'll make us all stink of chip fat anyway."

If I pointed out her top, jeans or hair probably needed a wash, she'd freshen up by spraying herself with Impulse. Not

49

just one squirt here or there, but a figure of eight without a pitstop until both of us were coughing and had to open the window. I smiled – life hadn't been all bad – but my smile faded when I realised I'd have to leave the house in daylight to find food.

My stomach began to churn, worse than earlier when I'd thought about driving. What if I bumped into *him*? Simon. My breath rasped between my teeth – faster, faster – making me light-headed. As dizziness overwhelmed me, I grabbed the edge of the kitchen counter. What if somehow the car had been discovered and those men found us. Stop it, stop it. *Stop thinking. Now!*

Keeping a tight grip on the edge of the worktop, I bent my head between my outstretched arms and forced myself to slow my breathing. To think, just this time yesterday everything had been okay – well not okay, but nothing like as bad as now. It could all start again, with those men hammering at the door, demanding money, threatening the children. But why would they come after me? They'd think the money in the tin was burnt in the fire.

Unless, Jez tells them.

Impossible. He was dead. I flinched, remembering the feel of his cool skin. He'd taken all those tablets, the coward, because he knew they were out to get him. Left his problems to me.

At the sink I splashed my face with cold water until my fingers and cheeks tingled. Calm now, I felt able to face what I had to do. I took a deep breath, dried my hands on my jeans and headed upstairs.

I'd folded the clothes into separate piles for each of us in the wardrobe. Beside them lay Jez's tin, half-covered by the carrier bag containing the photo albums and two folders. The tin was a quaint old thing with red tartan sides and a

50

picture of a castle embossed on the front. No different from any other one you'd find stacked ten high in the biscuit aisle at Christmas. I picked it up – surprised to realise it felt heavier than I remembered – and sat down on the bare mattress with it resting on my lap. Up close the grey castle with its austere turrets, thick chimneys and blank windows resembled a prison, especially with the grey mist that swathed the purple hills in the background.

My hands hovered as if a force field kept me from it, but I battled on.

As I dug my fingernails under the lid to lever it off, it came away with a pop. An unexpected smell rose. One I knew. Bile scorched my throat. I snatched the wad of notes and a small notebook and flung them to one side. Unable to tear my gaze from what lay beneath – no, no, he couldn't have – I slammed the tin to the floor. The silver underside reflected my face, mouth open. A small cellophane bag of white powder jutted from beneath the tin, while strewn round were a dozen or more small sealed pouches each holding pills. If Jez were here, I'd kill him. He knew how I felt about drugs. My hands balled into fists, my nails cut into my palms.

"Bastard!" I kicked the tin so hard it smashed into the bedroom wall. "You fucking bastard. You promised."

As I fell to my knees sobbing, Charlie called up the stairs, "Mummy? Are you okay?"

He couldn't see this. I made it to the door the bedroom door as his white face appeared at the top of the stairs. Anxious eyes peered into the bedroom behind me.

"Darling, I'm fine. I just dropped something, that's all."

I forced a smile, resisting the urge to dab the wetness in the corner of my eyes.

"I'll be down in a minute, after I've finished tidying up.

Tell Lily we'll be going out soon to get something to eat."

Once I'd stuffed the bags back into the tin, I clamped the lid on and tucked it by the door. No way was it staying here. As I tucked the cash under the mattress, the orange notebook caught my eye. The pages skimmed my thumb like a flickerbook. Names, addresses, telephone numbers and rows of figures, some crossed out, flashed by. None of it in Jez's handwriting, until the last page or two. Please no! I pressed my hand to my mouth. The notebook must have been Mick's, I was sure of it. Not only did it show a list of people who owed for drugs, but the loan side of the business and goodness knows what else too. Each page a dozen sad stories.

If I stopped to look, I'd find my name in there somewhere.

Chapter 10
– Summer holidays –

I LAID THE BOOK ON THE DUVET and sighed. What I wouldn't do for someone to appear right now and tell my mum they were taking me away to a school where I could learn magic and do exciting stuff. Even though I knew it was ridiculous, I couldn't help but take my little mirror from the bedside table, give it a quick wipe with my sleeve and lift my fringe. If I joined the spots, I could make a zig zag.

With a bit of imagination, my family might be the Dursleys. My mum would make a good Petunia Dursley – not being posh or anything – but always looking after her Dudley. That'd be Mandy, what with her always stuffing her face. She must have put on a stone in the six weeks since she'd been back here. Only Bill let us down. Not only was he too skinny to be Vernon, but sometimes he was nice to me, like letting me hide out here while they decorated the lounge.

Bill's whistling drifted up the stairs. I heaved myself to my feet and went down to see how he was getting on. As I entered the lounge, he climbed down the step ladder and smiled. His dark hair was all stuck up at the front like he'd smeared the paste brush along his face. White powder dusted his cheeks and eyelashes.

Hands on his hips, he surveyed his work. "Whatcha think?"

"That's right. Come in when we've finished," Mum said. She'd pulled her hair back into a ponytail, but a wisp had broken free and hung between her eyes. Irritated, she blew it away.

I'd never seen our lounge look so fashionable. The top half was papered in a mottled blue with a frieze pattered with navy diamonds and gold round the middle, while the same navy and gold ran in vertical stripes along the bottom. Only the ancient green and pink curtains ruined the look. A few weeks ago, I'd helped Mrs Hamilton do hers and she'd showed me how to pull the top strings so her curtains bunched together. Ours didn't. They hung at odd spaces. One corner flapped outwards where it had broken loose from its plastic hook to show the faded pattern on the back.

"Yeah, nice," I said.

Mum bent to pick up the bucket. "Here, make yourself useful. Wash this out."

I took it from her and went through to the hallway, where I sidestepped a flattened paste bag. In the kitchen a bag of plain flour sat beside the sink. How odd. I peered into the bag to check it was flour. The worktop looked like Mrs Hamilton's when she was making pastry, except she sprinkled the flour over the side for a reason. Here, the one clear patch on the top was a circle where the bucket had stood. I stepped outside. What were the odds I would be clearing up?

As I tipped the claggy water down the drain, the metal chain curtain at the back door clanked. Bill had brought it back from the betting shop last week to hang above the back door, saying it would keep the flies out and wouldn't blow about in the wind like our old plastic strips used to do. When all the chains settled together, it showed a picture of a horse and jockey racing up to a Tote sign. I wondered what Mrs Hamilton thought as she looked out of her kitchen window. She hated betting.

Behind me, a lighter flicked. Mum. I didn't turn around but banged the bucket against the concrete path. From the corner of my eye, I could see her leaning against the wall, taking a drag of her fag, her gaze on me. I made a show of banging the last dregs from the bucket.

"When you're done, you can take the flour back next door and say thanks. Don't be disappearing off with that Troy though. You need to clear this mess." She looked at the kitchen sides as if I'd done it. "Then you can explain where my fags have gone."

"How should I know?" I shrugged. "Ask Mandy. And anyhow, I'm not going nowhere. I told you, Troy's gone on holiday with his dad for three weeks. To Canada."

"Oh la de da. Some people get all the luck. Like that'd stop you buggering off." She pulled open the packet of fags and shook it, so I could see the six tips. "There should be ten. I've been keeping count."

She'd come out to here to have a pop at me away from Bill because he'd have stuck up for me and told her I hadn't stolen them. Okay, I'd snuck one of them last night, but there was a big difference between one and four. Either she couldn't count or Mandy was at it too. My money was on Mandy.

"I'm hardly going anywhere," I said. "Not when Nina's got a job."

I made sure I spat out the word 'job'. That was something Mum wouldn't let me have. Not a part-time one anyhow, as it might cause havoc with her benefits. She said it was bad enough Mandy being back home as she might get less money if they took Mandy's wages into account. That's if they found out.

In anger, I launched the bucket at the path, where it bounced several times before rolling to a stop by the fence. Refusing to look at her, I stomped past Mum to grab the bag of flour. Instead of jumping over the fence to Mrs Hamilton's back door, I headed out through our front door and down the path. Longer, but Mrs Hamilton would be in.

Within moments of knocking at Mrs Hamilton's front door, a pink shape appeared through the patterned glass, growing larger as she came closer.

"Who is it?" she said.

"Me, Cindy."

She pulled the door open and smiled.

"Cindy," she said, sounding pleased to see me. "Please, come in."

Mum would kill me if I took too long. I held out the flour and nodded towards my house. "I can't stop. I've got to clean the kitchen."

"That's a shame," she said.

The brightness faded from her eyes and lines appeared below her heavy foundation. Her pink lipstick had filtered like tiny veins into the skin around her mouth.

"It's so quiet without Troy. I can't believe he's only been away a few days. The next three weeks will feel very long." She gazed behind me and I twisted round to see who she was looking at – no one was coming along the road – not that I could see anyhow. Turning back, I found she was still looking beyond me, but then she smiled.

"Mustn't feel sorry for oneself," she said, her voice all cheerful. "It's a wonderful opportunity for him. You must come around sometime, Cindy. You can help me bake a cake."

"Will do." I turned to go.

I probably wouldn't. Talk about awkward being with Mrs Hamilton for hours. But as the door clicked shut, I felt bad. She might be stuck in the house all day, alone. I should bother with her.

♦

Later that afternoon, I was lying on my bed reading and listening to a tape Troy had loaned me, when I heard Mandy shout.

"You're a sodding liar, Cindy."

What now? Footsteps lumbered up the stairs and along the landing. By the time Mandy stormed into the bedroom, I was on my feet and ready.

"Why would I nick Mum's fags when I've got money?" Her face was all red and sweaty, matching the mahogany dye she'd put on her hair yesterday. She stabbed her finger so close to my face the tip blurred. "You're a liar, you are."

"No, I'm not," I yelled back. "Why would I take her fags?"

She shoved my shoulder and I staggered back, the back of my legs catching on my bed frame. Bitch. Who did she think she was coming in here and blaming me? My fist landed on something soft and squishy. When she clutched her boob and looked at me purple-faced and furious, I knew I was in for it.

"Bill!" I screamed.

Her hand whizzed past and my head spun round. A stinging pain ripped through my teeth and along my jaw. As the pain shot through me, so did my rage.

"Girls!" Bill's voice echoed up the stairs.

I grabbed her head and swung her on to the bed, blindly thumping and thumping her legs, arms, chest. I hardly noticed the blows that landed on me. All my anger poured into my fists and I became Rocky Balboa from the film we watched last week. She might be bigger, stronger and years older, but she wasn't winning.

"You're... the... thief," I sobbed between punches.

Arms wrapped around my waist and I was lifted in the air, legs flailing as I kicked out.

"She's the thief," I yelled. "I'm always getting the blame round here."

Bill let go and I bolted. At the top of the stairs, I stopped to look at them. He'd pulled Mandy from the bed and had tilted her face back to inspect it. A bead of blood ran from her nose and her face was blotchy. They both glared at me, like I was in the wrong. Even though I was fourteen, not sodding twenty-two like her.

Sprinting down the stairs, I bolted out of the front door and along the road, my arms pumping, my heart banging. A stitch brought me to a halt, where I found I was trembling. Hot tears rolled down my cheeks and I swiped them away. No way was anyone seeing me crying. My legs ached and my head felt woozy like last week when Nina and I bought that bottle of Thunderbird. Except that wouldn't have given me a whacking great big bruise like Mandy's fist must have done.

Not knowing where I headed – just that I needed to get away – I turned into Dogshit Alley. I needed a fag too. Something to ease the shaking. Then I remembered Simon and the promised cigarettes. For a moment his place became the promised land, until I recalled the forfeit.

But that was weeks ago and he was kind. If he saw me like this, he'd help. I knew that much.

Chapter 11
- late November -

ONCE I'D CHECKED NO ONE WAS AROUND, I left the keys in the ignition and hurried through the biting wind towards Troy's car. Through the beam of his headlights, I could make out the white of his fingers clutching the steering wheel but not his face. As I climbed into the passenger seat, he pursed his lips and tapped the Sat Nav screen, muttering something I couldn't make out. Running alongside the road sat high metal fencing, sharply pointed to deter intruders. Then it struck me. I'd taken him to the back of an industrial estate, away from watchful eyes, but what if there were security cameras?

"I'm sorry," I said.

"What for?" He tapped the Sat Nav. "This is useless."

"For asking you to do this."

He gazed at me. "You said it wouldn't get us into trouble and I believe you."

Had I mistaken the edge to his voice? I kept my answer brief, in case my voice betrayed me.

"Thank you."

Tears pricked my eyes. I swallowed. I'd said he'd be fine and I'd believed it, but that was before I'd opened the tin. Now we sat metres from a car with the spare wheel compartment stashed with Jez's drugs and in possible view of security cameras. As usual, I'd wrecked everything by leaping without a moment's thought. Why hadn't I binned the tin somewhere else? Flushed the drugs down the toilet. If it was found, Troy would be implicated – thanks to me and my selfishness. The children sat in the back of the car, their heads buried in the cushioned sides of their car seats. I sent a

59

silent prayer that we hadn't been seen. Poor Lily and Charlie had gone through too much already.

"At the junction, turn right into Stanwell Avenue," Sat Nav woman said, leading us a different route out of the industrial estate than the way I'd taken us in.

We moved forward, past Jez's car. The wing mirror reflected a charcoal silhouette against the night.

"Goodbye," I whispered as it disappeared from sight. My final link to Jez now a memory. While I hated myself for admitting it, I wanted it that way.

Just a week ago I'd have said I could spend a lifetime with Jez. But it would have been a life imprisoned by lies. What sort of man would be so stupid to choose an opponent like Mick? This was no David and Goliath trading stones in the open, but a spat in the sewers where thugs who hid in the shadows would do anything – *anything* – in the pursuit of power and money.

The road stretched ahead, lined by tall streetlamps that cast a yellow glow, illuminating rows of houses with dark windows and tiled frontages, chalet bungalows set back from the road and the occasional Victorian terrace. We overtook a car indicating to turn into a shopping precinct, all shadowy frontages except for the brightly lit Mighty Kebab shop where two customers leaned against white-tiled interior walls. My stomach rumbled. In the distance, a garage cast a halo of light, while beside it blazed the red dots of traffic lights.

"So, how long have you been driving?"

As Troy's words filtered through my mind, I guessed his underlying question.

"Not long."

"Normally I wouldn't dare to mention someone's driving but – oh my – twice, no, make that three times..."

60

Troy started to laugh but his expression changed and he shook his head. "I don't know what's happened or why, but nothing's worth putting you, your children or other people in danger."

I tensed. Did he really think I'd do this if I had no choice? Ahead of us the traffic lights turned green and he accelerated. Were they the ones I'd gone through earlier on a red? What if that truck hadn't tooted or if I hadn't hit the brakes like I did? I couldn't go on like this. Things had to change.

"Can we leave it? Please." My throat tightened. I couldn't speak or I'd cry.

He reached over and grasped my hand, releasing the tears I'd held in place. As they ran freely, I wished with every fibre of my being that I'd listened to him all those years ago.

Before I knew it, we were on the M25. Troy pulled past a lorry and I said a silent prayer of thanks that it wasn't the previous night when I'd sat behind the huge HGV for the whole of the motorway journey, too terrified to move. We sped beneath the motorway lamps where strips of light ran along the bonnet, across Troy's face. The corners of his mouth were upturned. His cute nose hadn't changed, even though I'd spent years twisting it as a joke. And although his eyes were mirrors to the light and dark around us, I knew their true colour. That I'd never forget.

Troy caught me staring and grinned. "I can't believe you're sitting next to me. For the past fourteen years I've wondered what happened to you."

"You wouldn't want to know."

"Try me," he said.

I shook my head. "How's your mum?"

He nodded. "Good. She said she hopes I'm not getting

into mischief with you. She'd love it if you came around to say hello. She still bakes, so your children will love her."

It was my turn to smile, until I remembered how Mrs Hamilton had looked at me during that final year, when she'd stand at her front window staring out. Her head would tilt towards my stomach and I would have to turn away because her eyes said it all.

"Your mum wants to see me? After everything?"

"Of course, Cin… Sorry, I can't get the hang of your name. What do you mean by 'after everything'?"

"What I did. To you."

"Cindy! You didn't do anything. You were a child."

I shuddered. Cindy. The sound revolted me. A plaything, a doll.

"Please call me Karis or Kari," I said. "I know it's new for you, but I've been Karis for years now."

"Sorry." He gave me the boyish grin of old. "I'll try harder."

He became silent, but moments later he thumped the wheel. "How can you think we wouldn't want to see you again? The best friend I ever had. I've never forgotten the first time I met you. You sitting on that lawnmower waiting for your cat and how bad I felt when I found the poor thing. And then having to face you that night."

I'd forgotten Tibbles. He'd become a haze in the past, when once he'd been the most important thing. The best present my sister ever gave me, although she didn't 'give' him. For a moment, I was back home with Tibbles warm beside me on the bed, his stomach vibrating as he purred so loud it sounded like Bill snoring.

"My first memory of you," I said and giggled. "Was seeing you in your white clothes and thinking that was your taste in fashion."

He chuckled. "What, my cricket whites?"

I nodded. "And your name. I thought your mum had called you it because you were Greek or something."

"Yes, you told me. Well, I thought you were called Cindy, after the doll."

Cindy doll. Cindy girl. An image flashed to mind. Me lying there, in a white room, surrounded by blurred faces. Huge tongues, wide eyes, dimples. You'll like this Cindy girl. Not just like it, you'll love it. Tell us you love it, Cindy girl.

I jerked away in shock. The memories, they'd come back! Unearthed after all these years.

Troy squeezed my arm. His hand lingered, resting on my skin. I clenched my teeth and forced myself not to shrug him away. *Cindy girl, sweet Cindy girl.* My heart thumped and prickles of sweat beaded my forehead. I dabbed my face with my sleeve and took a deep breath, and another, until I could manage to speak.

"It's hot in here."

"I wish you'd talk to me. I might be able to help."

I took his hand from my arm and placed it on his lap. "I wish you could, but I can't explain. Not yet."

Not ever.

Chapter 12
– Summer holidays –

As Simon opened the door, I burst into tears. Talk about stupid, but I was just so happy he was in. He signalled for me to go up the stairs and when I reached the lounge, he pulled me to his chest and cuddled me until I stopped crying. He smelt of aftershave and cigarettes, his arms thick and strong compared to boys my age. In the background, the TV commentator rattled on and a crowd roared.

"What's happened?" He lifted my face to look into his eyes. Creases cut into the corners, but I liked the way his black eyelashes curled upwards.

"Mum said I nicked her fags, but I didn't. Then Mandy slapped me cos I said it was her. So I gave it to her good and proper." Then I remembered he liked Mandy. "Sorry."

He stroked his finger across my cheek. "Is that sore?"

"A little." I shrugged.

"I'll get some cream. Do you want a drink?" He picked up the remote control and turned off the telly.

I hesitated, spying the cigarettes sitting on the arm of the chair beside an ashtray.

He gave me his typical lopsided smile, so his dimple cut into his cheek. "Tea, two sugars, and a fag, I guess."

The room was messier than the last time I'd been. Bits of fluff and ash were dotted over the carpet and two black socks, half-balled from where he'd pulled them off, lay near the settee. I picked up a cold mug of coffee and took it over to the windowsill where I shifted a load of papers and bills to make a space for it by the telephone. The woman in the house opposite was opening her bedroom curtains, but she stopped with her arm stretched upwards and stared. I backed away and sat down on the settee.

Through the alcove which led to the bedrooms and bathroom, a bedroom door stood wide open. The carpet there was a darkish blue compared to the mottled grey lounge carpet and the walls were whiter than the cream in here. I looked round, seeing things I hadn't noticed before, like the cobweb in the corner above the TV and the stains around the light switch. Finger marks, I realised, feeling pleased to be able to identify dirt. I'd check out our light switches later.

From the kitchen, came the sound of a teaspoon chinking against the side of the cup. A cupboard door clanged and footsteps came closer. I shuffled to the edge of the settee, not wanting to look like I'd made myself too much at home. He came through smiling and holding a cup in each hand. After giving the door a kick to close it, he headed over to the windowsill where he put both cups down on top of a pile of papers, leaving one cup tilted at an alarming angle. I expected him to sit down, but instead he disappeared through the alcove, where I heard him shuffling around.

"Got it." He reappeared holding out a tube of Savlon.

"I'm alright now."

He came over and leant my face to one side, so he could see where Mandy had slapped me. "It'll ease the bruising."

The cream was cold against my burning cheek but his fingers were soft, his touch gentler than I expected. It reminded me of last time. Flushing at the thought of his fingers stroking my tummy and the tingling sensation down there, I pushed his hand away.

"Thanks," I said.

He plonked himself down beside me and held out his fag packet. Once he'd lit both our fags, he lay into the back of the settee, his arm outstretched. His legs hung apart, unlike mine which I kept together so my knees touched.

"Having trouble at home, Cindy girl? You should make this your bolt hole. Come here whenever you like."

He tapped his nose and put his fag in his mouth. From the corners of his lips, he breathed out two long streams of smoke. It looked easy. I'd try it later. I reached up for my coffee and took a sip, watching him from over the rim.

"You don't have it easy at home," he said. "Mandy is great, but talk about hard work. Your mum too. I always thought you didn't fit in there. That reminds me."

He headed off towards the white bedroom. His shirt had come loose at the back, so it hung over his jeans and there was a small hole in the back of his socks. I was getting good at this noticing lark.

He headed back out, holding two books. The first he held up in a sort of 'dah nah' way, like he'd won the lottery. I recognised the cover. *Harry Potter*.

"For you," he said. "Apparently everyone's reading it. The other I think you'll like."

He dropped back onto the settee and handed me both books. I stubbed out my fag and took them from him. From the white grooves down the spine and the rippled pages, I could tell *Harry Potter* was second hand but who cared? I flicked through it, just to show interest, even though I had the library book at home ready to go back. The second one I'd not seen before, *Bridget Jones's Diary*. It looked brand new. The woman on the cover was smoking beside a blurb about alcohol, cigarettes and food. I ignored the urge to open the pages and start reading.

"Can I keep these?"

Simon nodded.

I grinned and turned the books over, enjoying the feel of their weight. They could go on my new bookshelf. "Really?"

"Have you time to stop and watch a film? I've got *Fifth*

66

Element. You seen it at the cinema yet?"

I shook my head. "What, you've got a copy here? But it's not out on video."

He gave me a secretive smile, bent over the edge of the settee arm to tug at something and handed me a video tape. There wasn't a box, but the white sticker on the front read *Fifth Element*.

"Go on, put it on. It's not a bad pirate either."

I shoved the video into the player and settled back beside him. He patted the seat for me to move closer, but I liked being against the settee arm. I curled my legs round and patted the cushion to get comfy.

"You won't be able to see so well from that angle." He leant over me to tug the cushion away and put it on his thigh. "Here, turn this way."

I hesitated, but then I saw what he meant. With the TV angled towards him I'd get a much better view, so I twisted round and put my head on the cushion. Sometimes I put my head on Troy's lap to watch telly or when we were at the park, but it felt weird being this close to an adult.

"If you like films, a mate of mine gets them for me."

As the noise blared and the film started to play, Simon's arm dropped to rest on my stomach and a burst of fear and anticipation ran through me. I went to push his hand away, but he lifted it to pick up his cigarettes and offered me one.

Once he'd lit the cigarette, I settled back, feeling quite the olden-day film star as I blew out a stream of smoke. To think, just this morning I'd been stuck in my bedroom alone with just a book. Now here I was surrounded by luxury: a film, a hot drink, my own books and a magic porridge pot of cigarettes. I shivered with excitement.

Simon must have picked up on my hidden pleasure, as he patted my arm. "Come round here anytime to get away from your family. No need to tell anyone. It can be our little secret."

Chapter 13
- late November -

I WAS IN THE LOUNGE with the children watching an auction programme when the doorbell rang. A strange off-key sound that suggested the batteries were about to die. With curious looks, the twins shuffled forward to get up from the settee, but I put my fingers to my lips and signalled for them to stay put. As I crossed over to the window, my heart began to thud. Even though it was likely our visitor could hear the TV, I tucked myself behind the curtains, so I couldn't be spotted, and peered through the synthetic-smelling nets.

Troy stepped back from the front doorstep and looked up at the bedroom, as if he expected us to be still asleep after our late night. I thought we'd agreed eleven, not ten o'clock. I tapped on the window and pointed for him to go around the back.

"Mysterious as ever," he said, as he stepped through the kitchen doorway. He held out a small bottle of milk which I put on the side.

"Well, you know me."

His eyes met mine and I turned away. We both knew the truth. He no longer knew me, any more than I knew myself.

"So, are you still up for an exciting afternoon at the supermarket?"

I held up the kettle and waited for him to nod before I flicked the switch. "Can we go to Chillington instead? I know it's a bit of a drive, but…."

I went to find the words to explain but found I couldn't.

Something had absorbed Troy's attention. He leaned against the worktop, gazing through the window to the frosted grass and grey sky. I couldn't see anything of interest in the garden, but he was another matter. Shadows stained the skin beneath his eyes. Just twenty-four hours with me and he looked worn out. I turned away and pulled two cups from the cupboard. While I splashed a generous amount of milk into mine, I let just a droplet fall into his, remembering how he liked it – strong and stewed. When I went to put the milk back, a hint of aftershave wafted in the air. Different to the one he'd worn yesterday.

The sound of the fridge door closing seemed to jolt him from his thoughts. "Wherever you want," he said.

Something about the way he spoke made me long to reach out to him. He'd been a precious friend, one of the few in my life. Friendship should never be a one-way street.

"How about I cook for you tonight, to say thank you?"

His eyebrows lifted.

"I *can* cook, you know," I said. "And you can talk. Swimming pool pasta dishes?"

"You'll never forget that will you? One little mistake."

I pointed the teaspoon at him. "One? Forgetting to strain the mince. Adding the onions at the end. And you said forty-five minutes to boil the pasta."

"No way! I'm sure that was you."

"Your mum's face when we dished up!"

When he laughed he tilted his head back, his teeth white against this tanned skin, his hair transforming from sandy to golden in the light. He made me want to giggle, to do madcap things again like cooking weird concoctions, to be young. *To go back and start again.* A shuffling sound came from the hallway and we turned to find Lily and Charlie by the kitchen door, mirror opposites as their heads rested against the wall, watching us with uncertain expressions. If I started again, I wouldn't have them. Which meant I had to go from here.

"Can we go out, Mummy?" Charlie asked.

I held up my cup. "Just let me drink this. Troy's taking us to the shops."

"How about the park afterwards?" Troy said.

As the children hissed 'yes', I shot him a look, but he put his hands up as if to surrender.

"I was thinking that if we're going to Chillington, we might as well make a day of it," he said.

I knew there was no point arguing.

♦

In the end it had been park first and then shopping, after we realised I'd need to buy frozen items. It meant the children had to run around the park in the too-small shoes with holes in the soles I'd collected from my flat. On the way home, they'd fallen asleep. Legs dangling, their new white trainers tapped the edge of the seat, mirroring the car's movement. Troy and I fell into a comfortable silence as he drove through the winding back roads, one minute we were enclosed by clumps of skeletal trees and the next our view transformed into a painting with rolling fields dotted with cows and criss-crossed by hedges. It was impossible to believe that this time last week I'd been living in the claustrophobia of a London estate, with graffiti as common as leaves. I corrected myself – as we passed beneath the bare boughs of a tree – leaves in summer.

As a child, I'd thought my council estate was huge and I lived in a town as big as a city. For a town, Mosston had its fair share of issues, especially our estate. No wonder Troy's mum had been so unhappy about moving there. Troy too. He'd looked so lost back then, nothing like the assured man sitting beside me, his grip loose on the steering wheel, his face in profile against the landscape. He suited my idea of a Canadian, at ease with the rugged mountains and bear-infested forests. The boyish plumpness had gone, giving a strength to his jaw and cheekbones I could imagine in the hardiest settler.

As he looked at me, I said, "You told me about your job but what's it like in Canada? Do you live in the countryside?"

He shook his head. "In the suburbs. Do you remember after I went there with Dad, I said I wanted to go back to live in a house near the sea? Well, I got my wish."

"I remember you going."

I didn't add that he couldn't have told *me* about his holiday. But he now recalled it too, as his tan couldn't hide the flush colouring his cheeks. His knuckles whitened and a knot pulsed in the corner of his jaw. He didn't look angry, more upset. But then he'd never had a temper, not like Jez, Mike or any of the others.

He slowed for the junction and we sat facing the sign for Mosston. Two miles, it said, although it would be less than a mile before we reached the outskirts. When the car didn't move, even though the road was clear, I turned to find him looking at me.

"Those weeks I was away may as well have been years. I've always wondered what happened."

As I went to speak, he held up his hand. "I know. You can't tell me. But, Ci..., you must understand... Last night, I didn't ask why I followed you to the depths of outer London. Always, I'll trust you. Maybe you could trust me too."

With that he pulled the car towards Mosston, while I sat prickling with agitation. Trust. An over-used word. Jez used to tell me to trust him. Just move in with him and he'd sort it all out. He'd look after me and the kids. Nothing bad would

72

happen again. Look where that had got me. Then it struck me. It had got me here with Troy.

Houses lined the road, where until recently there'd been fields. Cream rendered terraces snuggled next to three-storey town houses, while here and there stood a larger detached property, with a whisper of space between. A large board advertised properties for sale: four, three and two beds with part-exchange possible. On another board a housing association advertised properties for rent or share. If Troy's mum had moved now instead of back then, would she have chosen to live here rather than the social ghetto of my childhood estate?

She'd always been unhappy. I'd seen it in her eyes, in every step she took, in every sigh. How could a thoughtful man like Troy have left her alone in this country?

"Is your mum staying put or will she move?" I pointed to the new estate. "They look nice."

Troy smiled. "Mum's happy where she is, believe it or not. Tell you what, as you've invited me to test out your improved spag bol tonight, you can join us at Mum's tomorrow and have a chat about old times. She loves children. She'll adore your two."

I swallowed and turned back to the houses. The last thing I needed was a chat with Mrs Hamilton about the past.

Chapter 14
– Summer holidays –

TWO DAYS LATER I WAS IN BED at eleven in the morning and planning my day. I'd thought about going back around to Simon's – he finished his shift at three – but Mrs Hamilton's face haunted me. She'd looked so sad when I said I couldn't come in. Much as she made me nervous with her mustn't do thats or adding letters where I'd dropped them, she also helped me with my homework and let me lick the spoon after she'd been baking. Without Troy, she'd have no one to chat to apart from her church people on Sunday. I would go and visit. If not today, definitely tomorrow.

I crouched beside my bed and pulled out a small pile of books from underneath. Behind them lay my stash secreted in an old make up bag. Five cigarettes left, which should last the day. Simon had said to come back whenever, but I didn't want to look like a user. I'd have to find something to do for him, to pay him back for his kindness. Maybe Mrs Hamilton could help me bake a cake.

Downstairs Mum was screeching at Bill. Something about him getting off his arse and finding another job. He shouted back: 'At least he'd had one'. They'd had about six rows in the past week alone. Mum would be doing the usual finger-jabbing thing with her neck going all stringy as her sinews stuck out, while he'd be red faced with bits of spit bubbling at the corners of his mouth. If their row went on long enough, he'd end up like a rabid dog.

"I have to look after that friggin' cow upstairs," Mum yelled. "For all the thanks I get."

I paused, make up bag in hand. Great. What had I done now? I held my breath to hear better, but I couldn't make out

Bill's muffled response.

"What do you mean 'not her fault'?" Mum shouted. "Are you saying it's mine? You are, aren't you? Well, you can stick it up your arse."

The wedge-shaped bit of wood I'd found made a perfect door stop, better than wrecking one of my books. I jammed it under, hoping it would stop them bursting in and dragging me into their argument again. Talk about unfair – getting grounded yesterday – when they'd come in blaming me for being born. What did they expect me to say? Sorry? At least Mandy wasn't around today, standing at her bedroom door smirking to wind me up more. It was alright for her having a job to go to. But Mum probably told the social she was still living with Simon, like she said Bill didn't live here as he had his own place, which was true, except he rented it to his mate.

Mum's voice cut through the closed door. "Of course, I can't work. If I did, she'd be up to no good within minutes."

More muttering from Bill.

"Well, she's already stealing. Drugs? How should I friggin' know!"

Thank goodness, I hadn't heard the thunder of stairs but she sounded closer, as if she was backing into the hallway. How much longer before they remembered me tucked up here? Instead of aiming from a distance, they could fire their barbs at my face.

When I clenched my fists, like now, the tops of my knuckles stood out like mountains. Stealing? I'd only taken one cigarette in a whole fortnight. I punched my thigh. A fiery jag ran down my leg. Not enough, I could still hear them. I smashed my fist into my leg. Pain fired through my thigh, like hot bolts. Still I heard their voices, but through the fog of pain they sounded like 'waa, waa, waa'.

"Shut up! Shut up!" I shouted. "*Shut up!*"

Five more weeks of this until school. I crawled into bed and dragged the pillow over my head, pinning both sides to the sheet. The air became damp with my breath. If only I could suffocate, fall asleep, never to return. Imagine floating in the sky, no longer part of this shit family. I tightened the grip on the pillow, so my face pressed into the mattress and a muffled panting filled my ears. Just stop breathing. Sharp pricks of pain jabbed the backs of my eyes and it felt as if they were about to burst. If that happened I'd go blind and be stuck here forever. I flung the pillow to the floor, gulping air. Talk about a weak, gutless loser. I punched the mattress again and again and again.

♦

What felt like hours later, I found myself rolled up inside my duvet, my face hot and sticky. The top of my head was burning. I stuck my hand out to check the radiator. The heat stung the tips of my fingers. In summer? Mum must be on an urgent mission to dry something so she could go out later. Fingers-crossed she would.

I unwrapped myself from the covers and staggered from the bed to inspect my face in my mirror. I had a serious case of bed head with one side flattened and the other like I'd been plugged into the mains. Mascara speckled my face and sleep clogged the corner of my eye. I yawned and stretched. My bones clicked as my fingertips nearly touched the bare lightbulb hanging from the ceiling. Another inch and I'd be there. I couldn't stay this short forever.

Through the rain-splattered window, I could see Mrs Hamilton unpegging the washing in her garden. Her movements were frantic, but the clothes hung heavy with water. She must have just got back home. There was always something hanging from her washing line. I teased Troy when she hung out his pants, especially the time after Christmas a few years back when he had been given Mutant Ninja Turtle ones. Mum mocked Mrs Hamilton for putting her washing out in the middle of winter so it hung like cardboard, but it was better than piling every radiator with clothes, especially since Mrs Hamilton had told me why it wasn't good to have steam in the house with the windows shut. I lifted the edge of the curtain to inspect the mould which blackened the walls beside the window. Thankfully, it hadn't grown much since March. As Mrs Hamilton bent to pick up her washing basket, she spotted me at the window and gave a little wave. I did the same back. She smiled and, head down against the driving rain, strode back inside.

Sighing, I sat back down on the bed. There wasn't the usual echo of voices downstairs and the new kitchen TV didn't vibrate through the bedroom floor. I crept to the door and pulled it open just a crack to listen for noise. None. I grabbed my cigarettes and, taking the stairs two at a time, raced into the bathroom for a quick freshen-up. Then, snatching my coat from the hook, I made my escape.

A while later, I sat on the swing at the park with a damp bum, after grabbing the chains of the swing and releasing a zillion droplets of water. I inspected my rolled-up sleeves. Still soaked.

The dog walker on the other side of the field was on their second circuit. At first, I'd enjoyed watching the man's dog take acrobatic leaps to snatch the ball from the air. Now they'd become like a programme you had to sit through because there was nothing better on the telly. I'd always wanted a dog, but Mum said we had enough bloody mouths in the house. Nina's dog, Boris, was lovely. A Labrador crossed with something shaggy. I twisted my leg around to check the side of my jeans, satisfied to see the dog snot from earlier had been washed away by the rain. Lucky Nina. Imagine not only having a part-time job but going home afterwards to your mum telling you to sit down, have a rest, while she sorted the tea. My mouth watered at the memory of the sausages and mash smell when her mum had opened her front door. Perhaps I could find a quid or two in the house and grab something from the chippie. I pulled my cigarette from my coat pocket and straightened it. A quick fag, then home. Hopefully, Mum and Bill would still be out. No way could I face another row.

At the bottom of the alleyway, I paused to check my house. If they were in, I'd go elsewhere. Next door's hedge blocked the view of our downstairs' windows so, keeping to the opposite side of the road, I crept closer to crouch behind Mr Adams' car. As I picked grit from my knee, I wondered why I hadn't taken Simon up on his offer of a place to go.

The noise of a front door closing alerted me to Mrs Hamilton heading down her garden path. I ducked, although I didn't know why. Her gate clanged shut and footsteps tapped the tarmac, becoming louder.

"Cindy?"

My cheeks burned as I turned to face her. "Yes, Mrs Hamilton?"

"Are you okay?"

If I stood up Mum might see me, so I bent lower to show her I'd been checking under the car. "I'm looking for something."

"Can I help?"

"No thanks. Going somewhere nice?"

She patted her handbag. "Just to the postbox. Troy called earlier."

Troy? It would be lovely to hear how he was doing. I peered over the bonnet of the car to the house. Through the downstairs nets I spied darkness, while upstairs Mum's bedroom curtains were drawn. Still out, by the looks of it.

"I'll walk with you," I said.

"If you're sure." Frowning, she tracked my gaze to my house.

I got to my feet. "So, Troy's…"

"Oi!"

I knew that voice. I closed my eyes, wishing myself away to another place, another life. A place of happiness, warmth, and sausages and mash.

"Oi, you. Madam. Get in. *Now!*"

Mum stood at our front door, hands planted on her hips, in her denim miniskirt and crimson vest top with a face to match. The way she swayed told me she'd had a session down the club.

"I've got to go," I said to Mrs Hamilton.

She smiled sympathetically at me. "Come around for tomorrow. I'll update you about Troy and we can have lunch. One o'clock?"

I nodded. The horror of an afternoon alone with Mrs Hamilton was nothing compared to what faced me now. Mum strode towards me, her mouth like a snarling dog. We met by the gate where she grabbed me. I didn't pull away or anything, even when she pinched my arms as she dragged me inside. She slammed the door shut and turned to me, her eyes out of focus, her breath heavy with the stink of booze and fags. Pissed. No matter what I said or did, it wouldn't make a difference.

"What now?" I wrenched my arm from her.

Her hand flashed by, jerking my head to the side. Pain burst across my cheek. I gasped, my eyes watering. It must be Mandy again. Mum had hardly touched or even spoken to me until Mandy moved back.

"Go on, tell me. What am I 'supposed' to have done this time?" I put air quotes around the word 'supposed' and leant forward to stare her out. To show her there was no point her slapping me all the time. I could handle whatever she did.

She clenched her teeth and lifted her hand. White palm, fingers outstretched. Slow motion. I threw my arm out, to stop her. As her blow landed on my face, I shoved her in the chest. Hard. Through the haze of my tears, her mouth became a gaping hole that shrieked. She shot backwards, smashing into the wall. For a moment she stood there, stunned. Then she launched, grabbing my shoulders, shaking me.

"You and me are finished. *Finished!* I am not speaking to you and you are not speaking to me. That's it."

She stumbled off towards the kitchen and it hit me I had no idea what I'd done. I clutched my face, grimacing at the fiery jabs of pain. If I stayed here, there'd be no food or drink and Mum might come bursting in later, angry again. Perhaps I should go to Simon's? If I did, I'd get to eat, but I'd be stuck all night in a strange house. While he might be nice, it didn't feel right. I gazed from the stairs to the front door and back again. Then I traipsed upstairs.

Chapter 15
- late November -

I PICKED UP THE BOX of hair dye from the edge of the bath and gazed into the bathroom mirror. Natural brown it promised. Unlike my mink-coloured hair which, even in the dim light through the window, had a definite green tinge. What was natural about that? The pictures on the back of the box showed a warm brown in varying shades depending on the original colour. Except the palest of their colours was light brown, not bleached blonde.

I sat on the toilet seat and buried in face in my hands. I'd wanted to make myself unrecognisable in case those men came looking. But I looked ridiculous. With just one hour until dinner with Mrs Hamilton, I had no time to beg Troy to take me to the supermarket to buy another dye. Throwing the box into the carrier bag bin which hung from a cupboard handle, I headed off to check on the children.

They were lying on the lounge carpet, crayons in fists, scribbling on the colouring pads bought during our supermarket trip the previous day. At least the carpet was a little fresher after my spring clean this morning. Even though I'd emptied the cylinder before I started, banging clumps of matted dust and hair into the bin, the vacuum cleaner had filled before I finished downstairs. The rest of the house was in the same state. Cobwebs hung in room corners and the curtains billowed dust when shaken, adding to the layers infesting the carpet fibres.

Charlie rolled onto his side as I entered the room and gazed at my hair in alarm.

"It went a bit wrong." I swept my hand through my fringe. The dye had somehow smoothed the coarseness of years of bleach.

He clamped his hand over his mouth, but hiccoughed giggles broke through his fingers. Lily crawled over and patted my head.

"You look a bit like Timmy."

Timmy? I searched my mind, until it came to me. One of the women I used to clean for, Mavis Buchanan, had a mangy wire-haired terrier. I used to shut him away in the study, leaving the children to play in the conservatory, as he'd launch himself from under the desk, snapping each time I went near him.

"I'm surprised you remember that thing," I said.

"You've got Timmy's hair." Charlie sniggered.

"Cheeky," I said. "It's alright for you. I'm going to look a right one at Troy's mum's house."

I looked out of the window and up at the grey sky. If going around Mrs Hamilton's with green hair was the worst thing that happened – great – but I had a feeling this was the day's opening salvo.

◆

When Troy opened the front door of his mum's house, a flicker of surprise touched his face as his gaze levelled with my hair. He smiled and ushered us in.

"The hair suits you," he whispered as I walked past.

"Thanks. I thought so too."

The house was silent. No TV, radio or chatter from another room. Had Mrs Hamilton gone out? Then I remembered if she wasn't baking, she used to sit in the lounge reading. Back then, the quiet used to agitate me and I'd beg Troy to hurry so we could go. I glanced around. The anaglypta wallpaper in the hallway had gone, replaced by

82

plastered walls painted with a hint of lilac. As my feet sank into the beige carpet, I signalled to the children to take their shoes off, the opposite to what I told them each time we entered Mum's house. I stooped to help Lily with the buckle of her shoes, my fingers made clumsy by nerves. The more I thought about it, the more I was certain Troy must have coerced his mum into inviting us. She couldn't have forgotten what she'd said.

Troy stood by the lounge door, waiting to shepherd us into the room. Next to his shoulder hung a framed photo montage from years before. The largest photo used to be him beaming in his school uniform, but the oval space had been filled by a new picture. Troy cupped my elbow to lead me through into the lounge, but I pointed to the grey-haired woman in a purple suit, clutching a bouquet of white lilies, her arm linked with a man who wore a wide smile and white carnation in his lapel.

"Your mum got married?"

Troy nodded. "In there," he whispered, edging me through the door. "They didn't come out as they didn't want to crowd the children."

Lily and Charlie clung to my trouser legs, their fingers nipping my thighs as we walked. Unlike Mum's dirty nets which muted the sunlight, the nets in Mrs Hamilton's lounge glowed white, a luminous backdrop for the vase of yellow roses which sat on the windowsill. The walls were a warm cream, dotted here and there with family photos. I tried to assimilate this cheerful space with my memories, but failed.

Mrs Hamilton sat beside the man from the wedding photo. He smiled, his knees cracking as he lifted himself to his feet.

"Ralph," he said, sunlight glinting on his glasses. "And you must be…."

His voice had a bit of a country twang – Norfolk? – different to what I expected from a friend – husband – of Mrs Hamilton.

"Karis," Troy said.

Ralph wiped his hand down his trouser leg and reached out to shake mine. His fingers were thick and coarse, like the labourers I knew.

"Karis!" Mrs Hamilton came over and kissed my cheek. She smelled of lavender. Her voice hadn't changed – she still spoke as if each letter held its own within a word – but she'd aged more than I'd expected. Thick lines etched the skin beneath her eyes and creased her forehead and flabby jowls drooped above a crinkled neck. She bent to the children. "And who are these little people?"

"Charlie and Lily." I found myself thinking about how I spoke, making sure I ended my words. The children leaned back into my hands. "They're twins."

"Lovely." Mrs Hamilton sounded as if she meant it. "I've asked Ralph to get Troy's old train track down from the loft. It's over there." She pointed to a cardboard box beneath the window. "If the children wish, they can play while we talk. It would be good to hear how you've been. I've often thought about you."

In the dining area a table was set for dinner. On top of a crocheted lace tablecloth, a small vase of crimson daisy-like flowers sat between two silver candlesticks each holding long cream candles. It would be water for the children – and for me too – no way would I risk spilling anything on that tablecloth.

After a few minutes Mrs Hamilton got up to take care of the dinner, followed by Troy, leaving me with Ralph who, after helping the children to set up the train track, told me funny stories about his old gardening business and its customers. He'd been retired a year, married to Mrs Hamilton for four years, and they spent their time wandering around ancient ruins and monuments in various countries. They'd met on one of those singles holidays, he said.

I'd relaxed by the time we moved to the table, where Ralph poured the wine – white, thank goodness – and offered the children lemonade. They sat, a knife and fork upright in each hand, as Troy placed the plates in front of them.

"What's that?" Charlie speared at a green thing with his fork.

I blushed, unable to answer. I'd have said cucumber, but no one I knew cooked them.

"It's a courgette," Mrs Hamilton said. "If you don't like it, you don't have to eat it. You might prefer the sweetcorn."

As he pushed the green lump to one side, I hissed, "Try it."

While Charlie nibbled at the edges, wearing a pained expression, Mrs Hamilton turned to me.

"Have you been to see your mother?"

Troy shot me an apologetic look. I shook my head and Mrs Hamilton's eyebrows arched. She picked up her wine glass and took a sip.

"Of course, you've only just arrived. You will need to get settled."

I dabbed the back of my hand against my burning cheeks. I'd all but forgotten about my mum. My third day back here, living in her house, and apart from the strangeness of that first day or the odd thought about food or dirty sheets, I hadn't stopped to think about her or what she might be going through. Or that I might go and see her. A chill ran down my back and I shuddered.

"If you want me to look after your children when you visit, let me know," Mrs Hamilton continued. "She's improved since the stroke but she's still quite poorly. The little ones may find it stressful."

They would, but what did she think I'd feel? Surely, she remembered what had happened? I laid my knife and fork down and took a large slug of wine. Across the table, Charlie prodded at pieces of sweetcorn, impaling a line on a prong of his fork. The tip of Lily's tongue poked through her lips and her blonde ringlets bounced as she sawed her meat. I took another swig.

"What are your plans for tomorrow?" Troy asked Ralph.

"Marion's been nagging me to take her shopping before we go to Sofia. Why we need another shopping trip when we only got back from Rome last month, that I don't know."

"I'll need fur-lined boots for walking. Last year it reached minus fourteen one night. *Minus fourteen.* Can you imagine?"

Her voice melted away as I gazed into the coffin-coloured wood that gleamed beneath the fine crochet patterned tablecloth. Would Mum die soon? The thought of my mother lying there alone, staring into the distance, unable to speak – or goodness knows what she'd be able to do after a stroke – sickened me. But to see her meant I'd have to touch her, feel sorry for her, perhaps forgive her. I couldn't do that. Suddenly, I needed to find out about Ella. Was she happy? Who was looking after her? Mandy, I assumed, but if I raised the subject, Mrs Hamilton might ask me if I planned to see her. Then I'd have to confess, no, I didn't want to do that. Then they'd wonder what sort of person didn't want to see their own daughter.

"…the one thing I've said we have to see is the Alexander Nevsky Cathedral," Ralph said.

How much of the conversation had I'd missed? I tried to rewind it in my mind, but couldn't, so I worked on capturing the bits I'd heard. They must still be talking about Sofia. Not that I'd heard of a Cathedral by that name. My geography didn't stretch much further than the books I'd read as a child, my life in London, Mosston and the occasional school trip to the countryside.

"Have you been anywhere exciting?" Ralph asked, picking up on my thoughts.

"Just England. London mainly."

Charlie stabbed a piece of meat. "Is this a pig?"

"That's right." Ralph nodded. "Where's your favourite place?" he said to Lily and Charlie. With wide eyes they stared at him.

"The seaside?" Mrs Hamilton suggested.

"Where Postman Pat lives?" Lily asked.

"That's the countryside. You know the seaside. Where you build sandcastles," Ralph said.

From the corner of my eye, Troy shrugged in sympathy. He knew what I was about to say.

"They… they've never been."

Mrs Hamilton paused to look at me. Did she wonder what life I'd been leading where my children didn't know the difference between the country and the sea? But with years spent fretting about the next meal or heating the flat, days out had been the last thing on my mind. Jez had promised us a trip to the seaside next year. Southend, his childhood haunt, even though he'd been there all of three or four times. *Jez!* Was he lying cold on a mortuary slab somewhere? I swallowed.

Mrs Hamilton's frowned. "Don't worry, dear. There will be plenty of time for outings." She turned to the children. "You would love the seaside. Although I wouldn't recommend going in winter. Talking about that." She turned back to me. "I heard Ella is going on a ski-ing trip with the school. Your sister, Mandy, is so good to her."

Mandy and good in the same sentence? And to have Mrs Hamilton say so too. Envy rushed through me. Unable to think what to say, I pushed the food around my plate. I shouldn't have agreed to come for dinner. No, scrub that. I shouldn't have come back. Full stop.

"They've only been back a few days," Troy said. From his tone, I knew he'd closed the conversation. Thank goodness. "Mum, why don't you tell Karis about your trip to Australia last year when you were nearly caught up in that forest fire?"

"We left Jez in the fire." Charlie turned to Ralph. "We left him deaded. He wouldn't wake up."

I tried to hide the shock from my face. But my voice shook as I said, "Let's not talk about that now."

I reached across the table to squeeze his hand. Eyebrows raised, I held his gaze. We would discuss it later, my expression told him. He bit his lower lip and nodded. Around us Mrs Hamilton, Ralph and Troy sat as if Charlie had pressed the pause button.

"We had an accident at home," I said. "We're staying at Mum's while the house is sorted."

"Ah, you lost your pet. Poor lad." Ralph's eyes glistened.

While Charlie frowned, Lily opened her mouth and took a deep breath as if ready to correct him. This could be bad.

"We were just talking about pets earlier, weren't we?" I said. "About Timmy, when you two were laughing at my hair." I pulled at a strand. "What do you think? Does green suit me?"

Chapter 16
– Summer holidays –

THE SMELL OF BACON WOKE ME. That and the blurry presenter's voice that echoed through the floorboards. My mouth watered and my stomach rumbled, a loud gurgle from a pit of emptiness. I kicked the duvet cover away and stumbled from the bed, dragging yesterday's jeans and baggy shirt over the knickers and vest top I'd slept in, and headed downstairs.

Oddly, it wasn't Bill but Mum who stood beside the cooker, pushing bacon around the frying pan. Her hair hung loose: thin snakes that coiled on her shoulders. She stabbed the bacon with a fork, piece after piece, so the pan clattered against the ring, and shook the rashers into a tin. As one piece stuck to the fork, she reached out, grabbed a knife and scraped it free.

"Give me a break," she muttered, above the noise of the telly.

She opened the fridge, leaving the empty pan sizzling on the stove. As she pulled out the box of eggs, she spotted me. Her eyes were bloodshot and the skin below baggy like an old woman's boobs. Why I thought of my mum's eyes like boobs, I didn't know, but she looked old now she'd removed her usual ponytail and, with it, the free facelift.

Jabbing her finger at me, she said, "*You.* You can fuck off."

Great. She was still hung up about yesterday. Hadn't drunk enough for her usual memory loss, which probably explained why she'd made it down so early. I didn't know what to say, so I stood there looking gormless.

"You think it's okay to hit your sister, to hit me? If you

don't watch out, I'll get the social here. They can bloody have you. No one else will."

I wanted to tell her where she could stick it but the smell of bacon grew stronger, the sizzling louder, competing with the annoying TV voice. Maybe if I played it right, let her have her say, she'd give me some.

"I'm sorry." I lowered my voice and gazed at the floor, away from her angry eyes.

"Sorry's not good enough. I'm doing all I can with no money and now Bill ain't got a job. What I don't need is you stressing me out more. I've got enough on my plate."

My eyes watered, not from tears but from the smoke. I pointed behind her, to the cooker. "Look."

She shot around. "Oh, for fuck's sake!"

She held up the pan, turning it so I could see the blackened inside and a bump in the metal bottom. Smoke curled upwards into the grey haze. I glanced up to the smoke detector above my head, relieved to see it hanging open, a gap where the battery should be.

"See, it's you!" she screeched.

Her eyes bulged and the strings in her neck shot out like someone had tightened tent cords. Then she lobbed the pan at me. I ducked and put my hands up to shield my face, but it hit my arm. The pan banged as it fell to the floor, clattering until it came to a rest. Silence.

Then the pain rose! My arm, on fire, burning. I shoved past Mum's outstretched arm and rushed into the bathroom, where I threw the bolt across the door. Hot tears ran down my face. I gritted my teeth against the stabbing agony, barbs shooting up and down. I turned on the tap and pushed in the plug, plunging my arm beneath the cool water. Within moments I could unclench my teeth. Stupid Mum. What had she done? I twisted my arm around under the water, shocked to see a huge long bubble, a disgusting grey colour, surrounded by puckered raw skin. She'd scarred me. Probably for life too.

As the water numbed my arm, I lifted it out, only for the scalding pain to return. I shoved my arm back, banging my elbow against the side of the bowl.

A tap at the door. I ignored it.

Another tap.

"Cindy?" Mum said, sounding all worried. She should be. If I showed the social this, then she'd be the one in trouble, not me.

"I'm sorry," Mum said. "I meant to throw it past you."

She didn't care about me, just about what other people might say.

"You're not sorry!" I screamed, half from pain, half from anger. "You're never sorry. Just go away. *Go. Away!*"

She sighed and a moment later the stairs creaked. I gazed at the sloped bathroom ceiling, where black clouds of mould grew, tracking her slow steps until she reached the landing, and disappeared out of earshot. I lifted my arm to check the grey bubble and, wincing, dropped it back under. Would I have to stay here all day? The water had warmed – probably from the heat of my arm – and no longer stopped the pain. I turned on the tap, filling the sink until water gurgled down the overflow. The cold made my skin tingle, but I could cope with that.

The stairs squeaked, and footsteps padded down. Whoever it was didn't speak. Plates clattered on the worktop and cupboard doors slammed. Then the stairs creaked. Up, up, the person went. They didn't care. They'd probably forgotten I was here, sitting on the lip of the bath, my head resting on the sink edge, my arm a wrinkled sausage cooked on one side. Tears splashed into the sink. No longer tears of

91

pain, but sadness. Poor-me tears.

I wiped them away, the snot too, and rinsed my hand in the water. Then came the sound of muttering. Someone treading down the stairs. Maybe they'd come to check on me? A rap on the door, knuckles on wood.

"How long you going to be in there?" Bill said. "I can't hold on for ever, you know."

Even Bill didn't care about me. What did I expect? Ever since Mandy had moved back in, he'd been Mandy this, Mandy that, just like Mum. Or maybe Mum hadn't told him. That must be it! She wouldn't want him to know, wouldn't want to make herself look bad.

I leapt up. One-handed the bolt was a nightmare, but I wiggled it across and yanked the door open. Bill had his back to me, pouring himself a cup of tea – or maybe coffee – who cared? I held my arm out, grimacing as pain streaked up and down.

"D-do you know w-what she d-did?" The tears were falling big time. I couldn't stop them.

He swung around, mouth open, teaspoon in hand. He looked from my arm to me and put the spoon on the side.

"Come here," he said, his arms open and waving me into them. "I'm sure she didn't mean it."

"Mean it?" I slapped his hand away from me. "And where is she? Upstairs? Did she bother telling you what she done? No. Cos I'm nothing. *Nothing*!"

I had to go. Get away from them all. I tore down the hallway, out of the door, down the garden path, into the street. Sharp bits of grit dug into my bare feet. I looked up and down the road, seeing nothing but blurred cars through my tears. Through the open front door I could hear Bill calling up the stairs to my mum. I took off. The wind sliced my arm, a knife dipped in lava, jab, jab, jab. My front teeth cut grooves into my bottom lip. *Fuck*. The pain. Unbearable.

My foot landed on a stone and I winced. Not just *everyone* but *everything* hated me. Well, I hated them back. I half-ran, half-limped, coming to a stop when it struck me. Where could I go? Nina would be out at work, Troy was away. I had no one. I sank down onto the kerb and buried my head between my knees, sobbing so hard my chest jerked against my thighs. Who cared if kids from school saw? They didn't have an arm pounding like this – when would it ever die down? – or a Mum like mine.

Someone rested their hand on my back. I spun around, shading my eyes against the glare of the sun. Through my tears I made out a man-shaped silhouette. Simon. He squeezed my shoulder.

"You alright, Cindy girl?"

I shook my head and held my arm outwards, so the flabby underside faced him. The blister looked like a huge slug clung to my arm. Its fangs stabbed me. A breeze picked up and I gritted my teeth as the pain pierced again.

Simon's hand had shot to his mouth. It must be bad.

"You need to get that seen. Here, I'll get you to casualty. You can use my phone to call your Mum and tell her."

"S-she did it," I said.

He didn't say anything, but helped me to my feet. Smoke curled through the gaps of his fingers, as if he'd turned a fag in toward his palm like we did when the teachers were coming.

"C-can I have a f-fag?" A chill had settled, making me shiver.

Keeping his pace slow as I hobbled beside him, he pulled out a battered packet from the back of his jeans and popped one in my mouth, stooping over me to light it. He smelt of cigarettes, with a hint of beer and aftershave. We set off again, his keys jangling as he tugged them from his pocket.

"Car's just over there." He pointed across the road. I recognised it from the few times he and Mandy had picked me up, especially with one of the doors being a lighter red to the rest. "At the hospital, if anyone asks, can you say I'm your brother or something? The last thing I need is them asking questions about what I'm doing with a young kid."

Chapter 17
- late November -

TWO DAYS LATER, THE TWINS were in Mrs Hamilton's – sorry, Marion's – back garden playing football with Ralph and Troy. I'd been in goal, playing with them, but I'd snuck back to Mum's house to use the toilet and to defrost my frozen fingers. I found myself standing at her back door, wanting to watch the family scene as a stranger would. Red-cheeked, with glowing noses and bundled in the thick coats we'd bought the previous day, the children raced about. Charlie squawked as Troy dodged past his outstretched leg to kick the ball into the chain-link fencing, which rattled as the ball bounced away.

"Goal! Three-nil." Troy shouted and ran in a figure of eight, fists punching the air. He swung Lily around and put her down, where she tottered until falling onto her bum, grinning.

"S'not fair." Charlie pouted and crossed his arms.

"We'll get them next time, eh, Charlie." Ralph ruffled his hair.

Marion stepped from her kitchen door, holding a tray with four steaming mugs and two glasses of squash. "Coffee break. In or out?"

Troy rubbed his hands together. "In?" he asked the children. "We'll come back when we've warmed up."

It felt like a scene from one of those movies, where the poor kid sits out in the cold watching everyone having fun. But while the chill nipped through my jacket, the sight of my children being part of a family was beyond words. This must rate as one of the best days of our lives. As I stepped over the fence to join them back in the house, Marion spotted my leg lifted in mid-air and smiled.

"Old habits are hard to break, it seems."

"It seems they are."

I grinned and she disappeared into the kitchen, leaving me to hop over.

In the road, a car nosed into view. Blue and yellow squares along the side, a siren on the roof. I gripped the back-door frame. *Move on, move on.* But the police-woman in the passenger seat pointed at Troy's silver car in the driveway and grit crunched under the front wheels of the police car as it eased into the space outside – in full view of the lounge window. What would Marion say? I'd only been back a few days and already Troy was sinking into the quagmire that was my life.

With a trembling voice I called through Marion's door. "I'll just be a minute."

The policewoman got out of the car, facing her colleague who stood beside the driver's door. He pulled down his cap and looked at her, jerking his head my way. Clutching the top of her flak jacket, her fingers almost touching her radio, she turned and scrutinised me from top to bottom. I gripped the curled metal of the gate, both to hold myself up and to create a barrier. To stop them coming in. Her eyes drew level with my face. I had to speak.

"Can I help?" My voice quivered.

Guilty. They'd know I'd done something. But what? They could take their sodding pick: abandon Jez in the fire, steal his money, drive without a licence or insurance, abandon his car stashed with drugs.

"We're looking for Troy Hamilton." Her breath misted the air.

A door clicked shut behind me, footsteps grazed the concrete path and Troy reached my side. The glow on his cheeks from his earlier game with the children had become a red stain of anxiety. I'd done this to him. Why else would they be here, if not for the other night? Now he'd be in trouble for aiding and abetting a criminal.

"Troy Hamilton?" the woman said.

He nodded.

"Can we talk?"

Her gaze passed from Troy to me and back again. Get rid of her, she told him. Why didn't they want to speak to me too?

"Can you go inside?" Troy asked.

I eased my stiff fingers from the freezing metal and stepped back. Troy smiled to reassure me, but a frown pinched the skin between his eyebrows and a knot tightened on his jaw.

Heading back to the house, I glimpsed Marion who stood beside the lounge curtain, her fingers pinching the material. She and Ralph had been kind to me and my children and this was their repayment. I hesitated by the kitchen door, not wanting to face them. 'You've brought this on us,' they'd say. 'You haven't changed'. They would be right too. But I had to face them.

Heat buffeted me as I pushed open the creaking door and stepped into the kitchen. I stood, held back by a wall of silence, until Charlie's voice broke through.

"Can we go and see their car?"

"'Fraid not. They don't look happy. Best leave them to it," Ralph said.

I slipped off my shoes and took a deep breath. In the lounge, Lily knelt on the carpet, dragging a wooden train around the small track, while Charlie stood beside Ralph, well back from the window but, from what I could see, with a good view outside. Ralph gave me a brief smile and turned back to the window where Marion stood. Troy had his back to us but every now and then the policewoman would tilt her head and speak and Troy would gesture or shrug.

"Do you know what's going on?" Ralph asked.

I shook my head. "Sorry. I was asked to leave them alone."

His forehead creased. "I'm sure it's summat and nothing."

Again, his focus moved back to Marion, following her anxious gaze out to Troy.

Ralph accepted my answer, but if Marion had seen my face, she'd have known I lied. I stepped over Lily to lean against the mantelpiece beside the fire and to watch from a distance. On the table sat four untouched cups of coffee. Swallowing, I fought to ease the growing dryness in my throat.

Marion moved away from the curtain when Troy finally headed back inside, his mouth a thin line. Nerves buzzed inside me. A swarm of angry wasps, jabbing. Would Troy blame me? Had I got him into trouble? Ralph and Marion stood side-by-side facing the lounge door. What would they say? The kitchen door closed and a moment later Troy came in. One glance my way and I knew I'd been the cause of the discussion outside, but he smiled at Marion and Ralph and allowed the tightness of his shoulders to ease.

"A case of mistaken identity," he said.

"What do you mean?" Marion went over and touched him lightly on the arm. "Who were they after?"

Troy shrugged. "Not me, thank goodness. They thought I knew something about a car I'd had the misfortune to park near, but they soon realised I didn't."

"So, it's summat and nothing, then lad," Ralph said.

"It seems it is," Troy said.

He didn't look at me but I didn't need to see his eyes to feel his anger. I'd promised not to cause him trouble. Had the police told him what was in the car? Did he think the tin was linked to me? The one I'd insisted on holding and not let him carry when he'd helped me carry my bags in from the car.

"I'll make us fresh coffees," Marion said.

"I'll help," Ralph said.

I stood in silence, facing Troy, while I worked out how to apologise. Sorry wasn't enough. I could imagine him shouting, 'Is that all you can say?'. Not that I'd ever heard him raise his voice, but I'd given him enough reason to be fuming.

It slipped out. My whispered, "Sorry."

He flung his arms up in the air. "Sorry," he said in a low, flat voice. His arms fell to his sides. The room stretched between us; a gulf 'sorry' couldn't cross. He shook his head, more to himself than me. Was this it? Our rekindled friendship had been doused by a bucket load of my life. But I could change. Start thinking before acting and anyone else got hurt.

He came over and placed his hands on my shoulders. "I know, you *are* sorry. But Ci… Karis, I need you to tell me the truth. Not bits of it. All of it."

Chapter 18
– Summer holidays –

WE DROVE INTO SIMON'S ROAD, after four long hours of boredom and pain and questions at the hospital about how I'd burned my arm, with me lying and saying I'd caught it on the hob. Next to me Simon muttered something about a stroke of luck and pulled his car into a parking space opposite his flat.

"Look out, old Syphillis Norris is nosing again."

"Syphillis?"

"Her name's Phyllis, but you know…"

I gave him an 'oh yes' sort of nod. I wasn't going to admit I had no idea.

He pulled the key from the ignition and smiled. "I'll be gossiped about for weeks what with you coming into my house bandaged like that."

I shrugged. Who cared? I pulled at the door handle and eased myself out, taking care not to bang my arm against the side of the car. A warm breeze ran across my face, welcome after the stuffy A&E and ten minutes stuck in a car with a passenger window that wouldn't open. My sling blocked the view of the grass verge below and the likely dog shit, so I angled my bare feet to stand on the kerb stones and edged along like a beginner gymnast on a beam. At the hospital people had kept glancing at my bare feet but I'd ignored them.

As I hobbled across the tarmac, Simon muttered, "Great, that's all we need."

Mrs Norris peered through her window. Like the nurses and other patients, her gaze strayed to my feet.

I laughed. "What do you reckon the story will be? Man

steals girl's shoes and tortures her until she agrees to be his slave."

"Is that what you want?" Simon grinned. "Because we can start now."

I blushed, struck by the connotations. When he held the gate open for me, he outstared Mrs Norris who shook her head and shuffled off to do whatever old people did in their houses all day.

We went upstairs where I lay on his settee with my bandaged arm hanging off the side. Simon ignored the armchair and slid himself under my legs, so my dirty feet rested on his lap. One hand warmed my ankle, while he turned a pack of fags over and over like a square wheel in his other hand.

"Won't your Mum worry where you are?"

"I don't care," I said.

He shrugged. "Fine by me, as long as you don't grass me up about being here." He hesitated. "Not that I don't like having you."

"Give us a fag," I said.

"Uh uh," he said and waggled his finger. "You still owe me."

"Owe you?"

"Remember?" He shook the pack so the cigarettes rattled inside. Then he lifted my feet to one side and knelt on the floor. "Tell you what, finish the tickling bet and you can have all the fags you want today."

I'd forgotten about that. My eyes reflected in the gold packet as it spun between his finger and thumb. He pulled out a cigarette and put it between his lips and grinned, so his mouth shaped like the number eight as he sparked up. The tipped glowed orange and crackled as he dragged deeply. He leant over to blow the smoke into my mouth. The heat from his breath patted my lips, the taste of smoke made my mouth water. He did it again, this time closer. I moved my face away. Talk about agony, I needed a cigarette.

"Just tickling. No touching down there, right?"

He shifted up my top, lifting his eyebrows at the sight of my old stripy vest. I hoped it didn't stink from where I'd slept in it last night. He tugged it free. Cool air brushed my skin and I shivered. It took all my willpower not to drag it down, especially when he ran his finger along the hem of my jeans like he'd done before. I clenched my fists, gritted my teeth.

"When can I have a fag?"

"In a minute. Tell you what, you undo the button of your jeans and you can have one now."

"But you said you wouldn't touch down there."

"I won't. I'll just rub your tummy." He handed me his fag and I took a drag, while he pulled at the button of my jeans. My jeans popped open. I held my breath, checking his fingers didn't go lower down, but he kept the same line as before, rubbing up and down beside the loosened waistline.

"You're weird. What's the thing with stroking me?"

"I told you. I want to see how easily you tickle." He bent and kissed my stomach.

"No!" I tried to sit up, but he pushed me back – not nastily – but just so I couldn't get up. "Don't do that. I bet I stink. I haven't had a bath."

"Have one," he said and shrugged. "I can run it for you while you have a smoke."

I stared at him. What was he was playing at?

He got to his feet. "Your call. You do whiff a bit though."

I dragged my top down and leapt from the settee, unsure whether to laugh, run out or have a pop at him for being mean.

He burst out laughing. "Talk about sensitive. Look, you don't want to go back to your mum just yet and you said yourself, you feel a bit grubby. Stay there and I'll run the bath."

He was right. The last thing I wanted to do was face Mum right now. And a bath would be nice. Downstairs, the sound of a TV programme filtered through the floorboards. Mrs Norris was metres away. I could shout for help if I needed it, which was ridiculous as I wouldn't. This was Simon, after all.

"Okay, but no funny business, mind," I shouted as he disappeared through the arch. I stubbed out what was left of his fag, grabbed his packet and settled back on the settee to smoke.

Five minutes later, he called me through to the bathroom, where he handed me a blue bath towel like Mandy's. Softer than the scratchy ones at home. The bathroom smelt of parma violets and mounds of big glistening bubbles filled the bath. He showed me the shampoo and conditioner and, after telling me to watch my bandage with the water, closed the door and left me to it.

There wasn't a lock on the door. I stood for a moment wondering what to do and then decided to go for it. He'd agreed no funny business. I stepped out of my jeans, leaving them crumpled like a concertina on the floor. I eased my top and vest over my bandage and got into the water, savouring the silky heat on my legs. Simon had opened the bath window a bit, so the sound of birds chirping and the hum of lawnmowers filled the room. I leant back, making sure I hung my arm over the side, and closed my eyes while I wallowed, listening to the gentle lap of water.

A tap at the door. Then it creaked open. I shot up.

Waves crashed against the sides, splattering the floor.

"What are you doing?" I squealed and hugged my knees to my body. Good job I had my back to him.

"I just realised you won't be able to wash your hair, what with your arm."

"I won't wash it."

"If you stay like that, I won't be able to see anything but I can help you."

"Nah, you're okay."

"How else are you going to wash your hair, Cindy? Your Mum won't do it, will she, and I can't imagine Mandy'll bother."

"I'll work something out," I said. "It's not like I broke my arm. I can uncover it for a bit."

"You're being silly. They said to take care not to let it get infected." He edged into the bathroom. "Come on, let me do this for you."

The last thing I wanted was him in here with me, but I couldn't get up, not without him seeing me naked and I couldn't shout at him to get out, what with this being his home, so I huddled into myself while he fetched a plastic jug.

"You'll have to move your arm," he said. "Or else your bandage will get soaked."

With my good arm, I gripped my legs tighter and moved my bandage away but, when a breeze wafted against the edge of my boob, I made an L shape with my arm so nothing could be seen. He poured the jug of water over my head and I clenched my eyes shut. If water or, worse, shampoo got into my eyes, it would have to stay there. No way would I shift my arms. He massaged my hair, his fingertips moving in circles, to rub behind my ears, upwards to caress the top of my scalp, back down following the curve of my skull. My mind filled with the sound of his fingers against my skin, muffled by the foam. His thumbs grazed the nape of my neck. As my bits started to ache with the strange feeling from before, I arched back unable to bear the tingling sensation. This was wrong, so wrong. He gripped my shoulders, kneading them, and one hand slid lower, his fingers touching the hollow between my boobs. I wanted him. But I really, really didn't. I shrugged his hand away.

"Cindy." He sounded out of breath. "You don't know what you do to a man."

He leant against my arm and a thickness, like a bit of broom handle, pressed into my skin.

"Close your eyes," he said.

Warm water poured over my eyes and nose. I couldn't breathe. The jug tapped against the side of the sink and soapy water streamed down my face. I grimaced at the taste and wiped my mouth on my knee.

"Lean your head back, then it won't happen."

He pulled my shoulders back, so I could rest against his arm, with my head tilted and eyes shut. Cold air brushed my boobs. Which meant he could see them.

"Just one more," he said.

I tried to pull myself up. He mustn't see them. Water splashed my head, my mouth, choking me, stinging my eyes. I held out my hand, grasping for the towel I'd spotted on top of the toilet seat. Something brushed my nipple.

"Towel," I gasped.

Hands gripped under my armpits. He must be able to see all of me.

"No!"

I tried to push him off, but he lifted me from the bath and dropped me onto a soft rug. As the breeze from the open window nipped my naked skin, he pressed a towel into my hand. I turned away from where I guessed he stood and tied the towel around me, using a loose end to dab my face. The bathroom door clicked and I spun around. What was he doing now? Through stinging eyes and with blurred vision, I realised he'd gone. I sank down onto the edge of the bath, hugging the towel.

Did he fancy me? I shivered with excitement. No one had liked me before. Well, not like that anyhow. But he was old. Twenty-seven wasn't just old, it was ancient. Mandy would be sooo jealous if I ended up with him. She'd hate it. But much as I wanted to upset Mandy, did I want to be seen out with an old man? Chelsea Patterson in Year 11 had dated a twenty-four-year old and everyone in my class had called him a paedo.

I rubbed my back dry. What would that make Simon? Especially when he would have been thirteen when I was born. A year younger than me now. Freaky. I pulled on my knickers and shuffled my damp legs into my jeans. My vest smelt stale, my top not much better, although I hadn't slept in that. Probably the stink from the hospital. I hung the towel over the hook on the back of the door and crept out. The last thing I needed was to face Simon.

As I passed by his bedroom door, I heard him panting. Real loud, like he was doing weights. Then he gasped my name. *Cindy.* Not like he was calling me, more to himself.

His fags lay on the arm of the settee, so I took five.

"Thanks for having me," I called out.

"Hold on!" A creak, a bang, padding across the floor and then the bedroom door opened. "You're leaving?"

He'd taken his t-shirt off. Dark hair sprinkled his chest and his hip bones jutted out above the waist of his jeans, which sagged like he hadn't pulled them up properly. I flushed as I spotted his open zip and white underwear below.

"Yeah, better get back."

I didn't want to go home, but I couldn't hang around here. The way he looked at me made me blush. He'd seen me without clothes too.

"Come back soon, Cindy girl," he murmured. "I'm around later or tomorrow if you want. Anytime."

Chapter 19
- late November -

THAT NIGHT, TWO MINUTES LATER than planned, I opened the front door to Troy. He mumbled 'hello' and stepped inside but he didn't kiss my cheek. An icy wind blew and I stood for a moment, letting it cool my face, leaving him in the gloom of the hallway. I closed the door, shutting us in together. All was silent but for the slow thump of my heart. The landing light filtered down, touching the golden tips of his hair, leaving the rest of him shaded grey. I couldn't see his expression or gauge his thoughts.

We went through into the lounge. I wanted to sit in the dark, so he couldn't see me, but I pressed the light switch, grateful that the bulb needed time to warm up and brighten. Troy pulled at the knees of his trousers and sat down, the settee creaking beneath him. He tucked his hands between his knees, his back straight. He was nervous too.

"Coffee? Mine's only just made."

"I've had one, thanks."

The armchair angled towards the blank TV screen, away from him, so I sat there. Green numbers on the Freeview box still flashed 20.36. Troy and I had never been this uncomfortable together. Not so a minute felt like an hour. But then I remembered the time, years before, when Troy had gone back indoors rather than face me and the times I'd lingered at the end of the road or at the bus stop so I didn't catch up with him.

"Are the children in bed?" Troy glanced at the lounge door as if they might appear at any moment.

I flicked pieces of bit of fluff from the leg of my jeans. "They're asleep. I checked."

Tendrils of steam rose from the mug on the coffee table. I picked it up, cupping it between my hands. Sod coffee, I needed alcohol, to help me sleep later. But even if I could lay my hands on a bottle, I daren't touch it. If I drank too much, I might say things I'd regret or go into more detail than I should. I took a sip, savouring the bitter taste. Coffee would do.

My stomach fluttered with anxiety. "What do you want to know?"

He shifted forward and cleared his throat. "I want to know what's going on. I lied to the police, you know. Well…" He hesitated. "Not so much that as didn't give the whole story. You do realise they saw you driving in. We both passed a security camera. Thankfully, because we drove a different way out of the industrial estate, they didn't realise you'd got into my car. And they're looking for someone with blonde hair, not mink."

Troy didn't tell lies. Not once in all the time I'd known him. But thanks to me, he'd deceived his mum and Ralph *and* the police.

"What did you tell them?" I whispered, too ashamed to speak louder.

"I doubt they believed me, but I told them I was lost. They wanted to know what I was doing in the area. I said I was back in the country for a couple of months and took it upon myself to visit an old haunt."

"An industrial estate?"

"That's the lost bit. Luckily when I worked for Damon Mining I got involved with a woman who lived not far from there. They think I'm some saddo who'd gone off in search of past memories."

"They fell for that?"

"Well, they had to. What else could I say? *I'm* no good

at lying."

"And you're saying I am."

He thumped his fist into the settee arm, making me jump.

"Of course not, but something is up. I want to know what I – and you – have got ourselves into. For a start, the police were very interested in that car you drove. And twice they asked me if I knew a Jerome Jones."

I flinched. Jez hated his full name.

Troy's eyebrow arched. "Obviously you do. Look, I want to help you, but I can't if you won't help yourself. Can't you tell me what happened after you left Mosston? And what's going on now?"

He leaned back, placing his hands on his thighs in a relaxed pose, but every fibre of his being was alert, urging me to speak. I didn't know what to say. A ball of hurt filled my throat, cutting off the words. How could I explain the frigging mess my life had been? Still was. As tears pricked the backs of my eyes, I got up and walked over to the rear window. Through a gap in the curtains the moon lit up the navy-blue sky. Its smiling face somehow comforting. I rested my palms flat on the cold windowsill, shifting my fingers away from a dead fly. With my face veiled by the net curtains, I gazed into the darkness. The musty smell. Like… like…. *him.* A flash of memory. A man's neck above me, his eyes open, staring into mine, a strange smile on his face and his stench… *How could I have forgotten?* The stink of damp – like clothes after they'd sat in a washing machine for days – and fags. The churning pain in my stomach as… *Stop it!*

I couldn't let *him* back in to my mind. I *had* to shut him out. *Talk!* About anything.

"After I left…" My voice shook. I couldn't do this.

Or could I? As long as we talked about 'after'. 'Before'

110

with Cindy was hurtful, shocking, impossible to face. Although 'after' wasn't much better, I could deal with Karis's past.

"After I left." I tried again, adding a strength to my voice I didn't feel. "I made it to London. This man gave me a job in a café."

I kept my back to Troy. I didn't tell him about the weeks I'd spent sleeping rough, fending off advances from drunken slobs and evil-smelling lechers. I couldn't tell him how I cried myself to sleep at night, over the child I'd left behind, being the child I still was.

"He was foreign. He'd got hold of these fake documents, so I saved up my wages and got myself a new identity. I became Karis…" I squirmed. I couldn't tell Troy I'd called myself after him – Hamilton – my best friend, my only link to the past.

"Karis," I repeated. "I got a bedsit and after a while I met Steve, the children's father. We stayed together until the twins were just under a year old. He was a bit rough and ready, liked a drink and a punch up or two. I don't know what I saw in him really."

I didn't add that when Steve couldn't take his frustrations out on the lads down the boozer, he'd bring them home. Or that I'd ended up taking two jobs, because he pissed the money down the pub. Or that he'd left me for my neighbour, Sue, because the children squawked too much and I paid him too little attention. At least, I didn't have too long with him and Sue living next door and the indignity of their bed banging against my bedroom wall as, shortly afterwards, the council housed me on the Saints' estate, a mile away.

"When Steve left, I was on my own. But he came back when Lily and Charlie were about three. By then he wasn't

111

just drinking but gambling too. He ran up a huge phone bill and a massive debt with Mick, the bookie. I wanted him to go. I kept asking, but he wouldn't. Then, one day, three men turned up at the door. Mick's thugs."

As I told Troy how I opened the door that day, it felt like I'd gone back in time. The smell of fear, the nerves – I was there – gazing at three hulks, two skinheads and one with lanky hair and frizzy grey sideburns. Unlike the heavy leather jackets of the others, one of the skinheads wore a thin t-shirt, even though it was February, which showed off a tattoo of St George's flag. A puckered scar crossed his other arm.

The greasy-haired man had shoved the door open. His workman's boots crunched as he stepped into my hallway, leaving a thin layer of sand on the bare floor.

"Yes?" My voice trembled as the last of the three men stepped into my house. *Three!* I couldn't let this be a replay of what had happened the last time I'd been alone with three men.

"Steve Adams?"

"He's not here," I said.

The other skinhead pushed past me into the lounge, where he wandered over to open the back door which led onto the small balcony. Then he came back to check the kitchen. As he turned to go upstairs, I'd tried to stop him.

"The children, they're asleep."

He shoved me aside and thumped up the stairs. "We're not interested in your children. Just Steve."

They lied. When Steve didn't come back, they came after me. Goodness knows where Steve had disappeared off to – I don't think he went back to Sue – but, whatever he did, in their eyes his debt was mine. They reasoned he'd probably spent the money on me anyway, so it was only right I repaid

112

what we'd used. Except, with the interest they levied, it was impossible to pay.

When I came to the end of my story, Troy muttered, "You poor thing." Or something like that.

I pushed myself away from the window and went back to sit on the chair facing the TV. I needed space to think before I got to the next part. How would I explain what I'd agreed to do next?

"You'll think I'm terrible but Jez – Jerome – took a shine to me."

I couldn't believe I'd used an expression my gran would have said. But, somehow, it made my relationship with Jez seem better. Less dirty.

"He used to lower my repayments if... if..." I couldn't do this. I jumped to my feet. "Well, you can guess, can't you?"

This time I headed over to the fireplace where I ran my finger along the top. I flicked the thin ribbon of dust onto the carpet. Would this house ever be clean? Would I ever feel free of the grubbiness, the slime, the filth? I swung around to face Troy. Our eyes locked and, for a moment, he reminded me of the young lad I'd met all those years ago. Fresh-faced and innocent compared to the worldly-wise girl next-door. Except I hadn't been. I'd just thought I was.

"I am sick and tired of running from one fuck up to the next."

He got up and pulled me to him.

"You don't have to tell me more," he said.

His warm fleece smelled like the Troy of my childhood. Of Lenor, soap and homebaking. His thumb brushed my scalp in slow, circular movements and my agitation calmed. How many years since someone had touched me gently like this? I used to love having my head rubbed. *Simon!* I shoved

113

Troy away.

"I'll tell you."

I had to speak. Stop the memories that ebbed at the corners of my mind, threatening to overflow and swamp me. At least, talking about Jez meant I had to think about him. Not *them*. I turned back to the fireplace and stared at the wall, trying to block Troy's presence from my mind. His shadow reflected in the mirror.

"Two years this went on. With Jez coming... you know... and him somehow paying the loan interest. Not the loan, mind. Anyway, one day he came around with a proposition." I sniggered, more to myself than anything. Jez had actually said 'prostition' which, being a cross between prostitute and proposition, was the perfect word.

"He'd started coming around my place more often, for chats and coffee too, not just... that. One day he asked why I didn't move in with him, now his Mum was dead and there was room."

In the mirror, Troy's reflection shifted and the settee creaked. He'd sat down. Was this too uncomfortable for him? Well, he'd asked and – strangely – now I needed to tell.

"He was nice to Charlie and Lily, bought them gifts and he wasn't mean to me. Not like Mick's other thugs." Instinctively, I clenched my fist, remembering what they'd done. "Jez reckoned moving in would mean Mick would have to think about doing a deal. He'd get the debt wiped. I took ages deciding, but he promised he'd be good and sort himself out, leave Mick and get another job. And Jez had a garden for the children. So, I agreed."

I shrugged like that settled it. I'd moved in and it had been happy ever after. Except it hadn't. Beneath Jez's bravado lay bullshit. Three weeks after I'd moved in, he'd come in and told me it was sorted with Mick. The debt was

114

settled. But he couldn't leave Mick yet. He had stuff to sort, deals to make. That's when the phone calls had started and I'd answer to find somebody at the other end of the line, but they wouldn't speak or hang up. One time I stood in silence for ages, until I caught the sound of their breath.

"I can hear you," I'd said, but still they didn't hang up or respond.

Jez told me to stop answering the house line. He'd put his mobile on silent. Around this time, he started to disappear out of the house for hours – not unusual with his work for Mick – but he'd come back clutching a bag tucked inside his jacket. He'd shoot up to the bedroom and come down empty-handed or with a used carrier bag stashed in his pocket. There was something about the way he acted that made me follow him one day. I stopped halfway up the stairs so I could spy as he knelt to ease a plank open that skirted the wardrobe. He pulled a tin from the space, glancing back and almost catching me hovering there in the stairwell. I edged downstairs, a moment before he jumped up and shut the bedroom door.

When he went out later, I shot upstairs, determined to find out what he was up to, but I found myself creeping along to where the children slept top-to-toe in Jez's mum's old room. Charlie was huddled beside the wall in his new blue and red Spiderman pyjamas, while Lily lay stretched like a starfish, showing off her Princess nightie, bought during the previous day's shopping trip with Jez. Did I want to take them from the world of new clothes and trips out for pizza? I went back downstairs.

But a few weeks later – when Jez sat on the Formica kitchen table, his hands clasped behind his head, or stood at the lounge window peering out through a crack in the curtains, or checked his phone for the millionth time as frown lines dug into his forehead – I began to worry. Really worry. By then I'd all but forgotten about the tin.

"The tin. Is that why the police were so interested in him and that car?" Troy asked, bringing me back to the present.

I turned to face him. "There were drugs in the boot of the car."

Troy shot to his feet, his eyes wide. "Drugs? You–"

I leapt in. "I had no idea about Jez being involved with drugs. You have to believe me. There is no way – *no way!* – I would ever, ever get involved with drugs. Not after…"

"But you knew they were in the car. You let me follow you." His voice was monotone, like there was no reason to care anymore. He'd given up on me.

As he walked away, I wanted to grab him back, make him understand. But it was too late. I'd messed up.

He stopped by the lounge door. "You should have told me."

Shoulders slumped, arms hanging by his sides, he headed into the dark hallway. The front door opened and a draught of cold air reached me.

"I'm sorry. What else could I do? I couldn't leave them here," I called out.

But the door clicked shut and I was alone.

Chapter 20
– Summer holidays –

I GOT HOME TO FIND EVERYONE OUT, so I went upstairs where I dragged all but my knickers and vest off, throwing my top and jeans to the floor. Then I lay on the bed with my good arm flopped over my tired eyes. I don't know how much later I woke to find someone running their fingers along my forehead, brushing my hair from my face.

"Are you alright, love?" Mum whispered.

I groaned. My dream. Robbie Williams. I had to get back to it. I dragged the duvet cover over my head.

Later, I was woken by Mum's leg knocking against the bed and the swish of curtains being pulled open.

"Wakey, wakey, rise and shine. Look what I've got for you." She sounded like a mum from the TV adverts. The ones with the soft hands, flowery dresses and perfect smiles.

Through a crack in the duvet cover, the smell of bacon wafted. Sunlight stung my eyes as I peered out to find Mum holding a plate which she circled above. It wasn't so much the fact she'd brought food which surprised me, but the way she bent down and smiled. The same smile she used on strangers, similar to her telephone voice. She'd put on a different lippy, a soft pink which made her teeth look yellow. But her hair was the same, tied back, so the edges of her eyebrows rose, a bit like Spock from Star Trek.

"Bacon." She sat down on the edge of the bed. "How are you feeling today? Up to eating?"

I wiggled from the duvet and rearranged my pillow so only my shoulder blades touched the cold wall. She sat and watched me eat, her gaze flicking from my face to my arm. A splodge of lipstick thickened on her front teeth from all the lip biting she was doing. When grease dripped onto my chin, I dabbed it with my bandage.

"That woman next door, Troy's mum, she came around looking for you," Mum said. "About you going around hers for lunch. Don't you worry though. I told her something must have come up."

Mum jerked her head towards my arm. "Don't be telling the likes of her about that. She might not get that it was an accident. How about you rest up in here for the next day or two, just while you're feeling poorly?"

I stuffed the rest of the crust into my mouth. If she was going to bring me food and be nice, I could think of it as an accident. Poor Mrs Hamilton though. How long did she sit at home waiting before she came looking for me? The next time Mum went out, I'd go and apologise. I'd tell her about my arm, but say I'd burnt it on the hob or something. The hospital had believed me.

Mum smoothed the duvet cover around my legs and got up. "Will you be wanting a coffee?"

I nodded. Behind her, I spotted Mandy leaning against the door frame, glowering. She shifted to one side as Mum went past with the plate and then took up her position again, this time staring me out. I picked my book from the bedside table, settling back to read, but her rich auburn hair dye became an annoying glowing ball above the pages. She huffed and folded her arms.

"How did you get that bandage?"

I ignored her.

"Who took you to hospital?"

I turned the page even though I hadn't been able to read a word. Tracking the lines with my finger, I picked out the word 'cigarette' – I could do with one of those – and 'diet'. Judging by the state of Mandy's belly, she needed one of those. Her t-shirt rippled over her stomach.

"Who took you to hospital?" Mandy raised her voice.

When I kept reading, she stormed over, ripped the book from my hands and slammed it to the floor. Bits of spittle stuck to her teeth. She reminded me of Mr Banford, the maths teacher at school who foamed at the corners of his mouth when he got mad, except there were laws stopping him hitting me. Mandy on the other hand… She pounced, grabbing my shoulders, her fingernails digging into my skin.

"Get off!"

I smacked her away, wincing as my bandage made contact with her arm.

"You were seen with Simon. Yesterday. You stay away from him, you hear." She stabbed her finger so close to my nose, it made me cross-eyed.

The stairs creaked, but she either didn't notice or didn't care. I shoved her hand away and bent to snatch the book from the carpet where it lay upside down beside her purple-painted toenails. She beat me to it, her chubby foot clamping *Bridget Jones* to the floor.

"Get off, you'll break it!" I thumped her thigh as hard as I could.

She screeched and disappeared backwards, leaving me to rescue my poor, battered book. I lifted myself up to find her being dragged out cavewoman style by Mum. While their row went on in the landing – with lots of hollering about me being injured or just putting it on – I tried flattening the pages by bending them in the opposite direction to the creases. But it fell open, refusing to be anything other than a V. No longer new. I wiped the front across my duvet cover, ridding it of the invisible imprint from Mandy's sweaty foot.

"Look," I said as Mum walked into the room, holding my mug of coffee. "She's wrecked it. And it was brand new

119

too."

As I said it, I realised Mum would wonder where I'd got the cash to buy a new book. But if she did, she didn't say anything. Instead, she put the coffee down on the windowsill and reached inside her back pocket and drew out a fag packet. I sat, open-mouthed, as she put the cigarettes and a box of matches next to the mug.

"Your sister won't be bothering you for a couple of days. You just stay in here and take it easy."

♦

Three days later, I lay in my bedroom listening to the rain pelt the window while I flicked between the pages of *Pride and Prejudice* and *Bridget Jones' Diary*. Unable to think of anything else to do, I'd decided to look for the similarities between Mark Darcy and Mr Darcy. It involved reading *Pride and Prejudice* for the twentieth time, then setting myself questions. Boring, boring, boring. But anything was better than doing nothing.

I pushed the books to one side and got up to kneel on the pillow, my elbows on the cold windowsill, my chin cupped by my hands. Surely Mum would let me out today? I'd told her I thought it was an accident, so everyone else should believe it. But, although she didn't say as much, I knew she must be scared about me going on the social register again and this time being taken away. If that happened, she'd lose her benefits. But why would the social be interested in me now I was fourteen? It wasn't like I was a baby and couldn't look after myself.

Water ran in little streams down the window. As I opened it, cool air drifted in and rain splattered the windowsill. I stretched out my hand to catch the drops, letting them grow to become a pond in the curve of my palm. How many would it take to fill it? Six, seven – was I really doing this? – eight, nine. I slapped my hands together and dried them on my legs.

Downstairs the front door banged. Someone going out or in? I ran into Mum's room and looked through the nets. Anorak hood pulled up and her head down against the rain, Mum hurried in the direction of the precinct. Of course, it was benefit day, which meant she'd go shopping too. An hour to town and back again and maybe an hour in between, giving me two hours of freedom!

Back in my bedroom, I dragged on my jeans, flung a new t-shirt over my manky vest, and grabbed my hooded fleece. After fishing three library books from under the bed, I was about to leave when I remembered my cigarettes. Just two sat in the drawer, which meant I'd have to ration myself. I raced downstairs to fetch my shoes. The sound of snoring came from the lounge, along with the stink of beer and fags. Bill lay on the settee, his arms folded over his off-white t-shirt, mouth open, bare feet hanging over the arm. I grimaced at the sight of his ridged toenails lined with dirt and made a mental note to keep away from that side of the settee. Beside him on the coffee table, sat a can of Diamond White and an ashtray overflowing with butts, mainly his roll-ups – or rollies as he called them. I snuck over and opened his tin of baccy. Should I? As another snore ripped through his lips, I bottled it and carefully replaced the lid. He shifted around on the settee, so his bum hung off the side and his feet were now planted on the seat cushion. Euww. I took one final longing look at the glinting tin and left.

Once I'd fetched a carrier bag for the books, I stepped outside into the fresh air. Drops of water dripped from the door frame, one rolling down the back of my neck. Grinning,

I stuck out my tongue and leant my head back. Like the window upstairs, streams raced down my face, merging to become rivers that soaked my collar. I lifted my arm and, ignoring the heaviness of the carrier bag in my outstretched hand, spun around and around. Rain soaked my skin and pooled at the corners of my closed eyes. In my mind, I sang about singing in the rain and being happy again.

"Cindy?"

I juddered to a halt and opened my eyes to find myself facing the brick wall of our house. Still unsteady, I turned to the voice. Mrs Hamilton stood inside her open kitchen door, staring at me through a curtain of rain.

"Are you okay?"

"Yes thanks."

A raindrop fell from my nose into my mouth and I shivered as the wind chilled my back. My sleeves clung to my wrists and my top lay sodden against my chest. Behind her a buzzer rang.

"Do you want to come in? I've been baking."

I held out the carrier bag. "I've gotta go to the library and change these. Sorry, I mean *got to* go."

She smiled at me.

"I'm sorry about the other day. I burnt my arm on the hob and had to go to A&E." I shifted the carrier bag into my other hand and pulled at my sleeve, so she could see the bandage in case she didn't believe me.

"Your Mum didn't say."

"She didn't know." A half-lie. She didn't know I'd been at the hospital. "Anyway, I better go. Do you want anything from the library?"

She shook her head. "Please do come around anytime."

I gave her a little wave. "I will."

122

◆

My teeth chattered, an incessant brrr sound, and my sodden fleece hung heavy on my shoulders. I pushed the front gate open and swiped my dripping fringe from my eyes while I checked the lounge window for signs of Mum. I should have taken a coat and searched the house for money for the bus fare, rather than trying to race Mum into town and back. That way the books wouldn't have got soggy thanks to the rain dripping down my fingers into the bags, and that old cow librarian wouldn't have moaned. And if I'd been on a bus, Mum couldn't have spotted me running back with my new batch of books. I couldn't believe it when she'd pointed through the bus window, her mouth a circle as if mouthing the word 'You'.

'You' meant trouble.

I slid through the back door, tiptoed across the kitchen and into the bathroom, where I snapped the lock shut. I could hide out here away from Mum and get warm at the same time. After stashing my books in the corner, I gave the bath a quick rinse with the plastic jug and turned the taps on full. My jeans clung to my legs. I had to use my feet to stamp them free. The cold air prickled my skin, but it was luxury compared to the feel of my soaked clothes. My fleece, top and manky vest landed on top of the jeans, an island in an oozing pool.

A gentle tap at the door. "Is that you, Cindy love?" Mum asked, still using the sugary tone she'd been using for the past three days. Somehow my escape was forgiven.

"I'm in the bath," I said.

"Well mind as you come out, we've got a visitor."

That explained it.

After checking the temperature, I eased myself into the

bath, making sure my bandaged arm hung over the side. The heat massaged my goose-bumped skin. Above me, a forest of blackness grew along the ceiling. What was it Mrs Hamilton had called it? Mildew. She'd said to use bleach on it with an old toothbrush. I glanced across the four toothbrushes which littered the back of the sink between the taps, along with a tube of toothpaste and a sliver of soap. Maybe I could use Mandy's? It wasn't like she'd notice, with it being all splayed like parting waves. That'd pay her back for wrecking the postcard that had arrived from Troy yesterday. I knew she'd done it on purpose, putting her coffee cup over the writing side, so it became a smudged ring. An accident, according to Mum, but I'd seen Mandy standing behind her, smirking. Yes, I'd scrub the mildew clean. It'd give me something to do, especially later when I could watch Mandy brushing her teeth.

I lay there, turning on the hot tap each time the water cooled, until the water ran cold. Above, the immersion heater whistled but I couldn't wait the half hour needed to reheat the water. I went to climb out. Great. My towel! Bill's hung on the back of the bathroom door, mottled grey, but it would stink of damp and sweat. The only other option was my clothes and the hand towel. I picked up my dripping clothes and the bag of books and, burying them against the front of me, I unlocked the door while holding the hand towel around my back so it draped, I hoped, over my bum.

"I'm coming through!" I yelled. "Close your eyes."

Half-running, half-skidding, I fled through the kitchen into the hallway. As I rounded the stairs, I glimpsed Simon sitting in the armchair. *Not him, of all people.* What was he doing here? I hammered up the stairs, into my bedroom and slammed the door, dropping my clothes and towel into a squelching pile. Heart thudding, I leant against the bedroom door. Had Simon and Mandy got back together? I felt punctured, deflated, but I couldn't explain why. Probably that I didn't want Mandy to get back with him. Or was it more than that? It couldn't be. I mean, I didn't fancy him. But how could I forget the touch of his fingers against my scalp, the way they'd brushed my shoulders, caressed my skin? I blushed, remembering how I felt down there. How I'd wanted him. And I had.

Chapter 21
- late November -

EVEN THOUGH I'D WASHED MUM'S BEDDING, I woke to the scent of cigarettes and damp. A beam of sunlight broke through the crack in the curtain, through which danced specks of dust. Up and down they raced, buffeted between the cool draughts from the open bedroom door and the poor fitting windows, until they landed on the duvet cover to join the mountain of dust that would grow so large it would bury me. That's how I felt: suffocated and stifled in this house of memories. A chill wafted over my shoulder and I shivered and huddled deeper into the duvet, Mum's nylon sheets greasy against my bare legs.

Outside a car engine revved and a woman called out. Most likely one of the many people who'd moved in since I left. Then an indistinct male voice. Troy? I leapt out of bed and pulled the curtains to one side to peer through the nets, disappointed to see it wasn't him. A balding man with a pot belly stood on the verge opposite, a set of car keys dangling from his hand as he talked to a woman on the path below me. She faced towards him, so I couldn't see anything but her rounded back and lank hair draped over the collar of her coat. Something about the way she flicked a loose strand, reminded me of Mandy and I leapt back, my breath catching in my throat.

Not Mandy! Not coming here.

Praying I hadn't been seen, I tucked myself against the corner of the window, and angled myself so I could catch them both in the thin rectangle of vision between the wall and curtain. The man leaned back and laughed. A 'ha ha' sound filtered into the room. Through the haze of the net curtains the scene felt disjointed, like I was watching a TV programme with a blurry picture and speakers that wouldn't work, but I daren't switch it off, not while we were building to the scary part. Was she Mandy and, if so, would she keep walking along the road or come inside and catch me in Mum's house?

The woman waved goodbye and swung around to Mum's gate. I moved back, ready to run into the children's room and – hide? – but then I glimpsed a stack of leaflets in her gloved hand, her ruddy cheeks and the wrinkles cutting into the skin around her puffy eyes. Late forties or early fifties at a guess, so not Mandy, unless she'd aged terribly. The woman bent to stroke a passing black cat, tickling its chin and running her hand over its arched back. Mandy wouldn't have bothered with an animal, not unless age had dealt her a compassion gene.

I went to check on the twins. At the top of the stairs, I heard the snap of the letterbox. I paused until I caught the sound of card hitting the carpet, followed by the bang of the gate. She'd gone. The children's bedroom door lay open, the duvet strewn over the floor, the pillows at the top and foot of the bed still indented from the curve of their heads. I gave them a shake and flapped the duvet, so it billowed over the bed. When a child's giggle floated up the stairs, I set off to find out what they were up to.

It wasn't until I reached the hallway that I caught the sound of splashing coming from the bathroom. How had I not heard them? I picked up speed, racing along the hallway and into the kitchen, one part of me screaming – *No, please, no!* – while the other part reasoned – *Don't be silly, they're not in trouble, they're giggling*. Yanking open the bathroom door, I found Lily and Charlie sitting in a half-filled bath surrounded by a dozen or more crayons, a few lying on the surface of the water, the majority sunk to the bottom.

"Look," Charlie said. "We're playing ships and submarines."

"Get out!" I shouted. "Get out!"

Wide eyes gazed at me from beneath the water, mouth parted. *This bath, this exact spot, all those years ago.* I plunged my arm into the water, smashing through the nightmare of those baby eyes, to wrench the plug free.

"Never, ever, ever, get in here again without me. Water is dangerous, do you hear? *Do you?*"

My hands were on Charlie's shoulders, shaking him. His face scrunched, sobbing. I pulled away.

"I'm sorry," I said, as his cry became a howl.

As Lily joined in, I lifted them dripping onto the bathmat, and dragged a towel from the radiator. To the sound of bawling, I patted them dry, wondering how I'd forgotten the frustration I'd felt when they were babies. When one had cried it had set the other one off, leaving me little time to myself. The opposite was the case now. Mostly they were good, playing together, so I could get on with whatever I needed to do.

"I'm sorry," I whispered, kissing each of their heads in turn. "You scared me."

A bubble of snot burst from Lily's nose. "Why?"

"You might have drowned, been scalded, anything could have happened."

"B- but we were being good," Charlie said. "We didn't make a mess."

I glanced over at the sodden paper wrappings on the crayons, the battlezone of colour littering the bath.

"There's nothing to do here," Lily whined. "Can we go play football with Troy and Ralph? They're in. I saw them."

When Troy had walked out the front door, I'd known he

wouldn't be coming back, but still my mind played those stupid games each time the gate creaked or a shadow flitted past the door. I wouldn't let the children out in the garden either, too ashamed to face accusing looks from over the fence. Troy would have told Marion and Ralph and I didn't blame him. I'd messed up but my children shouldn't pay for it.

"What about the park?" I failed to hold back a shudder.

Lily bounced under the towel. "Yesss. Like we used to do at home."

♦

The football pitches seemed smaller, the hedgerows tidier, and a green fence now surrounded a much larger play area than the one I'd spent my childhood days mooching around. The swings were still there, maybe not the same ones as before – they looked too new – but the climbing frame and see saw had been taken away, replaced by a bird's nest swing, monkey bars, nets to climb over and a fantastic zipwire that ran along one side of the play area. Parents bundled in coats and scarfs pushed toddlers on the swings or stood by the zip wire watching children whiz past. Families were the one thing I didn't recall from the days I'd spent at the park. I hoped none of the parents would recognise me.

Lily and Charlie let go of my gloved hands and raced off towards the gate, leaving me running to keep up. Although adults were there, there still might be broken glass, syringes or goodness knows what. At first the children wanted me – Mummy push my swing, lift me onto the monkey bars – but shortly after they started one of their secretive games with rules I didn't understand. I went to sit on the swing, hugging my arms close to my chest, keeping my hands clear of the freezing chain. Memories of a time I'd sat here laughing with friends stole up on me – happy, welcome ones – until *he* crept in. I leapt up, desperate to get away from where he stood beside me, one hand in his jean pocket, his thumb out and pointing. How had I been so naïve, so knowing, so innocent?

I moved over to the monkey bars and wrapped my arm around the metal post, my sweater and coat a barrier to the biting chill. The children shrieked past, playing a game of 'It'. I gave them a little wave, taking pleasure from their wide smiles and glowing cheeks. Cold seeped through my shoes and my nose tingled, but I didn't want to drag the children from their fun. Instead, I stamped my feet and rubbed my hands together. I kept my back to the swing though, in case *he* might be standing there, taunting me, even though I reminded myself everything around me was new. Nothing came from *then.*

By the time the children were ready to leave, the playground was deserted. We traipsed back down the narrow alleyway once nicknamed Dogshit Alley by local people, but now free of the stuff. The children chattered away while I kept a tenuous hold on the back of their hoods, steering them to the right as we reached the road.

Then I saw – *HIM* – sauntering towards us. No longer a mirage but real. No one else I knew walked like that, half walk, half swagger. His dark hair was flecked with grey but even from where I stood on the other side of the road, I could see the crease in his cheek etched by his dimple. He pulled a cigarette from his mouth and flicked it into the road, where it landed burning, leaching smoke into the air. In the peripheries of my vision, the children looked at me, questioning our sudden stop. But my focus was on him. Slowly, he lifted his eyes until they met mine. For once those grey eyes with flecks of yellow didn't move to my chest. Nausea seared my throat. *Him. Here. In Mum's road.* I put an arm around each child, rolling them into me so I could pick them up. Then I ran. Towards Mum's house.

The children juddered against my chest and shrieked with shock.

"You're hurting me."

"Please, please be quiet," I panted.

I reached the point opposite Mum's house where usually we would cross, but I couldn't. If he saw me go inside, he'd know where to find me. The road was a dead end, unless I went down the other alleyway, the one that led to town.

But if he caught me in the alleyway, I'd be trapped.

I ran, blinded by unwanted tears. I had to be strong for the children. But I couldn't. Not with him.

"Mummy!" Lily squealed.

She flung her arms out, knocking against my ear. Another shriek. Why had I come back? Stupid. Of course, he'd still be here. Where else would he go?

"Troy!" Charlie shouted. Or was it Lily?

They writhed in my arms, their feet banging against my knees, but I tightened my grip, running faster, faster. Didn't they know, it wasn't Troy. It was *him*. The world swam around me, the verge and grass becoming a wavy streak.

"Karis!"

Someone grabbed my shoulder.

"No!" I screamed, jerking myself free.

Be brave, face him out. Here, in front of everyone. Better that than leaving it until we reached the darkness of the alley. Hampered by the children, I swung around, ready to boot him with my foot. Through the fog of tears, I found Troy standing there, arms outstretched.

"I was him," I whispered. "I know it was him."

And to my shame, I crumpled into Troy, sobbing.

Chapter 22
– Summer holidays –

AFTER A FEW CRINGING REMEMBRANCES, I'd all but forgotten my semi-naked dash past Simon. An hour later, wrapped in my dressing gown, I hung over the bed reading my new library book which lay on the carpet below. After serial bouts of pin and needles from leaning on my cupped hands, I'd put a heavy painted stone – one Troy had given me after his trip to the Lake District last year – on the edge of the book to hold the pages down. But it kept slipping off the further I got into the book, which meant the pages flicked together and I had to keep finding my place. Eighty pages already.

I paused, certain I'd heard a tap at the door. It couldn't be Mum as she wouldn't knock but fling open the door and storm in. I had the joy of that to come later, after Simon left. 'How dare you go out without my permission,' she'd yell. I'd tell her straight. No way was she keeping me prisoner, just because she was worried what people might say about my arm.

The door creaked open, brushing against the carpet.

"Are you decent?" Simon whispered.

Not waiting for me to respond, he shuffled sideways into the room. The door clicked shut behind him and he smiled. He wouldn't be smiling if Mum found him in my room. But then she let Troy in here, so why not him? Holding my dressing gown in place, I shuffled into a sitting position. He'd brushed his hair and gelled it into a side parting, something he did when he was going out on the town with Mandy. Unlike the fashionable shirts he'd wear then, today he wore a black Metallica t-shirt and a thick leather belt with a buckle in the shape of two playing cards.

"They're out talking to one of your neighbours. He's lost his dog or something."

"Poor Boris," I said. "Maybe we should go and help look."

"Maybe," he said, but he didn't move away from the door. "I came to see where you've been. I've missed you."

He came over and stroked my shoulder. My skin tingled. His finger ran down the towelling of my dressing gown to where it became a V on my chest. As my breath caught in my throat, I shifted further back, away from him. My cheeks burned. I couldn't look into his eyes. He picked up my book from the floor, placed it on the duvet and, turning his head as if listening for sounds of movement outside, knelt in front of me. I shivered as he laid his hands on my thighs. His warm fingers fired little pulses of excitement along my legs to my bits. I should push him away. *Now*. Mrs Hamilton always talked about a lady deserving respect, while Mum just called her an uptight cow. The respect thing sounded good. But hard work.

"Magician." Simon chuckled. "Harry Potter sequel?"

"Nah, it's a sci-fi fantasy. The librarian said I might like it."

He nodded but didn't seem that interested. "Shame I can't stop. It's not like I can say I was upstairs using your toilet, is it?"

His hands shifted a bit further up my legs, so I clamped them together and tucked my dressing gown between my thighs. He smiled and squeezed my leg to show he didn't mind and got to his feet.

"Come to mine later. Please. I'll get you something to eat. Something nice. We can chat if you like. I enjoy talking to you."

"I dunno." I glanced at the door. "I'll see if Mum lets me."

He shrugged. "She's going to the social tonight with Mandy. She won't know."

He checked outside the door, to make sure no one was around. One little wave and he disappeared. I pictured him holding onto the bannister so it took his weight, like I did when I didn't want the stairs to creak. He'd probably done that earlier when he'd come upstairs or else I would have heard him. We were so similar. I hoped he liked chips, because that's what I fancied tonight.

♦

Mum, Mandy and Bill went out about seven o' clock. They didn't call goodbye. Mum even held the door handle when she shut the door, turning it after the door was closed to make sure it didn't click and alert me. They didn't spot me standing at the top of the stairs, watching. Mandy even sniggered about something, to be shushed by Mum. It was a game to them: 'Let's trick Cindy'. Mum should have checked I was okay before going out and leaving me, especially as I'd said I didn't feel well and didn't want anything for tea.

Back in the bedroom, I stuffed my pillow under the duvet, along with my dressing gown and towel to make a perfect – if a bit odd – me shape. I drew the curtains, so not even a peek of light could be seen at the edges, not helped by the thin material which let light pierce the fibres. Mum wouldn't be coming back before it got dark, so why bother? With a start I realised exactly why. What if she thought to check on me during her middle-of-the-night trip to the toilet and found me out? I shivered with excitement. Was I really doing this?

In the bathroom, I brushed my teeth and gave my armpits and other areas a quick wipe to freshen up. The flannel had a strange damp smell, which overpowered the smell of soap, so I went in search of Mandy's perfume favourite perfume *LouLou* and found it tucked behind her open make-up bag on her dressing table. I squirted it on my wrists, armpits, neck, stomach and under my denim skirt onto my knickers, regretting the final squirt. Talk about obvious.

As I stood at Simon's front door with the strong scent wafting around me, I wondered if I could sneak into his bathroom and wash most of the perfume off. He opened the door, a grin widening on his face when he saw it was me.

"Come in," he said. As I passed him, he added. "*LouLou*. Nice."

I blushed. He'd know it was Mandy's.

We went through to the lounge. Hoover marks streaked the carpet and the smell of polish hung in the air. He'd even washed out the glass ashtrays. At home grey ash embedded ours, thick and bumpy at the bottom with a thin covering on the sides, so you'd have to look at the outside to know the ashtray started life white.

"You've been busy," I said.

He smiled. "No hiding from you. I had an hour or two."

The light seemed to be angled oddly in the room; one half bright, the other a diagonal of dimness. I looked up to find the pleated uplighter dangling to one side, the glow from the bulb picking out a strand of cobweb. Definitely no hiding things from me.

"I was just about to order a Chinese. Want some?"

"Can I have chips too?"

He brought in the menu and we sat together to look

through it. At home we only had egg fried rice, spare ribs and chicken balls, so I let him choose.

"It'll be half an hour." He put the phone on the arm of the chair. "How about I make you a drink while we're waiting. Vodka?"

I shook my head. "Just coke. I'm thirsty."

"Go on. A little won't hurt. I'll make it weak."

He came back a moment later, handing me a glass filled with coke and three ice cubes. Apart from a slight tang and a faint smell of glue, I couldn't taste the vodka. He bent down beside the video and pulled out three videos, telling me to pick the one I fancied. As I turned them over to read the backs, he sat beside me and held out a packet of cigarettes. Being thoughtful, he'd pulled out one of the fags out so the tip jutted from the pack.

My cigarette lit and video choice handed to him, I took a swig of my drink. A warm muzziness crept up on me, like the other day when I'd drunk Thunderbird with Nina. I liked the feeling. I gulped it back, gave an "Ah" and swiped the back of my hand across my mouth.

"Die Hard. *With a Vengeance*." He mimicked the voice-overs on the films. "Good choice. More?"

He took the glass from me and wandered into the kitchen, returning with one that had a lighter colour and a stronger smell than before. I took a mouthful and grimaced. The alcohol warmed the back of my throat and fuzzed my mind. What the heck. The food would soak it up. And it would be fun to know what it was like to not just be tipsy, but mind-zonkingly pissed. I took a gulp and giggled. Zonkingly. What a brilliant word. I'd have to use that on Nina and Troy.

"Hurry up with the zonking film." Laughing, I took a lug of my fag. I sat up straight so my boobs stuck out and

137

blew the smoke out in a straight line, like an actress would do.

Simon pushed the film into the slot. The video whirred and swallowed it. "You're enjoying the vodka, I see."

He sat down beside me and put his hand on my knee. Outside a car door slammed. He got up to glance through the window. "Chinese is here."

"Get the zonking door, my man," I said in my best posh voice. "One is hungry, one is."

We ate with our tea on our laps, like we did at home, except Simon gave me a cushion so the heated plates didn't burn my legs. Mrs Hamilton heated her plates too, but she put them on mats on the dining table and turned off the TV to eat. Something in the Chinese was spicy so, half-way through our meal, Simon got up and made me another vodka and coke which, he promised, wouldn't be strong. On the TV, Bruce Willis had a hazy twin behind his shoulder, following his every move. In fact, everything was double. I closed one eye, pleased to find things back in focus.

Simon laughed. "What are you doing?"

"Trying to see." My voice sounded blurred, distant.

He bent down and kissed me. On the lips. He smelt of beer and cigarettes and aftershave and food. The tip of his tongue circled my lips, making them tingle. I opened my mouth, so he could kiss me properly. He tugged the hem of my top loose from my jeans and his hand moved up, up, until his fingers fumbled under my bra. His breath was heavy, like mine. Everything prickled. My skin, my mouth. The desire down there grew stronger than I'd imagined possible.

Stop. He had to stop.

I pushed his hand away. "No. I haven't finished."

He took my plate from me and put it on the floor. Then he picked up his pint and handed me my drink. "We can eat later. Bet I beat you."

The brown liquid disappeared into his open mouth. He pulled away the empty glass and smacked his lips together. "Now you."

Mine tasted smooth like pop but, as I pulled the empty glass away and smiled victoriously, my vision shifted. Whoa. I grabbed the settee arm to balance myself and laughed – a muffled cackle. Simon had three noses now. *Three!* Imagine that. One semi-invisible, but the other two were definitely noses. Unless he'd grown one, which was impossible – I mean I wasn't that drunk or stupid – then it must be my eyes. Which one was real? The thick one, there, or… I jabbed it, hitting soft skin.

His head shot backwards and a row of eyes blinked. "Hah, you've got four eyes."

"You've got two very beautiful ones."

He pulled my hands into my lap where he held them tight. As he came closer I saw he had just the two eyes. And they were zonkingly wide.

Chapter 23
- late November -

TROY'S ARMS HUNG BY HIS SIDES but he'd balled his fists, so his knuckles whitened. A muscle moved at the side of his jaw. He turned from where I sat on the settee and headed over to the front window where he gazed through the net curtain. Nearby a radiator clicked, outside a car whirred down the road, then back to silence. With the children next door being looked after by Marion, the only sound was my breath rasping in my dry throat and the thud of my heart.

"You don't get upset like that about nothing," he said.

I shrugged, which was pointless as he couldn't see me.

I'd become like Jez. Saying nothing was wrong when, in truth, I should have answered *everything*.

"You're still shaking," Troy said. "That's not nothing."

I flexed my fingers in an attempt to stop them trembling. Inside, I churned. I'd known I would have to face this moment. But not like this. In my planned, sanitised version, I'd go and see Simon without the children and tell him to keep well away. Or else. But now Simon's threat from years ago hovered, like a predator circling its prey. *Blab to anyone and you're dead. And your baby too. Don't think I won't touch her, cos I will.*

Now he'd seen me, he might wonder if I'd returned to get my payback. He might panic, do something stupid. I hadn't heard the petrol glugging through Jez's letterbox. Only the smoke alarm had saved us. If Simon was desperate enough to do something like that to protect himself, would we make it out a second time? Unlike Jez's house, Mum's didn't have an outbuilding to climb onto, which meant I'd have to drop the children to the ground from the first-floor window. I shivered. It got worse. What if those men – the ones who'd poured the petrol through Jez's door, the ones who'd sprinted after us that night – found out we were here? Stupid, I know. How would they make the connection? But then it hit me. My name. *Karis*.

No way was I going back to being Cindy. *Cindy girl.* Maybe I had no choice. I couldn't use my current ID in case they traced me. I'd have to fetch the other folder from the bedroom. Rediscover myself.

"So, was it him?" Troy said.

My mind whirred. I couldn't absorb Troy's words.

"Simon, or whatever his name was"

If I left now, where would I go? Jez's money wouldn't last for ever. I couldn't access my bank account or anything, not from here, in case they tracked me down. My options faded. Maybe it was time to—

"Karis!"

Startled, I turned to Troy. He'd moved across the room, planting himself behind the armchair, his hands resting on the leather back.

"What?"

"I've been trying to ask if that was Simon you saw."

My bottom lip quivered. Talk about ridiculous. What was it with me and tears at the moment? I had to get a grip, pull myself together and fight back. I let myself finish the sentence Troy had interrupted the moment before – *Stop running* – then I nodded.

"Is he in any way connected to why you left?"

I stood up. "Yes, but let's not go there. I need a coffee. Want one?"

We went through to the kitchen. His eyes tracked me as I filled the kettle, pulled two mugs from the cupboard and, with unsteady hands, spooned coffee into the cups. Granules littered the worktop. He eyed me with concern. I swept the bits into my hands and threw them into the sink. It was a relief to open the fridge to get the milk. Cut off his scrutiny.

"I heard stories about him, you know."

Behind the open fridge door, I stiffened. He couldn't see my face, my burning cheeks. "Like what?"

"A while after you left, he was pulled into the police station for questioning about an incident." He stressed the word 'incident'. "Something about a young girl. Twelve, I think. Apparently, she said Simon came up to her at the park and propositioned her. But your sister said he'd been with her."

Bile seared my throat. A bottle of tomato ketchup rattled against the plastic shelf of the fridge door and toppled, saved by the metal rail. Simon tried it on with others after me. Younger girls too. And Mandy lied for him.

Troy cupped my elbow and eased my fingers from the fridge door. He pulled me to him, so I didn't have to see his face. The fibres of his jumper prickled my cheeks. He smelled of soap and aftershave. Familiar. Safe.

"I always wondered what happened to you during those weeks I was away. You don't have to tell me. I think I know."

♦

We talked all afternoon. Not about Simon but about other stuff. Fun memories from our childhood. Nothing heavy. Each time the conversation strayed too deep and I faltered, Troy would throw me the lifeline of another subject. But the more we talked, the more I realised I had to face my demons, starting with the man with the grey eyes flecked with yellow.

"Why don't we go for a walk?" Troy said.

142

I stared at him. "You are joking."

"Why not?"

I shrugged. He'd be with me at least.

He popped over to Marion's to see if she wanted anything from town and came back to tell me the children were up to their arms in flour, baking cupcakes. He'd put his beige suede jacket on and wore a dark scarf which hugged his neck. As he helped me into my coat, he laughed at my pink and purple striped bobble hat.

"I can see where they inherited their taste for bright colours," he said. "Mum's agreed to Lily's request for blue-coloured cakes. Charlie wanted black, but he settled for red. Something to look forward to later."

We had a lovely time wandering around the shops. At first, I searched for Simon in the clumps of people along the mall, through each doorway we passed, behind every hanging rail, but then I forgot to look. When Troy slipped his arm through mine, I smiled, and tucked myself close to him as we made our way through the crowds.

Outside, we walked past the library. Through the glass, behind the bookshelves, sat banks of computer screens, many obscured by the hunched backs of people doing what I needed to do. Nerves fluttered. I wouldn't like what I'd find, I knew it.

"Can we go inside?" I said. "I could do with using the internet."

"You could use mine," Troy said, but still he followed me inside.

We walked inside to welcoming smiles from the staff behind the counter, the sound of chatter and a child's giggle. Nothing like the morose place I'd slunk to when I needed time away from Mum. At the back, the children's area had painted tables and chairs and bean bags strewn around a

143

brightly coloured rug. Lily and Charlie would love to come here. While Troy went off to look at the books, I signed up for internet use and then went over to one of the desktops. Taking a deep breath, I input the password the lady had given me. I mouthed the words as I typed into Google, unable to keep them inside. Jerome Jones, fire. The newspaper article was the first in the list. I stared at the picture. The blackened brickwork, the gaping hole where once a door had been, the large pane missing in the downstairs window. And Jez? Dead. The word left me winded. I'd half-hoped – kidded myself – for a miracle. With trembling fingers, I scrolled down the page. In recent weeks, a woman and children had been seen living at the house, neighbours said. One of the calls received about the fire had been from a mysterious woman who'd hung up after refusing to give her details. Was she linked with the fire, the police were asking. My hand shot to my mouth. They were looking for me. They thought I was involved.

Footsteps grew louder. I closed the webpage, but I couldn't draw my eyes from the blank screen. The image of the fire imprinted on my mind. The sound, the smell, the fear.

"Cindy… sorry, Karis? Are you okay?" Troy asked.

I swallowed. Gave him a slow nod. But my mind whirred. They thought I could have done that. Burned the house, killed Jez. Now it wouldn't just be those men looking for me, but others too. They didn't know who the woman was, but it wouldn't be long before they pieced the fragments and realised it was me. The nursery would soon notice that Lily and Charlie had disappeared and then the police would go to my old home and find it empty.

I'd have to become Cindy again and face the past. I shuddered. I had no choice.

"Are you sure?" The hesitation in Troy's voice caused the man at the neighbouring computer to glance at the both of us.

I nodded.

When we were out of earshot, I said, "It's silly you having to remember to call me Karis. Just call me Cindy. I'll get used to it."

♦

After coffee in a small café away from the shopping centre, we strolled back. My thoughts had moved from Jez to Simon. How I could face my fear? No longer could Simon mock Troy for being a downy haired teenager, while offering himself as the mature model. As Troy laughed and pulled me up the hill towards home, I felt the power in his grip and imagined those fists pummelling Simon's face. If only I could be the one to smash Simon to the ground. But I had to use a different type of strength. But first, I had to build it.

"Can we go down Collerton Way?"

Troy frowned and his mouth puckered into a circle. I knew what he wanted to say. Why?

"I just want to see it again. With you here."

The houses in Simon's road were a different style to my Mum's. The mix of semis, terraces and two-storey flats had been built with a lighter brick. None of the houses in Mum's road were flats, thankfully, or he might have ended up living next door. Like all the surrounding roads, cars and work vans lined the street, with only the occasional break for a driveway. Many of the privet hedges and chain link fences had been replaced by brick walls or short wooden fences, while the windows were a miss-mash of styles: lattice windows, mahogany surrounds, the usual white frames.

Unlike my childhood, when new windows or doors meant a privately-owned home, many of these now had paint peeling from the fascia boards and clumps of moss on the roofs. The pristine uPVC windows and pink roof tiles now adorned the housing association homes.

With each step closer to Simon's house, my chest tightened. By the time we reached his gate, I could hardly breathe. Downstairs a curtain flapped loose missing a few hooks, like Mum's often did. A baby's bottle sat half-filled with blackcurrant juice on the windowsill. Poor Mrs Norris had either died or gone into a care home. Life moved on. Like I had to. I clenched my fists, took a deep breath and lifted my eyes to the first floor, taking in the brilliant white net curtain which arched in the centre to reveal dainty pleats. The net lifted and a face peered out. I stepped back into Troy who gave my arm a squeeze. It wasn't Simon, but a man in his twenties, maybe thirties, with a widow's peak and spiky hair. A friend of his? I froze, unable to draw my gaze away, even though I bristled with discomfort. I had to know. Did Simon live here? The man lifted the net curtain higher and a woman bent down beside him, a toddler in her arms. They wore the same puzzled expression. For a moment we all stood statue-like, until I realised I could move.

"He's not there," I said. "But he must live nearby or else he wouldn't have been up Mum's road."

But where? I wouldn't feel safe until I knew.

Chapter 24
– Summer holidays –

I LIFTED MY HEAD ABOVE THE MOUND of creamy flesh hunched beside me on the bed and checked the time on Simon's alarm clock. 6.10 am. Twenty whole minutes I'd been lying here. If I didn't do something soon, it would be too late. When I'd first woken, Simon had been a grey hump, but now he lay there in full colour. Bum. If only I'd looked for my knickers while it was still dark, rather than now where the chance he'd see me naked was heightened.

On the edge of his shoulder blade sat a whitehead, an island in the middle of reddened skin. Other smaller pimples appeared like stars, except the night sky was like the black velvet of a panther, not the skin of a plucked turkey with the odd straggly hair here and there. So, this is what an older man looked like.

My stomach ached. Maybe I was coming on my period. It felt a bit like that. I counted, in my head – definitely two weeks ago – because I hadn't wanted to go swimming with Troy before he left for his hols with his dad. But my periods were erratic. Last time it had been a gap of five weeks, the times before that just over four. Nina reckoned they would settle into a pattern. Hers had. She'd patted me sympathetically, pointing out that I hadn't had periods for a whole year yet, had I? Not like her being an old hand, having started at eleven. To think I'd been jealous of her. But she'd been right all along. They were a pain.

Simon shuffled around in the bed, kicking one of my legs which I'd parted slightly as my bits felt swollen and sore. Was it always like this – sex – or had last night been different? I closed my eyes, searching for the memories. I'd giggled when Simon had picked me up and thrown me over his shoulders, pretending to be a fireman, but I must have been knocked out or disorientated after my head had banged against the door frame as I couldn't remember much after then. As I rubbed the tender lump on the top of my head, my elbow tapped Simon's arm. Slowly his eyes opened – oh no, I'd woken him up – and he smiled.

"Morning," he said, his voice thick from sleep.

I shuffled under the duvet cover. His fingers brushed my stomach, so I shifted to the edge of the bed, clutching the corner to stop me from falling.

"I've got to go."

"Not yet, surely?"

He grasped my hand and pulled it towards him. Then he wrapped my fingers around his moist, stiff – I cringed – cock. Disgusting. More like a 'thing'. A clammy smell rose up from the gap in the duvet cover. I tried to jerk my arm away but his fingers overlaid mine. He moved his hand up and down, making mine do the same. My fingers and thumb didn't meet. Had something this wide really been inside me? Shit. No way were we doing that again. I had to get out. Now.

I yanked my hand away. "No!"

I leapt from the bed, dragging the duvet cover with me, horrified to see his – thing – standing upright. Its swollen purple head looked like it had been strangled by the tight brownish skin below and, just as Nina had predicted, his balls did look like manky plum tomatoes. She'd said a cock was sexy. Simon must have a defective one, but either no one had told him or he didn't care. He lay there smiling, his arms tucked behind his head, showing himself off like a peacock.

"Come back to bed, Cindy girl." He jiggled his hips so

his cock wiggled.

"My mum will be up soon."

On the floor lay his crumpled pair of jeans with something white poking from beneath them. From the corner of my eye I could see him running his hands up and down his thing. I had to get away. I kicked his jeans away to retrieve my knickers beneath.

"You don't know how sexy you are." Simon's voice sounded husky. His breathing heavy.

After I grabbed my knickers, I found my t-shirt strewn beside a chest of drawers and my denim skirt on the other side of the room. My bra? I looked around. Simon's hand moved up and down, his lips glistening. Leave the bra! I fled with my clothing, dropping the duvet outside his bathroom door.

Inside his bathroom, I tore on my clothes. The cold rim of the bath pressed against my leg as I bent to pull up my knickers. They chafed my swollen bits. Strange to believe the last time I'd looked in the mirror I'd been a virgin. Nothing much had changed from last night – no flashing sign to tell people what I'd done – except for the hedgehog hair, puffy eyes and creases down my cheeks from Simon's pillow. I dampened my hair and splashed my cheeks and eyes with water, using my t-shirt to pat my face dry. No way was I touching his towel. As I eased the bathroom door open, it juddered and scraped against the frame. I held my breath and checked outside. Only once I'd made sure Simon wasn't about did I tiptoe over to collect my shoes from where they lay beside the settee.

"See ya," I called while helping myself to three of his cigarettes.

As the bed creaked I shot out, taking the stairs two at a time. At the bottom it struck me that Mrs Norris might

149

glance out to see who'd been clattering about at that time in the morning but, by the time the front door crashed shut, I was halfway up the path. Panic rose inside me, making me sprint faster, leaping over kerbs, racing across roads, between cars. Why on earth had I stayed over? Mum would kill me unless, by some miracle, I made it down our road without being spotted.

I dived into a rarely used alleyway which led to Mottram Crescent, a cul-de-sac of bungalows for older people. Years before when I'd asked Mum what the cul-de-sac sign meant, she'd told me it stood for posh people not wanting our lot to go down there. I'd since worked out the real meaning.

I slowed to a jog until I caught sight of the tips of our leylandii hedge above a roof. I'd never seen the front of our neighbour's house. Not that they felt like neighbours. Just voices through the hedge. Their bungalow had a drive with two strips of concrete and pebbles in the middle. No sign of a car. At the end of the driveway there was a metal decorative gate beside a garage with green wooden doors. I could get to our back garden through theirs.

On either side of the front door the curtains were pulled tight across two large windows, while upstairs the curtains hung open in the small window. I couldn't make out anything but darkness through the gap. Were the owners away on holiday? Butterflies fluttered in my tummy. I checked around me, to make sure no one was watching. If I got caught, I'd get doubly murdered by Mum: not just for being a dirty stop-out but trespassing too. It took seconds to sprint up the driveway to the gate, which creaked open, so I didn't dare close it. At the back of the garden the old wooden fencing looked like it was losing the battle with the hedge, as it bulged under the pressure of the leylandii. I hoped the fence would hold my weight, like it used to do years ago when I'd squeeze between it and the thick branches to look over and see where Mr Tibbles disappeared each day.

Hunched over, I ran across the lawn and launched myself at the fence. It wobbled and cracked as if the wood would snap. I scrabbled to the top where, gritting my teeth against the soreness of 'down below', I eased myself into the thick hedge on the other side. The smell of leylandii smothered me and the branches snagged my hair, dragging my denim skirt up my back, while the fence scratched one side of my face. By the time my feet touched the ground, my arms, legs and face stung. Try explaining this one to Mum.

Our small kitchen window was open. I pulled myself up and put my arm through to unlock the larger window. Once in, I shuffled across the worktop by the sink and dropped to the floor. Luck made me look behind and spot the brown and green trail I'd left. I swept it up and headed through to the bathroom where, for the next few minutes, I picked bits from my hair and threw them into the toilet while the bath filled. Finally twig-free, I climbed in. The hot water stung my scratched arms and calves, but it was nothing compared to the burn of soap between my legs. My teeth cut into my bottom lip. *Fu…* With clenched teeth, I cupped my hands beneath the tap and slapped handful after handful onto my bits, until the pain eased to an itchy tingle.

Above me, the stairs creaked. I held my breath, tracking the steps down the slope of the ceiling. A moment later the bathroom door rattled.

"Who's in there?" Mum called and shook the door handle again.

"Me." My heart thudded. "I couldn't sleep."

"Couldn't sleep?" Disbelief in her voice. "Hurry up. I need the toilet."

What if she went back upstairs, into my room and found my pillow 'body' under the covers? The bath squeaked as I jumped up.

"You in the bath?"

"Umm, yeah. I had a, umm, period in the night." I cringed. "Won't be long."

She muttered something, like 'well hurry up' and shuffled away. Talk about a close call. Then it hit me. I'd done it again! My towel was upstairs, on the back of my bedroom door. No way could I ask Mum to fetch it.

♦

Ever since Mum had caught me in the bathroom four days ago, she'd been sniping. Did I have a thing about parading naked around the house in just a hand towel? She'd even suggested I'd done it on purpose just so Bill could catch me. Apparently, I'd been bothering with my looks recently, which was a bit difficult since she'd trapped me in my room for weeks.

"Don't be gross," I'd said, which got her back up.

I couldn't win. If I said Bill was old and ugly she hated it. The one time I didn't say anything, she reckoned my silence was guilt.

When she came into kitchen and leant against the worktop, puffing on her fag while I buttered my toast, I knew she was about to start. Troy had taught me that even when I kept my focus ahead, I could see what was happening at the edges of my vision. I don't know why we'd thought it was a good skill to master, but with practice we'd got good at it, although it made my eyes ache after a bit. Like now, as I watched her while taking my time cutting the toast. Maybe she'd get bored and leave. Then I could eat in peace.

"Did you see anything the other morning?"

I pressed the lid back on the tub of margarine. "When?"

"That morning you had a bath. Did you see or hear anything strange?"

I turned around. "Like what?"

She flicked her cigarette into the sink. A lump of ash melted into mush.

"Julie was telling me that there was an attempted break-in at Mottram Close. Dunno which house, but the neighbours saw someone suspicious and called the police. Probably something or nothing, but I said to Julie I'd found bits of twigs." She patted the windowsill. "Just here. To be honest, I thought you'd been up to something, but now I wonder. Perhaps you disturbed someone trying to break in?"

I looked straight into her eyes – a liar would look away – and prayed she didn't see my fingers tremble or the glow of my cheeks.

"Maybe the twigs blew in the window."

Mum shrugged. But then she pointed her cigarette at me. "Except I remember looking out of the window as I picked up those twigs. It was sunny, not windy, cos I went back up to Bill and told him he was taking me to that Fun Day in the park."

So that's where they'd all disappeared to while I'd lain in my bedroom faking period pains. Not that I'd had to pretend too hard as my insides had ached all day. I'd thought that was bad enough but now I had Mum thinking we'd almost been burgled. Worse, the police would have a description of the girl trying to break into that house and she'd look like me.

I shrugged and tried to look innocent. "Mottram Close is posh. We're not. No one's going to burgle us."

Mum stubbed her fag into the sink, where it sizzled and

153

died. She dropped the butt into the carrier bag hanging from the larder door. "Well, make sure you shut all the windows at night from now on. None of your airing the room nonsense."

Chapter 25
- early December -

I SAT ON THE FLOOR IN MUM'S BEDROOM, the 'Cindy' folder open beside me as I examined, absorbed and relived each sheet, photo and memory. Unable to bear any more, I let a photograph flutter to the floor where it landed on a grainy print-out of Ella. A blob with a large head and spindly legs. I had two more just like it; the scan pictures for Charlie and Lily, but they lived in the 'Karis' folder. I picked up the photo and forced myself to look again. Not just at it, but into it, absorbing each detail. If I was to be Cindy again, I had to face the past.

In the photograph, Mum sat on a rug in the back garden wearing a yellow flowery dress and a white cardigan. Strange how mumsy she'd become. Ella sat in her lap, facing the camera, her little body clutched like a teddy bear. I remember Ella's fists had opened and closed, reaching out for me. Or did I imagine it? She would have only been four months old that September. After I'd done as Mum had asked and taken the photo, she'd sent me inside to fetch Ella's bottle and then insisted on feeding her.

"Make me a cup of tea, love," she'd said, her gaze on Ella sucking at the teat. "I can't get up while I'm holding her."

"I'll feed her," I'd said.

"Nah, you go off and suit yourself." Mum turned to Ella and cooed, "Who's the prettiest little girl in the whole wide world. Yes, you are, yes you are."

Even as I sat here fourteen years later, I felt the old anger build. I wanted to wrench the baby from her grasp and shout 'No. I'll do it!' but like then, I balled my fists and turned away.

I pulled another from the pile of a dozen or so photos. Me and Mandy sitting on the old settee, the one with the holes I used to pick in the arms. Mandy wore crimson lipstick, which coated the tip of the cigarette she held between her fingers. I'd thought her so grown up. Compared to me she was, with her heavy make-up and cleavage-hugging low-cut tops. I'd spent ages trying to squeeze my arms together to achieve the same look. But *he* used to go on about how my boobs were wonderful, much nicer than Mandy's. I gazed at the photo. What boobs? My folded arms all but covered the small pyramid-shaped mounds. I'd tucked my head low, so my eyes lifted to the camera, and a flush stained my cheeks. Why was I blushing? Oh shit, that's why. I threw the picture to the floor. *Him.* He had taken the photo. This would have been when he and Mandy were dating, just before… before… *it* happened.

As the room blurred, I wiped my arm across my face, leaving a damp streak on my skin. I glanced at the time, surprised to see how long I'd been. I placed two items on the bedside table – my birth certificate and the picture of Mum and Ella – and shuffled the rest back into a pile, all the time keeping my gaze averted from the small jiffy bag which peeked from the folder.

I closed the bedroom door, making sure it clicked shut. Then I headed into the children's room, where I found the twins surrounded by a mass of paper – some tight balls, some crumpled – from the ream of paper Ralph had given them to use for colouring.

"I thought you were getting ready," I said, annoyed to see them still wearing their nightwear. "What on earth have you been doing?"

"Marion said it might snow, but it didn't, so we made

it," Lily said.

Charlie bent and scooped an armful of paper and flung it into the air. "It's snowing!" he shouted, while Lily giggled and clapped her hands.

I shook my head. "Well done. But you didn't want it to snow, remember, or else Marion and Ralph wouldn't be able to take you to the market. You've got…" I pretended to check my watch, even though I knew the time. "Ten minutes."

"Hurry!" Lily shouted, outdoing Charlie's usual level.

But he took up the challenge with a deafening, "Da nah nahhhh. Get ready!"

To the sound of banging wardrobe doors, I left them to get ready and headed downstairs with a smile wider than it had been for weeks. I'd never seen the twins so happy. Just a short time with Marion, Ralph and Troy had helped them become proper children. I hesitated, my nails digging into the white paint of the bannister. Should I feel ashamed that it was other people – not I – who'd helped them to step into a world of laughter. But I'd spent my life loving them, playing games with them and taking them to the park. I'd tried to protect them from my mess-ups and mostly succeeded – apart from the fire but I couldn't have predicted something as horrific as that.

I'd laid the best foundations I could. Ralph, Marion and Troy had provided another layer. But then it hit me. What would the children do when we had to leave? We couldn't stay in Mum's house for ever. Troy would be going back after Christmas. And what about me? I'd become used to being surrounded by kindness too.

"When you're dressed, come down and brush your teeth," I shouted up the stairs. "And hurry. You've got five minutes."

In the lounge I picked up the breakfast bowls from earlier and placed them in the kitchen sink. The children arrived downstairs breathless and with minutes to spare, allowing themselves to be shepherded into the bathroom where I brushed their hair and helped them squeeze the last of the toothpaste from the tube. As I zipped up their coats in the hallway, a shape appeared through the patterned glass of the front door wearing a black coat with dark hair. Ralph.

"Hold on," I said, loud enough for him to hear me through the door, while I funnelled Charlie's fingers into the individual finger holes of his woollen gloves, rather than his preference for two in each.

A moment later I opened the door, puzzled to find no one there. I stepped outside, spotting Marion and Ralph outside their front door; her in a lime green coat with a matching felt hat, while he'd hooked a black umbrella over the sleeve of his usual black anorak. Mirroring his glance towards the grey clouds, I pulled up the children's hoods, tucking a few wayward strands of Lily's hair beneath the thick material. After making sure the front door catch was on, we headed over to meet Marion and Ralph by their gate.

"Sorry for making you wait."

"You didn't, dear," Marion said. "Are you sure you don't want to come with us? Troy won't be back before we are."

She smiled as Lily's hand crept into hers. "The market is much better now. More variety than when you lived here."

Ralph nudged her. "She'll want peace without the children."

I fancied a trip out, but not Mosston Market. What if we bumped into Ella or Mandy or, worse, Simon? Plus, Marion had started dropping comments about the children missing school.

"Maybe next time," I said. "I've got tonnes of clearing up to do, starting with a mound of fake snow."

"Aw, please can we keep it?" Charlie said.

I sighed. "I'll find a box for it."

Arms wrapped around my chest to ward off the chill, I watched as they headed off. Hand-in-hand Marion and Lily took the lead, while Ralph walked behind his head bent towards Charlie, listening to his high-pitched chatter. Even when they disappeared into the alleyway, I imagined I could hear Charlie's voice. In a way I wished I'd joined them, but I had things to do. I turned back to the house where I released the catch so the door clicked shut. The dense silence cloaked me and I shivered at the thought of what I faced upstairs. I had to do this. Make myself go back and look through that folder until I accepted the memories for what they were. The past.

Caffeine. That's what I needed. Something warming before I settled down with the folder. As I lifted the kettle under the tap, the larder door creaked. Startled I glanced over to see fingertips curling around the edge of the door. It swung open and I leapt back. A scream ripped the air. Mine. The kettle clattered into the sink, water from the running tap hitting it and drenching my jumper. A figure stepped from the shadows. *He'd come back.* This couldn't be happening. Not now, not here. As I backed away, he edged forward, corralling me into the corner of the units. He turned off the tap and smiled. Brown stains edged the sides of his teeth, a crease forked his cheek.

"You!" I clenched my fists as I fought to stop my voice – my whole body – from shaking. "What are you doing here?"

Chapter 26
– Summer holidays –

I WAS COMING OUT OF NINA'S HOUSE when a bus pulled up at the precinct crammed with old biddies with their shopping trolleys, who clung to the handrail gasping as they edged down the steps. Market day, I guessed, as I squeezed through the gaggle of women having one last chinwag before going home. Then I noticed Mrs Hamilton walking alone, clutching a bulky tweed bag in one hand, a small white carrier bag in the other. Strange how she'd rather do old woman stuff than go to the social club and bingo like Mum. Even here she stood apart in her pink jumper and pleated grey skirt, unlike the curtain-fabric dresses of the other women. My instinct was to pretend I hadn't seen her, especially since I hadn't been around since missing her lunch. But guilt swamped me and I broke into a sprint, shouting "Mrs Hamilton" and waving my arm in the air.

She waited, smiling as I juddered to a stop beside her.

"You been to the market?" I pointed to the bananas, tomatoes and other stuff which stuck out of the brown paper bags.

"Yes, I have," she said, emphasising the 'have' which I'd forgotten. "How is your arm?"

I twisted my arm around so she could see the puckered skin surrounding the now-tiny scab, then realised my arm was covered in scratches from the hedge.

"It's better. How's Troy?"

I held out my hand to take her big bag, but she handed me the smaller one. While we walked, she told me about Troy's latest phone call and how he and his father had reached the final leg of their trip. Toronto. Was it just three

160

weeks since I'd sat in his lounge, flicking through the Encyclopaedia while he told me about the places he was going to visit? He'd mentioned Toronto and a possible trip to the CN Tower, but I'd been most excited by mention of the lakes. Would he see bears, I'd asked, so we'd turned the pages in search of them.

"He tried to call you the other evening," she said.

I'd missed Troy. When? Then I guessed. The one evening I'd been out. The night with Simon.

"I can't wait until he gets back. Just think, this time next week."

When Mrs Hamilton smiled, her face looked younger. She missed him as much, if not more than me. I really should spend a bit of time with her before Troy came home; not leave her alone and lonely while I sat next door doing pretty much nothing. We turned the corner into Kingsley Road, both of us sidestepping the lump of dog mess by the sign.

"Your Mum was saying that someone tried to break into your house."

Her cheeks bulged as she smiled. Was she laughing at the idea of someone wanting to burgle us, or had she spotted me clambering out from under the leylandii bushes? I said nothing and hoped she wouldn't ask.

Simon sauntered towards us, his jacket flung over his shoulder, even though it was t-shirt weather. Had he been to my house? I ducked behind Mrs Hamilton, as if to give him room to pass, cringing at the thought of having to say hello after what he and I had done.

When he got level with us, he grabbed my arm. "Have you got a minute?"

"I…" I gazed from him to Mrs Hamilton. "I…" I said, pointing as if to say, 'I'm with her', but then I remembered we'd been discussing the attempted break-in. It might be a good moment to leave.

"Okay." I shrugged and looked at Mrs Hamilton. "See you later?"

She pursed her lips. I got the impression she didn't like Simon very much.

"It was nice speaking with you again, Cindy."

She took the carrier bag from me and left, her heels clopping down the street. We stood in silence until she reached her house and then Simon signalled for me to follow him. He led me back out of the road and up Patterson Lane.

This end of Patterson Lane went nowhere, unless you lived along it or wanted a night out at the memorial hall. "Where are we going?"

"Nowhere. I just want to talk with you."

"Why are we going up here?"

He stopped by a tall privet hedge. "I didn't want anyone seeing us if they came out of your road."

He meant Mandy. He reached out to stroke my hand, but I pushed him away.

"Been to see Mandy, have you?"

"I came looking for you." He ran his finger down my arm. "I've missed you."

He leant forward. The warmth of his breath filled my ear as he whispered, "I need you, Cindy girl. You're all I can think of."

He pressed himself to me, so I could feel his hardness. The leaves of the hedge rustled, prickling my shoulders and neck. I couldn't move back unless I wanted to be covered in bits of twigs and insects like the other day. The hedge smelt sweet, like the leylandii had, but the closer Simon came, the less I smelt hedge, the more him. A strange musky smell. Huge black pupils swallowed the yellow flecks in his eyes. His lips parted and he sighed. An image flashed from the other night when he'd slumped onto me, dampening my body with his sweat.

"Come around mine. Tomorrow night," he said. "I'll make it worth your while."

I shook my head. "Nah, you're okay thanks."

His mouth drooped. Was he about to cry?

"Have I done something to upset you? That's the last thing I'd want," he said.

He brushed his fingers through my hair and tucked a strand behind my ear. Then he put two fingers to his mouth, kissed them and pressed them to my lips.

"Please come. Don't let me down. We... I've got a treat you'll love."

♦

Downstairs Mum and Bill were having a barney about some poxy statue he'd bought with the last of his dole money. I snuck out of bed and jammed my dressing gown under the bedroom door so Mum couldn't burst in and start on me. When I crept back, I glimpsed something white in the garden. The bed creaked as I knelt, elbows planted on the windowsill, to stare open-mouthed at the thing below. No wonder Mum was mad. This time he'd lost it.

A concrete statue of a half-naked woman had been plonked in the middle of the lawn. It leant to one side, as if about to fall over any minute. I smirked. Even I knew to cut the grass to make an even surface before putting something on it. I gazed at the woman's boobs, upright and pert with sticky out nipples just like Simon liked. Yuk. Is that why Bill had bought it, so he could stare at concrete boobs all day? Lucky her bits were covered with a piece of cloth.

"I thought you'd like it," he bellowed at Mum.

163

"Like it? Bloody like it?" Mum yelled back. "Eighty flaming quid for that."

"I got a deal."

"They should have paid you to take it away."

"I'm not having this."

I held my breath and waited. True to form, the door slammed. That left me and Mum alone in the house, with her in a right mood too. I jumped, hearing something crash below me. The sound of glass, or plate, hitting the floor.

"Oh, for fuck's sake," Mum screeched. "Now I can't afford to buy another one. I'm gonna kill him when he gets back." Another smash. "Fucking kill him."

A cupboard door banged, then another. I edged from the bed, heart thumping. Bill had *really* wound her up. If I didn't get out, I'd be in for it too. I grabbed my shoes and jacket and tugged the dressing gown free from beneath the door, tossing it onto the bed. At the top of the stairs, I heard the tinkle of glass and the slam of a metal lid. Mum was outside by the bin. I raced downstairs and out of the front door, taking a moment to put the key in the outside lock and turn it, so it didn't click and alert Mum.

I tried Nina first, but no one answered. They were probably at a family do or something. Unsure where to go, I wandered about until I found myself at the top of Simon's road. Maybe we could just chat like we used to. Not do *that* stuff. I headed towards his place, pulling off a bit of hedge here and there, flinging it into the path. When I reached his front gate, I hesitated. His lounge window was open, the TV booming. He said come around *tomorrow*. But, surely, he wouldn't mind? I pushed open the gate and, ignoring my growing nerves, I pressed his doorbell.

He'd be nice to me. Unlike Mum.

The door shuddered as Simon pulled it open. He gazed

164

through me, as if he didn't know who I was, then all-of-a-sudden his eyes widened.

"Cindy?"

"You said come tomorrow, but is today okay? Mum's being horrible."

He glanced behind him up the stairs. He must have someone there, a girlfriend or something, maybe Mandy. That's why he hadn't said about today.

"I'm sorry. I shouldn't have come."

"Don't be silly." He pulled me inside by the arm. "My cousin's here. I was going to introduce you tomorrow."

His cousin? The last thing I needed was to be stuck with Simon and someone else.

"I'll come back another time."

"You're here now." He ushered me up the stairs. Machine-gun fire belted out, followed by the sound of a bomb exploding. A war film. Things were getting worse.

Simon put his hands on my shoulders and propelled me into the lounge. My eyes watered from the thick smoke and the back of my throat tickled. He stood me beside the empty armchair, where I had to angle my feet so I didn't knock against the can of lager or the half-filled ashtray on the carpet. Two men slumped on the settee, each holding a cigarette in one hand, a can in the other. The chubby one's eyes widened and, as he shifted forward, the reflection of lamp light moved across his bald head. The other was around Simon's age, slim with muscles that bulged under the sleeve of his top.

Simon picked up the remote control and turned the TV down. "This is Cindy." He held me as if I was being presented. "She's Mandy's sister. Her Mum's being mean to her."

He spoke as if he was laughing at me.

165

"Hi Cindy," both men chorused.

I didn't need to be told which one was Simon's cousin. Fairer-haired, but with the same grey eyes and a dimple that cut into his cheek when he smiled. And just like Simon his eyes lingered on my boobs. I crossed my arms to cover my chest.

"Sit down. I'll get you a drink."

"It's okay," I said. "I'll come back when you're less... busy."

"Don't be silly." He pressed my shoulders down, so I couldn't do anything but sit. "Ade, look after our guest will you while Phil and I get the drinks."

The man grunted, not impressed to be the babysitter, while the other winked at me as he got to his feet.

At the door, Simon hesitated. "Seriously, don't look so worried. I'm glad you came. These two are boring farts at the best of times."

Chapter 27
- early December -

THE BUCKLE ON THE BELT OF HIS JEANS glinted in the light. He slunk closer. The worktop pressed against my back, the cupboard door handle jutted into my leg. Closer. Black stubble cut through the deep hair follicles shadowing his lower face. His eyes darted up and down my body, meeting mine. My skin crawled. *I hated him*. Hated every atom of his disgusting, sick-inducing self. I stepped sideways, but he mirrored my move.

"Nice welcome, thanks," he drawled. A triangle of black fuzz peeked from the top of his open shirt. "But you haven't quite got the point of a wet t-shirt competition."

My sodden jumper clung to my skin, agitating the prickling goose bumps. Water dripped from my sleeve, rolled down my hand. Like blood. Would he kill me? My hip knocked against the cutlery drawer handle, giving me an idea. I lowered my trembling hand behind my back as if reaching into the pocket of my jeans. Too obvious. He'd see I was up to something. I had to divert his attention.

"Go now!" Flinging my arm out, I pointed to the front door. Then I stepped towards him, hoping it would block his view of the drawer being pulled open.

"Or what?"

He grinned, but uncertainty flickered across his face and he glanced towards the hallway. Of course. He'd probably seen Troy chase after me down the street, after I'd fled in a panic. Maybe he'd even hung around to watch Troy bring me back here.

"Troy will be back soon."

Those putrid hazel eyes flecked with yellow lit up as he

smiled. "Will he indeed? Sorry, but I don't think so."

Had he overheard me talking with Ralph and Marion? Heard them saying Troy would be out all day? I couldn't believe we'd spoken loud enough.

"Think what you like" I steeled my voice, keeping my eyes level with his, while I fumbled in the drawer. How could I pick something up without making a noise? Impossible.

"Why are you here?"

"I thought we should have a chat."

"You hid in the larder to chat?"

His hand reached out towards my face. I smacked it away. Inside the drawer, the knives and forks clinked.

"Get out!" I shouted. My voice quivered.

"Cindy," he said. "There's no need to be like that."

I grasped what I hoped was a knife handle. As I pulled it out, it chinked against the other cutlery. Simon's eyes widened as he realised what I was doing. He wrenched my arm, bashing my hand against the drawer edge.

"You bitch." He tore the knife from my fist and flung it to the floor where it clattered against the tiles.

His eyes blazed. Like years before. But no way would he win this time. I twisted my arm, but he held tight. Bastard. Too busy showing his lecherous grin to notice my other arm whizzing through the air to land with a clap against his cheek. Saliva bubbles flecked his teeth. His eyes widened with fury and he grabbed my hair, wrenching my head back. Fiery barbs of pain stabbed my scalp, as if every strand would be ripped free. Pinned by my hair to the kitchen worktop, I tried to kick out at him, but he held me fast. The melamine stank of stale grease. Better that than his stench.

"You bastard. Get off." My eyes teared, my hand throbbed.

"We've been here before."

He pinned my wrists to the counter, pressed his crotch against mine. Disgusting. He bent down to stare into my eyes. Unable to twist away, I squeezed them shut.

"Why have you come back?" His breath puffed against my mouth. I pressed my lips together. Nothing of him would enter me ever again. I'd make sure of it.

"I've got a good life now. I don't need a slut like you coming back ruining it."

Me a slut? What sort of a freak was he?

"I was fourteen. Four, fucking, teen. And you did *that*."

I opened my eyes for the briefest moment but clamped them shut. His gaze was more than I could bear. A reminder of that night. Him above me. Or was it the other one?

"What, Cindy? Tell me?"

He was getting off on this. I could feel him hardening. Bile seared my throat. I had to stop him. While I had a chance.

What about the tape? But he might think to look upstairs to find it and realise it was broken. A moist warmth spread across my cheek. His tongue. I could smell his rancid breath. I jerked my head away, wincing in pain. He ran his finger along the waistline of my jeans, touching my bare flesh where my jumper had lifted. The worktop cut into my back. Nowhere to go.

"You used to like me doing this to you." He panted as he spoke. "Does it still turn you on?"

"Fuck. Off. Pervert."

"Why else did you come back if you didn't want this? Just imagine." He stuck his finger down my jeans, wiggling it so it brushed the lace edging of my knickers. "We could have it here, right now. You still turn me on, although…" He removed his finger from my jeans and ran it along my jawline. "You are getting on a bit."

I couldn't open my eyes. Not if it meant looking into his. But the world of darkness heightened my senses. Every touch, brush, whisper of breath. My heart pounded, blood pumped through my ears, my breath rasped. His smell. Excitement, lust. Would he rape me here, now, and then keep his promise from all those years ago?

I had to face him. Not hide in the darkness. I gritted my teeth, opened my eyes. His face was so close it blurred.

"Touch me and I'll tell everyone what you did," I snarled.

"Try it. I'll do what I said." He jerked a fistful of my hair as his spoke. "You've got two more, I see. Have you ever wondered what happened to the one you left behind? Nah, of course you didn't. Not you, Cindy girl, who only cares for what she can get from people. Unlike your sister Mandy. No way will I let you upset her."

"Me, upset her?" I choked on a bubble of indignation.

Why was he so concerned about Mandy? He and she were old news. But if they'd somehow stayed friends, it would mean he had access to Ella. No longer was she a chubby little thing, with a toothy grin and dimpled knees (and cheek). Her school photo showed her fresh-faced innocence. Just the way he liked them.

A mat of thick hair covered the arm that pinned me by the hair to the worktop. I needed to free myself. See Mandy. Find out where Ella was.

"So that's why you've come," I said, in as gentle a tone as I could manage. "I'm not here to upset Mandy. If I'd realised that worried you, we could have sorted this out ages ago. Let me go so I can explain."

He hesitated. Then he grunted something about no silly games and released me. My back cracked as I rose and squared up to him. Grey eyes, flecked with yellow, just like Ella. How often had I prayed she wasn't his? Not that the alternative was much better.

"I'm just here to see Mum." I rubbed my aching neck. Three red finger marks stained his cheeks. "I heard she was poorly and came to see her. I was going to say hello to Mandy too, before we leave."

He'd started to relax when I mentioned Mum, but now he tensed, fists balled at his sides. Gold flashed on his finger. Some poor cow had married him.

He didn't want me to see Mandy. Of course. He'd be scared I'd dredge up the past. I looked into his foul eyes and tried not to think about what they'd seen. What he'd done. Why did he care about Mandy so much? He knew she hadn't believed me all those years ago, so she'd hardly believe me now. But I hadn't told her the whole story. I hadn't been able to tell anyone; not after he'd threatened me with what he'd do.

"I don't want you going near her," he said.

The front door knocker creaked and tapped twice. I glanced into the hallway, through to where I could make out the shape of a man through the patterned door panes.

"Troy," I said. "He knows I'm here."

Simon shook his head. "I'm not falling for that."

"He's got a spare key if I don't open the door."

As he glanced towards the front door, his expression turned to alarm. He pointed a trembling finger at me.

"Say anything and you're dead. Your kids too. Just remember, I'll have nothing to lose."

He fled through the back door. As it slammed behind him, I locked it and ran to the front. Through the glass I could see a dark-coated figure walking away. Had Troy come back early? He had a brown jacket. I wrenched the door open to find a delivery man by the gate, a parcel tucked under his arm. He spotted me and sauntered back.

"For next door." He nodded towards Marion's house. "They're out. Can you sign for it?"

Behind him, Simon had reached the road and disappeared from view behind a large van. Now he knew it wasn't Troy, would he return? I knew the answer. Yes. But it wouldn't be today.

Chapter 28
– Summer holidays –

ADE'S THICK FINGERS RESTED on the settee arm. He didn't notice me staring at them. His attention was on the TV and the wagon that billowed a cloud of dust as it raced across the desert, followed by a dozen or more horses ridden by men in blue with flapping yellow scarves. One of the riders yelled something to his companion and Ade leant forward, frowning. Thick lines crinkled his forehead, ending where his hair line once would have been, but now there was just shiny smoothness against which the light from the TV reflected. He needed a cowboy hat. That way only the horseshoe of hair which hung over his ears would be seen and no one could tell he was bald.

He went to pick up the remote control and caught my eye. Did he know I'd been staring at him? I looked down at my hands. They gripped my knees so tightly, my knuckles jutted like the Rockies.

Ade took a drag of his fag and pointed the remote control at the TV. Music crashed into the room, the beat of a drum, the dah dah dahhh of a trumpet as two Red Indians popped up from behind a rock. Talk about old-fashioned.

"I can't hear," he said.

I nodded and turned away. What was I doing here with a bunch of old men? There must be somewhere better to hang out tonight. Even Mrs Hamilton's. Or with the goths at the precinct, although they hadn't been there when I'd walked past earlier. Hannah Curtis had become a goth and she reckoned they weren't as scary as they looked and much nicer than the chavs who laughed at me for being a swot. It wasn't my fault I was in the top set. Thank goodness I hadn't gone to Grammar or else they might pick on me like they did the other kids who got off that bus. They left Troy alone, but only because Issie Saunders fancied him. I'd seen the way she pushed her cronies to one side so she could flutter her eyelashes when he walked past.

I'd try the precinct again. Hopefully, Hannah would be there. As I stood up to leave, Ade turned to me.

"Not leaving already?" He grinned. "I have this effect on women."

"I've just got to fetch something. Nice meeting you."

He took a swig of lager and gasped. "You too."

In the hallway, I could hear Simon and Phil talking in the kitchen. Good. I might have half a chance of making it out without being seen. I felt bad for Simon. He was trying to be nice and looking out for me, but I'd apologise tomorrow. Carefully, I let the bannister rails take my weight and I snuck down the stairs.

"I dunno what your problem is. Ade might be up for it and I've got the stuff."

"You won't need it. Vodka did the trick last time. But I'm not sure about Ade."

"Just think how grateful he'd be. He'd owe us one big time. Here – insurance – stick it in."

Glasses chinked and the fridge door closed. I held my breath and crept further down, grimacing as the stair creaked.

"Cindy!" Simon stood at the top of the steps holding my vodka and coke and a can of lager. Behind him stood Phil who held another two cans.

I blushed. "I forgot I said I'd meet up with Hannah."

"She can wait a bit longer, can't she?" Simon put the drinks down on the side and came down to lead me back up the stairs. "I've made you a drink. Just another five minutes won't hurt."

He manoeuvred me back into the lounge and into the armchair and, after pushing the glass into my hands, he sat beside me on the arm, swinging his leg so his foot knocked the edge of the chair. Ade smirked and said something to Phil, and they laughed. I had to get out. The glass was wet and cold in my hands. I took a swig and grimaced. More vodka than coke by the taste of it. Was Simon trying to get me drunk? Maybe that's why his friends were laughing. They were having a bet on whether I walked or staggered out the door. Well, I'd walk. I'd make sure of that.

"I've gotta go," I whispered to Simon as I edged to the front of the seat.

He patted my shoulder. "Aww, at least finish your drink."

His hand stayed on my shoulder, his fingers brushing my neck. I tried to shrug him off but he bent down, murmuring that no one could see. The way I saw it, the faster I drank, the quicker I could leave. I took two gulps, then a third. The TV speakers vibrated like my cassette player did when I turned the sound up. A burning wagon lay on its side, while all around Red Indians whooped. Gunfire. So loud. An Indian fell from his horse, then another. The camera panned into a cowboy's blurred face. Great! That meant I was tipsy and those men would win their bet. I had to slow down. I stared at the TV, forcing my eyes to focus. With one eye closed I could just about see but I couldn't walk out squinting like a pirate.

Simon offered me a cigarette. I went to pull it from the pack, but my fingers plucked at thin air. He laughed and popped the fag into my mouth. For some reason, his hand rested on my forehead as he lit it.

The two men got up from the settee and wandered past us through to Simon's bedroom. Simon caught my eye and shrugged. He obviously had no idea either why two men were disappearing into his room.

"Gives us a chance to be alone."

He stubbed out the little that was left of my cigarette and kissed me on the cheek, leaving behind wetness. He smelt of beer, cigarettes and a musky warmth. His hand slipped beneath my top and under my bra strap. I twisted away.

"Tease," he said. But at least he removed his hand.

I knocked back the last of my drink and handed him the empty glass. Finally, I'd finished. I could go.

Whoa. A whirlwind hit me and I jerked back blinking and shook my head.

"Tha wash shong."

He laughed. It sounded like it came from the bedroom, but he sat beside me.

"Give me a few minutes more before you go. I wanted to tell you how much I like you."

He leant over and kissed me on the lips. Behind us on the TV the music pulsed. Dah nah, dah nah, dah nah nahhhh. I needed to dance. *Had* to dance. I jumped up but fell back, landing on Simon.

"Oops. Soz." I giggled and pushed myself up.

The room spun, around and around. I flung my arms out and twirled. I was a spinning top, making everything a whiz of colour: jags of brightness from the TV, Simon's white teeth, the shadows by the bedroom door. My legs buckled. I crashed to the floor and lay there, a starfish staring up at the ceiling. It rolled above like a wave. Hah! How funny was that. I'd become a spinning fish.

"A finnin spish," I shouted above the noise of the TV. "A finish pish."

Someone banged the floor so it vibrated.

"Do something!" Simon said. What did he want me to do?

I thumped the floor with my fists and heels. "Sshrup y'ol bag."

"Give her more. It'll quieten her."

"But we want her awake. Or we might as well use Ade's doll for all the fun it'll be."

Ade's got a doll? Hah! What sort of man was he? An old man who played with dolls. Wait till I told... um... told who?... who was I thinking of... nobody. Hah! I'd tell nobody about... um... nothing.

Another bang. The floor dropped beneath me and I was in the air.

"Sshrup y'ol doll," I screeched and cackled. I was a witch and I could fly. "Wheeeeee!"

"Well, you're the one who gave her it. I said just alcohol."

"Make her shut up. The old cow downstairs'll call the cops at this rate. We'll just have to make the tape look like she's with it."

Was I flying too fast? Were the cops chasing me? "Cops. Watshup cops!" I shouted at the shadows.

I was upright, surrounded by eyes. Millions of eyes. Something wet ran down my throat and I coughed. Vodka. Yum. With my magical witch powers, I'd floated under a vodka fountain. I opened my mouth and let it pour inside. My mouth wouldn't work. I shook my head. No more. Enough. The fountain spewed out, numbing my lips. Then it disappeared.

Simon's face loomed above me, his nose big like a... like a... big nose. Hah! Oh, Simon, what big eyes you have. Oh, Simon, what big teeth you have. Oh, Simon, what a strange smell you have.

177

Chapter 29
- early December -

THROUGHOUT THE FOLLOWING DAYS, I replayed the meeting with Simon, absorbing every word, every look and suggestion. Slowly I worked on drawing out my fear and horror from that summer, leading it around my mind, breaking it in until I knew I'd found the strength to delve deeper into the past. My fear became fury. I shook with outrage at what Simon had got away with, but I couldn't yet tame the memories. They leapt from nowhere. The gate had been opened and the past trampled the present.

"Bastard!" I found myself calling out one evening as the children and I sat watching *You've Been Framed*.

"What's the matter, Mummy?" Charlie had asked and I'd flushed, unable to explain that seeing an image of a video camera had pressed play on my journey into the past.

During the day I allowed myself to dwell on the fragments from *then*. When it got too much, when the new memories became a waterfall drowning my mind, I got up to do something – anything – to occupy myself. But night was different. When I awoke from nightmares in which grey eyes flecked with yellow loomed over me, I lay wide eyed, staring into the darkness, knowing what came next if I went back to sleep. Each recollection twisted my gut. Had that *really* happened? *To me*? With each memory came a smell. Sweat, cigarettes, beer and a strange intimate odour. Sex. I buried my face into the pillow and breathed in the fragrance of the fabric softener I'd bought, but Mum's scent clung to the fabric, a reminder of other pieces of the past. Her anger about the shame I'd brought on the family. The awful loneliness of pregnancy until Ella arrived, bringing with her a few months of happiness. Think about something else. Not her. Don't think about her.

Tears soaked the sheets, but I allowed myself to mourn the loss of my childhood self. And I felt myself grow stronger.

Chapter 30
– Summer holidays –

PAIN STABBED MY STOMACH and between my legs too, but it couldn't be my period. Far too intense for that. I shifted around, banging my knee on something. The shaft of light through the curtains stung my half-open eyes. Since when were our curtains blue? And the fabric didn't feel like a bed either. Clutching my aching belly, I took in my surroundings. The TV, the settee, the ashtrays. It wasn't ours but Simon's lounge. But where was he? Oww. I gritted my teeth against another wave of pain as a strange warmth seeped between my legs. Each muscle – more than that – every bit of me ached, right to the tips of my fingers and toes. I pushed myself to my feet. 'Down there' throbbed and stung. Why? I examined the pieces of last night, tried to fit them together, but nothing made sense.

Swamped by nausea, I sat on Simon's loo, staring at my knickers. Blood stained the fabric in two places but, weirdly, they were damp like I'd wet myself. I'd put them on back to front too. Talk about way too much drink last night. My wee dribbled out, shooting fiery needles of pain. Maybe I'd got that cyst thing Nina always went on about. That would explain the odd smell. She was right. It *was* painful. I needed some of that berry stuff she drank. My body trembled as I eased myself from the toilet seat until, hit by a wave of dizziness, I dropped back, gasping. Agony ripped through my insides, down my legs. I had to get home. Get to bed.

Everything became double. The door handle had a twin that shifted sideways depending on how hard I looked at it. The same with my hand, the walls, the floor. I stumbled into the lounge. My vision eased, a fog parting, and I could think.

My shoes. I couldn't go without them. I checked the hallway, the kitchen and back through to the lounge. Where were they? The sound of snoring came from Simon's bedroom. I'd have to wake him and ask if he'd put them away.

Simon lay huddled into his duvet in the murky room. The air stank. Sickly like B.O. Yuk. I hooked my top over my nose and crept over to grab my shoe from where it lay beside his dressing table. As I slipped it onto my foot, I spotted the sole of other one peeking from beneath the bed. It was jammed under this closed tripod thing, so I had to drop to my knees to tug it free. Odd that my shoes were in here when I'd spent the night in the lounge. Or had I? I couldn't remember. The bed creaked as Simon moved. No way did I want him to wake and find me in there. With the shoe in my hand, I crawled from his bedroom.

♦

Arms crossed, Mum leant against the kitchen worktop, facing the back door. She must have seen me coming up the path and been waiting, red fingernails tapping her arm. A draught blew through the open back door where I stood, wafting a loose strand of Mum's hair. She pursed her lips, raised her eyebrows. Well? I couldn't take my fingers from the door handle. If I went inside, I'd be stuck with no escape route. Behind her the kettle boiled, the bubbles churning, thumping the metal sides. On and on. At this rate it would explode. Why didn't she do something? Steam billowed, condensation ran down the cupboard door. It clicked off.

"Where've you been?" she said. "And don't try to lie. Your bed hasn't been slept in."

"I fell asleep round a mate's."

"Which mate, cos I'll check."

181

I shrugged. "It was some goth party. I bumped into them at the precinct."

My fingers tingled. Everything went… Woah! I fell against the door, heard it smash into the wall. I found myself on my knees, still clutching the handle. Shit. I was going to be sick. Hand over my mouth, I pulled myself up and staggered towards the bathroom. She didn't try to stop me. But I caught her sneer. Like I was filth.

"Serves you right for drinking," she said, as I shut the bathroom door. She raised her voice. "And no doubt shagging around too. You're grounded."

To the sound of cupboard doors banging, I leant over the toilet bowl, waiting to be sick. Years of shit clung to the sides, mottled patches, vertical lines as if something had slithered down. Euww. Even Simon's toilet was white. *Simon.* Why did the thought of him make me want to puke? I moved away and hung over the bath, my hair draping down the sides. The ceramic lay cold against my shaking chest. Flu. That must be it.

Someone knocked on the bathroom door.

"You make a mess, you clear it," Mum said. "Don't think I'm joking. If I find out you got up to anything last night, I'll have you. If it ain't you, it's Bill. I'm sick to the back teeth of it."

As she shuffled away, the sickness faded and I pulled myself up from the bath. Bill had upset her. Great. It couldn't still be about the statue, which left one thing. He must have been up to something behind her back again. Did that mean he'd move out for weeks like last time? I hoped not. She'd been a right nightmare to live with.

A spider sat at the bottom of the bath. I picked the toilet roll from the floor and pulled off a length. One bit was rippled, darker pink and damp. I grimaced. Probably Bill missing the toilet again during the night, which at least meant he was still here. I laid the sheets in front of the spider and touched the back of its legs so it ran onto the paper, then I shook it onto the floor and watched it scurry away.

The griping pain started again. Above, the stairs creaked and footsteps padded across the landing. I crept out of the bathroom. Just one tablet was left in the packet of aspirin. I threw it into my mouth and glugged the glass of water. Moistness oozed between my legs. What was happening? I slammed the glass down on the side and shot into the bathroom. The inside of my jeans and my knickers were soaked. Wee. Had the alcohol damaged me somehow? Wincing, I patted the tissue to my bits. Swollen, bruised, like I'd been punched. I pulled off more tissue and dabbed the around the back, flinching at the pain. I stared at the sheet. At the crimson dots. Really? I tried again, wincing. More blood. Bright, fresh.

I tried to recall the night before. Screwed my eyes tight. But the fog of alcohol had created a black hole which sucked up every thought. The harder I tried, the blanker my mind became. With my elbows on my knees, hands cupping my chin, I sat there and stared at nothing.

Then Simon's large grey eyes floated in front of me and I heard a strange panting. But as the memory faded, I realised it wasn't Simon. It was Phil.

Chapter 31
- mid December -

WE'D BEEN WAITING SO LONG in the aisle for the stream of jabbering school children to pour down the steps, that the chunter of the bus had lulled me into a dream of the past. A happy memory. One where I'd stepped onto the pavement to find Troy waiting, clutching his school bag and a pound saved from his dinner money. Issie Saunders had folded her arms and snarled something under her breath as she'd watched Troy drag me into the newsagents with the promise of first dibs on his pick and mix.

As we stepped onto the pavement, the hiss and clank of the doors closing behind us interrupted my thoughts. A group of teenagers milled around waiting for the bus to leave, while others had set off in clumps towards the precinct or nearby streets. Two men sat on the bus shelter bench, one clutching a bottle of lager. I'd already twisted the carrier bag handle around my hand, but now I gripped it tighter, in case someone should see the brand name and go to snatch it. Then I remembered: we were in Mosston not London. Old habits were hard to break.

The bus pulled away, leaving us in a fog of diesel fumes. Charlie waved his hand in front of his face. "Pooh-ee." But I liked the smell. For the first time in ages I felt alive. Cold pricked my skin, the wind whipped my hair into my face and a bird chirped in nearby trees. Beside me Lily hummed what sounded like the same three bars of a nursery rhyme, her gloved hand snuggled warm inside mine. Charlie kept his arms by his sides, insisting he was big enough to walk beside me without having to hold my hand. We'd brokered a deal. He'd stay close or else.

"Do you want to go to the park before home?" I asked when we reached the other side of the road.

We turned into Nelson Corner, which led to Collerton Way where Simon used to live. From there we could take a shortcut to the park through the alleyway. I shivered at the thought of going past his old flat. Stupid, I know. For a start he no longer lived there and secondly, hadn't I promised myself a new start? One where I'd look forward and not back. Simon could threaten me but I'd seen him run when he thought Troy was around. These past days had been spent working through the memories and the nightmares. I'd wrestled them into my control. He no longer held any power over me.

"Stop a minute," I said.

I unzipped my coat and stashed the carrier bag inside. No point tempting fate when we walked through the alleyway. When we got to the park, I would take the mobile phone out of the box. Then if anyone did decide to grab the bag, they'd be taking cardboard.

When I looked up, Charlie was way ahead, past the alleyway.

"Charlie," I called.

I'd tied his deerstalker hat tightly beneath his chin, so the flaps would keep his ears warm. But it meant he couldn't hear me.

"Charlie!" I shouted louder this time.

He spun around, puzzled to see us so far behind. Holding tight to Lily's hand, I jogged to meet him.

"Were you in daydream land?" I pointed down the road to an alleyway. "We're going up there."

Then I spotted *him* walking towards us – I'd know his walk anywhere – head bent as he chatted to a girl almost his height. She walked with the air of an older teen, but her hair

185

style made her look much younger. Fastened at the sides by gold clips, it fell in thick brown waves over the shoulders of her blazer. In Mum's photo it had been straighter. Darker in the flesh, her skin tone was more like mine and, although her head was bowed, I could see her long, thick eyelashes. I pictured her eyes, grey and flecked with yellow, and willed her to look up to show me her beautiful wide smile, but she turned to cut across the driveway of a house. Simon's leather-clad arm brushed her back, as if leading her. I fought the urge to drag him away screaming, 'Don't touch her!'. She moved ahead, taking long strides in her black trousers – thankfully not a school skirt – and pulled down the handle of the white uPVC door and disappeared inside. He followed her.

I stood, stunned. Crushed by a desperate sense of longing and need. And terror.

My daughter had grown up. But she was still a young girl and one in close contact with Simon. A bitter taste filled my mouth.

"Mummy." Lily yanked my hand.

In a fog of tumbling thoughts and memories, I led the twins across the road towards the alleyway. Would he touch a girl who could be his daughter or niece? Twigs snapped beneath my feet and branches snagged my coat, cracking as they broke free. A pebble ricocheted into the undergrowth. I'd left my daughter to a paedophile. We skirted a pile of dog crap and turned into Simon's old road. Paedophile. The word circled round and round. That's what he was.

"Yellow mini!" Charlie yelled.

"I said it first," Lily said.

The windows of Simon's old flat were closed but a tippy cup sat centrepiece on the windowsill, an ornament beneath the arc of the net curtains. Ella must live in Nelson

Road. She'd gone inside without knocking. But what about Simon? We paused while a car reversed out of a driveway, speakers vibrating to a thump-thump bass which overpowered the noise of the engine and the tinny strain of music. The car drove off, leaving us in a mist of exhaust fumes.

Marion had said Ella was living with Mandy. She hadn't mentioned Simon.

Ahead three pigeons sat on the lowest strand of wire that looped between two telegraph poles. One stretched and flapped its wings, causing the middle one to flutter away. The aggressor sidled into the vacated space, bent its head to nuzzle the other, while the loser watched from a neighbouring roof top. Like him, I'd given up too easily. My mind started to replay the same old excuses. Yes, I'd been young. Yes, it had been difficult. Not just difficult but impossible. Baby Ella couldn't have slept in the corner of the bin area or even in the luxury of the old shed I'd called home for six weeks. No way could I have got a job if she'd been there.

But I should have come back sooner.

Panting, the children trotted beside me. Charlie didn't shy away as I grasped both his and Lily's hands to guide them between the parked cars and across the road, towards the leylandii trees which now bordered the park. Green tips curled in the wind above the row of houses. Once the park hedgerow had been a muddle of thorn bushes and trees, I was sure of it. How had the leylandii grown so tall in the short time since I'd left? So many things had changed. Life had moved on.

But *he* was still here.

We reached the park. The children's hands slipped free and I watched them race off, little arms pumping. I'd missed

Ella's first steps, pushing her on the swing, helping her with her homework. But I could do something for her now.

If I wasn't too late.

Chapter 32
– Summer holidays –

"… COW." MUM'S SHOUT came through the door, waking me. Aimed at me or Mandy I couldn't tell.

The door flew open and Mum's head appeared, darker than the grey of the room. She waved her hand in front of her nose.

"For fuck's sake, Cindy. You planning on spending another day in bed? Lazy cow."

Her shirt draped over my face as she leant over to open my curtains, which snagged halfway, as they always did. She grunted, tugging harder. Her stomach stretched beneath the cotton and shadows covered the dip of her belly button. Skin, close to my face. I scrunched my eyes shut, unable to look. But the skin I recalled had been taut over the bulge of an Adam's Apple, accompanied by a strange 'huh, huh' like a steam engine gaining in speed. I flung my eyes wide open, desperate for relief from the images that crammed my mind.

"You're to get up now."

Mum snatched my cover away and let it fall to the floor. Hands on hips, she stared at me. Goosebumps pricked my legs and back, hairs pinged upright along my arms, but not from the cold. I curled into the middle of the bed, a C around the wet patch. Please, please don't spot it. I'd woken during the night to find I'd leaked but, too exhausted to change the sheet and turn the mattress over, I'd shifted to the edge of the bed by the wall and wrapped myself inside the duvet cover. Now I couldn't tell if the sheet was cold or still damp.

Mum bent down and sniffed. Her irises were like sticky dots plonked in the whites of her eyes. She hadn't taken her makeup off properly and a blue shimmer from last night's eyeshadow clung to the wrinkles that criss-crossed her eyelids, while mascara flakes sat on the bags beneath her eyes. Stubby lines spread in all directions from her down-turned lips.

I flinched as her nose touched mine. The taste of mint and cigarettes puffed against my lips. I held my breath. Her forehead crinkled, her mouth became a snarl.

"You've been taking drugs, haven't you? Bet that's why you're hanging out with those goths."

She snatched my jeans from the floor and lobbed them at me. "Get up."

Something about the jeans brought another memory. Mine being dragged off. Laughter. My white knickers on top of Ade's head. More laughter. Mine. This couldn't be real. I gagged and clamped my hand to my mouth. Three men and me. Me and three men.

"Didn't you hear what I said? Get up. No daughter of mine is spending another day on her arse."

She stomped from the room, leaving me to struggle from the bed. As I clutched the bedstead to help keep my balance, damp oozed between my legs and a teardrop of wee trickled between my knees, falling to the carpet. I gazed at the circular stain.

What on earth had they done?

♦

If anyone spotted me, they'd think I'd lost my mind, thanks to the dress I'd found in the back of Mandy's wardrobe. It shouted 'freak'. But while the dress was disgusting and frumpy, it was better than being seen with a damp patch or a huge pad bulging from between my legs. How Mandy could walk properly while wearing something half the size of a brick, I didn't know. She must have a period on the scale of Niagara Falls each month but, at least, that meant I'd be safe if I wet myself again. But, even if she'd had a normal-sized pad, I couldn't have worn my jeans. Anything rubbing between my legs hurt, even the gentlest dab of tissue.

They'd done something bad. That much I knew. I was going to see Simon and have it out with him. What I'd say or do when I got there was anyone's guess. I'd run through countless scenarios. Me punching him and yelling 'What did you do?' but he'd be too strong and probably grab my arm before I landed a blow. What if I screamed, embarrassed him in front of Mrs Norris? But then she'd know *something* had happened and she might tell others. Did I want everyone knowing?

I snuck out of the house without Mum seeing me. If she spotted me in a dress – especially a flowery one – she'd know something was up. The trainers made it worse, but no way was I wearing my school shoes. At the gate I gazed down the road, praying I wouldn't bump into anyone I knew. Especially Issie Saunders and her gang. I could imagine the jeers and bitchy comments. The dress flapped in the breeze and around my shins until it caught against Mandy's tights and clung on, refusing to let go. Every bump, every lump, was visible, including the pad. No way was I turning up at Simon's door looking like the dress was sprayed on. Static cracked as I pulled the material from my legs.

When I reached the sign for Collerton Way, I stepped back against the chain link fence to make room for an old woman. Stooped over, she wore a skirt with thick beige tights that barely hid the veins that bulged from her shins. In one hand she held a walking stick, in the other a lead for a small dog which trundled beside her, tongue out and wagging its tail. The woman lifted her head.

"Hi, Mrs Norris. I didn't know you had a dog."

"I don't." Her voice was tight, like she was annoyed about something. "Some of us spend our lives trying to help people, not upset them."

Her walking stick clipped the path. She paused at the kerb, her head a small hump above the mound of her back. Well, I'd learned one thing. If I went to have it out with Simon she wouldn't be on my side. You've brought it on yourself, gallivanting around like that, she'd say. No good comes from behaving like a tart. Her voice became an amalgam of all the condemning voices I'd read in Bill's newspaper. Girls today. Slappers. Slags. Deserve what they get.

Amalgam. Where did I get that word from? Of course, Science and Mr Potts. He reminded me of Simon the way he looked at girl's boobs, even when we had our sweaters on. Bet he read Bill's paper too.

A car headed towards me. Red with square headlights, a bit like Simon's. Two men sat in the front. Leaves brushed my head as I tucked myself beneath the overhanging branches of a tree. I could make out the passenger door, a lighter colour than the rest of the car. A chain-link fence bordering the footpath creaked as I pressed myself into it, desperate to not be seen. The car slowed and Phil's gaze met mine. He turned to the driver and Simon bent past him to stare out. They shared a laugh. As the car pulled away, Phil winked and held a smirk until the car turned the corner and disappeared.

Wave after wave of rage crashed down. Arseholes. I shoved the branch to one side, flinching as it sprung back. Bastards. My feet pounded the tarmac, my breath rasped in my ears. I fought the dizziness, ignored the ache between my legs. Before I knew it, I'd reached my gate, unable to stop until I smashed into the front door. My hand shook, the key slipped around the sides of the lock. Finally, it went in. The door smashed against the hallway wall. I took the stairs two at a time, raced into Mandy's bedroom, where I tore open the top drawer on her dressing table and ransacked the jumble of sprays and creams. I'd seen a key, a silver one, when I'd been searching for her pads earlier. I bet it was his. I slammed the drawer shut, yanked open the next one down, rifling through her underwear. Then I spotted it.

I didn't have much time. Mrs Norris would be back once she'd finished her walk and I had no idea where Phil and Simon were off to. The pub would give me a couple of hours, the bookies around half an hour, while the newsagents would give me minutes at best.

At the front door to Simon's flat, I paused to listen for the sound of a TV or movement. Nothing but the sound of me panting. There'd been three of them last time. Phil, Simon and an old bloke called Ade who hadn't been in the car. Was this a trap? I took a deep breath, crossed my fingers.

The key fitted. The door creaked open. I shot a final glance into the road – once I was in, there was no way out other than this door – and disappeared inside.

Chapter 33
- mid December -

TROY SMILED, WISHING ME 'good luck' without the need to say a word. The twins didn't take their gazes from the film, giving me a brief wave before they burrowed their hands back into the bowls of popcorn that tottered on their laps. The lounge door brushed against the carpet and clicked shut, swallowing the sound of the TV. Left in the quiet of the hallway, I took a moment to gather my thoughts. To plan what I would say. I'd told Troy I wanted to see my sister, Mandy. He hadn't asked why. Instead, he'd seemed pleased. Maybe I should have told him about seeing Simon and Ella, especially as there was a chance it might not go well. Might? There was no way she'd like what I was about to tell her.

I pulled on my coat and tucked my hair inside the hood, bracing myself for the gale Troy had warned me about as I opened the door. The chill slapped my face and I gasped. The dusk seemed murkier than usual beneath the dark storm clouds. With my hands tucked inside my pocket and my head down so the gale buffeted my hood, I started the trek to Nelson Close. An empty crisp packet flapped along until the wind flattened it against a brick wall. Thick raindrops splattered my face. Great. I bent lower, only lifting my head to peer out when I crossed the road. Thunder rolled in the distance, and gusts wailed down the alleyway, ripped through the trees, creating a banshee howl.

By the time I reached Nelson Close my legs felt like sponge, not from the rain – which had stopped – but nerves. I paused two doors from the house I'd seen Ella and Simon go into. Clenching my trembling fists, I took a few deep breaths. I muttered a silent prayer that this would be Mandy's house and she would open the door, but if this was someone else's house – a friend's perhaps – at least I could go home.

A light was on in the downstairs front window, the room inside veiled by net curtains, but I could make out white kitchen cupboards, a flowerpot on the windowsill and the outline of a black-rimmed clock on the wall. Seeing the bits and pieces of family life – worse, Mandy's – made it too real. Did I have to destroy the life she'd created for herself? Perhaps Simon had changed. I shivered. A paedophile didn't change its spots.

Water squelched through the cracks of a loose paving slab and splashed my foot. When another slab tottered and threatened to soak me, I side-stepped from the driveway onto the concrete path. Through the patterned glass in the front door, a shadow walked along the dim hallway. It disappeared.

A light flashed on upstairs, brightening the gloom. I pulled down my hood and swiped my sodden sleeve across my forehead to brush the droplets from my fringe. My heart thumped and my stomach fluttered. If I didn't do it now, I never would. The button squeaked. I held my breath and waited. At the end of the hallway, a crack of light seeped through the bottom of a closed door. I pushed the doorbell again. No sound. Instead I used the knocker. Tap-tap. It echoed around.

"Hold on!" a woman shouted from above.

I glanced up, for some reason expecting the window to open and a set of keys to be thrown down, but instead I heard a toilet being flushed and a click as the light turned out, dimming my surroundings. A raindrop rolled down the back of my neck and I shivered. Moments later a shape appeared in front of the glass. The door opened and warm air wafted out, bringing with it a stale cooking smell.

Mandy had aged better than I'd expected. She'd had her hair cut into a bob, a few centimetres too short for her round face, but much better than her lank teenage look. While never petite, she'd lost a bit of weight and suited the flowery top and black trousers she wore. Perhaps she worked in an office now? Or a fashion store. She gazed down to where I stood on the step below, her eyes widening, and for a moment the corners of her mouth lifted as if she was about to smile and welcome me in. Then she crossed her arms.

"It's you. What do you want?"

"To speak to you."

"Don't lie. You've come to cause trouble. Simon warned me." She kept her voice low, like she didn't want to attract attention.

A sudden gust splatted rain drops down one side of my body and face. I edged around, planting my back to the wind. It gave me a different view, past her, into the hallway. Two pictures hung from the wall. Poppies. A beige carpet led to a door at the end, from which the sound of a TV filtered.

"Is he here?"

She shrugged – yes or no, I couldn't work out which – and tightened her grip on her folded arms, squeezing her large boobs together. Legs parted, she stood like a prison camp guard. It seemed apt our first meeting in years should be with her standing at a doorway. Most of my memories involved her leaning against one door jamb or other, either barricading my way into a room or blocking my exit. The fights we'd had. But we were adults now and I was hardly about to push past into her house.

"I just want to talk to you for a few minutes."

"Say what you gotta say and then go."

I took a deep breath. "You've got Ella living with Simon, haven't you?"

A guess based on one sighting and the way she'd reacted when I'd asked if he was in the house but, when I saw her reaction, I knew I'd been right. She shook her head and I thought I heard her whisper, "No" but her eyes didn't meet mine. As she shifted to one side, I glimpsed a jacket hanging over the stair post. Dark leather. Like the one he'd worn the other day. Had I ever seen him without a leather jacket?

"Does he live here?"

Her head swung from side to side, her mouth opened, to lie again. He was in her sodding house. She was protecting the bastard. As always.

"You knew what he did to me and you've let him move in with Ella."

"Yeah, she lives here. Why's that? Oh, let me think." She put her finger to her mouth and made an 'umm' noise. "Cos her mum buggered off and left her. Now you've come back here with your la-de-da airs and graces, shouting the odds. Who am I to believe? You a liar, or Simon?"

"Didn't you give Simon an alibi when he was with the girl at the park? The one who reported him. So, you know what he's like."

Her fingers curled into fists. Her bottom lip jutted. I flinched as she jerked forward, even though I knew she wouldn't dare hit me. We weren't kids anymore. Instead she grabbed the door and swung it shut but I stopped it in time with my outstretched hand. We had to sort things out for Ella's sake. I jammed my shoulder against it, forced it open. Why didn't she scream for Simon to come and help? Instead, she made strange 'eurrghh' noises through gritted teeth. The door rattled. A push-me-pull-you between the two of us.

"He's Ella's father or uncle, as you well know. He raped me." My voice jerked with effort. "She's his perfect age.

197

That girl – the one at the park – was twelve. I was fourteen."

"He can't have children. Never could, so how can he be her dad? You're not just a liar, but a slut."

After all these years my sister continued to blame me – a fourteen-year-old – for something grown men had done. Would she stoop to blame Ella if Simon took advantage of her? And what did she mean, he couldn't have children? That didn't stop him. 'How can you be so stupid?' I needed to say but my throat tightened and I couldn't speak. Much stronger and larger than me, Mandy had begun to edge me backwards. If she gained momentum, I'd lose my fingers or my foot. I jumped back to the safety of the outside step. Caught off guard she flew forward, stopping the door just in time to prevent her fingertips being crushed. I noticed she still bit her fingernails to crescent-shaped slivers. Stress or habit?

She glanced from her hand to me and snarled, "Any other men you want to throw in while you've got the chance?" And slammed the door.

Through the patterned glass, the silhouette bulk of her body mirrored mine. Her cream hands hung by the side of her trousers. I willed her to reach out and unlock the door. How much longer could she deceive herself about Simon? She shifted and my heart jolted. Yes! But then she vanished from view. Seconds later the kitchen light flicked off, plunging me into darkness. The door at the end of the hallway opened, lighting her figure as she stepped into the room. Where Simon sat? She kept her head turned from me – towards him? – and closed the door, snuffing out all but a crack of light.

I stood there, unable to move. Soaked, frozen, scared. How could she be so blind to the danger facing Ella? My fist hovered. Should I bang the door, cause a scene, make her listen?

An engine whine grew louder. Tyres scraped the tarmac and a car bumped into the driveway opposite. The driver stepped out, gazing my way. She didn't turn from me as she pointed her fob at the car and orange lights flashed. Even at her door, she watched me. No lights flicked on. She'd need the night to spy on me. Of course, the people around here would be Mandy's friends and, no matter what I said, they'd defend her against the stranger.

I had to play smart and come back another day. I didn't have a choice. My conversation with Mandy had proved one thing.

If I didn't help Ella, no one would.

Chapter 34
– Summer holidays –

HEART POUNDING, I CLATTERED up the stairs and into his lounge, where I headed over to the window to check the road for cars. Not any old car. Simon's. Even though he'd left the small window on the latch, the room stank of stale lager and cigarettes. A stack of cans lined the windowsill, while others littered the carpet, alongside a filled ashtray. Two half-balled socks lay on the settee, half-covering a small pile of whitish things. I bent down to examine them and leapt back. Euww. Toenail clippings.

Then I remembered why I was here. They'd done something to me and laughed about it. Laughed about me.

I swept the cans from the windowsill. They crashed to the ground. Not enough. I kicked the ashtray into the wall. It cracked in two firing cigarette butts in all directions. I jumped on a can, smiling as lager dregs splatted onto the carpet. Another can. Caught at an angle, the rim crunched under my foot, forcing me to shake it off. This was too tame. Bored, I looked around for something else. Something to get payback, but not too serious. I didn't want Simon calling the police.

He'd been watching a film last night by the look of it. Wires trailed from the camcorder on the floor to the front of the TV. I glanced out of the window and picked up the camcorder. How did these things work? What appeared to be a little screen jutted out; beside it a set of buttons. I grinned as I spotted the 'on' switch.

"Just like a video recorder," I muttered.

The picture was blank, near the end by the look of it, so I pressed rewind, fascinated to see the dark screen come to life.

"Oh!" I gasped, as a man's bare bum jiggled on the screen.

I stifled a giggle. They were into porn. Through the open window came the drone of a car engine. A blue car drove into the driveway opposite. I went to switch the camera off, when I noticed it had moved on and someone – a woman – was sandwiched between two men. Yuk! Was that Ade? It couldn't be him, of all people, with his bald head and fat belly. I pressed play.

The 'huh-huh' sound – for some reason it was familiar to me – came from Ade. Disgusting. And the man on the other side… Phil… oh my… Shit. The film wobbled. The camera panned closer. That was *me* in the middle. *Me!* Jammed between those filthy old men. How? I gazed at my face, my half-open eyes. I looked dead. *Wake up!*

They were doing stuff to me. *Stop it, stop it!* My hand shot to my mouth. Tears rolled down my cheeks.

"No!" I flung the camcorder to the floor. "*No!*"

My voice sounded like someone else. A woman screaming in a horror movie, just before the knife plunged in. I wished it was me being stabbed, over and over. How could I live after seeing that?

"Are you going to give me a go anytime soon?" A man said and laughed.

Simon.

I couldn't breathe. I booted the camcorder into the wall. A fury, stronger than I've ever felt, built inside. Bastards.

"I hate you!" I screamed.

Like a car accident everything slowed. I part-heaved, part-slid the TV off the stand. It toppled over, just missing my feet to thud onto the carpet. The floorboards shuddered. What would Mrs Norris say? I stood for a moment, waiting for her to shout or thump her ceiling but the silence told me she must still be out. There was no one to stop me. I shunted the TV to one side, grabbed the video recorder. The wires snagged, but I wrenched them free. I lifted the video as high as I could stretch and smashed it down onto the humped back of the TV. Not enough. Again. Again, it crashed down until my muscles burned. No way would they be watching me or anyone else on it.

I stamped on the plastic. "I… hate… you!"

The phone was next. I tried to rip the cable out, but couldn't, so I sprinted into the kitchen and grabbed the sharpest looking knife from the drawer. A huge one, with a thick black handle. My red, swollen eyes reflected in the blade. He deserved this. With just two huge tugs the cable sliced apart. As another car rattled past, I paused to check outside. Not his, which meant I had more time. Gritting my teeth, I slashed the blade across the back of the settee and through each cushion. My arms ached, my legs shook. The knife handle dug into my palm. But still I hacked and ripped. Slivers of toenails shot across the carpet, pinging my feet. I leapt back, panting.

Yuk. This place needed disinfecting. And I knew just what to do.

He'd tucked the bleach behind the toilet. Not hidden enough. I carried it through to the lounge where I sprinkled it over the armchair, into the back of the TV, onto the carpet. Perv, I wrote. The bottle was half empty. Still so much to do. I moved onto to Simon's bedroom, where I opened the wardrobe doors. I shivered with anticipation.

A few shirts hung from hangers. Beneath them, a mound of clothes lay jumbled on the floor. I splashed the bleach over the shirts, watching as it dripped from the arms onto the clothes piled below. Then I swivelled around to face

202

the bed. Where *it* happened. My insides tumbled. The ache inside became a shooting pain. I wiped my arm across my face and gazed at the wetness. Since when had I been crying?

"I hate you!" I yelled. "I hate, hate, hate, *hate* you."

I showered the pillows and duvet with the last of the bleach, giving the bottle one final shake before I lobbed it on the bed. Outside a car whined, a gearbox crunched. Through the lounge window I spotted the red roof of Simon's car reversing into a space. I had to get out. My foot knocked the camcorder. I snatched it up and took the stairs two at a time, out of the door towards his back garden, not stopping to check if I'd been spotted.

Hidden from view behind his shed, I paused for a moment. I should dump the camcorder. Taking it was asking for trouble, especially if I got caught. But I couldn't leave the tape. No one must ever see it. If they did...

The fence blurred. Stupid tears rolled down my face. I dried my face with my arm and sniffed. As man's roar echoed, my heart jolted. He'd found my work. I tucked Mandy's dress into the sides of my knickers so it hung just above my knees and, clutching the top of the fence, pushed the tip of my trainer through one of the diamond holes, the other onto the top wire. The fencing bowed but in a split second I threw myself over, landing on next door's lawn. They hadn't spotted me. Yet.

I took the next fence quicker. Just a couple more and I'd be at the alleyway which ran down to Nelson Close. My trainers thumped over the ground, my breath rasped 'huh-hah huh-hah' like... not his, *not his*.... Onwards I sprinted, ignoring an angry "Oi" and the sound of knocking against a windowpane. Over the final fence into the alleyway.

The narrow path sloped downwards. I sped up, skidding on gravel as I turned into Nelson Close. Where now? He'd know it was me. Who else would wreck his video and steal the camcorder? He'd go to Mum's house, which meant I couldn't go home.

I headed in the direction of the precinct but juddered to a stop. I had nowhere to go, not if I wanted to hide from him. He could drive past at any minute, catch me at any time. Dizziness hit me, my legs turned to rubber. I clutched the metal post of a nearby streetlamp and held on until the feeling passed. Warmth spread between my legs. Not now. Please not now. I sank to my knees, sobbing.

"Are you alright, dear?" An old lady's voice asked.

I brushed pieces of grit from my knees. "I fell over."

"Of course, you did." She smiled and rubbed my shoulder. Through the haze of my tears, her white hair had a faint purple tinge. "Why don't you come in and have a cuppa?"

She'd call the police, then I'd be in for it. I shook my head.

"I had a girl just like you here a few weeks back. I've watched them since, that horrible gang of girls." She looked across to the precinct and shook her head. "Come in just for the one. When you get out, they'll be gone."

Chapter 35
- mid December -

MUTTERING TO MYSELF, I STOMPED through the back door into the kitchen. What had I expected Mandy to say? I wrenched my sodden coat from my arms and stood on tiptoes to hook it over the top of the bathroom door. Drips splattered the lino, mirroring the sound of the rain tapping the windowpane. My damp jumper clung to my back and I shivered. What I wouldn't do to have a bath right now. Two baths in one day? Decadent. But lying there in the peace and warmth might help me think through my next steps.

I checked my smile in the mirror – Troy always reckoned he could spot a fake one – and went through to the lounge.

"You lot okay? I'm freezing." I turned to Troy. "I'm going to warm up in the bath, if that's alright."

I nodded towards the empty bowls and crumb-littered coffee table. "Looks like you've been having fun. Was the film any good?"

Charlie shrugged. "A bit babyish. But Troy says he'll take us out for pizza."

"Did he now?"

Troy gave me a sheepish grin. "I hope you don't mind."

"Not at all. Give me half an hour. You weren't wrong about it blowing a gale out there."

"How did it go with Mandy?" he said.

I turned on the smile I'd practised in the mirror. "Oh, you know, so-so."

◆

The hot tap belched steam into the haze. Too lazy to sit up, I turned the tap off with my toes. My legs prickled, reddened from the heat, so I kept my feet balanced on either side of the ceramic rim while I sank down and let the water lap at my chin. All around was quiet but for the ping, ping of droplets falling from the tap, lulling me. A draught whispered over my shoulders and I opened one eye, spying the small window left on the catch after the children's earlier bath. Above, spots of mildew were starting to darken the ceiling. I should bleach them again.

Bleach. Strange how I'd forgotten about that. Had I really done that all those years ago? Covered his clothes in bleach and wrecked his flat? He deserved it. The bastard shouldn't be walking around free for what he did. And the threats he made afterwards. No way would I let him frighten me again.

But he'd be back here soon. Especially as I'd done exactly what he'd told me not to do and contacted Mandy. A day, two at most, and he'd be racing over to scare me with tales of what he'd do if I didn't push off and leave him to his cosy threesome. He'd wait until Troy was out and maybe even make sure Marion and Ralph were off somewhere too. My heart began to thump. Chances were this time the children would be here and he'd frighten them. Or worse. I clenched my fists, gritted my teeth and allowed the anger to build. Sharp and raw – but contained – unlike the day I'd played the video and seen Simon's true self. Mandy was wrong. He hadn't changed into a family man. He was a pervert protecting his quarry.

He wouldn't win.

Sweat beaded my face. I'd wanted a warm bath but this was too much. As I sat up to cool myself down, the water splashed the bath edges and lapped against my thighs. I had to do something. I couldn't just sit here while Mandy covered up for him. Cosy in her nest, Mandy would rather keep feeding the cuckoo, while ignoring the broken bodies spattering the ground because, in her eyes, a man like him was better than no one. Poor Mandy. I wouldn't allow her to judge Ella's worth as little as she measured her own. A man like Simon went for the weak ones. I'd make myself strong. Maybe now was the time to let Troy into my past. Stop running, stop hiding. Stop Simon.

"I'll get you this time, bastard," I muttered.

Then I smiled as the perfect idea came to mind.

♦

Later that evening, after tucking the children in bed, I found Troy in the lounge looking puzzled. He didn't notice the bulky folders I clutched or how I trembled. Instead, he held out two boxes he'd pulled from the carrier bag I'd left on the floor.

"When you rushed out of the pizza place, I thought you needed something really important. But Dictaphones? And why two?"

"I had to get them before the store closed."

I shifted the two steaming cups to one side and placed the folders on the coffee table. When I patted the seat next to me, Troy sat down, his earlier puzzled expression replaced by a look of concern. My hands shook, my tongue stuck to the roof of my mouth.

"I want to tell you something and I need you to not get angry or stop me." My voice quivered. I had to pause for breath. "It's going to be hard, but you need to know. And, please…" My voice thickened. "Please don't judge me."

"Is this about that Jez? Why would I…?" he said, but I

207

lifted a finger to hush him.

Where did I start? The beginning or the end? How did anyone tell a story like this, especially one that I'd spent the past decade and more trying to hide?

"Simon," I said.

His name punched the air from my lungs. I couldn't do this, *I couldn't*. Once he'd heard Troy would never look at me the same way again. What on earth made me think I was strong enough? I cupped my shaking hands over my mouth, breathed in and out, in and out, until the panic subsided.

The warmth of Troy's hand seeped through the sleeve of my jumper, but I shrugged him away. No sympathy or I'd cry.

"Simon," I said more slowly. "Is Ella's father or uncle. I don't know which."

During our confrontation, Mandy had said Simon couldn't father children, so perhaps I did know. But Simon might have lied to her to weaken my story.

The colour drained from Troy's face and two grooves cut into the skin between his eyebrows.

"I don't know which." I couldn't look at him. I had to turn away. "Because one night they drugged and raped me."

My hand quivered as I opened the Cindy folder and pulled out a stack of photos and papers. The picture of Mum smiling as she held Ella. My little Ella. I remember her chubby hand opening and closing, grasping for me. I flipped it over, thankful Mum had never been one for scrawling dates and memories on the back of photos. I upended the folder and shook it so a small cassette tape dropped onto the table. Two jagged slivers of tape protruded from the bottom.

"They taped it."

Light reflected on the black plastic. I remembered the feel of it in my hand, the anger, the tears. Did it really

208

happen to me? *The noise! Huh-hah, huh-hah. Not that sound, not that. Huh-hah, huh-hah, huh-hah. Stop it. Cover your ears. No, no! Stop it! The mound of flesh driving against my stomach. Ade. The hand gripping, squeezing my boob. Phil. 'Let me have a go.' Simon. Hah-hah. Laughter swirling, round and round. No matter how hard I pressed my hands to my ears, the awful noise wouldn't leave. Bearing down on me. Faster, faster.*

"No," I gasped. "No."

"Cindy." Troy tugged my shoulder. "You don't need to go on."

I stumbled to my feet and headed over to the other side of the lounge. That way Troy couldn't see my face, watch me pull my sweater sleeve over my hand, dab my eyes and nose. A trail of snot clung to the material. I wiped it down my jeans.

Think of happy memories, I told myself. Earlier in the pizza place, Lily and Charlie had crayoned pictures onto little chef hats and created their own pizzas with smiley mouths using ham and the eyes with pineapple. Later we'd walked out of the pizza place in a chain of linked hands. Troy and I had skipped with the children, swinging them into the air as they giggled and shrieked, "Higher, higher!".

Calm now, I knelt down on the carpet beside the coffee table and faced Troy again. The smell of coffee wafted from our untouched cups along with a hint of stale cigarettes, probably from the carpet. The skin glistened beneath his eyes and blotches stained his cheeks. I'd upset him. But I had to tell him the truth.

"You need you to know why I went to see Mandy."

His eyes widened. "Ella?"

I nodded. "Mandy's got Simon living there with her and Ella. She wouldn't let me in but I saw his jacket. We had a

209

row as she won't listen. I know I should have told you but Simon came here the other day telling me to keep away. That's why I went there."

"He *what*?" Fists clenched, he shot to his feet and stomped over to the TV, then he swung back round. "I can't believe you didn't say anything."

"Because then I would have had to tell you what happened. Mandy, Mum and you are the only ones who know."

"Your Mum and Mandy?"

His palms lifted into the air and he opened his mouth as if he wanted to say more. Instead, his hands dropped to his sides, smacking the sides of his legs. For what seemed like an age, he didn't say a word.

Then he shook his head. "They knew? But why didn't they do something?"

Chapter 36
– Summer holidays –

A WHITE HAZE SURROUNDED the huge moon. Its bright smile and wide eyes mocked me. You've nowhere to go. Did I prefer the leering moon or the pitch black of earlier when it hid behind thick cloud? I'd been thankful when it had reappeared a moment ago and the night had changed from black to velvet blue. But with it came the shadows. They slunk from the trees, casting dark lines as if I was inside a cage. As the wind rustled through a thousand hidden leaves, I shifted around to glance into the woods. A shiver ran up my back. Something was hiding, watching, ready to pounce.

"Do your worst," I muttered. "Do your frigging worst."

I shifted position on the park bench and rested my head on my knees. The narrow planks dug into my bum. I tucked my dress beneath my feet and wrapped my arms tight around my legs, but still the wind cut through the thin material. I wouldn't be sleeping tonight. Too cold. Not that I could shut my eyes either. Each time I did, the film would start to replay: me sandwiched between two old men. I could imagine them sitting together, laughing as they planned it. What shall we do? Oh, let's make a Cindy sandwich.

The corners of the tape dug into my hand. Harder and harder, I squeezed. It was useless. I didn't have the strength to crush it into nothing or to lob it into the bushes as I'd done with the camcorder. Something had made me keep it, but not as evidence. No way could anyone see it.

What would I do with it then? I didn't know.

Simon would be at Mum's house right now, sitting in her lounge, drinking tea and waiting for me. I knew it. He wouldn't tell her what I'd done to his flat. Or would he? I fingered the cold plastic. No, not while I held onto this. But he'd get to me somehow. I rubbed my arms, the heat smoothing the bristly hairs and bumpy skin. Bed. That's where I wanted to be. Tucked up all cosy with the duvet wrapped under my chin. But my bedroom stank of wee. I thumped the bench. I'd wet my bed. *Wet it!* What would my friends say if they found out? Worse, what about Issie Saunders and her gang? They'd see my face and they'd know. Here comes the bed-wetter, they'd laugh as I walked past them in the school corridor. Or worse. Arms crossed, they'd lean against the wall and sneer. Look at her. The slag sandwich.

If anyone saw me, they'd be able to tell what I'd let those men do to me. Just by looking into my eyes. Troy always said I was an open book. He'd know and he'd hate me. Like all the rest of them.

A tear splashed my arm. I wiped it away.

I wanted to bawl my eyes out, to howl and be cuddled and told everything would turn out fine. But no one would ever tell me that. Because it wasn't okay and it never would be. Everyone would hate me. Foul. Disgusting. I pinched my arm – hard – but the stab of pain wasn't enough. Instead I dug the corner of the tape into my calf and dragged it upwards. More, I had to do more. I deserved to be in agony for what I'd done.

"I hate you too," I whispered.

"I hate you," I shouted and punched my thigh.

A bird or something fluttered in the trees. I shot around, sensing my pupils widen as I strained to see. But I couldn't cut through the darkness. Anything could be hiding, watching me. What if Simon wasn't at my house? What if he was out looking for me? He might have heard me call out. My heart thudded as a twig cracked somewhere. I had to get away. From him. From here.

With legs stiff from the cold, I edged from the bench. The planks wobbled and creaked. My dress snagged on something – a nail? – and the material tore as I yanked it free. I limped away until the stiffness eased. Then I ran.

I had to leave Mosston. Before he came after me.

♦

The white sides of a lorry blurred as it zoomed past, so close it felt as if it could suck me under those huge tyres. Earlier I'd stumbled on the uneven verge, almost tumbling into the path of a car. It'd screeched around me, tooting, and a face had peered from the passenger window, mouth open and angry. At least now the morning light made me visible to drivers, while I could spot the dips in the ground, but it also meant *he* would spot me if he went past. He'd stop and grab me and then I'd be done for. I glanced back down the road, unable to see past the bend about fifty metres away. It wouldn't give me much time to hide. That's if I could. Between me and a prickly hedge lay a ditch. I grimaced. It looked no more than a hand deep, but there could be rats. But what was worse, *him* or rats? Him. Definitely.

My mouth tasted strange, metallic and sticky, like I was running out of saliva. I needed a drink. And a wee.

Another lorry clattered past, another fight with the wind. I held my hand up to shield my face from the grit and dirt and stumbled onwards. My legs ached. I must have walked fifty miles, maybe more. How many hours until London?

Oddly cars headed towards me with their headlights on. I couldn't have been walking all day. Then I spotted dark clouds in the distance, raining grey onto the hills. I scanned the sky, to see which way the clouds were heading. Towards me. At least it meant I'd get to drink. I could stand there, head tilted backwards, letting the drops fall onto my tongue, maybe even find blackberries or something along the way to eat. I'd be like that bloke on TV and live off the land.

What felt like hours later, raindrops ran down my face and caught in my eyelashes, making me squint through a beaded curtain. Tyres splashed along the road spraying me. Rivers of water ran down my legs to join the bubbles squelching from the sides of my trainers. My dress slapped my shins, clung to my thighs. As the wind cut through my dress, my teeth chattered and my lips wouldn't stay together – a non-stop 'brrrr' – but I staggered on.

"Walk, walk." I flinched as a blast of rain hit my face.

At the junction of a road I spotted a sign opposite. Camberton 3 miles. Mosston 14 miles. Fourteen miles. Was that all I'd managed? My legs became heavy, sodden, weights. I couldn't keep going. Not like this. I wasn't cut out for it. Just a week ago I'd been happy and warm in my own house. *One week ago.* And now I was stuck, never to go back, never to see Troy, Nina, Mum or even Mandy again.

He would. He'd see them all. He'd get to carry on as normal.

I'd make him pay one day. I knew that much.

I clenched my fists and the tape. Rain splattered my head, ran in channels between my boobs, down my stomach, making me shiver. A car slowed. I spun around as it pulled alongside, its indicator blinking orange. White, with blue and yellow squares. The siren on top flashed. He'd called them. My heart thudded as a policewoman stepped from the passenger side. She looked from the sky to me.

"What are you doing out here in the middle of nowhere?" she said. "Where's your coat?"

I shrugged.

214

"Where do you come from?"

I gazed in the direction of Camberton. Would they drive me if I said I lived there? Not that I had a clue about the roads, estates or even what it was like for shopping as none of the buses went that way. Mandy had gone there once, with *him*, in his car.

"Where do you come from, love?" She put her hand on my shoulder, holding me in place. Her radio buzzed, an indistinct voice. She moved it to her mouth. "PC Brown to control. White female. Red dress."

A lorry thundered past, drowning her voice. I watched it head towards Camberton. Maybe it was going on to London. If only I'd been braver and hitched a lift, I could be going to safety. Now I'd be taken back to Mosston. And trouble. Simon must have seen me running from his house. Given them my description.

"Are you Cynth…" She looked down at her notebook. "Cindy Smith?"

When I nodded, she smiled. "Thank goodness. You've got some very worried people looking for you."

Chapter 37
- mid December -

TROY STOPPED THE CAR AT THE JUNCTION and didn't pull away, even though the road ahead was clear in both directions.

"Please don't cancel your cousin," I said. "You can't be with me every minute."

He glanced into the rear-view mirror. "He can wait."

I turned around to check if there was a car behind us. Nothing but tarmac and trees. Charlie had fallen asleep, his head balanced against the door panel, which explained the occasional knock we'd heard when the car bounced over potholes. In comparison Lily looked serene as she gazed out of the side window, her lips stained red from the lipstick sweetie she'd been eating.

"There's no point," I said. "You're going back to Canada in the New Year. In three weeks, I'll be alone."

I didn't say it to seek sympathy. It was a fact.

He pushed the gear stick into first, turning the car towards Mosston. We drove on in silence but for the tap-tap of his finger against the side of the steering wheel. I could understand his agitation. He'd wanted to storm around Mandy's last night and punch Simon. I'd made him promise not to go, but his finger had shaken as he'd pointed and warned me that he wouldn't be responsible for his actions if Simon took one step near me or the children.

"You still haven't explained the Dictaphones," he said.

"They're just in case he turns up. Not that he will but they'd be evidence to use to stop him coming again." I noticed his pursed lips, so I changed tack. "I've got the

216

phone too, so I can call for help. Go and see your cousin. I'll be fine. Your mum is next door."

I kept my tone light. Tried to hide my fear. I knew what I planned to do was crazy – using myself as bait to get Simon to come to the house. Where we would be alone. I couldn't tell Troy. He would insist on being there and it wouldn't work.

He gave my thigh a squeeze. "How about you go around my mum's?"

♦

I kissed the children goodbye and headed out of Marion's lounge, meeting Ralph as he staggered down the stairs clutching a large cardboard box.

He took in my coat. "Are you off somewhere?"

"Too many chefs, so I thought I'd escape." I pointed towards the kitchen, where Marion and the children were preparing the ingredients to make Play-Doh.

He balanced the box onto the stair post. "I turn my back and she's stolen the children. The decorations will have to wait. Do you want me to save some for you?"

"Thanks, but I'm sure Mum will have them."

"Fair enough," he said. "We might go out later to get the tree. What time are you back?"

"I won't be more than a few hours. I thought I'd clean the house while I had the chance."

He grinned and hefted the box into his arms. "We'll be doing that later no doubt. Well if you finish in time, you can join us."

I pulled my up hood and stepped out into the drizzle, taking a moment to pat my pockets and check both the Dictaphone and my mobile were safe. Ahead a red car splashed along the road. Did Simon still have a car? I hadn't seen one in Mandy's driveway. A blast of wind cut through my fleece and I shivered. Perhaps I should rethink my decision to go straight to their house. If I went home first, I could have a hot coffee and put on another layer of clothing. At least then I'd be warm when I hung about in their road to lure him back.

I opened the back door to a wave of heat from the kitchen. As I unzipped my fleece and pulled down my hood, I caught the flicker of a shadow outside the window. A cat? I shook the door handle to check I'd locked it – I wasn't ready for *him* yet – and stepped over to the sink. Through the raindrop-speckled window, I could make out the bedraggled lawn and the leylandii which rose like a granite cliff into the grey mist. Certain I'd seen something, I heaved myself up to balance on the lip of the sink and, with my forehead pressed against the glass, I checked the length of patio. The statue lay sheltered beside the wall where Troy had moved it, while below water gurgled from a pipe into the drain. As the washing machine rattled into a spin cycle, it made my knees vibrate on the kitchen worktop, so I placed my hands against the window to balance myself. The pane shuddered in the wind, breaking the skin of a dozen or more droplets which raced down.

Something thudded onto the bedroom floor above. Holding my breath, I listened for footsteps or another noise above the din of the washing machine. Had I left a window open? I dropped back to the floor, wiping my damp hands on my jeans as I glanced into the hallway. For some reason, I expected to see Simon standing there, arms dangling, like some freak from a horror movie. But the hallway lay empty. I turned back to the kitchen window, unnerved to see an imprint of my hand surrounded by a fine haze. Similar to the handprint on the cover of a DVD I'd once seen, where a woman had been trapped with her family inside a house at the mercy of a psychopath. He'd toyed with her mind and just when she thought she'd escaped, he'd cornered her and her children in a lane and slaughtered them.

Goosebumps pricked my arms and I shivered and flicked on the kettle. I had no choice but to check whether I'd left a window open upstairs. If that's what the noise was. I switched the Dictaphone to record and dropped it back into my pocket, doing the same for the one stashed behind a box of cornflakes. My fingers wrapped around the phone in my pocket. Ridiculous, I knew, but I needed company while I went upstairs. I pressed Troy's number. It rang just the once.

"Are you okay?" he asked. He sounded worried.

"I'm fine," I said. "I just popped back home. I think I've left a window open upstairs."

"You came home for that?" He sounded suspicious. If I didn't take care he'd be racing back to check I was spending the day with Marion.

I found myself shrugging. "I'm going back out in a minute. How's it going with Mike? Has he still got that daft mutt you were telling me about?"

As I crept upstairs, I found myself caught between a need to lower my voice while making everything sound normal.

"Really? So, what did you do then?"

Usually the exploits of a man and dog I didn't know wouldn't be of so much interest, but this wasn't usual. I needed to keep Troy on the line. As I neared the small bedroom, the door juddered and a draught blew against my face. I had left a window open. Odd that I couldn't remember doing so. I slunk into the room, hoping my voice didn't betray my growing fear.

"What's Mike's house like?"

Raindrops splattered the windowsill from where the window had been left on the catch. I tiptoed over to fasten it shut. Then I moved from room to room, looking inside the wardrobes, behind the doors, even under the beds. When I closed the door to the immersion heater, I heaved a sigh of relief and headed downstairs. Steam had filled the kitchen, obliterating the handprint on the window. I tapped the side of the kettle, even though I knew it was hot, and dragged a mug from the back of the cupboard.

"I've got to go. You will go back to my mum's?" Troy sounded anxious.

"Ralph's talking about going out to get Christmas trees."

"Great." His tone lifted. "Probably the place he was talking about with a Grotto and lots of Christmassy stuff. Make sure you go, won't you?"

"Cross my heart." I tipped a spoonful of coffee into the cup. "What time are you back?"

"Around dinner, say s…"

I pressed the phone to my ear. "I missed that. Did you say six or seven?"

"Six," he said.

"Six? See you then. Have a lovely time."

I put the phone on the side and opened the fridge door. The smell of garlic and mince wafted from a small bowl of leftover lasagne. I checked the pork chops were defrosted ready for later and pulled out the milk. As I closed the door, I spotted him standing in the hallway, arms hanging by his sides, like I'd imagined earlier. He smiled at me. A disgusting, lecherous grin. The ground shifted beneath my feet and the milk carton slipped from my fingers, falling to the floor.

Simon's smile widened. His dimple scarred his cheek.

He shook his head. "Now, now, Cindy. Throwing milk at me. That's no way to treat a guest."

Chapter 38
– Summer holidays –

TWO DAYS IT HAD BEEN. Two whole days since they'd made me come home and Mum slapped me more times than I could count, calling me stupid bitch, cow, whatever. Didn't I know how much I'd worried her? What had she done to deserve me? When she'd finished, I'd gone up to my wee-stinking room and lay down in bed. That's when she decided I must have been taking drugs and needed sorting out. Hah! Talk about ironic. For once she was right, but so wrong.

She, Bill and Mandy mounted a guard of my room – Mum reckoned I'd made her do this – but I was glad. It meant he couldn't hurt me. But the memories could. The noise. Huh-huh-huh. The smell. Sweat and *that*. The images. Me sandwiched between Phil and Ade.

Why. Wouldn't. They. Go. Away?

"Go *away*!"

I wrenched the duvet cover from my head and looked around the room, desperate to think of anything other than that disgusting film. A spider, a fly, even a stain on the wall. My books taunted me. Read me, they said. *No way*. He'd bought me books to lure me in. Books and fags. I'd never touch either again. *Bridget Jones's Diary* sat on the floor, a secret smile on the face of the woman, a wisp of hair falling down the side of her face, and that fricking cigarette in her fingers. He'd known me better than I knew myself.

I grabbed the book, grimacing as I tried to pull the covers apart. The spine cracked as if it would snap, but nothing more. I twisted the pages, yanked them, but I didn't have the energy to break its back.

"I hate you. Hate you. *Hate you*." I ripped the cover

from the book.

With satisfaction I tore her face in half, then quartered her, again and again, until the page became confetti which I threw into the air. Then I set about doing the same to each page until I sat beside a paper mountain. I'd done this. I'd stopped her from taunting me. And I'd do it to every other book.

I picked up *Harry Potter*. "You deserve this."

♦

"Mum! She's gone mental." Silence. Then clomping up the stairs.

The door banged and the floor juddered as Mum stomped into the room. "What the fuck? You been on them drugs again? Have you? Have you?"

She tried to tug me from the bed by my arms but I held fast, scrunching my eyes tighter. I wouldn't look at her. If I did, she'd know. She'd know what I'd done. She grabbed my hair, wrenched my head back. I felt the twang of snapping hairs. Her breath puffed against my cheek. The stink of cigarettes. *No. Not them.* I ignored the pain and tore my head away, screwed my face so I couldn't breathe her disgusting smell.

"See, I said she'd gone mental," Mandy whined. "Do you reckon it was her who done over Simon's place?"

"I wouldn't put anything past her," Mum said. She yanked my hair again, so the back of my head pressed on the skin between my shoulders and a flicker of light broke through my eyelids. "Open your eyes, you stupid cow. What have you done? Do you want me to call the doctor and get you taken away? Do you? Do you?"

Would they shut me safely in my own room with clean

sheets and white walls? Please.

They knew about Simon's place. They'd worked out that it must have been me. 'Poor Simon. Look what Cindy did to your lovely house for no reason at all. It must be the drugs. Turned her mental.' Why couldn't they see him for what he was? Mum used to call him Slimeball Sime and she was right. But all that was forgotten and he was golden boy, while I was shit.

"Yes!" I shouted. "Call the doctor, the social, whatever. I want to go."

A slap knocked my face to one side, scalded my cheek. My closed eyes filled with wetness. I ached to shove the two of them from my room and scream *Stop hitting me!* But I couldn't look at them. I couldn't face anyone.

"Leave her," Mandy said. "Freak."

The door brushed the carpet and clicked shut.

"It's the drugs, I know it," Mum said, her voice fading as she walked down the stairs. "I should have been tougher on her."

♦

Four days later, I think – maybe five, no, four, I was sure of it – there was a knock on the front door. I heard muttering from the kitchen below, footsteps along the hallway, the front door scrape open and a familiar voice.

"Is Cindy in, please?"

A ball of tightness choked my throat and tears rolled down my face.

"She's grounded. She's not seeing you. She's not seeing no one."

When the door clicked shut, I buried my face in the pillow and sobbed. I wanted my friend back. To lie on his lap when sunbathing at the park; to listen to him moaning and doing that hand waving thing when he choked as one of my smoke doughnuts scored a direct hit. To tell him he was right about Simon, about cigarettes, about life.

But I couldn't tell him. Because then he'd know what I'd done.

♦

Hours later I heard another knock at the front door. Was Troy back again? For a moment my heart leapt but then it crashed down. I couldn't see him. Not today. Not any day. Footsteps lumbered down the stairs.

"Wow!" Mandy squealed. "Are those for me? Come in."

Mandy and her visitor went through to the kitchen, where I heard the slam of a cupboard and the pipes vibrate as she turned on the tap. Their voices droned, a hum through the floorboards. I turned back to face the ceiling and the mould that grew in the corner. Which country did it look like? Australia? I should go there. No one would ever find me. I'd be safe. *Not again.* I covered my eyes as that awful picture appeared – me, sandwiched between them – and the noise – huh-huh-huh. Desperate to shake off the images I swung my head from side-to-side. *Stop, please, stop.* Tears soaked my cheeks. I'd never be safe. Never be free. Wherever I went, no matter how far, I'd take it with me.

"Be right back!" Mandy shouted and slammed the front door.

A draught caught my bedroom door and it shuddered open. Footsteps padded up the stairs. But Mandy had gone out – I'd heard her myself – and Mum had gone into town an hour before. I pulled myself up and strained to see through the gap in the door. It brushed open and *he* stood there in a crisp, white shirt, open at the collar. As I squeaked in fear, he flinched, coughed and stepped back into the hallway.

"What on earth!" He grimaced.

His fingertips clutched the door post. I wished I could smash the door into them but my legs, my arms, my whole body had gone gloopy, except my heart which thumped the funeral march. This was it.

Twice more he coughed and then he stepped back into the room, covering his nose with his hand. He gazed at my snow mountain on the floor and shook his head. Those disgusting eyes turned my way. He wore an old leather belt with a buckle in the shape of two playing cards, but I hadn't seen the black chinos before or the wristwatch he now checked.

"We've got ten minutes," he said. "Not long, but long enough."

My tongue stuck to the back of my teeth. I sank back into the pillow, my jelly elbows no longer able to hold me up. He stank of aftershave. Sickly, synthetic. His foot knocked my bedside table as he grimaced and crouched down.

"You stink. You look disgusting. To think I touched you."

I clutched the duvet to my chest, shifted away from him, my back pressed against the cold wall, as far as I could go. I heard a sob, felt another rip through my throat. *Don't let him see your fear. Fight back, do anything. Don't let him win.* But my body trembled and tears stung the corners of my eyes. I'd lost.

"Your sister's right. You are a freak. You destroyed my house. You owe me big time and, believe me, I will make you pay. For everything."

226

"I've got the tape," I blurted.

He narrowed his eyes. The yellow flecks reminded me of a hawk's. "And?"

"And I'll show them what you did. *You'll* be in trouble then."

He tipped his head back and laughed. His Adam's Apple jutted out. "You're not the only one with the tape. We've all got one. But." He rested his elbow on my duvet cover and moved closer. "What will your friends will think if they see it? Troy, for instance. Bet he'd be shocked to know what his beloved Cindy got up to. Willingly. You asked for it, you know. The tape you've got doesn't show that. Mine does."

He pulled away, sneering. "You're still a girl. I bet your friends don't know how little you've got." He nodded towards my legs. "Down there. Just a bit of fuzz. No tits. Nothing. Do or say anything and I'll plaster posters of you all over town. Might even show everyone the tape of you begging for it."

"No, I didn't."

Tears dripped down, soaking the collar of my t-shirt. Perhaps he did have another tape somewhere. Or maybe he was a big, fat liar. But even so, I couldn't show the tape to anyone. No way could they see me naked.

"What about that girl you're scared of – Lisa, Louise, Lizzie?" He clicked his fingers. "Lizzie! She and her mates would love to know just what a little girl their friend is."

He got up and headed to the door. "I mean it, Cindy. You say one word, one word to anyone, and you'll wish you were dead. I'll make sure of that."

The door clicked shut and the stairs creaked. I held my breath and tracked his footsteps until I knew he'd made it downstairs. A moment later I heard him speak.

227

"You've got them, thanks love."

I dragged the tape out from beneath the mattress. No one, ever, ever, *ever*, would see me naked. No way. I yanked the film from the tape. My teeth bit into my lower lip, my hands shook with fury. When all the tape had spilled out, brown shit on the snow mountain, I tugged the two ends. As they snapped free an icy chill hit me. What if he did have copies of the tape?

Chapter 39
- mid December -

HEAD LOWERED SO HIS IRISES were a half circle beneath his eyelids, he reminded me of a bull about to charge. Except his gaze was more like a snake's. Dead, emotionless. I shuddered. His arms hung by his side and only his curling fists betrayed his anger as he slid towards me. I glanced from him to the door and the lock I'd checked earlier. Could I make it? No chance. He'd pounce before I got it open. My coat rustled against the worktop and caught on a cupboard door handle. I was being corralled into the corner. Then what? He smiled, took another step forward. My legs ached to run. But I had to go through with this.

The silver corner of the Dictaphone stuck out from behind the kettle. I took a deep breath. Forced myself to look at him.

"How did you get in?"

His voice oozed slime. "Your house now is it?"

Of course, Mandy. She'd have a key.

"What do you want?" My voice shook.

He slid towards me. His aftershave saturated the air. Sickly. Like always. I couldn't breathe. I had to get away.

"You wouldn't listen. I told you."

My legs quivered as if boneless, but the knock of my knees told me they weren't. I gripped the worktop. I had to fight. Make a stand.

"You told me." I raised my voice in case the Dictaphone couldn't pick it up. "You'd hurt Ella."

He sniggered and shook his head as if I was mad.

"That you'd… they'd r… r… rape me again."

His eyes lit up. The corners of his mouth lifted but it

wasn't a smile. "Is that why you came around? You still want me?"

"Believe me, the last person I want is you. Not after what you did. I was a kid and you and your friends – grown men! – drugged and raped me."

I held my breath. Had I gone too far? Would he guess I was recording him?

His eyes moved across my body, my neck, my chest, lingering on my crotch. I shivered and folded my arms, releasing them when I realised I'd pulled the waist of my coat tight so my bulky pockets stood out.

"Rubbish. You were begging for it. Wanted it."

The same old line paraded by perverts. How dare he tell me what I did or didn't want.

"No!" He flinched as I bellowed in his face. "If I wanted it, you wouldn't have had to drug me."

His arm shot out, grabbing the back of my neck in a pincer grip. I struggled but he forced me closer, so my eyes were a finger span from his. Those putrid flecks of yellow pulsed in my vision, while memories flashed with the brightness of youth. Him, bending over me. Cindy girl, he'd whispered. My Cindy girl. I looked away, as far as my gaze could stretch. Light shimmered across his forehead, grey flecked his stubble. And still those eyes burned into me.

"Cindy, you forget. I've got the evidence. I can prove you begged for it. Oh, Ade." He raised his voice to the pitch of a young girl. "More, more. Oh, Phil, you're so big. Simon, do what you did last time." Reddened gums arched over his clenched teeth. His voice lowered, becoming gruff. "You know why you could handle three men? Cos you were a slut."

Without thinking, I spat, "Begged for it? I was unconscious. You were a fucking paedo. Still are."

230

His fingernails bit into my neck, his face flushed the colour of danger. I'd gone too far. A knot tightened at each corner of his jaw and his lips bulged as if they held back a torrent. My heart thumped the seconds. Why didn't he do something? He squeezed harder, his nails cutting deeper into my skin. Inside I winced, my eyes teared, but I wouldn't let him see my pain. He put his nose to mine. His face a blur of moving lips, white teeth.

"No, I won't let you do this to me. Take this as your final warning. If you want the next film to be a snuff movie – you and your children – then go near Mandy or Ella."

He let go, leaving a burning imprint on my neck. But he didn't move away. Instead his fist opened and closed, opened and closed. He lifted his eyes to mine and then back to his fist, as if he wanted me to know what he had planned. I turned my face away from his. No way would I look at him. A thud made the worktop rattle and sent a breakfast bowl crashing from the pile on the draining board into the sink. I leapt back, the drawer handle banging into my back. Blood whooshed through my ears and my chest pounded. Thank goodness, he'd punched the worktop. Not me.

I'd had enough. He had to go.

He jabbed his finger. "Stay away. I mean it. We're happy, we've a good life. You're a fuck-up that's wrecks everything. Jealous, I reckon, cos you wanted me and I chose her."

He swung around, heels clicking across the kitchen floor, muffled by the hallway carpet. At the front door, he turned to find me standing by the open cutlery drawer. Ready, should he turn back.

He pointed. "Keep away from us. Or else."

The door clanged shut. I stood for a moment, unable to move. My neck, my body, my mind shattered. I needed a moment to piece myself back together. The Dictaphone glinted by the kettle. Fingers-crossed, I had what I needed.

On wobbly legs I ran to the door and twisted the catch. The bolt clicked. He wouldn't be getting in, even with a key. Back in the kitchen, my fingers trembled as I lifted the Dictaphone from my pocket and pressed play. At first the words were muted and I struggled to make sense but then I heard myself, voice trembling, fearful. 'You told me, you'd hurt Ella.' Would the rest be so clear? As the conversation ended, I shook from the horror of his words but success made me smile. I pulled the second Dictaphone from behind the kettle and went through to the lounge, where I slumped onto the settee to listen. Clearer, more distinct.

"Got you," I muttered. A shiver of delight over-rode my fear.

But then I spotted the now familiar school photo. Her happy smile. The dimple. The Elmhurst High School blazer. 'We're happy, we've got a good life,' Simon had said. What I was about to do next might ruin things for her. What was I thinking – might? – *would*. I went over to the photo. I looked into her smiling eyes, flecked with yellow. A lump formed in my throat and tears welled as I traced the outline of her face. I recalled the peachy feel of her skin, how she gnawed on her chubby knuckles when teething, the tramlines of snot from her constant colds. But most of all I remembered those arms outstretched in the photograph upstairs, grasping for me. I'd abandoned my baby and she'd become his.

Maybe one day she'd forgive me.

I put the photo back, touched my finger to my lips and pressed it to hers. "I'm sorry," I whispered. "I've got to do this."

.

Chapter 40
– Autumn term. Year 10 –

"YOU'RE NOT HIDING OUT in your bedroom all day. Get those clothes on and get your arse to school. You've got ten minutes before I come in there and dress you myself."

What Mum didn't realise was there was no need to come in and dress me. I'd done that. What I dreaded was leaving the house. Through the window, mottled clouds sat grey and motionless. Like me. As I sat on the edge of the bed, gazing at my trembling hands, I splayed my fingers as far I could. Still they shook. My body shivered, yet my cheeks burned. I was coming down with something. I shouldn't go out. It could be a bug and I'd pass it on. If I got cold or wet it would get worse. I'd get pneumonia and die.

I eased myself from the bed. What a shame.

Mum clattered about in the kitchen. I hesitated by the front door, hoping she'd say I looked ill, I should go back to bed, but she didn't. I sighed and turned to go. The door clicked shut, fresh air cooled my face. Above lay dark clouds thick and heavy with rain. I'd walk to school. Who cared if it made me late?

"Cindy!"

A door banged and shoes scuffed the path. I hurried away. He mustn't see me.

His panting told me he'd caught up. He threw his bag over his shoulder and grinned.

"Hiding from me?"

"No." I didn't look up.

"Well it's that or you've really upset your Mum. I've been round about ten times now."

My muscles ached. After so much time in bed my legs

233

were unused to exercise, let alone the strides I was doing now.

"Cindy." He grabbed my arm, pulling me to a stop. "What's the matter? What have I done?"

I didn't want to hurt him but if I looked up, he'd see into my eyes and he'd know what happened. What I'd done. My throat tightened. The last time we'd walked together in our school uniforms we'd been happy. His coach had arrived first – a posh affair with its fancy tie-back curtains – so I'd waited to wave him goodbye and then fought through a cloud of diesel fumes and the crowd of Year 7s to jostle for a place on our rattly bus. After school we'd met up with Nina and Josh in town and gone for a celebratory milkshake. No more school for six whole weeks. We'd talked about what we would get up to and Troy had reminded me about his fancy holiday to Canada while Nina and Josh had talked about the jobs they'd managed to get.

If only I'd ignored Mum – if I'd told her to stick it and got a job – I could have bought my own fags and books and I'd have been too busy to bother with Simon.

"Cindy?" Troy said, bringing me back to now. "Please tell me what I've done."

"Nothing." I shrugged. "Stuff happens. People change. That's all."

He bent down to look up at my face, so I turned to face the privet hedge. A ladybird crawled along the edge of a leave. Unconsciously, I put my hand out, hoping it would wander onto my finger, but the red casings opened and a long pair of black wings shot out, and away it flew.

A burst of anger flared. I hated it, hated everything.

"Is your Mum being mean to you?"

Troy put his hand on my shoulder to draw me around to face him. I shrugged it off.

"You need to get to school. You'll miss your bus." My voice wobbled.

"I can't go to school knowing you're angry with me."

"I'm not angry with *you*! It's… it's…"

I couldn't tell him. What would I say? A tear rolled down my cheek. I swiped the stupid thing with my sleeve. I had to get away. From him. From everyone.

"Leave me alone!" I screeched and sprinted across the road.

By the time I stopped running I was at the Rec. The last place I wanted to be and in the opposite direction to school. Fate. I wasn't meant to go. I kept walking. The breeze shuddered through the bushes that lined the edge of the playground and specks of rain patted my face. Nearby a swing creaked. I ignored it in case I found *him* sitting there, grinning.

At the corner of the football pitch a groundsman was wheeling a metal barrow thing along to make the lines whiter. He stared at me, so I hurried the other way, across the field and through the gap in the hedge that led to the rugby pitches. Troy had taken me to see a game once. I'd loved their red and black teeth and the way they smashed into each other with a loud 'whoomph'. Sometimes I wished I'd been born a boy. I wouldn't play cricket like Troy. Instead, I'd play rugby and bash my way through everyone to score a goal or whatever they called them.

I kept walking, under the big H post and over the rough studded ground, gashed in places like a knife had been ripped through the grass. My legs throbbed. Several pitches away stood an empty car park lined by brick buildings. The changing rooms I guessed. I could make out a couple of wooden bench tables dotted outside one of the buildings.

It was much further than I'd thought. My thighs burned

as I stepped over the squat wooden fence onto the tarmac of the car park. Exhausted, I slumped onto one of the benches which groaned under my weight. Splinters grazed my palms but, too tired to move to a better seat, I rested my arms on the sticky table top and buried my chin into my palms.

The bench faced the large window of what seemed to be a pub with dark wooden tables and chairs scattered around. I could just make out a purple banner stretched across the back wall with 'Mosston RFU' in big red letters. Probably a social club like the one Mum went to with Bill and her mates. A raindrop splashed the bench and I gazed up at the darkening sky. The breeze shuddered on my back, bringing with it more splashes of rain. I pushed myself up and went to see if I could find shelter. Along from a set of polished doors was a battered purple door with a bristly mat outside, littered with lumps of hardened mud and grass. The changing rooms. Behind I could just make out the edge of another building – a long garage-like building with rickety double doors held together by a latch. I dragged one of the doors open and peered inside.

The space stank of mud and damp, mixed with a plasticky smell. Thick cobwebs hung at a dirt-splattered window, while in the shadows sat a rack of shelving. I could make out rugby balls of all sizes, tins of paint, and a jumble of other bits and pieces. Opposite the window, a stack of thin metal posts leant against the wall and on the floor lay two rectangular bulky things smeared with hardened mud, each with a top bit that stuck out like a pillow. I pressed the heavy material. Not soft like my bed but at least they were squishy. Perfect. I glanced out through the drizzle, to the open fields, the empty car park, at the silent buildings. I'd stay here. Just for today.

◆

The kitchen was a fog of cigarette smoke. That and whatever was cooking. I pulled open the oven door and shut it again, coughing as scalding fumes scorched the back of my throat and made my eyes water. Burnt sausages and oven chips by the look of it. I lobbed my school bag onto the floor of the larder and went through to the lounge.

"I see," Mum said in her best telephone voice to whoever she was talking to on the phone. Flushed dots marked her cheeks. "Well, as I said, I'll have words with her. She won't be doing that again."

I began to back out of the room, but she curled her index finger, pointed to the settee and did her head-shaking thing. You're in for it, her face said.

'You,' she mouthed at me. Then she put her voice on again. "Yes, I told you. She's here, now. She'll be in on Monday, don't you worry."

She hung up and turned to me. "What's this? The effing welfare woman reckons you ain't been to school all week. You been hiding out with your druggie mates?"

"No."

She stormed across the room, slapping me hard across the face. As I clutched my stinging cheek, she held her hand like I'd hurt her.

"I am so sick of this." She flung her arm out and pointed towards the door. "Get to your room. And don't think you're coming down to eat later. I'm not wasting my money on the likes of you."

I leapt up, flinching – I half-expected her to thump me or something – and legged it out of the room. The key clicked in the front door. It swung open as I ran past. At the top of the stairs, I glanced back to see Bill stepping wearily

237

inside.

"What's for tea, love?"

"Tea, is that all you think about?" Mum said. "No hellos. Nothing. You're as bad as her."

I slammed my bedroom door and threw myself on the bed. Why couldn't I have a Mum who'd ask me what was wrong and help me? She must know there was a reason I couldn't go to school and face everyone. The shouting match intensified downstairs. I buried my face in my pillow and sobbed so hard my heart threatened to burst through my rib cage. As I heard her scream and a tin crash, I wondered if life could get any worse.

"The blasted dinner's wrecked!" Mum shouted.

As footsteps pounded up the stairs, I'd found the answer to my question.

Chapter 41
- mid December -

ONCE I'D CALMED MYSELF with a cup of tea and tucked the Dictaphones in a safe place, I went over to Marion and Ralph's. I made it just in time, arriving on their doorstep as they opened the door to go shopping for a Christmas tree.

"We were just coming to get you." Lily's gloved hand warmed my fingers. She looked all Christmassy in her red coat and little bobble hat.

"Shall we make a people paper chain?" Marion asked Lily and looped her arm through mine to lead me to the car.

I climbed into the back seat beside the children, forcing myself not to glance back at the dark windows of Mum's house or to search every car parked in the street to see if he stood there, hiding, watching. It was only when we left the estate that I found I could breathe.

The glow of excitement in the children's eyes, their jittery hops as we queued for Father Christmas and their joy as they tore the wrappings from their gifts, soothed the anxious buzz inside me. But each time my thoughts strayed to earlier, to him, and to what I had to do next, the angry wasp of fear stung deep. Today was a façade, a foil to be ripped away but my task would wait until tomorrow.

After both trees had been unloaded from the roof rack – and once Ralph and I had carted mine around to Mum's back garden – the children set about decorating Marion's tree in her lounge. Much later, she packed us off with a carrier bag stuffed with new tinsel and baubles, ignoring my earlier comment about not needing decorations as Mum would have them somewhere. Within seconds of her door clicking shut, the children's chorus started, reaching a crescendo of 'pretty pleases' which almost masked the sound of my mobile phone ringing. Troy. I put my finger to my lips. The twins stood with sealed lips but pleading eyes while I spoke to him.

"It looks like I won't make it back until seven at the earliest," he said. "The traffic is horrendous."

"No problem. I'll get dinner ready for seven thirty instead."

Before I said goodbye, I'd already decided to use the extra hour to please the children. With excited squeals, they followed me into the back garden. Net-wrapped and shaped like a mini-leylandii, the Christmas tree sat in the corner of the patio where Ralph had leaned it against the neighbour's chain-linked fence. Light from the kitchen window grazed the blackness turning the fence posts into man-size shadows and a breeze rustled through nearby bushes. Where *he* could lurk. I was being silly. Simon would be tucked up at home, drinking beer and staring at the TV like he always used to do on a Saturday night.

We dragged the Christmas tree along the patio and around the corner, a laborious zigzag with the children shoving each other in a battle to hold the tip of the tree. Several times I lost my grip and the tree crashed down, several times I pleaded for them to behave. When the branches snagged on the wall the net ripped, firing pine needles at me, I let go. The children gazed from the tree to my folded arms.

"What's the matter?" Charlie said.

"We can't do this if you're going to fight about it. Now we'll have to go through the front door or there'll be needles everywhere."

As I hefted the tree, both children leaped forward.

"No, you don't." I held my arm out. "Lily, hold the net but don't yank it downwards. Charlie, go and open the front

240

door."

Charlie sprinted into the kitchen, leaving Lily and I to stagger down the path. We rounded the corner to find Charlie standing by the gate, his face lit by the hallway light.

"Come on," I called to him. "You're meant to be holding the door open."

He pointed down the road into nothing. "He's ran off."

"Who?" Goosebumps pricked my neck.

"The man. He said..." He frowned.

Simon. It had to be. Who else would come over at this time of night? Much as I wanted to drag them both indoors, bolt us safely inside, I had to find out what he'd said before Charlie's attention moved back to the Christmas tree and he forgot.

"He told me to say... *I can see you*." Charlie shrugged. "Silly man. Everyone can."

I shivered. Simon would be watching us from behind one of the cars. I knew it. Seeing how I reacted, taking pleasure from my panic. I kept my movement slow, wrapped my arms around both children and shepherded them into the house.

"But..." Lily twisted around to point at the tree which lay beside the front door.

"Troy will be back soon. He can help us. It *is* a bit heavy." When Lily's bottom lip jutted and she folded her arms, I added, "You can both stay up late to decorate it."

As I closed the door, I caught a waft of Simon's aftershave. Then it disappeared. My imagination on over-drive. A cold draught wafted through the hallway and the kitchen door creaked. We'd left it open! I rushed to slam it shut, twisting the key in the lock. My breath hissed a long phew and my heart thumped. Through the patterned door panes, I could see the pink of Marion's jumper as she bustled

241

around her kitchen. Ralph would be nearby too. I pulled the mobile from my pocket and searched for their phone number, cutting it off before it rang. At least if I needed to call them, they were just one click away. The sound of the TV filtered through the hallway and I hurried back to the children, who'd settled down to watch celebrities being splattered by gloop.

"Just checking for Troy." I peered through a sliver of curtain.

I wished he'd hurry back. I'd left Charlie alone for no more than a minute and Simon could have snatched him. Behind me, the children giggled. *Simon.* His meeting with Charlie wouldn't have been a coincidence. He must have been spying on us from outside, maybe a car, maybe a friend's house. But whatever he'd been doing, I knew one thing. What I planned to do next would bring a furious Simon to our door, with nothing left to lose. And, like now, Troy wouldn't always be there to protect us.

◆

When I'd come to Mandy's house earlier that morning, the front garden had been dulled by rain. I'd stood at the door, nerves jangling, wondering if this would be a replay of the time I'd last confronted her, but no one had answered and I'd traipsed away, head down, to where Troy sat in the car across the road waiting for me.

"She must have a job," I'd told him. "We'll have to come back later this afternoon and try to catch her before Ella gets home."

I hadn't mentioned Simon. We both knew the risk of him being there.

Now damp patches mottled the pink and yellow paving

242

slabs edging the concrete driveway but, unlike this morning, the sun peeked from behind grey clouds to brighten the pot of winter flowering pansies beside the doorstep. Inside the radio played a song I didn't know. My heart thudded, I took a deep breath and lifted the door knocker. The rap of metal sliced the air and reverberated into the street. The radio cut out. Someone thumped down the stairs. Through the glass a shape appeared and the door scraped open. And I found myself gazing into grey eyes, flecked with yellow.

My heart jolted, my throat tightened. Shock fired every part of me. The empty pit that had been Ella fractured to become a cavern filled with loss and sadness. She should have been mine. I clenched my fists and swallowed.

Her smile faded, as if she had expected someone else.

"Do you want my mum?" she said.

She clutched a jacket by its collar. She must be going out. I longed to reach out, to touch her, but all I could do was nod. Her ponytail whipped around and I found myself gazing at the tendrils of hair on her neck. Remembering when all she'd had was fluffy wisps.

"Mum!"

Those beautiful eyes turned back to me. "She won't be a minute."

She smiled and her dimple sank into the smoothness of her cheek. I took in the new mole on her chin, the curve of her eyebrows, the earring glinting in her ear. Tears pricked my eyes. She did a half-smile, blushed and looked down at her feet. The pink nail varnish on her fingers matched her toenails. Stubby toes like mine. Her skinny jeans hugged her waist and collar bones jutted under the thin fabric of her jumper. In her school photo she'd had the plump face of a girl, but she was growing into a woman. Soon she'd be taller than me.

243

The stairs creaked and Ella smiled goodbye. As she walked away it felt as if a cord stretched between us – I couldn't let her go – until, severed by the lounge door clicking shut, it reeled back to smash into my chest.

"You," Mandy said. "I told you."

I couldn't breathe. I couldn't speak. All I could do was press my hand to my mouth and hold back the tears. Mandy's face blurred. Her mouth twisted. Sour.

"It's your fault." She nodded towards the closed door at the end of the hallway. "You chose this."

A tear tingled on my cheek. I wiped it away and shook my head.

"I don't remember much choice."

"Well, you wouldn't," she said. "Come here to cause more trouble, have you? To wreck her life." She jerked her thumb towards the lounge. "Well don't."

She reached for the door.

"Wait! Please." I tugged the Dictaphone from where it had got jammed into the corner of my coat pocket.

"Here." The metal glinted in my trembling hand. "You need to listen to this."

"I don't need to do anything."

She clutched the door but I could see she wanted to know more. After all, Mandy had always been a nosey cow.

"It's Simon. You need to hear what he has to say."

"You filthy bitch," she snarled. "You've been after him, haven't you? Trying to take him from me."

"For pities' sake." I waved the Dictaphone at her. "Listen to it."

The noise of the TV alerted us to the open lounge door and Ella standing there, wide-eyed. Mandy's face whitened. Lips pursed, she faced me.

"Go away." She lowered her voice.

"Not until you take this." I mirrored her tone. "I'm sorry but I'm going to…"

She snatched the Dictaphone, mouthed 'Now Fuck Off' and slammed the door. This time she didn't pause but stomped away. I heard muffled voices – Ella's high-pitched and enquiring and Mandy's gruff – but I couldn't hear their words. Neither did I want to. Mandy wouldn't be telling Ella the truth. With so many years spent covering up for Simon, she'd built a veneer of lies and buffered them until they shone.

Across the road Troy's elbow hung out of the window of his car, his hand cupping his chin. I shrugged and hurried over. As I got into the passenger side, he turned the ignition, clearly keen to leave.

"Didn't go too well?" he said.

"Understatement."

"At least he wasn't there."

I shuddered. I'd forgotten about him.

Troy turned the car out of Nelson Close, past the precinct where we used to wait for our buses to school, down Peters' Hill, towards town. Beside us people walked, women burdened by Christmas shopping bags, men with walking sticks, family groups, lone teenagers with their hands in pockets. From the safety of the car I surveyed their faces, searching for signs of familiarity, for the people I could have known in my youth.

We stopped at the traffic lights. The indicator ticked the seconds until the light went green. Was I walking into a trap of my own making? What if the police in London had put two and two together and worked out that Karis, who'd disappeared with her children, had once been Cindy? What if they'd found an old photo of me somewhere and circulated it? I pulled a strand of hair forward, taking comfort in the

245

brown. I'd become Cindy again and soon I would relive her life to strangers. I wouldn't let them lead me to Karis.

A mixture of police cars and other vehicles sat in the car park. Troy's lips tightened and I wondered if he was remembering the last time he'd had dealings with the police, thanks to me. A space lay empty opposite the blue entrance doors, as if someone was waiting for us and had ordered it to be kept free. The snaffle of tyres on tarmac grew louder, my heart beat stronger. A grinding noise. The handbrake. We sat there, facing a moss-covered brick wall. The car shuddered, the engine died. I had to do this. My fingers felt thick and heavy, the handle slipped from my grasp. But I couldn't. The door creaked open and Troy stood there, hand outstretched, ready.

My tomorrow had arrived. Today would change everything. My Christmas present to my daughter.

"Ella, forgive me," I whispered.

Chapter 42
– Autumn term. Year 10 –

AS THE BELL RANG, chairs scraped the floor. Above the bobbing heads and usual kerfuffle, Mr Peters stood at the front of the classroom waving a sheet.

"Don't forget. Homework in on Monday, no excuses. Enjoy the fireworks this weekend everyone."

Nina's chair knocked the front of my desk. As she stood to shuffle her arm through the sleeve of her coat, she gave me a brief smile. Beside her Millie Rogers stuffed her books into her bag and muttered something about checking out the café in case Harry and Carl were about. They swung their bags over their shoulders and took a pincer movement around the desk, meeting up by the classroom door. Without a single glance, they disappeared into the corridor.

Mr Peters had his back to the room, stretching to wipe the whiteboard. Outside shadows passed the door, voices echoed, screeches of excitement, the clatter of feet. I'd leave once it was quiet. Then I felt her breath. She couldn't have left without saying something.

"Poor Cindy, all alone."

I didn't turn to Issie, but I saw her teeth, the upward curve of her mouth, the flicker of her hand as she waved it in front of her nose.

"You should sell your hair to the chippy. They need some grease."

Her polished fingernails tapped the table. I curled mine into my palms, ashamed of the jagged crescents they'd become.

She sniggered. "Want to punch me, do you?"

Behind her, someone – maybe Isabel or Abi – giggled.

Maybe I should let her punch me. Hard, in the stomach. Her fingers were long and thin, designed to yank hair, pinch or scratch someone's skin. Maybe one of the others, Dawn or Kim, might join in and kick me if I went down.

"Go on then," I said.

She pushed herself away from the table. "I'm not touching you. I might catch something."

She flounced away, followed by her gaggle of bitches.

"Have a good weekend, Sir," they said and streamed into the corridor.

Mr Peters faced me. His shoulders sagged and he sighed so loud it echoed. Behind us lay empty rows of desks. Footsteps clipped the tiles. We were alone. If he reached me, I'd be trapped. I jumped up, snatched my coat from the back of the chair, my bag from the floor and, dodging the straggly chairs, leapt across to the next aisle.

"Cindy, wait," he called.

No way was I falling for that.

I slalomed past the groups huddled in the corridor, side-stepping the jutting bags. Not pausing to look back, I gripped the bannister rail and took the stairs two at a time, racing along the ground floor corridor, bashing my way out through the double doors, which slammed behind me. The freezing air whipped my face, cut through my jumper, but I couldn't stop to pull my coat on. My bag slid from my shoulder to my arm, so it knocked against my knees as I ran. My breath fogged the air. Huh-hah, huh, hah. *No!* As I pressed my hands to my ears, my coat slipped to the ground, almost tripping me up. Not that noise. Anything but that noise. The warmth of their bodies pressed mine. The smell. My face burned with the heat.

"Oi. Your coat!"

I swung around. A sixth-former stood there, arm

248

outstretched, my coat hooked over his finger. Nearby, a group of boys stood watching. A trap. I knew it. I'd go back and when I reached for the coat, he'd grab me.

He held out the coat. "You dropped it."

I took another step back, glanced from the coat to him. His lips curled up, like he was about to laugh. The group of boys shuffled closer. Definitely a trap. Mum would kill me if I came back without my coat, but no way was I falling for it. I sprinted across the road to the squeal of tyres and the blast of a horn.

"Freak!" A boy called to laughter.

They'd laughed too – Simon and his gang. I could picture the film playing, as if I was standing there watching it. Hear their laughter. Smell what I now knew was the stink of sex. Was I remembering the film I'd seen on his camcorder or was this another memory coming back? As I swung into an alleyway, my feet slid on a mat of damp leaves and I jerked, my arms flailing, but managed to keep my balance. I had to get away, from those boys, from the memories. My arms pumped, my breath rasped through gritted teeth. Huh-hah, huh-hah filled my ears. Stronger, louder. I shook my head, tried to fling it away. *Leave me alone.* Cramp wrenched my stomach, threatening to fill my throat with the acidic taste of sick, except I had nothing left to spew up after yesterday and this morning. Could this be really happening? I slowed to a stop beside a stubby tree. A nothingness sapped my mind and I staggered forwards. My bag thudded to the floor, my chest smacked against a thick bough, its bark scratching my arms. I clung to the branch. Below browns and yellows swam, slowly coming into focus as dirt and dead leaves.

In the distance a car door slammed and a breeze rattled the bare branches. I shivered. I couldn't go home. Not without my coat. Bits of moss clung between the cracks of the branch, along which a little bug stumbled. Would it die when the hard winter frosts came? I'd be joining it when Mum found out what trouble I was in. A sob escaped. High-pitched, like the wail of a baby. I closed my mouth, locked the tears inside. I wouldn't cry, no matter how unfair it felt. To go through 'that' and end up with a little Simon, Pete or Ade in there. An alien eating me from the inside. I had to get rid. Kill it before it killed me.

After a while I pushed myself from the tree and headed back down the alleyway, surprised to find how far I'd run. The queue of buses and clumps of school kids had gone, leaving an unfamiliar scene. Quiet, but for the distant hum of traffic. Beside grass verges imprinted with tyre tracks and brown puddles sat the occasional parked car. No one around to watch as I fetched my coat from where it dangled over the school fence. When I got close, I realised it had been hooked several feet above my head. Done on purpose to mock me? I pushed my foot through the gap in the fence and hoisted myself up the freezing metal rail. Grasping my coat with fingers raw and numb from the cold, I dropped to the ground and shoved my arms into the chilled sleeves. I longed for a bath. Something warming.

Then it hit me. Mum had just the stuff. And it would also kill the alien.

♦

A note leant against the kettle telling Mandy to meet Mum down the social, which meant they'd be out all night. Good. I tossed my school bag into the larder and went through to the lounge where I knelt beside the cabinet. One of the hinges was broken, so I took care opening the door. All I needed was Mum coming back to find the door on the floor. Three bottles sat in the cupboard, one creamy and yellow, while behind it sat Mum's vodka – no way would I get away with drinking that – but jammed at the back was an old bottle of brandy.

Brown speckled the edge of the cap and it scraped as I twisted it, like grit had got stuck inside. I sniffed. Eww. Tentatively, I touched my tongue to the edge of the bottle. Disgusting.

I had to do this. What choice did I have? No way could I let this thing grow inside me.

I pinched the tip of my nose and took a swig. Brandy burned the back of my throat and made my eyes water. Each time I burped a rancid taste filled my mouth. I was going to be sick. I knew it.

The sickness passed after a minute. I held my nose again and glugged back as much as I could handle. My tongue burned, my eyes watered, the back of my throat tightened. Gasping, I lifted the bottle, stunned to see how little had gone. This time I tipped my head back and let the foul stuff wash down my throat. As I coughed and wiped my mouth, a tear rolled down my cheek. My eyes blurred and my mind grew woozy. I smiled. Finally.

Gripped by cramps, I clutched the corner of the unit until they passed. My stomach heaved.

"No, no!" I leapt to my feet, covering my mouth as I raced to the bathroom.

I dropped to my knees and clutched the cold toilet seat. The stench made me spew. As the water turned brown, the air became acid and my world toilet shaped. If I couldn't get rid, what would I do?

Outside a figure walked past the patterned bathroom window. Behind them another taller person. The key turned in the back door and the kitchen light flicked on.

"Cindy!"

Mandy. All I needed. I wrenched the toilet handle down and dived over to the sink where I cupped my hand beneath the tap. Icy water stung my face, washed my mouth.

"I've got lov…"

Mandy stood at the open bathroom door. Eyes narrowed, she gazed from the toilet to me, until she walked over to examine the bowl. I'd lifted my sleeve to wipe my face but as she turned to me I froze, arm mid-air. Drips rolled from my chin and splashed the collar of my jumper.

"Again?" she said. "You've been sick every morning this week. I've heard you."

She stabbed her finger at the person who'd followed her in. From where I stood by the sink, I could just make out a dark blazer.

"You haven't, have you?"

A palm raised upwards. Troy's.

"What?" He half-laughed.

I snatched the towel from the side of the bath. We hadn't talked for more than two minutes since he'd come back from holiday, so what did she think he'd done? As I stepped into the kitchen Troy's eyes widened and his mouth fell open. Too late, he recovered and gave a small smile. But he couldn't hide his thoughts. I knew him too well. Disgust, confusion. What had I become?

"You've got her up the duff, haven't you?"

My face had dried but I couldn't pull the towel away. The musty smell intensified as I stood, caught in the horror of Mandy and Troy's faces. Poor Troy. He didn't deserve this.

"Leave him alone!" I flung the towel at her. "It wasn't him."

The kitchen light reflected in his teary eyes. He looked from Mandy to me, his mouth a circle of shock. He shook his head. Disbelief. Stumbled towards the door. For a moment the tips of his fingers gripped the door frame as he swung onto the path, but then they slipped away, replaced by the sound of his pounding footsteps.

"Troy," I called. But I didn't go after him.

Mandy shook her head. "You stupid cow."

Chapter 43
- mid December -

"IT'S OVER. YOU DID IT." Troy squeezed my shoulder, his voice thick with emotion.

Several times during the interview, I'd caught him dabbing his eyes. His fingers entwined mine as I dug up buried memories and grasped for the words I needed to explain. I hadn't been a bad child, just naïve. When I'd handed them the Dictaphone, it had quivered in my fingers as if it too was afraid of what it would spurt.

"It's just the beginning," I said.

He stretched out his arm to hold the door open. I lifted my head to let the breeze cool my cheeks, the smell of warming pavements and sodden grass heaven compared to the stuffy dry air of the police station. A thick-set man stepped to one side, waiting for us to pass. As I smiled thanks our eyes met. His irises were unusual, one hazel, one blue. I'd seen them before. I glanced back to find him frowning at me. An old friend from Mosston? Too old. Perhaps one of Mum's or Bill's mates?

Troy had slowed alongside me. He hadn't picked up my confusion about the balding man who paused by the police station doors, watching us. When he released my arm to fumble in the pocket of his jeans for his car keys, I glanced back to find the man had moved inside to become a shadow peering through the glass. My unease grew. Why couldn't I place him? Maybe because when I'd been a child he would have had hair. I shook my head. He didn't fit into the jigsaw of Mosston memories.

"You're quiet," Troy said. "Tired?"

I nodded and shifted around in the car seat, so I could

watch the figure by the window.

"When we were in there…" His voice broke and he swallowed. "I'm sorry. Even when you told me the other week, I didn't get just how shocking it was. I mean..."

He lifted his hands from the wheel as he struggled to find the words. "I knew it was awful, just not… *This*. It explains… *Everything*. Cindy, I am so, so sorry."

I flinched. I'd told him to call me Cindy, but the interview had made me realise just how much I loathed it. Cindy. Cindy girl.

"My Mum," he said. "She's going to find out on the local grapevine, I mean about Simon. I'd rather we told her first."

I shot around. "Your mum?"

Troy gripped the steering wheel, his knuckles white, his face strained. He'd supported me, bottled what I told him, screwed it inside. The least I could do was to offer him a release valve. I cringed. If I'd thought talking to strangers – the police – would be difficult, Mrs Hamilton – sorry Marion – was another level. I flushed, remembering her harsh words from years ago and the way her eyes had glittered with anger as she'd surveyed my belly. My stomach churned.

♦

Specks of yellow pollen surrounded the vase of pink lilies on the table. Air bubbles clung to the green stalks, magnified by the round glass. I'd finished my story and sat waiting, hoping, that someone would break the silence. Marion pressed a soggy corner of tissue to her eyes. The varnished tip of her nail peeked through a tear in the paper now stained black from her mascara and beige from her foundation. When she swallowed, the folds of skin on her neck rippled and her jowls sagged as if weighted by what I'd told her. Little did she realise I'd given her half the tale – the sanitised bits – saving the full horror for myself.

"Your poor thing," she said. "How can you ever forgive me?"

"What do you mean? You had nothing to do with it."

Troy sat across from me at the table, holding his mum's hand, just like he'd held mine at the police station hours earlier. He shrugged and upturned his palm.

She cleared her throat and fingered the tissue. "That time… when…"

A tear cut a silvery path down her cheek. Troy's chair knocked against the table leg and he wrapped his arm around her shoulder.

"Mum, I'm sorry. I was being selfish."

"You dear? Why?" A fragment of tissue fluttered to the table.

"It wasn't selfishness," I said. "He thought it was best to tell you now I've told the police, just in case you heard any gossip. Anyhow, the past is past. I'm dealing with it thanks to Troy."

"But." Marion shook her head. "What I said to you that time. I've never forgotten how… judgemental I was."

She blushed and I knew we were both back there, squaring up to each other. What had she called me that day? Fog clouded her actual words but her expression grew vivid. Her foundation-clogged pores, the thin lips, the way saliva clung to her teeth as she growled at me. A she-wolf protecting her son. Stay away from him, from us.

"After you left, I wondered if there was more to the story. Why would a mother, even a young one, leave her child behind and with…."

'Them', she wanted to say, but couldn't.

As she picked at the tissue and ragged pieces littered the polished table, Mrs Hamilton finally became Marion. Flawed but real. She'd dabbed her foundation from beneath her eyes to reveal a bed of matt grey skin. She looked old. A side effect of years spent alone bringing up a child in a world she didn't fit. Mum had belonged but hadn't fared much better. Would years of smoking, drinking and looking after me have caused her stroke?

Mum.

Her shadow hovered as if she were standing beside me, her hair pulled up into a tight ponytail, her eyebrows arched upwards. 'You lying again, Cindy?' She put a cigarette to her mouth and, with a sneer on her lips, she blew a long plume of smoke.

I shuddered.

"Would you like a cup of tea?" Still clutching the ribbon of tissue, Marion pushed herself to her feet. "I expect Ralph will be back with the children soon."

Something outside caught her attention and she hesitated, craning her neck past the Christmas tree to look to the right of the window, into the road. All I could see was a balding man who sauntered past, a newspaper tucked beneath his arm, his lips shaped as if he was whistling. He disappeared, leaving a view of parked cars beyond the crimson and green poinsettia on the windowsill.

But then I realised Marion and Troy weren't looking in his direction. Troy frowned.

"Oh dear," Marion said. "I think the news is out."

Chapter 44
– Spring term. Year 10 –

I FLICKED THROUGH THE PAGES in the book I'd promised myself I wouldn't read, turning to 32 weeks. 'Your baby's eyes can focus now' it told me. The picture showed a baby with its arms and legs squished into its chest and its eyes closed. A bright purple cord twisted around linking it to me, taking what it could. Just like an alien. Right now, the thing was inside me all squashed up, head tucked downwards like the midwife said, getting ready to come out. She'd given me this book, saying she didn't do that for everyone, but it might be nice for me to see what was happening. I popped the pen in my mouth and pulled off the lid and scrawled the date on the page. 20 March. The first day of Spring.

The thing shifted and something – a foot? – dug into my rib. I turned the pages to 38 weeks with the woman with the stretch marks on her stomach and the sticky-out belly button. Then I clamped the book shut, so I wouldn't see the scary picture of the woman with the sweaty face and open legs on the next page. The midwife had told me not to worry, but I did. Would it be Ade, Simon or Pete who popped out or a monster that looked like all of them? Would it rip my insides and pay me back for trying to kill it?

I let the book slip from my lap, where it thudded to the floor, and slumped back into the pillow. Above, the mould stretched along the ceiling above the window to cluster in the corner of the room. A growing black mass. Now I looked at it, I could see a face: two eyes and a mouth leering at me. An alien friend for my thing. Watching out like everyone else did for this baby. Stuff me. I could die for all they cared. They probably hoped I would too.

I shuffled awkwardly to my knees, not wanting a repeat of the shooting pains in my pelvis after I'd sprung up to go to the toilet in the middle of the night. Keeping my elbows away from the pools of water on the windowsill, I rested my chin in my cupped hands to gaze out. Behind the bubbles of condensation on the pane was a deep blue sky. I could make out a vapour trail from an airplane, puffs of candy floss. My stomach rumbled.

Downstairs was quiet. Mandy had left for work two hours ago, followed by Bill who had stormed off to the sound of Mum calling him a 'fat, lazy sod'. I hadn't heard her leave. I strained to listen for the sound of the radio or TV. Nothing, so I stepped from the bed and crept to the bedroom door. No clang of pans from the kitchen or whistle from the immersion heater, which would tell me Mum was in the bath.

I tiptoed down the stairs, using the bannister to take my weight, but still they creaked. In the lounge a newspaper had been left on the settee, open at the TV pages, while on the floor Mum's lipstick-stained cup sat beside an ashtray. Her fags weren't in their usual place on the settee arm. She must be out. I moved onto the kitchen, where I spotted Bill's abandoned mug and inside it a crumpled teabag which had soaked up the splash of milk he liked. It must have been some row for him to stomp off without having his morning cuppa. I fetched a bowl and the cornflakes. Dregs lined the bottom of the plastic bottle I pulled from the fridge. That explained it. They'd rowed about milk again. Either Bill had put the empty carton back and Mum was down the precinct buying more or – worse – he'd put his money on the wrong horse, like last week, and we'd be back to drinking black tea for the next few days. Great, no bread either. My stomach grumbled. I grabbed a handful of cornflakes and pushed them into my mouth, kicking the ones I dropped under the side.

The door clicked and brushed open. I shoved the cornflake packet to the back of the worktop just as Mum stepped in.

"Sodding parky out there," she said. "Put the kettle on."

"There's no milk."

She tugged the scarf from her neck. "Oh, for fuck's sake. Have you used it all up again or is it that lazy sod? Bet it's him. I asked him to do one thing." She shook her index finger at me, in case I couldn't count. "One sodding thing and he's off down the bookies, I bet. Not only…" She popped a cigarette into her mouth, flicked the lighter, and took a drag so the tip glowed red. "Not only has Simon got me the paint for nothing, but now he's been lumbered with the painting too."

"Simon? Paint?"

She pulled a screwed-up fiver from the pocket of her jeans. "You won't want to be in the house with the fumes. Go down town. Get yourself a burger or something."

She stuffed the money into the palm of my hand and curled my fingers around it.

"Simon's going to paint here?"

"If I had my way, Bill would be out the door. Lazy shit. It's not like your room will take long. Now, go on, get dressed. He'll be here soon."

Simon? In my room? I stood, open-mouthed. Please say I'd misheard.

She jerked her head towards my belly. "No one will see you if that's what you're worried about."

"You know it's not. And you know why."

"Not this again."

From the lounge came the sound of the phone ringing.

Mum sighed as if it was another thing she had to deal with and stomped off, leaving me leaning against the kitchen worktop. My legs shook so much I thought they'd crumble under the weight of me and *It*.

Simon was coming here. The alien churned, scraping the underside of my rib cage. *Simon was coming.*

Here.

I grabbed my coat and raced out of the house. The wind slapped my face, making me gasp. As I lifted the gate to pull it open, the hem of my coat caught on the latch and I bent to unhook it, straightening up to find Mrs Hamilton beside me, lips pressed so they'd become the colour of her powdered skin.

"Cindy," she said, as if it was a statement.

"Mrs H-Hamilton."

She'd hooked her handbag over her arm and stood with her gloved hands linked together like a belt across her coat.

"I've been hoping to have a chance to speak with you. About Troy."

Troy? She shifted away from the glare of the sun, but now it cut across her shoulder, blinding me. I shaded my eyes and found she gazed at my bulge.

"I can't understand why someone who masqueraded as a friend would want to hurt my son the way you are doing."

My throat tightened. I missed him. Like Nina, he had his own gang now. His was a group of lads from his grammar school. Often, I stood a bit back from the nets and watched them walk past laughing and joking, with Troy in the centre, an inch or two taller than the rest. I half hoped he'd turn and spot me, while praying he wouldn't.

"I'm not."

"Don't play games with me. You know what people think."

"W-what?"

She pointed at my bump. "My Troy had nothing to do with that. But until you start telling the truth, he's the one being blamed."

"I haven't—"

"For goodness' sake, Cindy. Who was it?"

Ade, Simon or Phil – you choose – a voice mocked. The thing inside me shifted. My throat constricted and I tugged at my collar, to loosen it, to get air. The material scratched the back of my neck. Simon would be along any minute. He'd see me. See my bump. His devil spawn, like *Rosemary's Baby*. A gust of wind punched me and I grabbed the concrete gate post. Don't think of him. Think of something else.

"Cindy!"

Her shoes were square-fronted and shiny, unlike my scuffed trainers. Where I'd rolled down my grey school socks so they looked like trainer socks, her beige tights were smooth under her coat which flapped open at her knees to show a tweed skirt. I didn't have to look to know my legs were stained with a hairy fuzz the colour of the elasticated skirt Mum had found in an Oxfam shop in town, along with a pair of pregnancy leggings. I should have worn the leggings. At least then Mrs Hamilton wouldn't be sneering at me the way she did now.

"You and I both know it wasn't Troy who did this to you. Please – for Troy's sake if nothing else – tell the truth. Don't leave people thinking…"

I shook my head. What could I say?

"You won't do it, will you?" Mrs Hamilton said. "You're quite happy leaving everyone thinking it's my son. Because it suits your purpose, whatever that it is. You. You..." She jabbed her finger at my face, making me flinch. "Are not the Cindy I knew. You have changed. Become nothing but a… tart."

Her hand shot to her mouth. Then she swung around and clopped away, pushing her gate with such force the hinges clanged. I'd never seen her so angry before. I should run after her, tell her. But a car engine caught my attention and I spotted a flash of red between the parked cars. Simon. The car braked, whining as he reversed into a space on the opposite side of the road. He was coming. Here. To my room.

I found myself running, panting, towards the one place I could go.

Chapter 45
- mid December -

"YOUR SISTER IS AT YOUR DOOR," Marion said.

I'd been so busy watching the man walking past, I hadn't realised both she and Troy were watching someone else. I pushed the chair from the table and walked over to the front window, shocked to see Mandy standing by Mum's door. Crumpled and older looking, her cheeks blotched and eyes red-rimmed, she clutched her elbows as if in the grip of a terrible cramp. She stepped away from the porch to gaze up to Mum's bedroom, and back to bang the door knocker – hard – so I could hear it from inside Marion's lounge.

Marion laid a tentative hand on my shoulder. "Are you going to speak to her?"

I nodded and lifted the net curtain to tap the window. Mandy swivelled around, her gaze meeting mine but, when I raised my index finger to tell her I'd be a minute, not a flicker of emotion showed in her eyes. With simmering nerves, I set off to meet her. Three times in one day I'd have to face up to what Simon had chosen to do, what he'd forced on my child self. I wouldn't apologise to Mandy, even though I was sorry she and Ella would be hurt. Anyhow, her deadened eyes said she was beyond pain.

I didn't skip over the fence, but went the long way, giving myself a few seconds more until I had to deal with her. Across the road an ornamental Santa dangled from the roof of Mr and Mrs Wilson's old house while inside lights twinkled on a Christmas tree. A young family lived there now. For others, life moved on, while the past held me in its clutches.

Mandy huddled inside her coat. "The police came," she

said, her voice flat.

I ushered her around the side of the house to the back door.

"Mum, Mum!" Charlie called from across the fence. He held up a line of Christmas lights which led to Ralph, who stood on top of a ladder buried in the bare branches of a tree. As Lily joined in waving, the ladder wobbled. She gave me a whoops face – shouted "Sorry" to Ralph – and planted her hands back on the ladder's sides.

"Looking good," I called. "I'll just be a minute."

"Yours?" Mandy said in the same monotone voice

I nodded. She didn't glance back to the children. She didn't look at me either. I was glad. It gave me time to prepare for her blame. How I'd ruined Ella's life, not once by leaving, but twice by coming back. How, thanks to me, the neighbours would find out. But if she'd heard the recording I'd given her, she'd know I had no choice. I had to do something.

After filling the kettle and pulling two cups out of the cupboard, I turned to her. "They've been to see Simon?"

"He wasn't in."

"Oh," I said. "So—"

"They went to his work too. I guessed what they'd come about, although they wouldn't tell me."

Her eyes lifted to meet mine. A crimson rash covered her cheeks. She dabbed a knuckle into the corner of her eye and sniffed.

"Ella came back when they were in the house looking through his stuff." She unzipped and zipped up her coat. Up and down, up and down. Zip, zip. Background music to her words. "After they went, she asked me about them. I- I decided to tell her t-that he might have done something years ago. Involving a young girl."

265

She paused and her fingers fell from her zip to reach for a tassel that hung from her coat. Her silence made me prickle with unease.

"Ella said…" She took a deep breath. "That Simon made her nervous."

Her voice quivered and a tear rolled down her cheek. She brushed it away. "When I asked why, she wouldn't say."

A pit of ice settled deep inside. Mandy's mouth contorted as she searched for the words she needed. I wanted to comfort her, to shake her, to slap her. This was my sister, the woman who'd turned my story of abuse into one of jealousy, who'd protected Simon from the accusations of the twelve-year-old girl at the park. Her lies could have meant he was free to abuse Ella and other young girls. But he was to blame. *Him.* Not her.

Her eyes welled. Again, her lips moved but no words came. My turmoil grew. We'd both played our parts, worked together to keep him safe. I'd stayed away, not caring about the girl I'd left behind. She was a baby. What harm could he do? I'd let the memories fade, so Ella became an occasional pang of remembrance at Christmas or the times I remembered her birthday in May. As long as I was safe. Free from him.

I couldn't just blame Mandy. Not when I'd failed Ella too. I had to ask.

"Do you think…?"

Mandy shook her head. "I got mad with her. Said she had to tell me what he'd done. Nothing, she said. Though he'd have liked to. He told her how pretty she was, how he liked her…"

Steam billowed behind her head. The kettle clicked off. The sound took me back to the time I'd been sent out to make Mum and Bill a cup of tea years ago. I'd been

266

stretching up to the cupboard to fetch down a mug when I'd felt a warm hand on my bum. I'd swung around, shocked to find Simon standing beside me.

"Nice legs," he'd said and grinned, his hands held up in mock surrender.

When I'd blushed and smiled back, he'd bent closer. His breath had patted my skin. "You don't know what you do to a man."

Then he'd run his finger along my jawline, down my neck, stopping at the collar of my t-shirt. "You're the most beautiful girl around here. Do you know that?"

Me, beautiful? No one had ever called me that. I'd gazed up at his face, his eyes framed by dark lashes, the dimple which cut into his cheek, his smile, and I'd felt a tingle of excitement. That moment had signalled the start of the end.

"He hasn't touched her." Mandy exhaled. I found I could breathe too.

Then she began to wring the bottom of her coat. Winding up to tell me more. I knew. And I tensed with her.

"I've come to say sorry. I- I saw his laptop. After you came round."

She must have seen the shock in my face because she shook her hand. "No, no. You're not on it. I don't know what made me want to look, but I did. I guessed his password. Those pictures. He's… *filth*, disgusting."

Her hands flew to her eyes, leaving a triangle of face, her nose, her gaping mouth, lips wet with saliva and tears. I ached to hold my sister.

"Cindy, what am I going to do? What will people say when they know Simon's a paedo? What he has on that laptop? It's horrible. What is going to happen to Ella and me?"

I reached out and she fell into my arms. Her warm body shuddered with each sob. My sister, so close. I couldn't remember a time we'd touched other than to fight. But there was more at stake than childhood grievances. She was right. By association, people would say she must be guilty. After all, they'd lived with him. Ella would be bullied at school. She'd become different, an outcast like I'd been, someone to be despised and hated for what another person had done.

Then it hit me: the reason why Mum had refused to listen to what I'd told her about Simon, even though she must have known the truth. She'd wanted to fit in down the social club and with her gaggle of friends who she queued with every week at the Post Office. One of the gossips herself, she knew how dangerous it was to stray into the territory of people who stood out. As long as she buried the secret, she'd stay part of their circle – be one of them – and not have to confront the shifting net curtains, the accusing looks, the whispers.

Unlike Mandy.

Chapter 46
– Spring term. Year 10 –

I WOKE TO THE SMELL of synthetic and damp. As I opened my eyes, sunlight filtered through the cobwebby window and a million bits of dust danced in the air and floated onto the shelving unit and the rugby balls, poles and paint pots. It was still light, which meant Simon would be at the house, unless by some miracle I'd managed to sleep until tomorrow. I grimaced as my bladder twinged. This thing inside wouldn't let me sleep for more than a couple of hours at a time, so it must be today. I peeled my cheek from the plastic covered foam and eased myself around to get more comfortable. The skin under my eyes felt puffy and sore from all the crying. It hurt to keep them open so I let them flicker shut and, fighting the urge to go to the toilet, I drifted back to sleep.

Simon's hands were on my face, pressing down on my nose and mouth. Smothering me. I want you and it dead, he told me. The flashes of yellow in his eyes glowed and his pupils became cone-shaped, while his blackened fingernails transformed into claws which shimmered in the sun. He ran one claw down my face, slowly as if caressing me. As the blood trickled down my cheek, I saw him turn to my stomach. He grinned. He was going to steal my baby. I knew it. I had to stop him.

"No…." I bent double in agony from where I'd tried to sit up too fast. The plastic material creaked as I lay back down, clutching my stomach. I kept my eyes open. No way would I slide back into that dream.

A beam of light cut through the gloom. Not the daylight of earlier, but – shit – floodlights. I could make out voices, men calling to each other and the slam of car doors. With difficulty, I rolled off the foam rectangle onto the concrete floor and crawled to the door. Grit bit into my knees and the palms of my hands. Through the crack I could see a small group of men in shorts huddled by the huge H post and others pulling sports bags from cars. Headlights shone in the darkness and a car came into view, two beams turning my way. I pushed myself to my feet and stepped back, so I couldn't be seen. I had to get away. They might come in here soon. The headlights now faced the doors, shining on the shelves and the tins of paint. Paint!

The sound of the engine died and with it the headlights. Plunged into darkness, I stood there, breath held, while a man hoisted himself from his car. He pulled a bag from the rear seat and slammed the door. A beep, two flashes of orange and I was back in the dark and alone. Not for long, I knew that much. I went over to the shelf and lifted the tins, shaking them in turn to listen to the satisfying gurgle of paint. I chose the two heaviest. Inside I smiled. I had painting of my own to do.

When the car park had emptied, I slipped from the shed, heading away from the pavilion, even though it meant a much longer walk home. I ducked behind the cars until I was well into the shadows and I could stumble into the woodland bordering the pitches. My shoulders ached, the plastic handles bit into my hands and the tins banged my legs. Twigs crunched nearby. I paused, heart thumping and tried to hold my breath, but found I couldn't. Air broke through my teeth, through my nose, making me gasp. Goosebumps pricked my neck and I shivered, desperate to turn around but too scared to move. I'd been here before – not here – but in the dark, alone and afraid. The night after…

Bastard. Tears stung the corners of my eyes. If I'd never met him, I'd be warm in bed and Troy would be my friend, and Nina too, and Mrs Hamilton wouldn't hate me. Everyone hated me. Everyone.

A stick snapped and I ran. Not towards the fields and the rugby players – who might see me with the paint – but along the edge. Brambles tore my arms, ripped my dress, tried to slice the paint pots from my hands. But I couldn't let go. I needed them. Branches scratched my face, snagged my hair. I lifted my legs higher, and stomped through the woods, while the thing inside stabbed at me with every step. Even it hated me.

By the time I reached my front gate, dried blood crusted the scratches on my legs and my fingertips were swollen and numb from where the thin plastic handles of the paint pots had eaten into my skin. The house stood like a dark hulk, unlike nearby houses where light glowed through curtains or shone through nets. I could make out the back of Mr Wilson's head as he sat on his settee watching TV. He turned as Mrs Wilson walked in with that one-shoulder-higher-than-the-other walk she did and handed him something. A cup of tea? She looked my way, craning her neck as if she'd spotted me. I pulled the paint pots in front of me, into the shadows so she couldn't see them. Finally, the night had become my friend. I pushed the gate open with my foot and walked round to the back door. The pots clunked as I put them on the ground and rubbed life back into my sore hands.

"Mum," I called into the dark kitchen.

The house stank of fresh paint. A flash of anger hit me as I pictured *him* in my room. Did Mum really think that whenever I woke up or walked in, I would want to face the walls he'd painted? Well, I had the answer to that.

I flicked on the kitchen light. A ripped piece of paper leant against the kettle. *Gone to the pub with Simon and Mandy. Mum*. I swallowed down the ball of hurt and let the

271

note flutter to the floor where it landed on its back, displaying my school logo and the first line of a letter – Dear Parent.

School. The place I used to love but now couldn't bear. Thanks to him.

"I hate you!" I screamed

I grabbed the paint pots from outside the back door and raced upstairs. My bedroom had become a show room with a new duvet cover to match the baby pink walls. Since when had I liked pink? That was Mandy. I dropped to my knees and tried to push my fingers under the lid of the paint pot. Impossible. I tried the other pot. Then I raced downstairs to grab a knife, ignoring the jab, jab of the thing under my ribs.

Back in the room, the lid came off with a satisfying clomp. I gazed at the deep purple and breathed in the fumes. The other lid opened to reveal a pillar-box red skin which I popped with the knife. Liquid glowed halfway down the tin. My room would be Mosston RFU colours. Except I didn't have a brush. I lifted the red pot up. The paint slurped around the edges. I grinned and shivered with fear and excitement. I could do this. I would do this.

I tipped the tin at an angle. A small puddle of crimson plopped to the carpet, the shape of smiling lips. I flicked the tin towards the wall, where it splattered like a child's painting. Three lines of red raced down reminding me of the drips of bleach falling from Simon's clothes. Except this time I was adding colour. I shook the last of the red onto the duvet and picked up the purple. Unused and full, my muscles ached as I lifted it. At first, I could only manage small throws, with most of the contents glugging onto the carpet or my trainers but, after a while, the paint splashed the wall, the windowsill, even the back wall behind the bed. Thick beads dripped onto the skirting board, rolling into the edge of the carpet. I upended the tin on the floor and sat down on the bed, the wetness soaking into my skirt.

Outside someone laughed and something clattered.

"Shush!" A whisper so loud I could hear it.

Another giggle. The key turned in the lock and the front door opened. My bedroom door creaked in the draught. I gazed at the wall, at my handiwork and shivered. A bubble of paint glimmered on my thigh. I brushed it away but it smeared crimson, bright against the dried blood. The stairs creaked. My hands trembled.

"Mum! Mum! MUM!"

Footsteps hammered up the stairs.

"What the fuck?"

"I told you she was mental."

"What the fuck have you done?"

Mum's face burrowed into mine, her angry eyes cut in half by her eyelids. Thick lines creased her forehead. She grasped my shoulders and shook me. I let her.

"Cindy."

A palm flashed, stinging my cheek. I gasped and clutched the side of my face – protecting myself from her hand that wavered outstretched, ready to strike again – my tongue tasted blood.

Then I saw *him*, standing behind Mandy at the door. *Him*. Here. In my room. I could smell him. The stink of his aftershave above the paint.

"Get him out of here," I screeched.

The knife glinted on the floor, tipped red. I grabbed it, pushed past Mum.

"Get him out!"

Warily, Mandy stepped back, into him. Her eyes flicked from me to Mum.

"You should go," Mum said as I took another step

273

towards them. "I'll sort this."

She grabbed my wrist. I spun around, twisted my arm to shake her free.

"No, you don't, madam." She gritted her teeth and, using her other hand, tore the knife from my fist. "I don't know what the hell is going on, but no way are you getting away with this."

"You brought *him* into my room, when I told you. *I told you*…."

"And that's another thing. You can stop this right now. He's your sister's boyfriend. Not yours. I don't know what your sister's done to deserve you spreading muck like that."

From the hallway, Mandy whined, "She's jealous, Mum. She was always after him."

Mum jerked her head towards my belly and pressed her lips together. "But it stops here and now. You're a kid. He's a grown man. And he's with Mandy."

She stepped towards the door. "How you and the baby are going to squeeze in this room is beyond me. But there's no way Mandy can move in now. I can't speak to you. I'm too angry."

She gazed at the streak of paint on her palm, turned to look at the walls and shook her head. Her hands shook, like mine.

"But I can tell you one thing, you owe me for the paint and her for a duvet cover."

Chapter 47
- mid December -

I WILLED MANDY TO LOOK UP, but instead she gazed into the mug which trembled in her cupped hands. Outside the sky had turned a luminous pink behind mottled grey clouds. Inside the room was tinged grey. I checked the time on my mobile phone. I'd told the children I wouldn't be long, but an hour later here we were still in Mum's lounge, digging deeper trenches, unable to find common ground, even over Ella.

"Seriously? You can't hide it forever," I said, shocked by Mandy's insistence Ella shouldn't find out who I was. "She'll see her birth certificate one day."

"It's not the right time." Mandy shrugged. "She's just about to find out Simon is a paedo. She doesn't need to know…" She cleared her throat. "Well, you know."

We sat in silence. Mandy lifted her head towards the window. She sniffed and dabbed her nose with her sleeve. Her eyes glittered with unshed tears. I bent to pick at my fingernails. Ella would be left to find the truth from a piece of paper or gossip on the street. Was Mandy so naïve to believe she could keep it secret for much longer? Poor Ella. How would I have felt if someone in the street had come up to my teenage self and told me my mum was someone else? Delighted. But Ella wasn't me.

Mandy interrupted my thoughts. "I didn't lie to her. She knows I'm not her real Mum. She's just never asked who is. She's happy."

She burrowed deeper into the armchair, withdrawing further into 'Poor-me-ville'. I wanted her to leave. I'd had enough of going backwards and forwards and getting nowhere. But then I remembered our earlier conversation. She wasn't just hiding Ella's parentage but the weapon that would nail Simon's guilt. My fury spiked.

"I can't believe you hid it."

"It's alright for you," she said. "You didn't see what's on there."

After everything, she still protected him. I shook my head, more to myself than her, unable to believe she'd left the laptop with a friend. If she really didn't want that piece of filth in her house, the police had given her the perfect opportunity to rid herself of him.

"I didn't know they were coming round," she whined.

"But they did, and you didn't tell them."

"Give me a day to get my mind straight." Her finger circled the rim of her mug. "I need to prepare Ella."

A day? Simon might be out before then. Just like Mum all those years ago, she was putting herself first. I opened my mouth to argue but found I had no words. Was she so wrong in wanting to protect Ella from the bullies by keeping quiet about the laptop, while I – her mother – would gift her to them? The laptop would disappear, I was sure of it. I should warn the police. In the armchair, Mandy sniffed loudly and swallowed. She swiped a tear from her cheek. No, I wouldn't call them and get her into trouble. But neither would I take any more of her excuses. I jumped up and headed towards the hallway. Behind me, the armchair creaked. Good, she'd taken the hint.

When I opened the front door, she turned to me. "You go on and on about me doing right. But what about you? You haven't been to see Mum. Not once. She knows you're here."

She didn't wait for a response but wrapped her arms around her coat and stomped off, head bent into the wind.

The front door clicked shut to the sound of the gate scraping on the footpath. My breath hissed like a deflating balloon. Finally, she'd gone. Through the panes in the door, the headlights from a passing car flickered across the wall and into the kitchen. I fancied I saw Mum standing by the kettle and caught a whiff of her cigarette smoke. She didn't smile, but pointed a shaking, crooked finger at me. *You.* Her voice, sharp but frail, made me wince. *After all I've done for you.* I tried to banish her scowl, remember her smile, but nothing came. Of course, it wouldn't, not when I'd buried the good memories – there must have been some – beneath a mound of anger. Numb, hollow, after the day's events, I needed to feel again, to be with my children, to cuddle them and tell them how much they were loved. To make sure they remembered that.

Dusk had turned everything in Marion's garden to grey, except for the white lights that twinkled through the branches of the tree Ralph had decorated with the children. Had he taken them out to buy some more decorations and given them something to do while I dealt with yet another problem? Every time something happened it was left to him or Marion to look after Charlie and Lily. This couldn't go on. I couldn't keep imposing on Troy and his family.

I shouted "Hello" through the kitchen door to let them know I was coming in. The kitchen smelled of cooked meat. Stew, I guessed. My stomach rumbled. Heat from the chuntering oven wafted over my legs. I bent to look at the ceramic pot on the gleaming rack, glancing up as the lounge door creaked. Troy stood there, one side of his face illuminated by the glow of the Christmas tree. He smiled and beckoned me into the lounge. Like a scene from a 1950's Christmas, the twins lay on the floor in front of the fire, coaxing trains around the wooden track, watched from the settee by Marion and Ralph. Marion had been reading or so I guessed by the book she'd placed beside her. A bookmark stuck from its centre, while on top lay her glasses. When I'd left earlier, the coffee table had been empty but for a centrepiece bowl of nuts. Now two empty glasses, a plate of crumbs, a teapot, four cups and assorted children's bits and pieces had been added.

"I'm sorry for dragging you into all of this," I said to Marion and Ralph.

"Don't be silly," Marion murmured.

I dropped to my knees beside the children, kissing Lily on the cheek and ruffling Charlie's hair.

"You said a minute," Lily said.

"Troy said she couldn't count," Charlie told her.

Grinning, Troy plumped the armchair cushion and sat down. "Well remembered."

Lily shifted closer and rested her head on my thigh, while Charlie made 'choo-choo' noises and chattered away, sometimes lifting an engine to tell me a story about it crashing or going out to rescue trapped passengers. I listened and caressed Lily's warm scalp. Her eyelashes fluttered shut and the corners of her lips lifted. Behind Marion, Ralph and Troy murmured. The Christmas tree lights blurred, each dazzling like the Star of Bethlehem, and above a golden angel looked down, her silky wings spread wide as if she was protecting us. This place was heaven.

Ralph's laughter drew me back. In one hand he held the kernel of a nut in his palm which he offered to Marion, in the other a nutcracker. Fragments of shell chinked as he dropped them onto the empty plate and reached for another nut. Troy caught my eye and smiled. As I smiled back, sadness filled me. Not long now until Troy left. One happy Christmas and then the children and I would be on our own again. I'd been kidding myself if I thought this was anything but a temporary stop. A respite of sorts. The men who killed Jez would be looking for us, especially if they'd worked out I'd taken Jez's car. But it wasn't just the car that linked me to him. I still had the tin, tucked at the back of Mum's wardrobe, along with the money and the notebook Jez had stolen from them, the one with contacts, amounts and dates. I shivered. I should get rid of it. Carefully this time. Not like the drugs. If only I'd tipped them down the toilet rather than stashing them in the boot of Jez's car to be found by the police.

A chill crept up on me. The man at the police station. The jigsaw piece slotted into place and the chill turned to ice. One of Mick's cronies. In the early days he'd come to my house with Jez a few times. What was he doing here in Mosston? I entwined a strand of hair around my finger. His puzzled look must have meant he hadn't recognised me, but how long would it be before he did? His gang were dangerous, even more than Simon. They wouldn't think twice about harming the children. After all, they'd set fire to the house in which the children and I slept.

Now the tree lights blurred for all the wrong reasons. I wiped a silent tear from my cheek. Mosston wasn't big enough to hide in. We had to leave or risk being found. Our Christmas would be like all others. Alone.

Chapter 48
– early May. Year 10 –

THE BABY'S FINGERS CURLED around mine. So cute. I ran my other finger down her cheek, over the soft hairs. A white cream coated the creases of her skin and matted in her scalp. My baby. All around me were mums sitting in beds, dads and families gazing wide-eyed at little bundles tucked inside see-through cribs. The woman opposite could start a florist shop on her bedside table. A baby boy according to the helium star that floated above. I wanted a pink balloon. Fat chance of that. The man who'd been sitting at the edge of her bed picked up the baby and nestled it into his arms. He wandered about, rocking and shushing it even though it looked asleep to me. I hoped for the baby's sake he was the granddad, especially with those thick glasses and his fashion sense. A striped sleeveless jumper over a checked shirt? But I mustn't think like that. I was no longer a girl who judged people by their clothing, but a mum.

Baby let go of my finger, so I shuffled back up the bed and dropped onto the pillows. The curtain around next door's bed bulged like a pregnant woman's belly, the effect ruined by the backs of shiny black shoes which stuck out at the bottom.

"Well done, Mum," the nurse said. "That's much better."

A hand shot through the side of the curtain, followed by a plump body. The nurse grinned at me and I couldn't help but smile back even though I knew it might lead to the breastfeeding lecture. No way. From what I'd heard, it sounded like a right palaver. Painful too according to the woman with the cracked nipples opposite. This time the nurse didn't come over but headed off, her bum swaying from side-to-side as if she danced.

The tap-tap of stiletto heels echoed from the corridor outside. I knew that sound. I leant over to pull the cot closer, blocking the chair beside the bed.

"Nah, you're okay," Mum said to the nurse as they crossed by the door. "We've bin before."

Her voice sounded so different to everyone else here. As if grit from all the fags she smoked had stuck to her vocal chords. Mandy clomped behind her holding a carrier bag, her greedy eyes on my baby. They reached my bedside. Mum smelt of perfume and stale fags, while Mandy stank like she'd stopped at the chippie on the way here. I studied her hands. Her fingers shone with grease and tell-tale hand-wipe marks streaked the thighs of her jeans.

"Oh coochee-coo." Mum tickled baby's chin. "How's my little grand-daughter then? Did you miss me? Did ya, did ya?"

She burrowed her hands under the blanket and hoisted my baby up. Mirroring the man opposite, except she was in leggings and a denim jacket, she walked around the bed bouncing my baby. A wail, a little arm shot out and baby's fist opened and closed, grasping for my finger. I shifted forward, ready. My baby wanted me, not her. Mum tucked baby's arm under a corner of the blanket, swaddling her like the nurses had shown me.

"I think you're hungry. Aren't ya, aren't ya?"

"She's just had a bottle," I said.

"Bet you're hungry. Oh." Mum's nose crinkled. "I think she needs changing. Didn't you notice?"

"She was fine a minute ago."

"I'll do it." She sighed like she was hard done by.

I ignored Mum and left her to huff as she dragged a

nappy from the packet and baby wipes from the top. Instead I let myself be drawn to the laughter which spilled from across the ward. The man grinned and dabbed his face with a towel while his wife – daughter? – smiled and pushed him to one side to take over the nappy change.

"For goodness sake, Cindy. Why isn't she wearing those mittens I got you? Look she's scratched her face."

Mum clipped the final popper on the baby-gro and lifted my baby to kiss her cheek.

"Just wait until you get home," she cooed. "I'm going to show you off to everyone. I nearly forgot. Mand give Cindy the bag."

The bag landed on my lap. I pulled out a pink envelope, then a bib with the price tag in place. £1.75. A posh one. I held it up. No clues needed as to who'd bought it.

"I love my Granny," I said.

"Cos she does." Mum kissed baby's cheek.

I ripped open the envelope and pulled out the card.

"It came through the door. Don't know who it's from." Mum shuffled closer to peer inside the card.

'A baby girl', it proclaimed, above a picture of two teeny feet. The message inside read 'May her life be filled with love' and below was scrawled, 'To Cindy. Congratulations. From Troy.' No love, no kisses, just five words. What did I expect? We'd not spoken since he rushed off the day Mandy had told him I was pregnant. The last time I saw him – a fortnight ago – I'd stepped out from the back door as he opened his. For a brief moment, our eyes met and our cheeks reddened. But while I'd pretended to drop the key so I had to bend and pick it up, his door had banged shut. He hadn't walked down the path. He'd gone back inside rather than face me.

"Are you sure he's not the father?" Mum said.

Mandy sniggered and her cheeks bulged so her piggy eyes became slits.

"You *know* who the father is," I said.

I stared at Mandy who turned away. Yes, she knew.

Chapter 49
- mid December -

MANDY TRAIPSED AHEAD, talking without the need for a response. It was as if she'd told this story to numerous hospital visitors over the past months, even timing the words so she could speak and pant while she climbed the stairs to the first floor. How Mum used to look after Ella at weekends until she had her first small stroke, how life had changed for all of them since the second stroke – she left me hanging at this point while she pulled a door open to let a porter push an empty wheelchair through – when she'd found Mum lying on her bedroom floor unable to move.

"It was awful. I thought she was dead."

For the first time since we arrived, she stopped speaking and we took the next steps in silence. Until she swung around.

"I forgot. I think a man was asking about you. Not that I knew it was you at first. He called you Kerry or Kalis or something odd like that."

"What?"

"While I was waiting for you outside Marion's house earlier. He had a clipboard, but he didn't look like no salesperson to me."

"What did you say?"

"He said Hamilton, so I thought he'd got Marion's name confused. But then he said you were also known as Cynthia." She chuckled and shook her head. "*Cynthia.*"

I grabbed the arm of her jacket, forcing her to stop. "Look, it's important. Did you tell him about me?"

Bewildered, she looked down to where I gripped her sleeve. "No, course not. Anyhow, it was only later I realised he might have been meaning you." She patted my arm and I let go. "If this is about Simon, don't worry. I'll still do what I said."

She turned into the ward. Hadn't she heard my footsteps falter as my trembling legs refused to go on? But, no, she disappeared through the open double doors, leaving me standing beside a vending machine stacked with bottles of coloured water and fruit juice cartons. I pressed my forehead against the cool glass, the light filtering through my closed eyes. Mandy's words from moments earlier smashed into me again, wreaking a tsunami of fear. Jez's old gang had found me. I had to get away. I should be packing right now, moving the children to safety. But where was safe?

Blood red bottles blurred through the glass. A chill ran down my spine. I pushed myself from the vending machine, glanced up and down the corridor. I shouldn't be here. I needed to get back. Now.

Mandy came back out of the double door, confused to see me standing there.

"Come on." She waved me inside.

As I hesitated, her frown softened and she came over to link her arm through mine. "Don't worry. She's much better now. I mean, she still can't speak properly but you can tell she likes visitors. She'd *love* to see you."

She led me through a corridor that reminded me of school with the navy line painted the length of the wall and the waft of old food smells. My legs ached to turn around and I cursed Mandy's cheery voice. "Do you remember when…?" How long would she go on until she noticed that she was the only one in the conversation? We passed a squat, artificial Christmas tree, dressed with a few strands of tinsel and a lop-sided angel. I needed to get the children's presents. A square metal trolley clattered by, pushed along by a balding, thick-sct man. Just like the man who'd watched me at the police station.

He smiled. "Afternoon," he said, in a cheery voice.

I needed to get home. Back to the children.

"They're still having lunch," I said. "Perhaps we should come back another time?"

"They're alright in this ward," Mandy said. "Nowhere near as strict as the last one she was in. They're moving her again soon. To this place that's like a care home. I would look after her but…"

She paused as if she wanted to tell me something, but then she sighed. Her shoulders slumped and her hands dropped to her thighs. Even though my instincts told me to leave, my legs followed her into a small ward, just like the one I'd been in after I'd had Ella, except here there were no flowers. Slack skin clung to the skeleton of a woman who slept below a 'Nil by mouth' sign, lips parted to reveal gums the colour of veal, while opposite her an elderly lady hunched over her bedside table eating what appeared to be crumble and custard. Mandy headed towards the two beds by the window, one hidden behind a curtain. At the other, a visitor sat so she obscured all but the grey hair of an elderly patient. Breath held, nerves over-riding my earlier agitation, I walked towards where Mum must be tucked behind the curtain.

"Hello Mum. Look who I've brought," Mandy said in a too-loud voice.

I spun around to find Mandy at the other bed, standing beside the woman in the chair who was using a spoon to wipe food from the lips of…

No! Not Mum. Impossible. The frail thing in the bed couldn't be. Fifty-somethings didn't have lips that sagged and glistened with saliva or eyes that were murky pools of nothingness. No spark of recognition where there'd once been life, anger, vigour. The last time I'd seen Mum, her eyes had flashed as she'd snarled. *Get out!* My hand shot to my mouth, clamping the hiss of shock. It *was* her. But strokes didn't turn hair grey. Her hair colour became black by her ears, as if she'd leaned back to dip her hair in dye and missed the top section. She must have gone grey years ago.

"Mum, this is Cindy. You know, Cindy. Your daughter." Mandy spoke as if Mum was a child.

The eyes widened and a lump of custard spilled from her mouth. I had to blink back my tears, bite my lip to stifle a sob. Now I knew why they called it the past. It was over.

"...nee," Mum said, or what sounded like it.

Her fingers clawed the bedcover. "...nee," she repeated.

She looked at me – really looked at me – and a tear rolled down her cheek. I knew we both remembered. And we were both sorry.

Chapter 50
– May. Year 10 –

THE RAT-TAT, RAT-TAT OF MUM'S FINGERNAILS on the wall counted the seconds. A reminder she stood at the doorway to my bedroom, waiting for an answer, even though her gaze stayed on Ella asleep in her Moses basket. The one thing we had in common. All day I could sit on my bed watching Ella's tiny chest go up and down, see her pucker her lips, spot each cute yawn. I didn't want to miss a thing. Mum sighed. I ignored her. The crusted paint on the carpet scratched my feet, but I carried on picking at it with my toenail, in sync with her tapping. Rat-tat, pick, rat-tat, pick. It took my mind off her. A crumb of red broke away. I pushed it to one side. At this rate I'd clear the room.

"Well?" she said.

"What?"

She huffed like Mandy did. From the corner of my eye, I could make out her arms folding, her leaning against the wall. She'd sit this out. Stay there forever until she got her way. I couldn't let her win.

"No," I said, when the tension got unbearable. "She's mine."

"I'm not taking her from you," she said. "But she can't stay in here."

She looked from the red and purple splattered walls to the carpet. Her lips pressed into a line.

I crossed my arms, copying her. "I'll get my own place then. And what would Bill say?"

Hand raised as if to slap me she leapt forward. Her eyes blazed. "For fuck's…"

Too late, her hand flew to her mouth. Ella jerked away

to restart the non-stop wah-wah-wah she'd spent most of the night doing.

Mum bent to take Ella from the cot, but I snatched my daughter into my arms and hugged her to my chest. With each wail her body tensed and a knife twisted through my heart. Mum held out her hands. *Give her to me.* I rocked my daughter – hush, hush – kept my focus on her and not the fingers which itched to steal her. When she quietened, Mum started again, this time with a dramatic whisper.

"You'll do no such thing. Besides, you're too young." She pointed at me. "We'll talk later. When you're in a better mood."

She stomped from my room. "And make sure you feed her properly this time. I'll sort the bottle."

"No need," I shouted as she clomped down the stairs.

Her voice filtered through the kitchen ceiling followed by Mandy's drone. I reached across to the windowsill where I'd left the bottle from which Ella had been drinking thirty minutes earlier. She clamped onto the teat and sucked greedily. Phew.

Ella's eyelids had fluttered shut and she was mouthing the bottle when footsteps broke through my daydream. Mum came into the room holding a full bottle. She frowned and shook her head.

"I told you I didn't need one," I said.

"You stupid cow." She snatched the bottle from Ella's lips and threw it on the bed. "You can't give her old milk. You'll make her sick. Is that what you want?"

"Course not."

She dragged Ella from my arms, firing me an angry look as Ella began to cry.

"You poor thing," she cooed. "Was Mummy silly? Well Granny's here now."

Without asking, she took Ella away.

"I didn't know," I called. But she didn't hear. The stairs creaked followed by the burst of TV and the thump of the lounge door being closed.

"I didn't know," I muttered to myself.

The ache. It felt as if Mum had wrenched Ella from inside me. In the cot her blanket humped over an invisible body, the sheet still warm. I dragged it out, put it to my face, breathed in her smell. She'd be cold without it.

I found myself standing at the top of the landing, clutching the woolly material. I had to fetch my daughter back. Somehow. Make sure she was warm. Three steps down a knock at the door startled me. A shape moved through the patterned glass. It coughed. *Him.* It couldn't be. Mandy came out of the lounge door, a smile plastered on her face. She reached out to unlock the door.

"No!"

She flew around, surprised to see me taking the stairs, two at a time. I had to stop her. No way. *No way* was that bastard getting near my daughter. She twisted the doorknob. It clicked. Palms outstretched, I slammed into the door. The pane shuddered. He leapt back. I could make out the white of his shirt, the blue of his jeans. His disgusting body.

"Go away!" I shouted at him, as Mandy clawed my shoulder.

Through the bubbled glass, his head shifted and a flame flashed. He lifted something – the orange glow of a cigarette – to his face and stood there. He was enjoying this.

I swung back to her. "He doesn't come here. No way."

"Piss off, mental."

Mandy gritted her teeth. Tried to wedge herself between me and the door. I pressed my arms against either side of the wall and clung on, battered this way and that. No way would she win. No way. Mum came through the lounge door, cuddling Ella. Both were blurred. I was crying. I hadn't realised. Even though my chest hurt.

"Please." I sobbed. "Please."

"Mandy!" Mum's voice was sharp. "Leave it."

◆

Later, Mum came into the lounge, where I sat watching TV with Ella asleep in my arms. She stank of stale ciggies from where she'd been holed up in the kitchen, the new smoking area. Without taking her gaze from Ella, she sat down beside me. I shifted along and tucked myself into the corner with my elbow on the arm of the settee, so she couldn't get closer. Pointless really. By the time the programme finished, Ella would be cuddled up with her.

"I've told Mandy he won't be coming in the house," she said. "We're a family. We look out for each other."

I looked into her eyes to see if she was for real. She smiled and nodded. A warm feeling spread through me. Now she'd seen how upset I was, it must have made her realise what I'd been saying about Simon was true. My mum believed me. At last.

"Thanks."

Ella yawned and arched her back and stretched out two mittened hands. The dark eyelashes flickered and her lips smacked together, as if she dreamed of sucking a bottle. Mum slid closer to caress her forehead.

"She's such a cutie," she said. "You must look out for her. Like I do for you."

I tensed, waiting for what would come next. The reason for her niceness.

"You can't keep her in that room all day. It isn't fair."

291

Mum bent to kiss Ella. Her hair hung like curtains covering Ella's face, leaving me to aim dagger stares at the back of her head. We were back to this. The niceness? A ploy. Worse. A lie. Her finger traced the outline of Ella's lips. I wished I could wipe the damp stain of betrayal from my baby's forehead. My baby. Not hers.

She smiled at Ella. "Your mummy needs to be going back to school. To get an education. Then she'll get a good job one day and you can have nice things."

School? How could I face that again? The sneers, the catcalls. Look who's got herself preggers, up the duff. Slag. Slut.

One of Ella's eyelids fluttered open. The corners of her mouth lifted. Wind, they said, but I didn't believe them. That was a definite smile. She knew who her Mummy was. She stiffened in my arms, her face reddened, then a squelching sound. Okay, wind.

"Not yet. I need more time with her." Mum hovered, her mouth parted as if she had something more to say. Why wouldn't she go away? "I've got to change her nappy."

"I'll do it," Mum said.

I shook my head and pulled the changing mat out from under the settee.

"You'll have to go back soon," Mum said. "School's important. You said as much yourself. I'll look after her for you. I'll even have her in my room on your school nights." She held her palm up, cutting me off before I could speak. "Just school nights. She'll be yours the rest of the time."

I ripped the tags from the side of the nappy, pleased to see the earlier noise was just wind. With a quick lift of the legs, I slotted the new nappy under her.

"At least this means you've got someone you trust looking after her."

292

Trust? Hah! Funny, coming from her. As I pulled on the legs of Ella's babygro, I spotted the faded pink of my old frying pan scar, now just the size of a leech. Thanks to her, *he'd* taken me to hospital. *He'd* become my friend because she hadn't been. Not that she'd listen if I told her. The frying pan was an accident she'd said, and the rest – the screaming, the slapping – she'd had to do, because I'd given her no choice. Being a mother wasn't easy. Apparently. I clipped the poppers together. It didn't make sense. If she found it difficult being a mum to me, why did she want to be with Ella? Even if I said yes to Ella moving in with Mum – which I wouldn't – surely Bill would have something to say about having Ella being in their room at night?

"What about Bill?"

"He's gone." Her knee clicked as she pushed herself up from the settee. She stood there, creating a shadow over us while she flicked bits of fluff from her arm.

"Think about it while I have a fag," she said.

I waited until the lounge door clicked shut and then I carried Ella over to the TV where Mum had left the remote control. No way would I think about what she said. I stabbed the sound button. Twenty eight, twenty nine, thirty – probably a bit loud – twenty eight. The news flashed in front of me – a woman holding her hand to her mouth as she wailed – and I found my own hand pressed against my lips. Bill had gone? Just like that. Where? Why? Was it to do with mum losing her money after the benefits people found out about him being back in work and living here? Did that mean… no, it couldn't. Surely not? Not even my mum would do that. Or would she?

Outside Mrs Hamilton hurried past, the skirt of her supermarket uniform peeking from under her coat. I shrank back into the curtain folds in case she spotted me, forgetting

293

she wouldn't be able to see through the nets into the darkened room. Mrs Hamilton worked, Nina's mum worked. But Mum? I pulled the blanket tighter around Ella, to protect her from the dread I felt. I'd be back at school within weeks. I knew it. And Ella would be looked after by Mum.

A win-win, Mum would say. Of course, she would. It meant she didn't have to get one of those shitty paid jobs she moaned about. Not while she had my daughter to look after.

Chapter 51
- mid December -

AFTER AN HOUR SPENT in Marion's cosy lounge, I'd all but forgotten the earlier shock of seeing Mum, but when I walked into the kitchen – Mum's kitchen – followed by Troy and the children, sadness overwhelmed me again. The frail creature in the hospital bed – not a creature, *Mum* – might never be well enough to come back home. Even if she did, I wouldn't be here for her. Before old wounds had time to heal, I'd be slicing them open. Cutting myself and my children loose. But I couldn't risk Jez's old gang members finding us. Instinctively, I rubbed my hand. If I hadn't agreed to their demands, spiral-shaped burns from the electric hob would have been the least of my worries.

"Drink anyone?" My voice shook. Tears pricked the corners of my eyes.

Troy's hand rested on my shoulder. 'I know', it said. He thought I cried for Mum. Little did he know that in a few hours I'd rip the children from the world which in six wonderful weeks they'd come to love and trust. If only there was another way.

"Tell you what," Troy said. "Why don't I get us a take-out from Ansons?"

"It doesn't open till six." Damn my wobbling voice. I stretched my lips into a smile and turned to the twins, who stood either side of Troy with mirror expressions of uncertainty.

"I could do with getting some last-minute bits before the shops close." He wrapped his arms around the children's shoulders. "They can come with me."

I didn't want him to go. I wanted to spend our final

evening together. To pretend we were a family with a future. But, thanks to my past, staying here would put the children and Troy in danger. When the children's father, Steve, hadn't settled his debt, Mick had imprisoned me with promises of what would happen to my children. Lily and Charlie were the only people I had never run from, but I would run because of them. I loved Troy too, but doing so meant I had to leave him. I had no choice. If Mick discovered us, we would become the chinks in Troy's armour. Troy would want to protect us and Mick would take advantage of his chivalry. Richer pickings could be gained from him than me. That's if, after what I'd done, Mick would let me live.

"You're shattered," Troy continued. "Have a bath, clear your head and we'll have a nice night in."

A few hours alone would give me the chance to pack while I worked out how we could leave without being seen. I hugged the children and let him shepherd them back outside, where they stood silhouetted against the brilliant peach and grey sunset.

"Go inside, keep warm." Troy bent to kiss my cheek. His warm breath puffed against my skin. "Come on, guys."

I couldn't speak, couldn't smile, in case the tears broke free. The door clicked shut, muffling the children's excited chatter. I twisted the key in the lock and turned away. Troy would be out preparing for a real family Christmas, while I betrayed his kindness. But I had to.

Or did I?

In the gloom of the hallway, the kitchen light glowed like a flame on the brass back of the letterbox. If I risked staying even a few days longer, I'd have to tape up the letterbox in case they tried to burn this house like they'd done to Jez's. A tremor jolted me. They'd hoped the children and I would die too. After all, I was a witness to what they'd done – not just to Jez – but to all the families they'd forced into debt. That's before the police even got started on their drug dealing activities. Much of it listed in the notebook upstairs.

The beam of a car's headlights brightened the hallway. Troy and the children leaving, I guessed. It would be at least two hours until they returned, which gave me time to pack, just in case we had to leave. What was I thinking? We couldn't stay – not when that man had been asking questions about me outside this house. I hooked my coat over the stair post, wrenched my boots off and padded up the stairs into the dark landing. At the top, I flicked on the light and blinking, headed towards my – Mum's – bedroom.

I pressed the bedroom light switch. Nothing. Not even a pop as the bulb went. Something or someone sniggered. Outside? I stood frozen in the spotlight glow from the landing and listened, but all I could hear was my heart thumping. Shapes began to form: the bed, the wardrobe with my dressing gown hanging from the handle, the bedside table. Light from the streetlamp filtered through the thin curtains and something glinted on the duvet. I grabbed the tin, shook it even though I knew it would be empty, and let it fall to the bed. It chinked against the light bulb. As I glanced up to the empty light fitting, goosebumps pricked my back. I wasn't alone.

I edged from the room and peered into the landing. My old bedroom door stood ajar, leaving a shadowy strip into which I couldn't see. A floorboard creaked. I swung around, straining to pierce the gloom of the room behind me. Nothing moved. Or nothing I could see. Frantically, I patted the pockets of my jeans. No use. I'd left my mobile in my coat pocket at the foot of the stairs. My heart hammered. Crushing each breath. I wasn't alone, I wasn't alone. But I'd never been more alone.

The only option was to make a run for it. Head for the stairs. Get out. I took a tentative step and then raced across the landing, screeching in shock as my old bedroom door flew open. The shimmer of his belt buckle, the whites of his eyes, his grin. I grasped the stair rail, flung myself down the stairs. His pounding footsteps matched mine. I reached for the front door handle, but he grabbed my shoulder and yanked me back. My head smashed against the corner. Pain fired through my jaw. He pinned me by his elbow to the wall and something flashed in his hand.

"No, you don't," he hissed.

His breath stank of rancid milk, while his eyes gleamed above the dark forest of his jaw. He pressed his body into mine. I could feel him. His heat, his disgusting smell. I lifted my knee into his thigh, forcing space between us, eased my elbows into his chest to lever him away.

"You've got to tell them." He grunted and dug his elbow between mine, driving them apart. "Tell them you lied."

"How did you get in?"

"Tell them, Cindy. Or else."

His arm pressed my throat. Saliva flecked his gritted teeth. I could go along with him, pretend I'd do as he said, but I couldn't betray my childhood self. No way. He had to pay. And I'd make sure he did.

"It's too late. Mandy's giving them your laptop. She'll be there now."

"She wouldn't."

His teeth bit his lower lip, turning it white. The pressure of his arm intensified. I gasped for the air that taunted my tongue. Harder he pressed. Harder. Crushing my windpipe like a straw. My eyes filled my sockets, about to burst. This was it. I'd die here. Now.

"You're a liar," he hissed. He whipped his arm away.

Between coughs I sucked in mouthfuls of air.

"What you said … to the police. … Bitch."

A white-hot pain ripped through me. My leg. What the fuck had he done? Was that me screaming?

He clamped his hand across my mouth, bashed my head into the wall. Shards of agony continued to fire through my legs, my groin. My glistening tears made his teeth sparkle, the gold flecks in his eyes glitter. He brought a blood-tipped knife to my face.

"Just one little prick hurt, did it? You'll know real pain soon."

I should have lied. Said I'd tell the police anything. Now I wouldn't see my children again.

"You bitch. You've wrecked my life. Taken everything."

I had to say something. Stop him. I tried to open my mouth, but the words wouldn't come. Speak, Cindy, speak. Think of something.

Behind his head a shadow shifted at the door. My heart leapt.

"Now you'll…"

I jammed my teeth over his fingers, catching a slice of skin.

"Troy!" I shouted. "Tr…".

His fist smashed me to silence. I couldn't breathe. A warm trickle ran from my nose to my lips. The metallic taste of blood. My mind blurred, my eyes closed. I longed to drift away. To stop the pain. From the back door came the tinkle of glass, the click of a key turning and the creak of the door. Troy was here to save me. I must stay awake. I couldn't let him fight alone.

"What the…?" Simon muttered and loosened his grip.

I waited, breath held. Footsteps crunched glass, tapped the floor. Hope turned to horror as the figures of not one, but two men, moved into the hallway. The kitchen light reflected on a bald head.

"*Karis*. Long time, no see."

Chapter 52
– September. Year 11 –

I'D SLOWED MY WALK almost to a stop as I reached my street, but it wasn't enough. Somehow, I seemed to be catching up with him. If I did, what would I say? I let my PE bag slip to the ground and pulled off my trainer to shake out an imaginary stone. He'd grown. His shoulders filled his blazer so it stretched across his back, while his trousers had fallen out with his shoes. White socks filled the gap. Yuk. He needed someone to tell him they'd gone out of fashion with the ark. I would have told him. That's what mates did for each other. He reached his gate and turned to me. The corners of his mouth twisted up and he shrugged and shuffled away.

For the first time since Ella was born, I wished I could turn back time. When was the last time someone had cuddled or joked with me? Okay, I got to hold Ella each night, but it wasn't the same. If only I could be with Troy, playing music and chatting about school. Or hanging around town, like Nina's crowd were right now, flirting with the boys. As my trainer blurred, I swiped my eyes with my arm and checked to see if anyone had been watching. The road stood silent, apart from the sound of birdsong and the distant hum of cars. I stifled a yawn. Maybe Mum would let me have a bath after I washed Ella. Relax before bed and, hopefully, get some sleep. Mr Anderson wondered why I wasn't paying attention in class. He should try listening after an hour's kip. Thank goodness for my secret shed, the one place I could hide out at lunchtimes or when school got too much.

I'd go there tomorrow, so I didn't have to face him and Maths. Just a few hours of luxury resting on the foam

301

cushions while I looked at pictures of Ella and imagined our new life together. Just me and her and no school, no bullying girls or Mum telling me what to do. I'd take some more stuff there tomorrow, ready so we could leave when I'd saved up enough. Thanks to the secret cupboard I'd found behind the shelving, I'd stashed quite a bit of stuff: photos, my birth certificate, even the ripped-up camcorder tape. I couldn't leave it behind, in case anyone found it and worked out what it once showed. I fingered the fifty pence in my pocket. With this I had over ten pounds saved too.

A stone caught the edge of my foot and skittered, hitting our gate post with a clank. I held my breath, ready for the wailing, and cringed. How stupid. Ella would have to have bionic hearing for that to wake her. I walked around the side to the back door, spotting the edge of a blanket on the grass. We'd done that in summer – sat on the grass, while Mum and I took it in turns to hold Ella – but back then it was hot. Mum had needed to fetch her Lambert & Butler umbrella to shade Ella.

"Nice day at school?" Mum sat in the garden. She smiled and pulled at the hem of her new dress. Mum in yellow? "I took Ella shopping and we found this in Oxfam. A right bargain."

She lifted Ella from where she lay on the blanket and sat her down on her lap, facing her outwards towards me. Goosebumps pricked Mum's arms, but Ella was snug in a knitted cardigan I hadn't seen before. A glistening trail cut across the dimple on her plump cheek, fed by the bubble of snot from her nose. She chuckled and her grey eyes sparkled. My daughter loved me. Even though I disappeared off to school each day, she knew who her Mummy was. I dropped to my knees on the rug and held out my arms to take her, but Mum left me kneeling there while she yawned – a long one which involved her squishing her eyes shut and stretching her mouth so far I could see the deep red of her throat. When she stopped, she blinked and smiled at me.

"Fetch the camera, love. We've been waiting to get a picture of us in our new garb."

Later, after I'd made Mum a cup of tea and she'd fed Ella, I sat in the lounge watching TV with my daughter snuggled in my arms, snuffling gently. As the sound on the TV dipped, the hairdryer blasted upstairs. Just a few minutes more peace before Mum came downstairs. Even though it meant I had to twist my neck to see the TV, I edged around on the settee and stretched my legs, so my feet pressed against the arm rest on the other side.

Mum came bouncing into the lounge a short while later, the ends of her hair still damp. She hovered beside the armchair.

"Mand not in?" she said.

I shook my head. Why she had to pretend, I didn't know. Did she think because I'd been tucked away upstairs changing Ella's nappy, I hadn't heard her telling Mandy to 'Have a nice time.'? When the front door had clicked, I'd gone through to Mum's room to watch through the nets as Mandy had got into *his* car. A conspiracy. Just don't tell Cindy.

Mum stood there, her gaze like a magnet, drawing Ella from me. I tucked my arm over Ella's warm little body and hugged her tighter. Her eyelashes fluttered and her mouth twitched. She knew I held her. She loved *me*.

Mum tapped my knee. "Budge up."

I gave her a bit of room, but kept my legs curled, so my feet created a buffer. It didn't work. It just meant Mum's thigh pressed my toes into the cushion when she leant over to stroke Ella's cheek

"I left hot water for you. Why don't you go for a bath?"

Earlier the adverts had shown a woman running creamy soap along her arms as she wallowed in steaming bath water. I'd have done anything then to lie in a bath of silk. Mum held out her hands so I would pass Ella to her.

"Nah, you're alright," I said.

♦

Mum poked her head around the door and blinked at the brightness of my bedroom light. She'd pulled on a pair of jeans, but her 'bed' t-shirt hung loose on one side where she hadn't tucked it in.

I rocked Ella in my arms. "Shush, shush."

I took the bottle from the windowsill and coaxed the teat into her open mouth, but she shook it away, screwing up her face to continue the incessant, hoarse 'wah-wah' that cut through me. Her face matched the purple and crimson bedroom walls. Again, I touched the teat to her lips, to her raw gums.

"Please, please drink," I whispered, although every bit of me screamed 'Please, please shut up'. What sort of Mummy was I to think like that? Perhaps she sensed my thoughts, felt my agitation and it upset her more.

Mum turned sideways to edge between the door and the cot. She gave me a look and put her hand to Ella's forehead.

"I thought the doctor said it was teething. Since when do teething babies wheeze like that?"

"That's what he told me."

"Didn't you tell him about her not feeding?"

"He said it was normal. All babies are like this when they're teething."

I didn't tell her how stupid he'd made me feel. The way

he'd sighed when I'd walked into his surgery this morning. What twice in two days? For teething? So what if she's got red cheeks, is grizzling and irritable. They're typical teething symptoms. Of course, babies don't like teething. It's painful. Blah-blah-blah. He'd talked slowly and used words a child would understand because that's what he thought I was. A girl playing at being a mum.

Mum went to take Ella from me, but I swung away. I had to do this. Not her. But if I did let her take Ella, the noise, the stress would go and I could slink into bed, close my eyes and drift away. But if Mum managed to calm her down and make her stop crying, I'd feel worse.

"Teething babies don't wheeze like that," Mum said. "Give her to me and go and call the doctor."

I shook my head. "He said…"

"Stuff what he said. If you won't phone him, I will."

♦

The white top of the drip needle jutted from Ella's hand, held in place by a criss-cross of tape. Poor little thing. I shifted my chair closer to the cot and pressed my face into the metal bars. They'd said I could pull the side down to touch her, but I couldn't. She might wake and cry again or, worse, scream like earlier when they'd stuck the needle in. A tear rolled down my cheek. It was my fault. They all blamed me – I could tell. I'd seen the looks on their faces when Mum had told them I wasn't going to call.

"Teething, my arse," Mum had said. "I knew it was something serious."

The short nurse had turned her back to clear a few bits and pieces from the side, but I thought I'd heard her tut and she'd definitely shaken her head as the movement rocked her ponytail. Later, when the doctor lifted up the x-ray, pointed to a milky patch and said it was pneumonia, they'd all looked at me. Not even winter and, somehow, I'd given my baby pneumonia. They didn't need to speak, their eyes had said everything.

The clip-clop from outside our side room grew louder, breaking into my thoughts. The door creaked open and a nurse smiled at me. Not the one from earlier. They must have changed shifts. She nodded towards the bed.

"Are you getting some sleep, Mum?"

I wiped my sleeve across my damp face and shook my head.

She came over and touched my shoulder. "She's a beautiful baby."

A lump grew in my throat. I tried to swallow, but I couldn't. Instead, I buried my head in my arm to hide my tears. What sort of Mum cries when they should be caring about their child? A bad one. I was selfish and bad. Thanks to me, my baby could have died. I couldn't breathe for crying. Sobs jerked my chest. At this rate I'd wake Ella. I had to get away. Blindly, I pushed myself backwards. The chair scraped the floor. Before I took another step, the nurse wrapped her arms around me, buried my head in her warm chest.

"Babies get ill for many reasons," she said, like she read my mind. "She's in good hands."

Not mine. I didn't choose to think that, but as soon as I did, I knew it was true.

By the time Mum came back, I'd finished the hot chocolate the nurse had brought in and my tears had dried. Mum staggered through the door with the two carrier bags from home for Ella and me. The bed opposite creaked as she sunk down and we faced each other through the bars of the cot – our eyes on Ella asleep between us, linked by tubes to the drip.

"Perhaps now is the time to think about it." Mum's gaze didn't leave me.

I stiffened. I knew what was coming but still I said, "What?"

"Your bedroom. It's too small. It's no good for her. She needs air. And the mildew—"

"Okay." She didn't need to say more. I knew.

"It's no good—"

"I said *okay*." I spoke through gritted teeth. "You don't need to go on. You win."

"It's not about winning, Cindy," she said. "It's about what's best for Ella."

She was right.

Chapter 53
- mid December -

JOHN. THAT WAS HIS NAME. I remembered now. One below Mick in the hierarchy. I knew the other guy too. Hadn't he come to my house in the early days, before Jez took me as his own? His lank hair still dripped to his shoulders. The same sovereign ring on his finger. The one I'd gazed at as his clawed hand had pinched my mouth into a circle of silence, shoved my head into the wall, pressed my fingers onto the cooker ring and turned the dial from one to four. Pay up, or else it'll be six. Lanky: the man who'd made me decide Jez was my future.

"He was outside earlier." Lanky pointed at Simon. "Reckoned he didn't know her."

Simon backed into me. He clutched the quivering knife handle to his chest, the tip angled towards the men. A bead of sweat ran down the side of his face. His leg pressed my thigh, firing shafts of pain in all directions. I eased him away, but he sprang back, pinning me to the wall.

The two men edged forward, their arms hanging like apes at their sides, fists curled. I had to do something now. Once they reached us it would be too late. Lit by the glow from the landing, my coat hung over the stair post, the pocket and my mobile phone more than an arm's length away. I twisted around, using my shoulder to lever myself free of Simon while his attention was on the men. A hissed 'No' gave me little warning before he grabbed my hair and the knife lay cold against my neck. His chest heaved against my mine. Stubble rasped my cheek and his panting breath soured the air.

"No point saving her, mate." John laughed. "Look after

yourself."

John stood the other side of the stair rail, palms outstretched in mock surrender. Simon hesitated, his fingers bunching my hair. He let go and stepped towards the door, his knife pointed at the men. He took his gaze from them for the briefest moment as he patted the door in search of the handle. Through the door pane light from the outside streetlamp reflected on his glistening brow. I looked from the men to him. Surely, they wouldn't let him go? Then it hit me. Mick wouldn't have sent just two men. There would be others outside, watching. They'd take Simon away, help him disappear – no witnesses – do to him what they planned for me. If he went outside, we were both dead. We had to stay and fight. As the door clicked open, I spotted the rolled-up orange book which poked from his jacket pocket.

"He's got the notebook." My throat hurt after he'd choked me, making my voice thick and muffled.

The men shrugged. So what? their expressions said.

I pointed to Simon's pocket. "The one Jez took from Mick. He's got it."

Would they leave him to the men outside and let them deal with it or…?

John leapt at Simon. In the half-light, I watched Simon's eyes widen and the colour drain from his face. The knife flashed, imprinting my vision with a silver blur. I swung around to my coat and, with trembling fingers, pulled the mobile phone from the pocket.

The door rattled and Simon screeched a half-wild, "Get off! He—" Cut off by an 'oof'.

While Lanky banged Simon's arm and the knife against the wall, I swept my finger across the phone screen. Blue light radiated. I gazed in despair at the password request – think, think! – then I saw the emergency call button. A shriek

309

pierced the air, quickly muted. One of them had been hurt but, not stopping to find out who, I pressed call and headed upstairs.

Spotting me, Lanky shouted, "Oi!".

A hand grabbed my ankle. As my chest smashed into the stairs, the mobile phone bounced free and thumped back down.

"Help!"

Wrenched backwards, each knock, each step, sent shards of agony through my leg. I snatched at the stair rail, but it slipped from my grasp. Again, I flung my arms out and managed to cling on. Lanky tugged my ankles, but I tightened my grip. The glossed wood squeaked, juddered against my arms. I was losing hold.

Charlie. Lily. I had to stay alive for them. *Ella.* I had to say sorry.

"No!"

I put all my strength into one vicious kick, knocking Lanky's hand from my ankle. A second boot to his knee. He staggered back into the wall but, before I could lift myself up, someone – John – grabbed the collar of my sweater, dragging me, choking, towards the door. My foot clipped something and I fell against John.

"Shit," he said. He signalled Lanky over. "Move him."

Below Simon lay in a pool of blackness – mouth open, eyes wide, the hilt of the knife sticking from his neck – blocking our exit.

"You've killed him! I can't believe you've killed him." I tried to wriggle from John's clutch.

I would be next.

Lanky muttered as he kicked Simon's arm away and stepped over his legs. His arms around me, John waited for Simon's body to be shifted from below us. As he stepped forward, the collar of my top loosened and I dived down to grab the knife. It didn't budge. I gritted my teeth, gripping it tighter. I would do this.

"No, you…" John grunted.

As he hefted me up, the knife shot free and I swung around, slashing his wrist. The wound opened like a smiling mouth and dark liquid oozed.

"Bitch!"

He threw me across the hallway, where I crashed into the wall and the knife clattered to the floor. Stunned, winded, I half-sat, half-lay there, gasping for just a moment before I snatched the knife away from Lanky's reach. Pointing the quivering blade at them, I edged backwards into the kitchen.

John's teeth gleamed. He moved closer into the brightness of the kitchen. The dark oil seeping through his fingers became crimson. Drip, drip, onto the floor. Join the dots and they would lead from Simon to me. Glass crunched under my feet and a draught brushed my neck. I glanced behind, hoping they'd left the back door open after they'd broken in, but it stood closed. A barrier. The air rushed through a jagged hole in the door pane.

I had to stay alive for Charlie, Lily, and Ella. I couldn't die. I wouldn't die.

"I would like to say we've got all we need." John lifted his hand from his wrist to pat his pocket. He'd taken back the notebook. "But we haven't."

Lanky stood by the front door. Blue streaked his face, along the hallway walls. As he opened the door a sliver, his eyes flickered sapphire. Outside a distant siren wailed and men shouted. He threw a panicked look at John. They both turned to me and John reached into his jacket. I had to get out. I sprinted to the back door. Behind, footsteps clattered. I wrenched the handle, but a hand grabbed my shoulder

311

flinging me back and I smashed into the worktop. Pain exploding through the back of my head to my teeth, my jaw. With its handle sticky from Simon's blood, the knife peeled from my fingers and slipped to the floor. As the back door burst open, a gust of ice slapped me. Black and white filled the room.

Angry voices. "Get down. Put it down."

My mouth filled with a metallic taste. I felt sick. Put what down? I wasn't holding anything.

Slowly I began to spin round and round. Yet I didn't move. Round and round, sinking deeper. I closed my eyes, let the warmth drift in.

♦

Above a man and a woman in green hovered. I grimaced and gritted my teeth against wave after wave of agony. I needed to go back to sleep, to the place without pain. A tear trickled down my cheek.

"You're safe." One of them said. "We're just taking you to the ambulance. You'll be right as rain soon."

Frosty air nipped my cheeks, the tang of diesel filled my nose. As the ambulance doors opened, Mandy appeared beside me, panting, her nose tipped red.

"I'm sorry," she said. "I did what I promised. Told them about the laptop but they'd already let him go."

"He's dead."

As she clamped her hand to her mouth, a sob broke through her fingers and she staggered back into someone's arms. Sorry, I wanted to say, but I couldn't. I let my eyelids flutter shut and welcomed the calm. The peace.

She faced her whole life ahead without Simon.

And so did I.

Chapter 54
– Christmas. Year 11 –

MANDY STROLLED INTO THE LOUNGE humming some strange tune. She smiled at Ella, who sat in her babywalker gazing at the Christmas tree lights from behind a barricade of upended chairs. Rewarded with a toothy chuckle, Mandy dropped to her knees and started tickling and 'coochie-cooing' Ella, until she noticed me tucked into the corner of the armchair and her smile became a snarl.

"Where's Mum?"

"We ran out of milk."

She glared at the window, where rain splattered against the pane. "And you couldn't go? Lazy cow."

I bent to pick at a jag of nail from my big toe and flicked it onto the carpet. When I looked up again, Mandy stood by the fireplace with Ella in her arms.

"Look." She picked up a Christmas card and let Ella hold it. "A card to Auntie Mandy from her friend Jessie."

When the card headed towards Ella's open mouth, Mandy snatched it away.

"And this one," she said, waving another one to distract Ella. "Is from Julie to your Grandma. And this..."

A khaki-covered figure ran past the window, bowed under the weight of rain. Perhaps I should have gone to fetch the milk like Mum asked, but then I wouldn't have been able to sit here alone with Ella and watch her eyes mirror the twinkle of the Christmas lights. We'd spent the past ten minutes giggling at her new trick, where she would knock her walker against the wooden chair so it tapped the glitter bauble which spun around and flashed a disco ball of splintered light. The shapes had raced across our faces and circled the room. When the bauble came to a stop, she'd bashed the walker against the chair and it had started again. That is, until a moment ago when she'd heard the stairs creak. Now, I had to listen to Mandy being her usual bitchy self. I itched to thump her, to tear the cards from her hands and screw them up, but I wouldn't upset Ella.

"But we can't find a single one for Cindy, can we?" Mandy cooed. "Is that because Cindy has no friends? Poor little Cindy."

Mandy gave me a spiteful smile and took Ella over to a Santa Claus decoration. "But Cindy doesn't like other people having friends. Oh no, she can't have other people being happy."

The silver and black of Mum's umbrella bobbed outside the window. Thank goodness. It gave me a break until tomorrow, the next day, or next week, when Mandy would be back to dig the needle in and restart the whining. I was to blame for her relationship going sour, even though I'd done nothing other than to get Simon barred from the house. I hid a smile behind a yawn. No point winding her up more.

"Simon and I were happy. Yes, we were. And Cindy wrecked it. Cos she's a sad cow. Yes, she is." Mandy stroked Ella's chin and wiped her finger on her jeans.

The front door clicked open, followed by what sounded like the umbrella clattering against the wall.

"Tipping it down out there," Mum shouted. "Anyone fancy a cuppa?"

Mandy stooped to put Ella back into the baby walker and tweaked her cheek.

"I'm off out now, with my friends. You take care being stuck alone with her." Mandy cooed to Ella and nodded in my direction. "She wrecked things for Mum and Bill. Then me and Simon. People around her end up alone. She makes sure of it."

Acting like I didn't care, I stuck out my tongue at the Michelin tyres of her back. But her dig about Mum and Bill hurt. That wasn't my fault.

"You off out now, Mand? Have a nice time," Mum said.

Moments later Mum came into the lounge. She swept damp strands of hair from her forehead and slumped onto the settee. "Put the kettle on, Cind."

With the remote control aimed at the TV, she switched it over to a children's programme.

"Come to Granny." She held her arms wide and flapped her hands at Ella, who grinned and trundled over. "Look, it's Teletubbies. Our favourite."

By the time I reached the lounge door, Mum had stretched herself along the settee, her arms wrapped around Ella, who lay with her thumb in mouth as if she'd been there for hours. Jealousy twisted inside me, its stranglehold fierce. I should have cuddled Ella while Mum was out shopping, instead of watching her play with the tree. No wonder my daughter preferred Mum to me. Didn't everyone? I glanced over to the Christmas cards. A few had my name scrawled, an afterthought after Mum, Mandy and Ella. Mandy was right. None were just to me. But what would they write? To weirdo Cindy. To Freak Girl. I shivered. If Mandy found out what they'd started calling me at school, my life would be hell.

♦

My fingers had crinkled from washing all the Christmas dishes. Just a few more to go. Beside me, Mandy dried a saucepan and chanted "Dah na na na na na na nahhhh, Freak Girl" under her breath to the Batman tune. Hardly

315

Christmassy. In my head I turned up the sound of Sleigh Bells Ring, imagining I could see Christmas scenes in the bubbles until one-by-one they disappeared in a sea of carrots and bits of stuffing. With the last of the pans balanced on the draining board, I pulled out the plug and wiped my soaking hands down my top, ignoring Mandy who gave me a final burst of "Freak Girl, Freak Girl!" as I walked off towards the lounge to join Mum and Ella.

Mum sat on the carpet, with Ella tucked in between her legs banging a cardboard box on the floor. I hesitated. Could I take Ella with me over to the settee or would she cry? Instead, I plonked myself on the floor in front of her.

"You're blocking the fire," Mum said.

I shuffled to the side of Mum's foot and picked up Ella's new telephone on wheels.

"Look, Ella." I rolled it up and down, so the bell dinged. She grinned and thumped the box harder.

Mum huffed. "Ella was looking at the tree. Now she can't see. What's wrong with sitting on the chair like normal people?"

I heaved myself onto the settee and bent down to pull the telephone along by the string. It jangled and Ella giggled.

"Look." I turned the dial and picking up the phone. "Mummy ring Ella."

"For goodness sake. Can't you give us a moment's peace?" Mum whacked my knee with the back of her hand. "I can't hear myself think."

I folded my arms and sat back into the settee. A moment later Mandy came in. Her knees clicked as she dropped to the floor beside Mum.

"What you playing?" she said in a low voice and picked up the telephone to hand it to Ella. When Ella banged it against the box lid, Mandy grinned. "A drum kit, eh?"

"I was thinking of taking her for a bath," I said.

Mum swung around to me, frowning. "Don't be stupid. She's just eaten."

She shook her head at Mandy, who lifted her eyes to the ceiling and tutted.

"Not this min…" I started to say, but I was cut off by Mum turning up the sound on the TV.

Later, when Mum and Mandy had disappeared upstairs, I snuck over to where Ella slept on the settee surrounded by cushions. Her cheeks glistened and a lump of something brown – chocolate? – stuck to her chin. Gently, I scraped it off. Her eyelashes fluttered open and she gazed ahead, unseeing, but then she reached out to be picked up. She smelt of sweat and excitement.

"Want a bath?" I said.

She gave a wide smile showing her two bottom teeth. "Mamma," she said.

I kissed her hot cheek and took her through to the bathroom where I sat her on the bathmat. The room stank of damp, so I left the door open. I turned on the taps and squirted her bath foam into the water. Behind me came a clump, clump sound.

"I can't leave you for one minute." I took the empty toilet roll centre from her mouth and popped it in the waste basket.

After I'd unclipped her babygro and taken off her heavy nappy, I checked the temperature of the bath water. Just right. I let her toes dangle in the water and she kicked in delight, flicking droplets my way. When she wouldn't bend her legs to sit – enjoying soaking me – I bribed her with the little duck that lived in the corner of the bath. She bashed it into the water and giggled, splashing us both. Again. This time harder. Spray splatted her face. She gasped and opened her mouth, ready to wail.

I turned to grab the towel but realised I'd forgotten it. The hand towel hung beside the toilet, stained white where Mandy had wiped toothpaste from her mouth so I used my sleeve to pat Ella's face dry, rewarded by a smile. She held the duck by its head and pulled it around. At first, I kept my hands behind her back, but she stayed upright without my help. Tiny goosebumps pricked her shoulders. I glanced at the dirty hand towel and back to Ella. She'd scream if I took her out now but soon she'd get cold and I couldn't get her out without a towel. The bathroom door stood open. It'd only take a minute to run upstairs to the airing cupboard. Ella chuckled and put 'duck' in her mouth.

"Mummy will be one minute," I said.

I raced upstairs, reaching the airing cupboard as Mum came out of her bedroom.

She yawned. "Fetch me a towel, love. I could do with a bath."

I tore the towels from the pile. When I turned back to hand hers over, I found she'd moved and now stood the other side of me, blocking my path. Slowly, she padded down each stair – if she went any slower, she'd stop – her hand on the rail, barring my way.

"Excuse," I said.

I spoke louder. "Excuse me."

She ignored me. I clenched my fists and gritted my teeth. If I told her about Ella, she'd move. But she'd be furious. Just two stairs more. That's all.

When she finally turned into the hallway, I squeezed between her and the wall. Too late. Ahead Mandy walked into the cloud of mist from the open bathroom door. I sprinted the last steps, desperate to get to Ella before she did. How could I have been so stupid? We reached the bathroom door together. Startled, I gazed at the bath. Ella had gone. Then I saw her chubby arms flailing beneath the water. Her grey eyes, wide open. The pale belly, heaving.

I leapt forward, but Mandy knocked into me and dragged her from the water. Ella's head flopped back, her arms hung over Mandy's hands. The room fell silent but for the ping-ping of water dripping from her little body. I'd killed her. Shit, I'd killed my daughter. Mandy swung her over her shoulder. I couldn't breathe. Mandy mouthed 'come on, come on' and patted Ella, staining her frail back with faint handprints. A moan. Please let it be Ella. A sob. It rose to a wail. The most beautiful sound. Mandy snatched the towel from my hands and wrapped it around Ella, joined by Mum who caressed Ella's crumpled, angry face.

"Sshh, sshh," she said.

As Ella's tears quietened, Mum stabbed her finger at me.

"You! You shouldn't be allowed to have a child. Get out and don't come back."

She lifted Ella from Mandy's arms and rocked her. My legs froze. Mum didn't mean it. She was angry. Ella's head fitted the curve of Mum's neck and her tiny fingers – moments earlier they'd scrabbled for life – clutched Mum's shirt. Mandy turned her back and huddled closer into them, as if protecting my own daughter from me. Of course, she would. If it wasn't for her, Ella would be dead.

Mum frowned. "You're still here?"

I legged it out, grabbed my coat and shoes. As the front door slammed behind me, a chill slapped my face. Where could I go? I dropped to sit on the step. The frost bit through my trousers. I brushed the wetness from my cheeks and shoved my hands into my pockets, pulling my coat tight. If I said sorry... But what good would that do? Thanks to me

Ella had pneumonia in summer and nearly died on Christmas Day. Talk about a crap Mum. Whatever I did, I hurt her. How much longer would it be until I did something stupid again? Next time, there might not be anyone around to save her.

I should get away. Far away.

I'd go to the pavilion, collect my stash and the little money I'd saved for my planned escape with Ella. Tomorrow, I'd leave my daughter behind. Safe without me.

Headlights reflected on the black metal of Mrs Hamilton's gate posts and tyres crunched over bits of gravel as her car pulled onto the driveway. Troy sat in the passenger seat, his face blurred by condensation on the window. I huddled closer into the doorway, hoping they couldn't see me. Mrs Hamilton got out and muttered something to Troy, who dragged two large bags from the boot. Leaving the boot open, he followed his mum into the house.

I should go before he came back and spotted me. I got up as he stepped from his front door.

"Cindy?"

I stood, unable to speak. My breath misted the air.

"Are you okay?"

"Yes, fine." My voice quivered.

"I meant what I said in my card," he said.

I gazed at him. What card? The wind shuddered through the hedge, lifting the tips of his fringe.

"You're letting the heat out," Mrs Hamilton called.

Troy pulled the boot shut and walked over. He twisted a broken piece of wire that jutted from the chain-link fence.

"Come over sometime. What I said – I wasn't joking – I… I miss our chats."

Mrs Hamilton peered outside the door, startled to see me. She pursed her lips. "Come inside, Troy. It's bitter out there."

He shrugged and followed her inside. The door closed and I was left in the darkness. One person wanted me. In the whole world, I had one friend. From the side of his house, a shadow appeared. Too short for Troy. The figure moved into the dusky glow of the streetlamp. Mrs Hamilton. She cleared her throat.

"I don't want you seeing Troy again," she said, her voice cold as the night. "He's doing well at school. He's got good friends. If you were a true friend, you'd stay away."

She disappeared around the back as silently as she'd arrived, while I stood stunned. She was right. What sort of friend was I? What sort of person, full stop? Inside Ella wailed and a light flashed on upstairs, leaving me in an unwanted square of light. I dragged the gate open and turned to see Mum silhouetted behind the curtains, rocking Ella. My throat tightened. I could barely breathe.

"Goodbye," I whispered to Ella. "I'm so sorry. I love you."

Chapter 55
- Christmas -

"BUT YOU CAN'T," I SAID. "It's not fair on you."

"I want to."

"But you've a whole life out there. Your job, your house, everything."

"I'll have to go back and sort a few things out. But I want to be here with you, for the trial. Then we can decide what to do."

I pulled two cups – almost forgetting the saucers – from the cupboard. "I'm not worth it. Your mum will be furious. It's bad enough already."

Through the patterned windowpane glass of Marion's kitchen door, I could see the blue and white tape fluttering outside Mum's house.

"No, she won't. She likes you. She'll understand."

I went to argue but gave up. Maybe he was right. No one had forced Marion to put us up for Christmas. She could have sent us off to Mandy's where I would have been faced with the paraphernalia of Simon's life – his clothes, photographs, smell – or, worse, had to fake sorrow while Mandy wept for him. Poor Mandy and Ella.

"Has Mandy called to let us know about tomorrow? If she's coming for dinner?" I said.

"Does she know the police kept your phone?"

My hand flew to my mouth. "I forgot about that. I just said to ring and let me know whether they want to come. She'll think I'm hiding from her."

Troy chuckled. "I'm sure she won't."

I wasn't so sure. Mandy had been in an awful state when she'd come to the hospital: eyes raw from crying, her

322

face sallow from lack of sleep. When I'd passed on Marion's offer of coming for Christmas Day, she'd looked grateful but dubious.

"We'd ruin your Christmas. You're better off without us. All this." She gestured from my bruised face to my bandaged thigh. "Wouldn't have happened if it wasn't for me."

I'd clutched her hand, told her not to be silly but, although I meant them, my words sounded wooden. She may have hidden the laptop, but at least she'd kept her word and taken it to the police. When she found they'd released Simon, she'd shouted at the sergeant and wouldn't leave until they understood that no matter what conditions Simon had agreed to pending his court appearance, he'd lost everything. The first thing he'd do would be to pay me back. I'd never know if it was her pleading or the emergency call I'd made that had saved me, but there was one thing I did know. If she'd told the police about the laptop sooner, it wouldn't have stopped John and Lanky from coming after me and, without Simon there to mess things up for them, I may not have survived. Thanks to Simon, John had the notebook when the police arrested him and, thanks to my call, the police had heard everything.

Troy wrapped his arms around me, drew me close into the warmth of his body. He smelled of fabric conditioner and soap from his earlier shower. Taking care not to touch my still swollen cheek, he kissed the top of my head and bent to my lips. Hearing a tap at the kitchen door, we broke apart.

Ralph harrumphed. "Your sister called. She and Ella can make it tomorrow."

From the hallway came strains of Charlie and Lily singing, "Mummy and Troy sitting in a tree. K-I-S-S-I-N-G."

Lily giggled. "One, two, ready?"

As they started singing again, I grinned at Troy. "Are you sure you don't want to stay in Canada?"

♦

Crumpled wrapping paper was strewn over the children's put-me-up bed. Blinking in the early morning light that streamed through the open bedroom curtain, I gazed at their empty bed for a moment before it dawned on me that I'd somehow slept through the children opening their stockings. I swung around to the alarm clock – nine fifteen – and threw my duvet cover aside. Knowing my luck, the twins would have been awake by five and up to all sorts of mischief. I shoved my arms into my dressing gown, pulled the belt tight, and hurried downstairs to where choir music filtered through the open kitchen door, along with the smell of roast turkey.

Potato peeler in hand, Marion waved at me and called, "Merry Christmas."

As I wished her a Merry Christmas, Troy appeared from behind the door, a tea towel draped over his shoulder. He came over and kissed me.

"Happy Christmas to us," he murmured and nudged me towards the lounge. "I'll be through in a moment."

Ralph sat watching a Christmas film in a lounge warm with the fug of a coal fire. Beside him the children lay on the carpet playing with a wooden train track decorated with colourful Lego tunnels and houses.

"Look, look!" they shouted, holding up various constructions.

"I hope you don't mind, love," Ralph said. "But I let them open our present. We'd run out of things to do by seven o'clock."

"Not at all." I cringed. "I wish you'd woken me."

324

"We've had a lovely morning," he said. "What's Christmas without kids?"

He patted the settee cushion but I eased myself down onto the carpet beside Lily and Charlie, where I kissed them both and whispered, "Happy Christmas". In the fire, coals smouldered and baby flames danced, their reflection mirrored in the golden baubles. I sighed. This time a week ago I was planning to take my children away. To leave the love, hope and kindness behind and move to a supposed place of safety. We weren't out of the woods but, as Troy had pointed out, thanks to the notebook, I wouldn't be giving evidence the police didn't already know.

The lounge door brushed open and Marion poked her head through.

"There's someone at the door for you," she said to me. "They won't come in yet."

She signalled for Ralph to stay seated. Puzzled, I followed her into the hallway to find Troy at the front door, chatting to Ella. He smiled, patted my shoulder, and followed Marion back to the kitchen.

"Happy Christmas, Ella." I peered behind her, wondering where Mandy was. "Is everything okay?"

"Yes." She looked down to where she twisted the hem of her coat. "Mum – erm, Mandy – said I could come here first."

Her breath misted the air and the tip of her nose glowed like the Rudolph decoration on Marion's sideboard.

"Come inside. It's lovely and warm."

She shook her head and glanced at the lounge door I'd left ajar, although I noticed Troy had closed the kitchen door.

"Mum – Mandy – she's told me everything." Her words spilled out. The shock I felt must have shown on my face, as she hesitated and screwed the hem of her coat in her fists.

325

Her bottom lip trembled. "I'm sorry. I didn't know."

She clenched and unclenched her fists. What had Mandy said to cause her such upset? And at Christmas, of all times.

"I don't know what your Mum has told you," I said. "But–"

"That you're my Mum. My real Mum. She told me why you left. About Simon and what she and Granny did to make you go."

No one had forced me to leave. Or had they? I'd been so mixed up and confused. Everything was shrouded in the fog of time. Exactly thirteen years ago to this day I'd walked away. Left my daughter. I couldn't blame myself any longer. First Mum and now Mandy had said sorry. Simon was gone. I had a future. One where I could be a better Mum for Charlie and Lily. Now, the child I'd tucked in the depths of my heart, so her memory couldn't hurt me, stood at the doorstep.

I pulled Ella close, feeling her rigid body begin to relax. For the first time since that Christmas so many moons ago, her chest heaved against mine.

"I'm sorry too. I loved you then, I love you now." I held her out to gaze at those beautiful grey eyes flecked with yellow, now shimmering in a well of tears. She allowed me to draw her back into my arms.

I smiled as I rocked her. "You've got two Mums, if you'll have me, because I'm never leaving you again."

Printed in Poland
by Amazon Fulfillment
Poland Sp. z o.o., Wrocław

49608764R00193